By humans. For humans.

◆ ◆ ◆ ◆ ◆

NOT YOUR EVER AFTER

AN ANTHOLOGY OF
CROOKED FAIRY TALES

Ash Whitaker • Debbie Lynn • Hana Maren Godfrey • Charlie Morgan • C. P. Ashton

Damn
Delights
PUBLISHING

Published by Damn Delights Publishing, an Imprint of Watermeadow Press.

Paperback Edition ISBN: 979-8-9886697-3-9

Ashes & Alibis

For B, C, & D—the loves of my life.
-Ash Whitaker

By Any Other Name

To Robert B.—For all your help. With everything.
-Debbie Lynn

Clever

For those who believe that kindness is magic—
don't let the darkness diminish your spellwork.
-Hana Maren Godfrey

All That Glitters Is Not Gold

To those who've fought in the face of darkness,
may the sun always kiss your cheeks.
-Charlie Morgan

Code RED

For those looking up at glass ceilings,
and for those who are shattering them.
-C. P. Ashton

Content Advisories

These are not your typical bedtime fairy tales. Each story deals with content that some readers may choose to avoid. We encourage you to make the best decision for your personal enjoyment, whether that means reviewing the following advisories or skipping ahead to avoid potential spoilers.

Ashes & Alibis

sexual harassment
death of a loved one
suicide, off page

By Any Other Name

(none)

Clever

physical and mental abuse by a parent
magical subjugation
mention of child marriage
witch burning, off page
death of a parent, off page

All That Glitters Is Not Gold

deception
blood, gore, violence
death of a loved one, on and off page

Code RED

bioterrorism and quarantine
sexual harassment, divorce, cheating, manipulation
mention of alcohol abuse, off page

Contents

ASHES & ALIBIS

ASH WHITAKER

Ember and her family aren't villains, just thieves with questionable morals and a talent for survival. Bound by the debts her late father left behind, they've made a life out of clever disguises, quick hands, and near misses.

When a mysterious noble offers Ember a job too tempting to refuse—attend the Royal Ball and pick a pocket—it sounds like the score she's been waiting for. Not only is it a chance to buy freedom for her and her family, but to strike back at the man who's shown them nothing but cruelty for years.

For Ember, it's no longer just about the job.

It's about getting even.

Ashes & Alibis is a "Cinderella" inspired retelling where the women are all a little wicked.

This damn wig was starting to itch. I could feel the sweat collecting under it from the midday heat and had to resist the urge to scratch at my head. Or better yet, rip the thing off. An impulse that was becoming difficult to ignore as I waited for my target to leave her endless lunch.

Ms. Lilia Hartwick was the daughter of a wealthy merchant, the kind of girl who never once worried about the price of anything. Her chosen restaurant was a high-class establishment that required its clientele be draped in fine silks and a noble surname. Needless to say, I'd never set foot inside.

"Hold it together, Ember," I muttered under my breath, shoving down my growing frustration and re-minding myself why I was here. Why I hoped the wait would be worthwhile. Through the tall window, I caught sight of Lilia laughing, wine glass in hand as she indulged in her second bottle with a friend. Her necklace alone would cover three months rent, but I wasn't leaving with just that. If she was tipsy, even better. I smiled for the first time that day. This was going to be fun.

I was sitting on a bench across from the restaurant. Book in hand, posture relaxed, just a woman passing time. The nearby coachman hadn't spared me a single glance as he tended to his horse. Like me, he was no doubt waiting on a wealthy noble, though I imagined for very different reasons. A subtle tingle sparked in my fingers, a signal I was following a target. The thrill of the plan. The timing. The dance of it all lighting my body up, a rush as natural to me as breathing at this point.

Still, there was no accounting for the itchy wig, the strands sticking to my face and hiding my long, golden hair beneath. I needed it to conceal my identity and, if that didn't do it, the unfashionable hat I wore would. Several seasons old and frayed at the edges, its wide brim covered the majority of my face. It was the kind of choice that would draw the eye. Women in this neighborhood, like Lilia and her companion currently lounging across the street, would notice the fashion misstep. Meanwhile my hands, sheathed in plain gloves, would go unnoticed.

The restaurant's bubblegum pink exterior shimmered in the mid-afternoon sun, one in a tidy row of brightly colored shops and cafés. The whole upscale street reminded me of the gems I so often sought. Each store like a stone nestled neatly in its place, I saw amethyst in the deep violet of the tea shop, emerald in the soft green glow of that adorable gown store, and bright ruby in the sparkle of the bakery.

With summer in full bloom, the shops of the Jewel were bursting with flowers, creating a scene straight out of the fairy tale books I loved to read as a child. Lilac and wisteria vines cascaded with vivid blossoms, while roses and jasmine spilled from every windowsill, weaving a tapestry of color and fragrance that drifted on the breeze.

Even when I wasn't working, I was drawn here, to the sights and smells. They tugged at a secret, beautiful place in my heart. A place I reserved for my mother. She would have adored this place of color and light, a place where flowers grew wild.

I remembered her in the garden during much of my childhood, golden hair braided down her back, sun hat

4

shielding her delicate face as she knelt in the dirt. She walked through the garden naming each bloom as if they were old friends, voice bright with joy. We strolled barefoot together, hand in hand, brushing past blossoms in a world only we knew. My chest tightened at the memory, at the familiar ache of her loss.

I forced it down, shoving the pain aside to focus on my task. The girl I'd once been, my mother's little Emberlynn, was gone. That chapter of my family's story had not ended well. After my father remarried, everything had gone to hell.

I sighed through my nose and shook the memories from my limbs. In the haze of the past, I'd lost sight of Lilia. My eyes swept over the restaurant, finding her table empty, and my heart skipped a beat.

"Shit," I muttered, already in motion, stepping up from the shadowed bench into the bright sun.

During the past five years, I'd learned a lot about stealing. Chief among them was timing. You had to meet your mark on your terms or not at all. And although it would break my mother's heart to know I now schemed and stole and lied with ease, my circumstances had left no choice. The price of safety from my family's past involved a few of Lilia Hartwick's valuables.

I heard her laugh, loud and uninhibited, before I saw her. Thankfully only a few steps from the restaurant's front doors, her gloved hand intertwined through her friend's arm. *Good,* I thought, gauging where I could intercept her before she met her carriage. I was barely off track, my painful visit to the past not throwing me off by much.

I kept my eyes on Lilia and her companion as I crossed the street with deliberate calm, the book tucked into the crook of my elbow. A lady didn't run, and an innocent lady? Why, she never did more than meander gracefully through the world.

I stifled my snort at the thought. I was no innocent lady.

The two women strolled across the cobbled walk, lost in chatter. I trailed behind, taking in the small details of the pair. Lilia's auburn curls were pulled back, leaving her neck, with its sparkling jewels, blessedly bare. Her pink silk dress seemed to glow against her skin. The other woman was just as striking, with her long blonde hair, so similar to mine, tumbling down her back in gentle waves, complementing her blue gown. The color would suit me, if I ever had cause to wear it.

"I cannot wait. Only three more days!" Lilia exclaimed, swaying slightly as pink bloomed across her cheeks. She was well on her way to nap and a blurry recollection of the afternoon, which suited my needs just fine. The words *prince and castle* drifted past me as I closed the gap between us. Just as they turned to enter Lilia's polished wood carriage, they collided into me.

The small, unstylish old lady.

My fall wasn't entirely staged. As I hit the ground, a sharp pain jolted through my elbow while my book slid down the walkway, aided on its journey with a little push from me.

By the time my body stopped moving, I was already richer. A silk coin purse, neatly lifted in the stumble, tucked in the pocket of my gown.

I groaned, clutching my arm in obvious pain. Standing over me, Lilia let out a startled gasp. "Oh, Fates! Are you all right?" she asked, words pinched high in surprise. She bent toward me, her brown eyes scanning my body, and, I noted with satisfaction, lingering on my hat.

Her companion stood a few steps behind, concern knitting the space between her brows.

"Just the clumsiness of an old lady," I let my voice shake. "Would you be so kind... my book...?" I pointed toward where it lay, feigning helplessness.

Lilia turned and gestured quickly to her friend, "Maribelle, the book."

Maribelle's slippered feet whispered across the stones as she went in the opposite direction. Good manners made such lovely little weaknesses.

Reaching out a red laced hand, Lilia clasped my own. Her touch was warm and unguarded as she helped me to my feet. I leaned into her, fingers unclasping the necklace at her long throat before I gripped her shoulder. After steadying myself, I released my hold, slipping the necklace up my sleeve with a grateful sigh.

My second mark, done.

"Bless you sweet girls for helping an old lady," I gushed, voice dripping with the honeyed warmth of a doting grandmother. "The world needs more like you two." Maribelle returned with my book, and I gave her a lingering, motherly pat. My fingers brushed her wrist, settling on the bracelet she wore.

That was the final piece.

Lilia and Maribelle beamed, flattered, glowing under the praise. I knew they would remember their moment of charity, their goodness on display and acknowledged. I imagined they'd recall their heroism as they charmed some nobleman. I, however, would remember our interaction differently. With my act completed, it was time to get the hell away from these two. With a small wave goodbye, I hobbled away, head bowed and back bent.

I slipped into the mouth of an alley, hidden from view, and finally let it hit me. Five minutes at most, a small part of their day really, but a crucial step toward my freedom.

The smile came fast, unrestrained and real as I closed my eyes and sighed. I allowed myself to feel it. A rush of warmth blossomed in my chest and spilled into my limbs, relief and triumph flooding through me in a brief, exhilarating wave. This is what winning meant to me now. Not glory or applause, just the sheer, private bliss of survival.

But the moment couldn't last. It never did.

Time to go.

I loosened the ties at my waist, fingers moving with practiced ease. The outer layer of my skirt slid free, and with a well rehearsed flip, I turned the fabric inside out revealing the rough cotton underneath. I re-tied the laces, first at my neck, then at my waist. It was now a faded green apron.

I took off my hat and tucked the book inside, then shoved the wig in next, groaning in relief to be free of it. With the wig gone, my braid tumbled down my back. The hat's ribbons were already knotted and I silently thanked my stepsister Lark for thinking ahead. Slinging them over my shoulder, I carried my new bag, slightly misshapen but passable enough that no one would look twice. Precisely the point.

A sheen of sweat, now cooling in the breeze, still clung to my neck. I ran my fingers through it, using the wetness to smudge the cosmetics on the lower part of my face. What had once been carefully applied wrinkles now looked like dirt and exhaustion, merely grime from long hours of hard work.

In less than a minute, the clumsy old crone was gone. My transformation to sweat stained laundress, invisible among the dozens in this district, was complete.

The side streets were empty of wealthy merchants and silk-clad ladies. Their stately pace had given way to the bustle of laborers and servants navigating the narrow streets that bisected the city of Aurelia. The farther I walked from the wealthy Jewel District, the uglier the world started to look. The scent of flowers no longer drifted through the air, replaced by the smell of sweat and debauchery. There were more sins than souls crammed into the run-down row houses and sagging apartments. My eyes scanned alleys and shadowed doorways, a habit ingrained in every street rat who knew how quickly this city turned cruel.

I slipped a hand in my pocket, reassured by the dagger I kept on me at all times. Its familiar weight was soothing, a silent warning against another thief's stupidity. With my jeweled cargo in tow, I preferred to make it home without a fight.

Keeping my head down, I picked my way over the uneven red and brown cobbles, avoiding the drunk man sprawled across the walk. He muttered something I didn't catch, and I didn't care to hear. Whether he was after my pity or my time, I had none to spare.

All of this, part of my familiar route to an area unlovingly referred to as the Heap. The area where the poorest and most downtrodden scratched and clawed out their lives in the shadow of Aurelia's otherwise beautiful city. But no one asked questions here, and if you minded your own business and didn't piss off the wrong people, you could survive.

It was my father's fault we had ended up here ten years ago, because of the debts and reckless investments that came to light after he died. The banks had come first, taking my father's house, the land with my mother's gardens, and anything of value they could get their hands on. But after they took their cut, what was left behind was far worse. Debts owed to the kind of men who didn't care that the debtor was buried. They wanted payment and looked to his widow and daughters to make it right. So we did. Year after year, we chipped away at what my father left us and stashed what we could for ourselves.

The familiar outline of our rowhouse came into view, the crumbling exterior a stark reminder of its former beauty. I couldn't help but wonder, not for the first time, what it must have been like here before neglect and poverty created something altogether different. The façade, whose color must have once resembled fresh clotted cream, was streaked with weather stains and chipped in places, exposing the rough brick underneath. The tall sash windows were now covered in grime, missing panes replaced by boards long since bleached by the sun. Our neighboring houses had fared no better. Repairs required money, and families in the Heap had little to spare.

I climbed the crumbling steps, ignoring the wrought iron rail that wobbled precariously. Reaching into the pocket of my apron, I pulled out my key. The door was solid oak and reinforced with steel bands, the only new addition to the house's weathered exterior. Standing in stark contrast to the decay around it, I knew it could withstand a battering ram and had been worth every damn crown. Between that and the reinforced lower windows, we slept better at night knowing they helped protect our home. The Heap's nightmares would have a harder time clawing their way inside.

I braced myself for the impending inquisition and unlocked the door.

Inside, the grandeur of the house was similarly faded. The high ceilings, once adorned with intricately painted patterns, were dulled and cobweb-covered. The wooden floors creaked underfoot, and you had to know which boards to avoid if you wanted to move quietly up the stairs. I skipped the first floor entirely, heading instead to the place that felt like home, the second floor.

Standing at the top of the stairs, leaning on the faded wooden bannister, stood Raven. Tall and lithe, my older stepsister looked regal, even in her worn leggings and tunic. Her corset, cinched to emphasize her slender waist, concealed at least three small daggers that I knew of, likely more. Once, in a seedy pub, she'd coolly threatened to strangle a man with the leather ties of that very corset. I'd laughed so hard that ale shot out of my nose, a memory she still teased me about.

As I drew closer, her features were no longer wrapped in shadow. Dark brown hair cascaded over her shoulders in loose waves, framing her delicate face. High cheek bones and a full mouth gave her a sultry type of beauty. Her gaze swept over me, lingering on the elbow I cradled before locking onto my face.

"Just a bruise, Mother Hen." I grinned.

"How was the grab?" she asked, ignoring my attempt to rile her. "Two marks?"

"No," I said, reaching the top of the stairs beside her, savoring the momentary suspense before adding, "three." My grin widened as the word landed.

Raven's brows shifted, her otherwise stoic face revealing no other sign of shock. It was impossible to rattle her, though I tried almost every day.

"Lady Greed is a needy bitch, Em," she warned beneath the calm.

"'Twas not greed, Dear Sister," I replied, pressing a hand to my chest in mock offense. "Though I am touched by your concern. Merely a lucky opportunity I chose not to squander." I handed over my precious cargo.

Raven tilted her head, amber eyes locking onto mine, weighing my words. Sister or not, my pulse quickened. It was instinct, like facing a predator.

She gave the smallest nod.

I let out a quiet, relieved breath.

She smiled, white teeth on display as if to say, I *saw that.*

"Shut up," I mumbled before turning to walk down the hall.

"She's going to kill you," she called after me.

I froze mid-step and glanced over my shoulder. "You think?"

"You might truly have done it this time. And with what you took, it's not something even I could save you from."

"Thanks for the warning," I replied, starting again toward the washroom. "I'm going to get cleaned up."

"You should fold your costume and hang the wig this time," she said in a whisper that was far too amused. She held up the misshapen bag. "It might be the only thing that saves you from her."

I snorted. "Relax. It won't be that bad."

But I knew the truth. I might very well get my ass kicked, and I might just deserve it.

The thought had barely settled when something launched out of the shadows and slammed into me. I hit the floor hard, hands shooting out to catch myself. The wood scraped against my palms, but at least my face was spared. Air rushed from my lungs and I cursed myself for not paying attention. I just hadn't expected vengeance to come so soon.

"Did you take my book again Em?" hissed the specter crouched on my back. My younger stepsister's voice had lost its usual singsong melody, replaced by a growl.

"Ach, Lark," I wheezed, cheek mashed against the floorboards. "That actually hurt, devil woman. I've already fallen once today."

"Where is it?" she demanded, each word clipped, sharp like the knives she carried. Her long chestnut braid trailed over my face, and I had to spit out several strands before I spoke.

"Raven has it," I grumbled and, without warning, I twisted my hip and threw her off. She fell in a small heap among her ruffled skirts, a little gasp of surprise escaping her mouth. Satisfied at the sight of her, I turned over. "In the hat." I waved vaguely down the hall.

Lark untangled herself and stood in one motion. "It better not be scuffed from your little distraction bit. The walkway is so brutal on the leather."

I was already halfway to the washroom, my whispered confession trailing behind me, "I may have accidentally skid it across the—"

"WHAAA—"

"For Fate's sake, girls stop that fighting," came an exasperated voice from the sitting room just ahead. My stepmother. "Ember, come in here please." I looked wistfully down the hall, imagining sinking in the hot bath and washing off the cosmetics and sweat.

As if reading my thoughts, my stepmother continued, teasing, "Nice long baths are for girls who follow the rules, which you did not." Lark and Raven snickered behind me. "Come sit, love."

I looked at the two of them over my shoulder, the glee evident on their faces. A shiver worked its way up my spine. Lark had gotten too close without me noticing. I should've heard her. I always did.

And then I remembered Raven. Her warning. That sly smile. She'd distracted me on purpose. Set me up.

Assholes.

A laugh burst from me. "Assholes!" I whispered in their direction.

The answering laughter, one low and rich, the other bright and wild, echoed from behind me as I entered the sitting room. I'd have to get them back.

My stepmother was standing just inside, a warm smile on her face. In middle age, Rosalind was beautiful. I could see both Lark and Raven in her high cheekbones and the dusting of freckles on her fair skin. Her rich brown hair was swept up neatly, a few rebellious strands loose from work. Despite the long, thin scar that marred the side of her face, she carried herself with a confidence I hoped one day to achieve.

She walked toward me and brushed a strand of hair from my face, her touch loving. "The makeup is perfect. Lark really outdid herself this time." Affection colored her tone.

I leaned into her hand, meeting the brown eyes that held nothing but love. I had called her Mother since I was nine, two years after she married my father. I still remembered the tears in her eyes the first time the word left my lips, she said it was an honor. Yet it was she who'd honored me, and at twenty-two, I could see the history of her unwavering love.

These wild and brave women were my family, not by blood but by bond. They had buoyed me in a life that would have otherwise drowned me. Mother always said we fit together like we were always meant to be. She called me her spring, said I reminded her of that first bloom after winter's chill with my golden hair and sky blue eyes. Raven, her winter, was sharp and enduring. Lark, her summer, was fierce and bright and warm. We were the seasons of her life. But then she was our autumn, deep and comforting.

"Come sit." She moved to one of the patchwork velvet armchairs. I joined her, choosing to sink into the blue sofa across from her. The sitting room, like everything in the house, still carried echoes of elegance. Faded emerald wallpaper curled at the edges, and the wooden floor bore the scars of countless footsteps. Yet this room was our safe place, where we read by the fire and laughed. Where we shared tea and secrets, where the sunset shimmered in through the windows, bathing us in golden light. The first floor was a shield against the world, the place where we greeted visitors, which was a rarity in the Heap. People here didn't do parties. Not the kind our family used to throw, with wine and dancing and tables full of food. There wasn't enough to go around. Weddings were quiet affairs, funerals somber and lean.

My gaze flicked to the doorway as Raven and Lark joined us. Lark's green eyes met mine, sparkling with joy, a wide smile on her face.

"Tell me I'll have more things to laugh about with you two," said Raven, voice filled with amusement. She sat in the armchair next to Mother and removed a dagger from the sheath at her ankle. Picking a whetstone up off the table, she began the rhythmic work of sharpening the blade. "I mean, you're the one who decided to steal from our little book hoarding dragon over there." She smirked, gesturing toward Lark with the tip of her dagger.

Lark and I locked eyes, assessing. I arched my brow in question. Was she going to spring onto the couch for round two? She grinned, a familiar blend of sweet and wolfish. *Maybe.*

We both spoke at once, voices overlapping. "I'm sorry."

"The book's not scuffed, which saved you, but admit it, I got you," Lark said with a grin. I tapped the cushion next to me, offering her a seat.

"Yes you did," I muttered. She flopped down beside me on the sofa, book in hand, bumping into me playfully. I let out an exaggerated huff, needling her with my sharp elbow, which I counted as a win. "But my quick thinking saved my face."

"Here," she said as she handed me a small glass jar. I blinked at it, brows pinching in question. "For your elbow," she clarified. "You're okay, yeah?"

"Yes," I said. "Our information was right as usual," I added, directing my words to Mother. "Lilia had a soft spot for a little old granny." I unscrewed the jar, the smell of lavender and eucalyptus drifting up to meet me. I rubbed the salve gently onto my elbow. "She was quick to help and didn't ask questions."

"Her grandmother is a special person in her life," Mother murmured. "Lilia reads to her every week." She sat with perfect posture, hands neatly folded in her lap. Lady Rosalind Trevion had been born and raised a noble, and even after all the years of poverty, the habits stuck. Of the three of us, Lark followed those manners most often. I sat up straight when required, mostly when I was working. Raven rarely did, her stubborn hatred for the rich making it physically impossible, I think.

"It was easy," I said, glancing at Mother nervously.

"I'm glad," she replied, meeting my eyes, "but it would have been best to wait for someone. A runner, a distraction, someone watching your back." She didn't need to raise her voice to communicate her frustration. It rang clear. "We work best together, Emberlynn."

And there she was. The other side of our mother. The one cultivated by her wealthy family but honed and sharpened by the Heap. Stern. Edged. Her warm face now hewn of stone, her scar more pronounced.

Raven whistled low through her teeth. Our birth names—Ravenna, Emberlynn, Larabelle—were rarely used, echoes of the girls we once were. Pulled out only when we were in trouble. Those names were such soft, delicate things, and those girls didn't belong here. Not in the slums. By some unspoken agreement, the three of us never used them with each other. The day we moved into this house, we killed that part of us and became someone new. Because once we discovered the kind of monsters that prowled these streets, we grew teeth of our own and there was no going back.

I held my mother's gaze, refusing to wilt even though I wanted to. "I get it," I said, measuring each word, "but I knew Lilia was having lunch with a friend. She would dress well. Raven and Lark both had work. But I planned and scouted with Raven last night. I was quick and careful. In and out in scarcely five minutes. In seven, I was someone new. Disguised with—"

"Geraldine," Lark interrupted. She was trying to spare me Mother's wrath and the impending lecture. I shot her a grateful look. I could have kissed her.

Mother's brow pinched, her eyes leaving my face. I breathed a sigh of relief. All things considered, I'd gotten off easy, even though I had broken one of her cardinal rules. *Stick close.* Meant to keep us from death or the City Watch's cells, they were family lore at this point. Some families memorized prayers to the Fates, but we recited Mother's wisdom. *Eyes sharp. Hands swift. Leave shadows, not handprints.*

"Geraldine? What are you on about, Lark?" Mother asked.

"She named the wig Geraldine," supplied Raven. Her mouth pinched, and I knew she was holding in a laugh.

"Oh, Lark, another silly—" sighed Mother, exasperated by our neverending antics.

"It is silly, isn't it?" said Lark dreamily. "But it's so fun."

I cut in before the lecture could resume. "I'll be careful," I said and meant it. While I wasn't stupid enough to believe I'd always get away, I was good. Damn good. "I won't go alone if I don't have to."

"I love you," Mother said, her voice gentle but firm. She held my gaze for another tense moment. "I won't have you arrested or hurt for being foolish."

Relief loosened something in my chest, and I knew the worst of the storm had passed. I thanked all Seven Fates for my sister. I shifted the conversation. Outlining the interaction with Lilia and the subsequent take, the quiet precision of my wardrobe change. Lark beamed as I told her how well the hat worked, as both distraction and bag, her idea entirely.

Raven placed my prize on the chipped wooden table between us. The bracelet, necklace, and money pouch were worth more crowns than most people saw in a year. They looked obscene, gleaming against the scarred wood. But I felt it then, the shift in the room. A ripple of something wordless.

Hope.

We were one step closer to paying off the debt that had cost us our old life. The debt that chained us to one of the Heap's most dangerous cutthroats, Lord Jasper Wickham, our final creditor. Owing him was the knife point on which our lives balanced, every choice threatening to cut us down. More dangerous than gathering intel on our targets through Raven and Mother, more than the disguises Lark wove, or the grabs I executed, was the constant, unrelenting weight of what we owed Wickham. He would take his payment too, whether in coin or flesh. I had to force my eyes not to drift to Mother's face at the thought, at the damage he was capable of inflicting. Every time I thought about him, fury, hot and jagged, unfurled in my chest. It made my fingers itch for a blade. We never spoke of the scar Wickham had given our mother after a missed payment. Or how, the very next day, I had stolen my first coin purse. Sloppy and desperate, but enough for that month's debts.

Lark masked her anger behind easy smiles, but it simmered beneath the surface, ready to erupt the moment his name was mentioned. Raven's rage, however, was colder and sharper than even mine, a blade that never lost its honed edge. She would be the one to deliver our revenge. After he grabbed her ass at eighteen and suggested another way that she might settle that month's debt, I knew she was biding her time. She'd be the blade in the dark.

Mother scrubbed her hands raw in the laundries at the Glass Palace and the homes of wealthy nobles just to keep us fed and Wickham appeased. What had started as survival had become something more, a constant source of gossip. That gave us our marks. Little thefts, little victories. Jewelry, antiques, and once, to Lark's horror and our unending joy, a rare book we were forced to sell.

No matter what, every month, we paid. But we kept our thefts a secret or Wickham would demand his cut, or worse, that we work for him. Too much money, and he'd ask questions. I tried that once, and he'd demanded to know where the extra money had come from. My courier job couldn't explain it, so I lied and said someone dropped it. It was a balance, paying him slightly more than we had to each month, but never enough to make him pry. One day, though, we'd be free of him.

Mother stood then, smoothing her yellow skirts, the only sign of nerves she ever showed. "Better not delay the inevitable," she said. "Let's get this over with."

And just like that, the fragile joy was gone. Popped like a soap bubble.

Raven's gaze met mine, concern etched on her face. "I'll do it," she said, though she'd made the delivery last month and Wickham's advances toward her had grown bolder, more predatory.

"No," Lark and I snapped together.

"We take turns. It's mine," Lark declared. "Now, here, put my book on the shelf." She handed me her book. "And hang Geraldine, or I'll cut your hair in your sleep," she tossed over her shoulder as she followed after Mother.

"Well you heard the witch, better get on it," Raven said, unfazed by Lark's threat. She jerked her chin toward the hallway, then leaned back in her chair, resuming her work with the whetstone.

With an exaggerated sigh and a muttered curse at my sisters, I scooped up the book and hauled myself off the sofa. The weight of Lark and Mother's departure hung heavy. We wouldn't rest until they returned.

As I headed toward Lark's room, I flipped through the pages of the book she guarded so fiercely. Maybe I'd finally read the story, see what drew her in. I'd only ever read a few of the naughty parts.

I froze.

My breath hitched in my throat. Something slipped from between the pages and floated to the floor. Something I knew with absolute certainty hadn't been there this morning.

Ivory paper. Thick. Expensive.

I bent over and picked it up with steady hands. Hand-cut and inked with swirling, decorative writing, it was an invitation. To the upcoming Royal Ball. From seedy taverns to the finest shops, it had been the talk of the kingdom for weeks.

But it wasn't just the invitation that made my blood run cold. It was the quick, hasty writing on the back.

I could use your skills.

Midnight, tonight.

Pier 7 warehouse.

My throat went dry. Someone had seen me.

All that planning this morning, gone to hell. Short of being hauled off by the Watch, this was the worst thing that could've happened. Whoever left that note had used my fall as their own distraction. Clever. Dangerously so.

Panic clawed at my chest, and the air felt heavy, too hard to breathe. A hot wave of fear and shame tangled together, threatening to consume me. Did I just bring danger to our doorstep with my carelessness?

Three breaths, that's what I needed, what I'd always done when my chest felt tight.

One.

Two.

Three.

Bit by bit, the panic ebbed. The tightness loosened its grip until I was clear-eyed and ready. Certain. I'd been in tight spots before. I could get out of this, I just needed a plan.

A floorboard creaked behind me. Raven. She'd heard me stop; of course she had. I didn't need to look to feel her watching, waiting.

I shifted the paper and saw more writing.

PS I won't bite.

A dry, humorless laugh escaped me. Arrogant bastard. Definitely a man. Cocky too. That, I could work with. He might not bite, but he'd soon learn I had teeth.

I met Raven's worried gaze, and my heart hardened in resolve. Midnight then. I'd go, but not alone.

And sure as hell not unarmed.

◆ ◆ ◆ ◆ ◆

The roof was slick beneath me, the cool night breeze a gift after today's heat. My leather-soled shoes were well worn, trusted tools I'd used for this exact task time and time again. The warehouses along the wharf all looked the same, making scouting simple. I'd been at it for an hour. Crouching low, I jumped from roof to roof, scanning the darkness surrounding Pier 7. Three circuits of the roof told me no one waited to ambush me and not a soul entered or left. The darkness might conceal movement, but the silence reassured me. No shuffled footsteps, no whispers, nothing but the lamps that lined the street, each offering small halos of light in the inky dark. My pulse was steady, but a sheen of sweat formed on my neck as instinct and doubt warred inside me.

The warehouse at Pier 7 stood just across the walkway, a perfect place for a secret meeting. The smarter choice was not to go into the building at all, to turn back.

I couldn't.

The uncertainty about this stranger gnawed at me, relentless, like a splinter burrowed under my skin. It pushed me forward despite the risks. Despite the warning in my head of meeting strangers in the dark. But I had to know, was it luck that our paths crossed today? What did he know about my family?

I had a rough plan, several actually, crafted in the hours since the invitation arrived. I didn't like working for strangers, better to get out of it. If that wasn't an option, I'd tolerate it for the right amount of money. There was also a small chance I was about to take a knife to the ribs, though that seemed unlikely. He could have done that in the alley while I'd changed. He needed me, and that gave me an edge. My fingers traced the rough clay tiles as I inched closer, keeping watch.

I heard them before I saw them, the light scuff of a boot over stone, voices slithering on the wind. Two men, hooded in black cloaks, walking and whispering. Their steps were in sync, strong and sure as they walked my way. The taller of the two looked up, scanning the surrounding buildings, and I sank further down, flattening myself against the roof. I was not as skilled as Raven at this game of shadows and stealth, but that was the reason I was out here and not her. She was needed elsewhere. The men entered the Pier 7 warehouse without hesitation, a sign they expected nothing to go wrong.

But still I waited.

Minutes passed with nothing but the sounds of the lapping water against boat hulls and the creak of masts. I drew a deep breath, summoning the liar I always became before a job. That's what this was, I reminded myself, just another target. I shuffled across the roof to start my climb down. I'd walk right through the front door, and if they thought me naïve and stupid, all the better. It was part one of my act, after all.

I shimmied down the drainpipe I'd climbed earlier, using the large iron rivets as hand holds. My skirts were bunched up around my waist, tied with small ribbons Lark had sewn into the hem. Climbing two stories in a dress hadn't been my best decision, but I had no choice. They knew I was a woman, they'd expect the dress. What they wouldn't expect were the daggers strapped to my thighs, ankles, and corset. I imagine it would be quite a shock to find out my hair, styled in a loose updo, was pinned in place with a hairpin sharp enough to slice through skin. And those were just the weapons I carried on me, not the only ones I'd brought.

I dropped to the ground and retrieved the black cloak I'd stashed hours earlier behind a stack of wooden crates. I smoothed my skirts before sweeping the hood high to obscure much of my face. Darkness meant he wanted anonymity as badly as I did. A noble, surely. It would explain how he saw me in the Jewel. Nobles were a pain, but at least they paid well, and most of them couldn't throw a punch to save their life. All good things for me.

I made no attempt to soften my footsteps as I crossed the threshold, announcing myself into the darkness. I'd scouted the warehouse hours earlier and knew the layout. Every instinct braced for what lay ahead, tension coiling tight beneath my skin. Alongside it thrummed the familiar thrill that came with a job. I might walk away with my own treasures tonight, maybe even a bit of leverage. First, I had to hear what this bastard wanted.

"Hello," I called out timidly, letting a subtle quiver creep into my voice.

A lone lantern flickered in the warehouse's depths, its glow pooling on a desk, a small beacon in the dark. Leaning against the desk was a tall figure, arms folded, ankles crossed with the casual ease of someone meeting a friend. That thought rang through me like a warning bell, almost stopping me from going farther. My eyes swept the shadows, searching for the unseen partner I knew lurked nearby. I took comfort that my daggers were all within reach.

No one came out this late, into this kind of isolated place to meet a stranger, and felt this comfortable. Not unless they were confident in their ability to defend themselves. He was dangerous. Smart, too, bringing someone to watch his back. This must be the author of my note. Both carried the same arrogance that made me clench my jaw.

"You came." His words drifted from below the hood, voice low and rough, colored with surprise. "I wasn't sure you would." He gestured to a pair of empty chairs with a slow, deliberate sweep of his hand. "Please sit."

I hesitated for a heartbeat, long enough for it to seem deliberate. The shadows obscured everything but the faint curve of his lips and the sharp line of his jaw beneath the hood.

"I promised I wouldn't bite." His voice dipped, teasing, like he was sharing a secret with me. And dammit, I could actually hear the smile in his words. My spine straightened before I remembered the role I was meant to play, and I walked toward the table, feigning unease.

The room stretched around us, dim and cavernous. My eyes scanned the familiar jagged silhouette of the railed stairs that ran the length of the warehouse, often used by runners from the harbormaster's office on the second floor. The office loomed just behind us, a perfect place for someone to hide. Nothing was out of place.

He stood a foot taller than me, cloak slung over one shoulder to reveal he was broad and well-built. His leather boots, scuffed from use, were the finest quality. A small gold ring sat on the pinky of his left hand, and I fought to keep my steps even. My heart lurched to my throat to see my assumptions were correct, the ring confirmation enough. Strange that he wore it on his left hand and not his right, likely to throw me off. Only nobles wore those rings, each engraved with a family crest. Stealing one sent you straight to the castle dungeons and King Leopold was a notoriously harsh bastard. Mother's rule was to never touch a noble's ring, yet another one I might just break.

My solitary footsteps cut through the silence as I closed the distance between us.

I stumbled, cloak tangling at my feet. Strong hands caught me around the middle, just as I had hoped. Nobles and their compulsion to help was something I depended on often during my little performances, something I weaponized. This was no different. With his fine cloak and boots, I was depending on the rules he had been taught since birth. His grip was strong, steady, his body firm at my back. I swayed closer, grasping his hands for balance, a seemingly thoughtless gesture that let me brush my fingers against his ring. Our bodies were pressed together so closely, I could smell his deep, smoky vanilla scent, so rich and unexpected I had to resist the urge to inhale deeply.

But this was exactly where I wanted him.

"I'm so sorry, sir." I let the words tumble out in a desperate rush as I went still. "Thank you. It is difficult to see in the dark."

He cleared his throat, awkward and uncertain, betraying his discomfort at how close we were, how intimately he was touching me. The noble class and their rigid sense of propriety was a constant source of ridicule. The Heap may be a lawless place, but it was free in ways the highborn could never understand, at least in public. As long as you were smart, you could have as much fun as you wanted. My sisters and I certainly did. One of us was always alert, or close enough but we had a lot of hazy nights pressed up against partners, nights we never regretted. His hands slid from my body, his touch lingering slightly. Then, with a deliberate step, he was gone, leaving me wrapped in the ghost of his heat and scent.

"I, uh, yes. It's no problem." His voice wavered, uncertain.

I smiled, safe in the cloak's hood, unable to help myself. I felt more in control now that he was off balance. I turned to face him, letting the silence grow.

"Thank you for meeting me," he said at last.

"Yes, sir," I replied, voice small and fragile. The awkward pause hung heavy. He was having doubts. I could feel it.

He studied me, searching, then muttered as if to himself, "I may have been mistaken."

"Oh?" I tilted my head, feigning curiosity. "About what, sir?"

He shifted uncomfortably, the scuff of his boot loud on the wood floor.

"You're not what I expected." His words tumbled through the air. "I'm... I'm sorry. You can go."

"Yes, sir." I dipped my head and spun away, stunned at how easy this had been to get out of.

I hadn't gone five feet though, before a low, throaty chuckle slid across my skin. I stopped.

"You almost did it again, damn you." His voice cut through the air, sharp with something I couldn't place.

I turned to face him. If I couldn't get out of this, fine, time to hear him out. I stood to my full height, spine straight, a citizen of the Heap once more. But, my little act had already served its purpose.

"The woman I saw today was confident. Strategic. An excellent thief... nice grab by the way." He sighed, holding up his now ringless hand, staring at it as if the ring might reappear. Lifting that same hand to his mouth, his thumb skimmed his lower lip, drawing my eyes to the half-smile there. "I'm going to want that back by the way." It was respect I heard now.

I smirked, ignoring his request for the ring as I dipped into a mocking bow. "Why thank you, *my lord.*" I lingered on the title, making it clear I saw through his act too. My tone was light, almost teasing, though my pulse quickened. The real game was beginning. I looked into the shadow of his hood, where I knew his eyes were. "Took you long enough to notice. I was starting to wonder whether you were worth my time."

A quiet laugh, almost pleased. "I hope to be."

"You followed me. Left a note in my book," I said flatly. I wasn't going to give him the satisfaction of my admiration. "Most men wouldn't survive that."

"I'm not most men." Amusement laced his tone. "As for watching you, I couldn't stop, you were magnificent."

Something traitorous fluttered in my chest at the compliment. His admiration of my skill, not my looks, was a dangerous thing. So I quashed it. "What do you want?"

"It's simple enough." His voice steadied, the playfulness gone. "I need you for a job."

"You've seen me work one time. You're rather trusting rather fast."

"This isn't about trust. It's about necessity." The simple, unguarded truth. I was an asset, which suited me just fine. Lines were clear in those situations, both of us using the other. "And I've seen you work more than once. This morning and just now." He stepped forward with the deliberate calm of someone approaching a coiled snake. "Tonight. You became someone else, just like the old lady this morning. You played the part so well I started to doubt my own memory. I need that."

He reached into his cloak and pulled out a slim black envelope. The deep red of the Royal seal caught the dim light. He extended it toward me, but I didn't take it. He'd yet to convince me this was worth my time.

"What's that?"

"Money for supplies and a clean invitation to the ball." He tapped the seal, drawing my eyes. "Though I suspect you knew that already."

I gave a soft, incredulous laugh. "And what exactly do you want me to do once I'm inside? Dance with the prince? Steal the crown jewels?"

"Nothing quite so fun, I'm afraid," he replied. "Though if you feel like dancing with the prince, you should. He's obligated to attend, poor bastard. Another of his father's schemes to marry him off." He scoffed. "There's a letter. Lord Atticus Thorne will have it on his person. I want it."

I stilled.

Thorne.

That name carried with it whispers of blackmail, of disappearances. Thorne was the worst kind of noble, hiding his evil deeds behind the mask of a saint. He was a usual topic of conversation in the Heap, equally admired and feared. He even scared men like Wickham. If this stranger wanted a letter from Thorne, it wasn't just important. It was dangerous.

"Why not get someone closer?" I asked. "A servant. Hell, you could do it, you're clearly skilled enough."

He smiled wide, his white teeth glinting, "You think I'm good?"

A scoff slipped out, despite the grin tugging at my mouth, he *was* good.

Robbing Thorne of his little prize did have a certain appeal to it. I'd rather take from someone who deserved it, and Thorne certainly did. He was powerful, dangerous, yes, but I might just be able to use it to my advantage.

"I have my own role at the ball that will keep me busy, and Thorne keeps his distance from me. He suspects I'm watching him." He leaned closer. The dim light caught on a faded scar on his chin. "A servant doesn't have your skills. The ability to read someone and use their expectations against them. When I saw you this morning, I knew you'd be able to do it."

I swallowed, my throat tight. "I know how to survive," I said, and this time, the words weren't a game I was playing. They were the truth, raw and bare. I don't know why I gave them to him, but for some reason, they felt safe out here in the dark.

"I believe that." His voice softened, as if he saw the truth of my words. He offered the invitation again.

This time, I took it. The parchment was thick and expensive, the edges embossed in gold. Somehow, he had access to one of the most coveted pieces of paper in the kingdom. They'd been hand delivered to all guests. Had he stolen it?

"There's just one problem," I murmured, turning the envelope over in my hands. "Thorne will remember my face after this. That's not something I'm willing to risk. His wrath is the stuff of legends."

His answer was immediate. "I happen to know the ball will be a masquerade."

I raised a brow, impressed. "That hasn't been announced yet."

He smiled, slow and self-satisfied.

"Arrogant," I scoffed. "What's even in the letter?"

"If I knew, I wouldn't be talking to you." His tone turned grave. "I have my suspicions, but I need to see it. I know that it matters. He'll be delivering his note to his contact at midnight. So, steal it before then."

"And if I say no?" I asked, even though I already knew my answer. I was already working through the job, cataloguing the possibilities. My fingers twitched, the familiar thrill creeping into my blood. Stealing from Thorne would be dangerous, but he'd feel safe at the ball. His guard would be down, he'd be drinking. And with all that wealth on display? I smiled, this could be fun.

He gave a one-shouldered shrug, like my answer didn't matter. But it did. I saw it in the tightness of his jaw. This was somehow personal to him.

"Then I find someone less talented, and you walk away from an offer people don't get twice." This was it, the part where I saw what kind of status this man had. "Ten thousand crowns," he said without pause. "Enough for your silence, and anything you've ever wanted."

The number hit me like a punch to the chest. Ten thousand crowns. That kind of money could change everything, settle all our debts.

But freedom... real freedom? That was harder to buy.

Wickham wouldn't just let us go. He'd started treating us, especially Raven, like possessions. Like he had some twisted claim. Getting free of him wouldn't be as easy as disappearing with a bag of gold. He'd find some way to keep us close, so I'd have to find a way to cut ties permanently.

I tapped the invitation against my palm, considering. "If you've got this much influence, can you get another one of these?"

He tilted his head, curious. "Do you have some lover you wish to impress?" he asked. "You'll be too busy for romance."

I ran my finger along the edge of the invitation, dipping my voice just enough to make him wonder. "Who says I can't multitask?"

That earned me a smirk, like he wasn't sure whether to laugh or test the theory. "I have no problem believing that."

"Get Sir Jasper Wickham an invitation. Then we have a deal."

"The lowborn noble?" he asked, in disbelief. "You can do better."

I didn't answer.

He studied the shadow beneath my hood, like he was trying to read something written behind my silence, but it wasn't a story he needed to hear. After a beat, he exhaled and nodded once.

"Done. I'll have it delivered in the morning," he muttered. "I'll find you at the ball."

My brows arched, uncertainty in my words. "How the hell will you find me in a room full of masks?"

"I'll have eyes." He stepped near, his hand brushing my neck and sending a shock down my spine. He caught a strand of my hair, winding it around his finger, watching it sparkle in the lamplight before letting it go. "I imagine you'll be hard to miss." He huffed a laugh. "We'll be watching Thorne all night. You won't be alone."

"I'm never without backup," I said, thrown by the feel of his skin against mine.

He chuckled, gesturing to the empty space around us. "Like tonight? You walked in here alone. Unguarded. If I was someone else, you could be dead."

"Oh?" I asked, voice sharp. I caught his self-satisfied smirk. "You mean a shadow, silent and unseen, watching my back? Good idea," I stepped back, tilting my head, "don't you think, Wraith?"

A dagger slid across the floor with a soft scrape, coming to a halt near us.

I smiled, slow and dangerous. "Timing really is everything."

"She had backup," came a deep, amused voice from the shadows above us. His ally, near the harbormaster's office. Right where we expected when we scouted hours before. Raven had played her part well.

A flicker of genuine shock came from the shadow of his hood. He pointed to the dagger, "That looks strangely familiar, like my friend's." He paused, seeming to struggle through his thoughts. "You really are unbelievable, you know?"

I was glad the dark hid the heat in my cheeks at his compliment. "Since you'll be at the ball, place my payment in the washroom on the south side of the ballroom. The one with the tacky purple wallpaper. There is a bin there for laundry collection." I didn't explain how I knew about that washroom. How someone from the laundries emptied it daily. "Let's go, Wraith," I stepped back into the shadows. "We've got business."

I heard the distinct sound of a kiss smacking on someone's cheek, followed by the quiet rhythm of boots on stairs. Raven sauntered over, looking every bit the wraith she was with her hood down low, cloak trailing behind her. Together, we moved toward the exit.

"And little thief?" he called after me. "I'll want my ring back."

A laugh was my only reply as I stepped through the door and into the night with Raven.

◆ ◆ ◆ ◆ ◆

Raven and I were quiet for the first half of our walk. The Wharf District gave way to the Heap in crooked turns and broken cobblestone. We kept our eyes and ears open, daggers clutched in our hands.

Raven spoke first, her words muffled by the hood she had yet to lower. "Good to see your little falling bit got the job done." She chuckled. "Well, almost."

"Yeah, kind of," I replied. I pulled the ring free of my pocket and slipped it on my finger. I knew he'd notice its absence, I just hadn't expected him to notice so quickly. The blue stone caught the lamplight, flashing. Strange, I'd never known a noble ring to bear a gem. Likely a house I hadn't crossed paths with or stolen from yet. He'd get it back at the ball if all went well. A small, sparkling clue about the man pulling the strings, a little leverage of my own.

Raven hummed cheerfully beside me. "His hands lingered a little, didn't they? And unless I'm mistaken, you leaned into him." She waited, looking for a response I was not about to give. "I didn't know if you two were about to fight each other or fu—"

"Shut up, I was just distracting him," I cut in, feeling my heart flutter at her words. The worst part was she wasn't wrong. I'd leaned in, just a little, before I caught myself. I'd hoped she hadn't noticed, but of course she had. Damn her. Damn me. And damn him for smelling that good.

"Sure. Sure," she said, unconvinced. "Admit it, you were having fun."

I bumped her with my shoulder. Hard.

"Fine, fine." She threw up her hands in mock surrender, but I could hear the smile in her words. "His friend though? He's thick and delicious. I enjoyed silencing him in the dark."

"Fates, Raven." I stopped walking and pulled my hood down to stare at the side of her head.

"What?" She threw back her own hood, face filled with wicked glee. "Once this whole thing is over, I might treat myself to a ride." She winked, and continued her chipper humming for another block. I knew she was thinking of the man from the warehouse. What the hell had she done in the dark?

I hurried to catch up as she fit the key into our front door. She didn't open it though. She just stood there. Shoulders tight, eyes fixed on the door as though it held answers for her.

Then, she spoke, barely above a whisper. "Why invite Wickham?"

The question hovered between us. I knew it was the safety of the quiet street that allowed her to voice it in the first place. To see Raven like this twisted something deep in my chest.

It wasn't often I saw her afraid.

I stepped in front of her, planting myself between her and the door. When our eyes finally met, there was none of her usual fire. "Because I know what he offered when you dropped off our payment a few months ago," I whispered. "What he's always wanted. Or rather... who."

She looked away, jaw tight. The silence heavy with things she didn't want to revisit.

I pressed on. "Your hand in marriage to clear all of our debt," I searched her face. "I know you had to have thought about it."

She gnawed her lip, unease flickering across her face. My fierce, protective big sister had thought about it, of course she had. Curse Wickham for putting that choice on her.

My hands curled into fists. "That monster thinks he can buy you, own you. He can't. I won't let him." Fury lined every word.

"Me neither," she said, firmer now.

We stood in silence for a moment, the weight of so many unsaid things passing between us. Then I said it, the only thing that really mattered. "Then we take him down. Together."

Raven released a breath, some tension easing. "Have you figured out how?"

"Not yet," I admitted, the corner of my mouth twitching, "but I have some ideas."

"Good." She nodded, eyes on me. "I trust you Em."

Like I trusted her. "Come on," I murmured, reaching for the door. "Let's get some sleep. We're gonna need it."

✦ ✦ ✦ ✦ ✦

I gave up chasing sleep when the morning sun spilled gold across my room. I'd stayed up too late, mind spinning around the meeting, the deal I'd struck, and the consequences. Sleep had come in restless fragments.

Now, in the quiet of morning, my gaze found the ring I'd set on the nightstand. His ring. I hadn't meant to think of him, but he crept in anyway, smirk and all. I hadn't realized how much I enjoyed our banter. The way he'd taken to being outmaneuvered, with amusement, not anger, was dangerously appealing.

The soft creak of my door pulled me from my thoughts.

"You awake?" whispered Lark. Raven followed, shutting the door with practiced quiet.

I didn't answer, just tossed back the quilt and made room. My bed was small, but I'd long since given up any hope for personal space with two sisters.

Lark slid in first, stealing half my pillow as always. Only a year younger, she'd struggled the most with the move to the Heap, sneaking into beds for weeks. Even now, at twenty-one, she never refused the chance to snuggle. Raven plopped down at the foot of the bed, sprawling across our legs. We lay there in silence, taking comfort from being close.

"How long have you two been awake?" I whispered.

"Long enough for Raven to fill me in on your meeting," Lark said, voice thick with sleep. "The note you left last night had some key details missing."

"Yeah, well, we had to scout the spot," I murmured, rubbing at my eyes.

"Mother's worried," Lark added.

"I'm curious what she'll say," Raven said, voice thoughtful. "She might be furious you're working with a stranger or proud. Depends on if she hears about the gold or the danger first."

"She'll most certainly yell," Lark said flatly, "especially with Thorne involved."

I felt it then, the weight of what I carried, not just for myself, but for them. Not money or protection but something deeper. A promise I'd lived by since my father died, to fix what he'd broken.

After an illness stole my mother, it was more than I could have dreamed when he married my stepmother, a house filled with family. For the first five years, things had been good, filled with laughter and sister squabbles. Then came the business deals Father claimed would secure our future, but the ship of goods was lost at sea. He grew more desperate, and the drinking got worse. That final year, he was someone different. We were told he'd jumped from the Eastmore Bridge, but I'd always wondered if an unpaid loan had sealed his fate. We didn't know how bad things were until his debts came due. With no extended family, we were truly on our own. I still blamed him for all of it. But if this job, this risk, could make it right, I'd take it. I'd bear the danger. I would not fail them like he had.

41

"You're really going to do it?" Lark asked.

"I already agreed," I said. "It's done."

Raven sat up at the end of the bed, hair a mess of tangles, eyes sharp. "Then we're in. Obviously."

"We don't even have a plan yet."

"We will," she said, pretending to unroll a scroll. "According to the rules set forth by our queen Mother, we work best..." she looked at us expectedly, brows raised.

I cut her off, "Be serious. If this goes wrong..."

"We know," Lark said, hand finding mine beneath the blanket. "You are not alone in this. We work best together."

"I know," I replied and meant it. I couldn't do this without them.

A well of emotion clogged my throat, and I blinked hard, forcing back the tears. They would never abandon me. I looked at them. Raven, with her wild grin, looked ready for a fight. Lark, steady, already thinking through what we'd need. Something in my chest loosened. Just a little.

A sharp knock cut through the stillness, three sharp taps.

Mother's voice followed, clipped. "If you're all done skulking around, maybe we could speak like actual humans? Kitchen please, ladies."

Raven winced. "Morning meeting with the queen it is."

We walked down the hall together, a unified front, though more like guilty children summoned by the headmistress. The kitchen smelled of cinnamon and clove, warm and familiar. If the second floor of this house was our refuge, the kitchen was undeniably our mother's domain. Worn butcher block counters, carved with years of knife marks and dusted with a fine layer of flour, told stories of countless meals made by loving hands. Copper pans, dulled by time, hung from hooks above the iron stove. The curtains, made by Lark, were embroidered with Mother's favorite flowers, the little bursts of color making the room feel even more alive.

The air was charged with the weight of what she already suspected.

Mother stood at the counter, hands kneading what I hoped was dough for her scones. Though judging by the angry way she handled the messy mixture, I probably wouldn't be getting one.

"I assume there's a reason you three felt the need to creep around before sunrise?" she asked coolly, eyeing us all with the lethal precision gifted to all mothers.

Raven opened her mouth, no doubt ready with some sarcastic remark, but I stopped her with a look. She swallowed the retort, propping herself against the counter. Lark, brimming with her usual energy, folded her arms and brought a hand over her mouth, as if physically holding back her words. I lingered in the doorway, guilt pressing heavy in my chest. I made the deal, starting this conversation fell to me.

"I took a job," I said, stepping forward.

Mother stopped her food prep, wiping her hands on a rag with slow, deliberate movements. Only she could look intimidating with flour dusted across her cheek. "I assumed as much. Explain."

"It's enough to clear our debts to Wickham," Lark said, stepping beside me. "Dangerous, yes, but it's something we can do."

Mother's gaze flicked to each of us. "What kind of job pays that much? And who is paying you?"

I hesitated, not quite ready to voice my suspicions about the shadowed stranger, suspicions I hadn't yet shared with my sisters.

"A noble," Raven supplied. "Show her the ring, Em."

I placed it on the counter between us all, and Mother sucked in a breath, surprised by the sight. "Blue topaz?"

"Yes, it's not a house I'm familiar with," I answered.

Our mother's expression darkened, a deep furrow between her brows. "There was only one noble house that used blue stones in their seal. The late queen's line, Emberlynn," Mother said, enunciating each word. She shook her head. "To honor her, no one uses it anymore. That is not a noble ring." She pointed at the glinting band. "That is a family heirloom." She snorted, like she couldn't believe it herself. "You may very well have gotten hired to do a job by Prince Rowan himself."

I nodded. That same conclusion wouldn't leave me all night. When he mentioned details about the ball, details not yet announced, I wondered. When he didn't hesitate to get me another invitation, I had suspected. But when he named my payment, the figure so absurdly high, I knew.

Mother's gaze drilled into me. "Do you trust him?"

"No." My answer was immediate. "I don't trust anyone outside of this house. But I'm not foolish. He needs us, this is personal to him. And we need a way out from under

Wickham before he demands something we're not willing to give."

Mother stiffened. She was the one who'd told me about Wickham's proposal. The flowered curtains swayed softly in the morning breeze as she stared out the window, quiet for a long moment before she spoke. "We keep control by choosing the jobs we take. A pocket here, a jewel there, small thefts when the wealthy are tucked away at their country homes. But this?" Her voice dropped, heavy with warning. "This is royalty. That world... few people dare to steal from it." She looked at us, eyes filled with worry. "What if something happens to you girls?" She knew, if one of us was doing this job, we all were.

"Then we handle it together," Raven said, fierce certainty lining her words.

"We're not children anymore," Lark added, her voice calm but resolute. "We've taken risks like this before. It's only the venue that's changed."

Mother's gaze landed on me, the weight of her love and worry near unbearable. "Ember." Her voice broke slightly. "Tell me you can do this. That you know what you're leading them into."

I swallowed hard, my throat tight, but I didn't look away. "I've thought of little else all night, and I'd rather risk everything than wait for Wickham to take by force what he's only asking for now." Her expression flickered and I could see the emotions wash over her, the fear, the fury, and then resolve. "I won't fail us," I finished and meant it.

Mother studied us, her daughters grown and defiant, standing side by side like an unbreakable wall. A small smile pulled at her lips. "Fine." She let out a breath and returned to her dough. "Tell me everything. Leave nothing out."

So I did. And, for the rest of the day, we planned.

⋄ ⋄ ◆ ⋄ ⋄

We'd strategized well into the night, pulling the scheme apart from every angle, running through contingencies until the words blurred together. I'd fallen asleep fully clothed on top of my blankets. The only real point of conflict had come up, unsurprisingly, at the mention of Thorne. Lark had been right, Mother had started yelling then. Even I had to admit she was right to be worried. He was dangerous, but we'd approach him like any other mark. We'd stalk, we'd learn, and we'd find his weakness. Raven and I planned on spending the rest of our day and night doing just that.

The sun had barely climbed above the rooftops before we were out of bed. The morning air still held a crisp bite, and golden light spilled across the streets as we made our way to a familiar tailor in the Jewel. Our history with her was… complicated to say the least. But, we had to look like we belonged at a Royal Ball, and I knew she could make our dresses quickly. Besides, she owed us. Otherwise, Raven might follow through on her long-standing threat to burn the shop down.

"I cannot believe I am going to visit this bitch," Raven hissed for what must have been the tenth time.

"I told you," I said, annoyed. We'd had this conversation already. "Abigail's the only other tailor willing to work with people from the Heap, and she has the skill to make a dress for a royal event. Greaves was stabbed last week."

"Was it bad?" Raven asked, brows raised, clearly unconcerned for the man we usually dealt with. "The stabbing?"

Lark and I stared at her in stunned silence.

"Yes," Lark replied, as if communicating to a stubborn infant. "The stabbing. To his *chest* was bad."

"Seems like something he could soldier through," Raven muttered, stomping along the cobblestones, fury radiating with each step.

"If anyone should be pissed, it's Lark," I chastised, knowing it'd make no difference, "but she isn't being a rage-filled maniac."

"Well," Raven scoffed, "it's a well-established fact that Lark is a far kinder person than me. And you, for that matter."

She wasn't wrong. Still, like it or not, we were headed to Abigail's shop.

Abigail happened to be Lark's ex-girlfriend, and her last real relationship. It hadn't ended for lack of love, but Abigail's parents wanted a better match for their daughter. Someone from the right family to raise their standing. Abigail had caved to the pressure, leaving them both heartbroken. Especially Lark.

We reached the shop just as the bell tolled the new hour, before the streets filled with people. I paused at the shop's threshold, glancing at Lark.

"You ready?" I asked.

Lark drew in a slow breath, smoothing her hands down the front of her simple dress, a nervous habit she shared with Mother. "How do I look?" she whispered, voice uncertain.

"Too damn beautiful," I said and meant it. She looked radiant, the light shining through her chestnut hair like a halo, her cheeks rosy from our walk. She was color and life and could easily pass as a lady of the Jewel.

Lark stepped forward, took the handle herself, and was the first to enter. The bell above the door chimed a bright, cheerful note into the otherwise quiet shop. It smelled faintly of lavender and starch, the air already warm from the iron pressing tables in the back. The early sun filtered through the windows, catching on bolts of fabric arranged in careful rows along the walls. Dresses in every color hung from wooden pegs, their jeweled skirts catching the light like little stars. The space was pristine and organized, Abigail's mark in every polished surface and perfectly folded ribbon. That relentless pursuit of her craft was how she'd claimed a prime shop in the Jewel despite her youth, outpacing tailors with twice her experience. She settled for nothing short of mastery.

Abigail was standing inside, a dress in her arms. She froze when Lark entered, lips parted on a surprised exhale, a stunned expression on her face. Her red hair was pulled back in a braid away from her fair face. She took a step toward the door, hand outstretched like her immediate reaction was to reach for Lark.

Then Raven came in, and Abigail dropped her hand quickly as if burned.

Abigail cleared her throat, eyes never leaving Lark's face as she drank her in. "Lark, what a surprise," she said breathlessly before her eyes flicked to me. "Ember, hello," she added, polite but distant. "Raven," she finished, voice devoid of any warmth.

Raven's answering smile was sharp and wolfish, enjoying Abigail's obvious dislike. I stayed quiet, letting Lark lead. She held the most sway here, and I trusted her to handle it.

"We need dresses, Abi," Lark said, voice steady despite their history. My heart swelled with pride at the sight.

"Really?" Abigail blinked, caught off guard. We'd never needed fine dresses, not in all the time she'd known us.

Lark huffed out a small laugh. "Yes." She was smiling now, as if they were sharing a joke. "For the Royal Ball."

Abigail's eyes widened. "That's tomorrow night. I can't possibly make three new dresses in that time! The palace just announced it's a masquerade, every seamstress in the city is scrambling to make masks. Gold or silver. It's absurd." She looked frazzled, hair escaping her tidy updo, apron askew, so unlike her normal polished appearance.

Raven stepped forward, looking ready to use this as an excuse to finally torch the place, and with it, our chances. I threw out my arm, holding her back.

"We can pay you," I said, producing some of the Prince's money, but Abigail didn't even glance my way. She just watched Lark.

"We can use ones you've already made," Lark offered. "I'll help tailor them to fit us. All night if I need to. Please, Abi. It's important." Her voice was soft now, earnest.

Abigail sighed and I could see she'd help. She couldn't say no to Lark, and we all knew it. "Okay, for you, Birdie.

I mean, Lark," she stammered. My jaw clenched at the use of Lark's old pet name. "Yes. Let's go see what I have." She turned toward the back of the shop, Lark close behind.

"Can you try a little harder here please?" I whispered over my shoulder to Raven. I trailed after the pair, careful not to be overheard.

"Considering I haven't tried at all, sure, I guess I could," she muttered, leaning close enough for me to feel her breath on my ear.

I shot her a sharp look.

"Fine," she hissed. "I'll be nice." But from the glare she gave me, she didn't believe that any more than I did. "Though, I could have sworn I heard *your* teeth crack when she said 'Birdie.'" She *tsked* sarcastically. "Best behavior, Sister."

The back room was lined with rows of completed dresses, silk and taffeta, jeweled and pleated, bursting in every color imaginable.

"I always thought you looked beautiful in red," Abigail said to Lark, her voice soft and familiar as she handed over a bright ruby gown. She leaned in, and Lark didn't move away. From the corner of my eye, I saw Raven roll her eyes theatrically.

Fates, I cursed. This was going to be a long day.

"I just need something dark," Lark said to Abigail.

"In case she needs to hide away and take a moment for herself," I explained, seeing Abigail's puzzled look. Lark never wore dark colors, it wasn't her style.

"A deep crimson would be great, if you have it," Lark said, claiming the dressmaker's attention once more.

My eyes scanned the row of dresses until one caught my attention. A rich blue, strikingly similar to the gown I'd seen on Lilia Hartwick's blonde friend.

"What about this one?" I asked, unable to keep the awe from slipping into my voice. The sweeping skirt, the subtle train, it was stunning. The kind of beauty we rarely got to touch, let alone wear.

"Oh, I made that for Maribelle Leander," Abigail said. "She ended up choosing something else for the ball. Said she was tired of wearing blue. Spoiled brat." Abigail had to work with the elite of the Jewel. We used to laugh and gossip over the requests her clients made. "She still paid for it, though." She held the dress up to my body, brushing her fingers over the intricate beading and layered bodice. "I worked my fingers numb making this, but it'll suit you with your coloring. Just a warning, the neckline's low. You might end up with a proposal by the end of the night."

Good. Breasts did tend to make men, especially men like Thorne, stupid.

"Maribelle," I said absently, imagining myself in this dress. "Is she one of Lilia Hartwick's friends?"

Abigail raised her brows. "Yes. You know her?"

I nodded, remembering the blonde whose bracelet I'd claimed two days ago. "Sort of. We crossed paths recently."

Then Abigail turned to Raven, her tone icy, edging on disrespect. "And you?"

"She'll take something green, please," I said quickly, stepping in as Raven went rigid at Abigail's tone. Best to keep their interactions to a minimum. Green was the color of Wickham's family crest. These dresses weren't just for appearances. We were choosing strategically, they were part of the roles we meant to play.

"Let's try these on and I'll pin them for the alterations," Abigail said, ushering us behind silk screens. "Should be quick fixes and I can have them done tomorrow. Especially with Lark's help." She paused, then added shyly, "I always loved working with you, Lark."

A distinct ripping sound came from Raven's direction. "This dress needs mending by the way, there's a tear."

"Abigail?" I cut in, pointedly, tugging off my cotton shift. I redirected the conversation from the impending argument with Raven to my second reason for this visit. "Did you hear the rumor that a group from the Heap is attending the ball?" I looked over my screen, giving Abigail a playful wink.

"I hadn't," she admitted, her tone uncertain as she looked at me. Wondering. "How far would you like that rumor to spread?"

"Pretty far," I replied, glad she caught on so quickly. Like most who served the elite, Abigail traded in gossip and secrets as easily as thread and silk. I'd need her little network to do their part before this was done. I wanted her to pass the information on and let other people spread this news. By the end of the ball, it'd be common knowledge that masked thieves prowled among the dancing crowd.

"Can you believe it?" Lark chimed in, feigning shock from behind her own changing screen. "Cutthroats and street rats at the Royal Ball?"

My pulse picked up. The beginnings of our plan were set in motion. I couldn't believe they'd let the likes of us through their gilded doors. But tomorrow, we'd be at the ball. Masked and dressed as nobility, ready to see if we could actually pull this off.

The day stretched long before me. Before the sun set, I had to stalk Thorne. Learn his patterns, his likes, and become someone he'd not only notice, but want close. A role I'd played before, slipping into the shadows to collect secrets, but today a different sort of thrill ran through me. The thought of taking on Thorne twisted my stomach, fear and excitement mixing together at the challenge. It was what Raven liked best, the danger of getting close to a target, finding their weaknesses. Thorne was a dangerous adversary, but one I intended to exploit.

Meanwhile, Lark would stay in the Jewel ensuring our dresses were finished. She needed to collect the rest of the supplies for the ball: cosmetics, shoes, and jewels. My heart swelled with joy at the thought of her spending what might very well be a Prince's fortune, weaving through the streets of the Jewel all day. I pulled the soft blue silk up my body, luxuriating in its softness and smiled.

◆ ◆ ◆ ◆ ◆

It was the sharp knock that woke me the next morning.

I groaned into my pillow. "Go away."

"It's noon, you need to start getting ready," Lark called through the door she'd already nudged open. "Raven's getting her hair done and arguing with Mother. Trust me, that entertainment alone is worth waking up for."

That got me moving, though every muscle begged for more sleep. After our dress fittings, Raven and I had trailed Thorne past midnight. We followed him from one meeting to the next, using my knowledge of the city streets from my courier job to stay hidden. A lavish lunch, then his favorite gambling den where I watched him cheat at cards. Later, a high-end brothel, where he made a visit to his favorite courtesan before going home to his wife. We also listened to what people said when he left the room. Asked just enough questions to get information without prying. People were eager to talk in hushed whispers over a pint about the dangerous man. I'd learned enough to make him notice me, enough to use against him tonight. Fortunately for me, he seemed to have a weakness for blondes.

"How'd dressmaking go?" I asked groggily as I stepped in the hall.

"About as well as you'd expect," Lark sighed. "It was fine. Abi was sweet, fun. It's easy to see why I loved her so much. She wants to see me again, but in secret." She stopped, weighing her words before she added, quieter. "But, I won't be hidden. I don't deserve that."

My throat tightened for my beautiful sister. "You're right. You deserve to be seen and loved out loud. Adored."

"I thought Raven might kill her."

"We remember how she made you feel," I said. "The only reason I didn't threaten her was because I knew you could handle it."

"Tell that to Raven."

"Yeah, right." I smirked. "But seriously, I'd get violent for you, Little Sister. And... you look beautiful." She must have been first in Mother's chair this morning. Her hair was woven into an intricate, full braid, jeweled pins glinting like diamonds throughout.

"I have your back too sister," she said fiercely. "And... thank you."

We entered the sitting room to find Mother wielding a hot iron at Raven like a weapon, slicing it through the air in sharp, erratic motions. The scorched tang of singed hair lingered in the room.

"You're done," Mother declared, triumphant as if she'd tamed a wild animal. Judging by Raven's stormy expression, she probably had.

"Thank Fate I don't have to do that again," Raven said, springing from the chair. She didn't so much as look at the mirror before she stormed toward her room.

"You're lucky I didn't slip and burn your ear," Mother called after Raven's retreating form. She looked at me. "Ember, dear, your turn." She motioned for me to sit in the seat Raven had just vacated.

"I'm off to get dressed," Lark said as she slipped from the room.

Mother started working a brush through my hair with gentle, measured strokes. I almost closed my eyes at the sensation, lulled by the rhythm of her hands.

"Half up, I think," she murmured to herself, lifting sections of my hair with thoughtful care. Still groggy from sleep, I caught her reflection in the mirror, and something shifted in me, sharpening my thoughts. She was already dressed for work tonight in the Glass Palace laundries.

"You were able to change your shift?" I asked. "No one was suspicious?"

She scoffed dismissively. "No one really cares, as long as the work gets done."

I hummed my agreement.

"I work until midnight," she said, meeting my gaze in the mirror, her eyes full of meaning. "And I've told them it will be my last night working." A small, proud smile tugged at her lips.

"You're that confident we'll succeed?" I asked, needing to hear it, to feel the weight of her faith in us.

"I believe in you girls," she whispered. "Whether because of the hardships you've faced, or in spite of them, you'll do what it takes to finish this job."

I believed her. We could do this, we could pull it off. By midnight, one way or another, we'd all be out of that castle.

She worked on my hair for over an hour, sectioning and braiding until the sides were swept back and the rest fell in gentle waves. A dusting of rouge warmed my cheeks, kohl darkened my eyes, and a soft pink tint made my lips look full and inviting. The result was striking and alluring. A flutter stirred deep inside me at the sight. Maybe soon I'd have time to feel pretty, to explore a part of myself I so often pushed down.

"All finished and much easier to manage than Raven," she teased, giving my shoulder an affectionate pat. Our reflections gazed back from the mirror, side by side. My features were unmistakably my mother's, her deep blue eyes and the same golden hair I kept long like hers. But

I carried something of Rosalind, too, her devotion, her strength. "You look beautiful, love."

I smiled broadly.

"Now," she whispered, a beautiful secret between us two, "you're perfect."

◆ ◆ ◆ ◆ ◆

Dusk had given way to full darkness during our carriage ride later, the castle a glowing beacon against the star-scattered sky. The gentle breeze whispered over our skin, but did nothing to calm the unease that had grown as we neared the castle gates. My palms were clammy, and my chest felt tight. I found myself counting to three more than once to steady my breathing. Raven kept flicking her right hand, over and over, as if opening an imaginary blade. I was pretty sure I'd seen Lark smooth her hands down the front of her dress at least fifty times. Nervous energy radiated off them both in waves.

It wasn't just the idea of lifting a letter from Thorne that had us on edge. If all went well, we'd be done with Wickham tonight, too. Mother hadn't been there to send us off but had given us each a lingering embrace before she left. She was already inside the castle doing her part, and we were about to join her. The valet opened our carriage door, his gloved hand smooth against my own as he helped me dismount the shaky steps first.

Raven exited next and was a vision in green. The gown was fitted through the bodice, tracing the line of her long waist before cascading into layered skirts that shimmered with every step. The round neckline and slim sleeves framed her toned shoulders, accentuating the regal poise she always carried effortlessly. With her gold mask in place, she looked elegant and undeniably seductive. She gnawed on her lower lip, concerned about the upcoming encounter with Wickham.

Lark glided down the steps last, as if her feet barely touched the ground. Her red gown clung to her slight frame, the fabric catching the light and shifting from crimson to the deepest wine as she moved. A subtle slit in her full skirt gave the barest hint of her long leg. The square neckline and full sleeves were detailed with delicate gold beading, mirroring the gleam in her gold mask. Where Raven was dark and mysterious, Lark was a living flame, wild and untamed. Only the restless tug on her sleeve betrayed her unease.

My own dress was the blue of a summer sky just before dusk. The off-the-shoulder neckline dipped into a soft sweetheart shape, revealing the graceful line of my collarbones. The skirt flared from a cinched waist, and though I hated the stiff boning, I couldn't deny it carved out a striking silhouette. Silver thread wound through each layer, catching the light like sunlight dancing on the water. My silver mask, crafted from the same shimmering thread, framed my face, making my kohl-lined eyes glow.

Our looks served as both armor and distraction, tools for the layered plans we were about to set in motion. The extra pockets that lined my skirts, thanks to Lark's handiwork, would certainly help. But the pocket she had hidden at the back of my bodice would be the most useful. With the wealth that would be on display tonight, I was about to have a lot of fun.

There it was, the familiar thrill, as addictive as any drink. I glanced to my right at Lark and gave her a fortifying look. She stopped fidgeting and offered a mischievous wink. Raven to my left gave me a playful air kiss before turning forward again. We were ready.

Carriages rolled up in a steady stream behind us, wheels clattering against the stone, footmen leaping off to open doors with practiced ease. Guests spilled out in glittering waves, quiet laughter and perfume drifting with them as they swept toward the entrance. We slipped among the masked crowd, becoming just another noble family arriving for the ball.

The palace gates were swung wide open to welcome guests. The doors towered above us, four times my height, and were intricately carved—serpents, roses, and battles long since won. At the center, gleaming in the torchlight, sat the Royal Crest, the lion etched in the wood seeming to watch us as we crossed the threshold.

A valet in scarlet and navy received our invitation with gloved hands. His face betrayed nothing, though his eyes lingered on the Royal Seal before he gave me a low bow and gestured forward. "This way, ladies."

We moved with the stream of guests along the lantern-lit walkway, weaving our way toward the castle's grand archway. The ballroom opened up before us like a dream, vast, and glittering. Marble floors gleamed beneath our feet, reflecting the light of towering chandeliers that dripped crystal light from a ceiling so high it seemed to vanish into the heavens. Gold trimmed columns lined the perimeter, each carved with delicate floral patterns and the ever-present lion crest. Between the tall windows hung heavy tapestries in royal blue and crimson, rich with history and power.

At the center of the dance floor, a royal messenger unrolled a scroll, his voice slicing through the excited murmurs of the crowd.

"Welcome, most noble guests, to the Royal Ball honoring our beloved Prince Rowan. May you find delight in this evening's festivities."

On cue, servants flowed into the room like a tide, balancing trays of glittering glasses and delicacies in their practiced hands. Music swelled, a graceful melody drifting through the air like smoke.

I leaned into my sisters, gripping their hands tightly and drawing them close. "Remember," I whispered, my voice low and firm, "at the stroke of midnight, you'd better be outside those gates, in the carriage." They nodded once, solemn. I let them go.

Raven drifted toward the edge of the room, green skirts billowing in her wake as she plucked a flute of champagne from a passing tray. She lounged against a pillar like a panther basking in sunlight, daring someone to come closer. Lark, on the other hand, disappeared silently into the crowd, on the hunt for prey of her own. As for me, I slipped a bracelet from a woman who brushed past me and lifted a jeweled clip from a gentleman's collar before I'd even reached the hors d'oeuvre table. My fingers tingled, my blood sang.

The game had begun.

For a while, I let the current of the ball carry me. Music rose and fell, a song of strings and lifting flutes. I plucked delicious confections and savory bites from passing trays, enjoying every decadent bite. Across the ballroom, Lark danced with a man in a silver mask, her dress a living flame as she moved in time to the music. I caught the subtle nod she aimed in my direction. A confirmation that she had visited the washroom with the purple wallpaper. Our payment was there. My pulse quickened with excitement, ten thousand crowns, a shiny gold prize if we could pull this off.

Drifting in and out of conversations, I collected gossip like the jewels beginning to weigh down my pockets. Prince Rowan seemed to be a main topic of conversation. Some swore he hadn't arrived yet, while others insisted he was already hidden among the dancers, his mask allowing him a taste of freedom at his own party.

I positioned myself just inside the ballroom, near the open windows overlooking the bubbling fountain and palace gardens. There, I let Lady Thorne draw me into a long conversation, nodding and murmuring politely as we gossiped. She couldn't wait to tell me the news that someone from the Heap had infiltrated the ball. But her gasp of surprise when I mentioned the man was rumored to be named Wickham assured me her friends would hear all about this. Her husband, Lord Atticus Thorne, lingered at her side for a time, his pale gaze sliding toward me too often to be an accident. I watched him pat the front of his jacket intentionally, as if checking its contents. *Perfect*, I thought. *He has his letter.*

When he finally excused himself, I let my gaze linger on him a heartbeat too long. Just enough for him to notice, before quickly looking away, embarrassed to be caught. His lips curved into a grin, and I knew he'd seek me out again. From his courtesan, I'd learned he craved the chase itself, savoring the tension in being admired and the thrill of spoiling purity. It probably played to his already inflated ego and cruel nature.

"Can you imagine, my dear?" Lady Thorne asked me between sips of her nearly empty glass. "I do hope we are safe here."

"I assure you Lady Thorne, you are completely safe this evening," a deep voice replied from my right, familiar, though I couldn't quite place it.

I had to tip my head back to meet his gaze. He was tall, broad-shouldered, with tousled blonde hair that looked as though he'd just run his fingers through it. His green eyes were sharp and watchful behind his silver mask.

"Oh, Commander Hawthorne," the woman said warmly, relief visibly softening her features. "With you on watch, how can we not be? Allow me to introduce you to this sweet young woman, Lady Ashcomb."

"Lovely to meet you, Commander," I said, extending my hand with a polite smile.

"How do you do, Miss Ashcomb?" His much larger hand engulfed mine, and his bow was formal as he pressed a short kiss to my knuckles. He lifted his eyes to meet mine. "Though if I'm not mistaken, we've met before."

"I'll leave you to chat," said Lady Thorne before she walked off to the drink table.

The voice clicked in my memory at last, one short sentence, spoken in the dark three nights ago. No wonder I hadn't placed him right away. I searched for where I knew Raven stood across the ballroom, her gaze locked on me and the commander. He followed my eyes and looked at her too. She smiled coyly and lifted her champagne flute in a teasing toast. He smiled back, wide and unrestrained, before lifting his glass in turn.

"She will eat you alive," I said to him, half warning, half jest.

He didn't take his eyes off Raven. "Fates, I hope so," he said with a quiet sort of intensity. He drew a slow sip from his drink before turning his attention back to me. "Is everything going well?"

"Yes, *Commander* Hawthorne," I replied, placing a special emphasis on the first word. "Where is your hooded friend this evening?"

"Call me Silas." He looked at me, eyebrows raised above his mask. "Hooded friend? Am I to believe you don't know his name?"

"How could I possibly know that?" I asked, feigning ignorance, "I only just found out who you were."

"You didn't take my ring. And if I'm involved, it narrows down the possibilities, doesn't it?"

I drew a sharp breath, interrupting Silas. A flicker of movement at the edge of the room drew my attention, and my stomach clenched as I spotted Wickham slithering through the crowd. He wore a tailored green jacket, so similar in color to Raven's dress, they were almost a matching set. My shoulders stiffed, as I watched him make a deliberate path straight toward Raven. "I take it you're the extra set of eyes watching this evening?"

"I am," Silas answered, immediately noticing the change in my demeanor and looking toward Raven once more.

"Then be sure to keep an eye on her too," I said, my voice sharp like a blade. "She's going to have a worse night than me." I touched his arm, "Enjoy the rest of your evening, Silas."

Though it physically pained me, I pushed my concerns aside and turned my back on Raven and Wickham. She could handle herself, but I felt better knowing Silas was nearby. His presence confirmed what I had suspected, Prince Rowan was my mystery employer. It seemed we were all playing someone else tonight. But, confusion muddied my thoughts. *Why did he want the letter?* He was the prince, couldn't he just demand to see it? There was clearly something larger going on in here, but it must be important for Prince Rowan to hire me.

I moved toward the far side of the ballroom, skirting clusters of guests bent close in conversation. The laughter of the crowd, the clink of crystal, and the steady swell of music wove together in a symphony of a party done well. My gaze swept the gathering, looking for Lark in the sea of masks. I finally found her and, with a tilt of my head, made my way to the washroom. I smiled and averted my gaze like a good noblewoman as appreciative glances were thrown my way. Lark followed me into the washroom, locking the door behind us to steal a moment of privacy.

The purple wallpaper was as ugly as Mother described, though I couldn't tell if her hatred came from the pattern or the fact that she was the one always hauling linens out of here. A dizzying array of oversized lilies and looping vines, each outlined in metallic gold. Regal in theory, but something created out of a fever dream. Lark's lips twitched as she pointed out a small purple frog hidden in the wallpaper's foliage. We shared a stunned look.

"Here," I whispered, hands moving fast as I emptied my pockets. The bounty clattered across the marble counter, jewels and brooches tinging on the hard surface. My pulse was a thunderous beat in my ears. Now that the first part was over, I had to do the job I was being paid for next. "Mother will be here soon to collect the linens."

"I know, Em," she said, steady as ever. "It's going exactly as planned. I saw Raven with Wickham. I'll drop the bag of jewelry near her. She'll make sure he sees it, he'll think it's his lucky day."

I let out a short, nervous laugh. Part of me worried for Raven, but I also knew she'd relish being the one to outsmart him. "Acting like a lousy thief, getting caught, that's what's going to piss her off the most."

Lark snorted, shoving the final piece of treasure, Lady Thorne's ruby necklace, into a small bag.

"Can you handle the last part? With Thorne?" I asked, concerned for her.

"Of course," she replied, words firm and sure. "I've seen him with a drink in his hand all night. He'll be sloppy and angry, unfocused, after you're done with him. I'll be quick. That's why my dress is dark. Besides," she added with a sly edge, "I've gotten good at attacking people from the shadows, as you well know." I smiled, I certainly did know that. "I'll see you on the dance floor before you meet with Mother at the fountain." She gestured toward the door, tucking the bag under the slit in her skirt.

We stepped out of the washroom and were swallowed by the noise of the ballroom again. In the few minutes we'd been gone, the party had taken on a sharper edge of excitement, the music and chatter now louder. The entire room had stirred to life. Lark peeled off, searching for Raven.

"I am telling you, I am certain I saw Prince Rowan," said a short brunette to my right.

A flutter stirred in my chest at the mention of the prince. Had my mystery employer finally arrived? I didn't have time to dwell on it. He'd seek me out. With Raven and Lark busy trapping Wickham, it was time I found Thorne.

I saw him with an empty glass in his hand, making his way toward a servant bearing a tray of tall crystal flutes. Time for him to meet his next dance partner. The young doe eyed girl, who'd caught his eye earlier. The one who found him attractive and—I tasted bile at the back of my throat—wanted his attention. With his wife nowhere to be seen, now was the time.

I closed the distance between us, meeting him at the tray of drinks. Letting my body brush firmly against his, I reached for the same crystal flute while my other hand skimmed the front of his jacket. Every instinct screamed to pull away, yet I leaned in.

"Watch it," he snapped, jostled by our contact.

"Oh, forgive me, my lord," I purred, cutting off any question about the light touch where his letter was stored. My body was nearly flush with his as I peered up at him through my lashes. "I didn't see you there."

"Well... accidents do happen, my pet," he murmured, the corners of his mouth curling in a predatory smile. He dismissed the servant with a lazy, practiced flick of his fingers. "I had hoped to see you again this evening, Lady..."

"Ashcomb, my lord," I replied, letting a small smile pull at my lips. "I'm pleased to see you as well."

He lifted the glass in a slow, deliberate sip, not breaking eye contact. I held his gaze for a beat or two before lowering mine. When he finished, he smacked his lips in exaggerated satisfaction. "So good. So sweet," he said, his meaning unmistakable. I felt his gaze like a physical touch on my chest, and resisted the urge to punch him in the throat. I'd have to thank Abigail. She'd earned her pay.

I offered him a soft smile before taking a delicate sip of my own drink, unable to enjoy the way the bubbles kissed my lips. Thorne watched my every move, his gaze hungry. I gave him a shallow bow, keeping my eyes downcast.

"Thank you for your graciousness, my lord. Please enjoy the rest of your evening." I turned to go, heart in my throat. This was the moment, the moment I saw if I had him.

"Now, now." His hand clamped around my arm, firm and far rougher than necessary as he spun me towards him. He pulled me closer. "Surely you wouldn't deny me a dance after all that," he murmured. His breath, warm and laced with champagne, ghosted across my cheek.

I fought the urge to recoil from his closeness, from the oppressive feel of his body against mine. This is exactly what I wanted, for him to invite me close. Summoning a flirtatious grin, I murmured, "Why, my lord, how could I possibly refuse?"

He plucked the flute from my hand and touched his lips to the spot mine had just been, smearing the lip stain I left behind. Finishing the drink, he handed both glasses to a passing servant before wrapping an arm around my waist. Possessive. I drew a measured calming breath, nerves and anticipation battling.

He pulled me close, far closer than was appropriate, and inhaled deeply near my hair. "*Hmm*, lilacs. My favorite," Thorne whispered, his breath hot against my ear.

I know, I thought. *That's why your favorite woman at the brothel wears it.*

As he spun me with the music, the crowd beyond came into focus, swirling skirts of every hue slid across the marble, couples lost in the revelry. I saw Wickham guide Raven across the dance floor, and a coil of tension wound up my spine. Others might admire Raven's perfect posture as a sign of noble breeding, but I recognized the tense line of her body for what it was, barely contained rage. Given the way Wickham held her, it wasn't hard to guess the cause. *Soon*, I thought, *so soon.*

Amid the other dancers, a figure caught my eye. Tall, black hair tousled, a silver mask doing nothing to hide the familiar shape of his jaw. His gaze found me, intense and unwavering. On the next rotation, he winked. My breath caught. Prince Rowan. His perfectly tailored jacket, deep blue with silver threads, clung to his muscular form, and I felt his gaze like a brand as Thorne pulled me closer.

Thorne's hands roamed freely now, fingers brushing too low, lingering too long. The first time he grazed my backside, I stiffened at the touch. "So sorry," he murmured, the false apology curdled by the smirk in his voice. I forced a smile in response, though my fingers itched for a blade.

My gaze drifted past him searching for one face. Lark. She should have been here by now. A ripple of unease curled low in my stomach, if she'd been delayed, we'd be in trouble. No, I reminded myself, she'd come. Just as Raven had played her part, Lark would not fail us. I just had to endure Thorne a little longer. The next part was important.

But as his hand lingered on my ass again, I was so intent on scanning the dancers for Lark that a small gasp slipped free, my step faltering and pressing me flush against Thorne. He stilled instantly, mistaking my reaction as desire.

"Were you overcome?" he asked, fingers pressing possessively into my side. He tilted my chin until I met his gaze, lust flickering in his pale eyes as he wet his lips. My stomach twisted. "It's only natural to want me," he whispered. "I've seen the way your eyes have lingered this evening."

I wanted to recoil. To shove him away, instead I smiled and lowered my gaze. I must play this just right, this game of cat and mouse he enjoyed so much. Each second stretched taut like a bowstring. I needed him to dance just a little longer, I needed to wait for Lark.

"We'll find a more private place to finish our dance," he murmured, seizing my hand.

"Near the fountain, my lord?" I asked, feigning eagerness. That was where Mother would be waiting, where the next turn of our plan was meant to begin. Even if I missed Lark, I could still set Thorne in place for the final part.

He pulled me through the ballroom, dragging me in his wake like a doll, past servants balancing trays of emptied crystal flutes and dancers spinning in jeweled circles. His stride was quick, anticipation thrumming in every hurried step.

A flash of red brushed my side, walking just behind me. Lark.

Her hand slid quickly into the secret pocket at my back. In a heartbeat she was gone, vanishing into the sea of masks and jewels, on her way to meet our Mother. That meeting, what they would need to do, had to happen before I saw Mother at the fountains. I needed to delay Thorne to give her a little more time. My chest was tight as my thoughts swirled. Thorne continued to drag me forward, his focus so single-minded he hadn't once glanced back.

We passed Raven and Wickham, half-hidden behind a stone column. He stood rigid with anger as he gripped a familiar canvas bag tightly in his fist. He leaned in close, invading her space as he hissed words I couldn't hear. To anyone else she might have looked cowed, her posture bowed as her eyes welled with tears. Guilt tugged low in my belly, instinct demanding I rush to her side, to pull her away from him and his anger. I couldn't, but I caught the flick of her right hand, subtle and sharp, as though testing the weight of an invisible blade, just before the crowd hid them from view.

"He seems to have the right idea, but I know a more private place, away from prying eyes." Thorne said, "The gardens will be better. Easier for us to... talk."

Talk. Right. His grip on my hand was too tight, his steps too eager. I knew exactly what he wanted in that garden, what he'd feel entitled to. Panic clawed at my throat, I couldn't let him take me there. We were near the edge of the ballroom now, so close to those open doors I could see the fountain, almost feel the cool night air.

"My lord," I tried, one more time, careful to keep the panic from my voice. I pulled my hand slightly, slowing our pace, buying me precious seconds to think. "I would love to rest near the fountain for a moment, perhaps have another glass of champagne."

"No, no," he said dismissively, tugging more forcefully. "I know what you need."

The crowd around me blurred, a swirl of sound and color pressing in, as my heart beat violently in my chest. I wanted to scream, to wrench my hand from his grip, but we wouldn't be safe without this next piece. Thorne must never know I'd taken his letter. If the fountain was off limits, I needed something, anything, to erase the evidence of my crime.

A servant stood in front of us, balancing a full tray of drinks in his hands.

I smiled... timing really was everything.

As we passed, I reached out and, with a swift motion, up-ended the entire tray. Glass and champagne flew through the air in a messy arc, landing squarely on Thorne, drenching him and sending a clatter of broken glass across the floor. Several women nearby gasped. The commotion drew every eye in the ballroom and a hush fell heavy over the music. All that remained was the steady drip of champagne sliding down Thorne's coat.

I'd considered many ways I might ruin his jacket, fire from one of the ballroom candles or water from that damn fountain, but champagne... this could work. And it just might make Lark's next job easier, if I could survive Thorne's wrath.

Each soft plink of liquid on the marble floor seemed to deepen the fury etched on Thorne's face. His eyes snapped to the servant, a boy barely older than eighteen, whose expression twisted in horror. Thorne's hand rose, his intent clear in the rigid set of his shoulders and the tight line of his jaw. He was going to strike that boy. Right here, in front of everyone.

I stepped between them without hesitation. Whatever else happened tonight, I would not let that blow land, not for me.

"I'm terribly sorry, my lord," I stammered, voice faltering. Anger boiled in me, a desire to lash out at his cruelty, but I swallowed it. Now wasn't the time. "It appears I was clumsy."

Thorne's furious glare landed on me, his hand stayed raised, tense and threatening. I clenched my jaw, bracing for the smack he clearly wanted, the one I knew he would relish. Then, suddenly, a hand shot out, seizing his wrist in a crushing grip. Thorne grunted, the sound betraying real pain.

"Why, Lord Thorne," a familiar voice snapped, sharp and furious, "it looks like you were about to strike this woman." Prince Rowan *tsked*. "If you raise your hand to her, or any woman, I will remove it. Understood?" He released Thorne's grip.

"Yes," Thorne said through clenched teeth, lowering his hand. "I was merely... overcome."

"Funny," Prince Rowan hissed, the threat in his words clear, "you've spent much of the evening failing to keep your hands to yourself." The accusation hung in the air, he'd been watching us for longer than I'd realized. He pivoted to the rest of the room. "Please, continue to enjoy your evening, just a simple accident." The crowd returned to their conversations, dancing resumed, and the room swelled with noise once again, as if the whole situation had never happened. Nobles... they'd pretend it wasn't a spectacle, but I had no doubt that our incident would be gossiped about for days.

Before Thorne could respond, a woman approached. Clad in the apron I had tied myself earlier this evening, was my mother. She had obviously noticed that the plan had shifted, but the objective was the same. I kept my face neutral, betraying nothing.

"My lord, I work in the palace laundry," she said demurely. "Allow me to take your coat and show you to the washroom to freshen up."

"Of... of course," he stammered, shrugging off his now drenched jacket. She folded it neatly over her arm and started walking away. I noticed, only because I was looking,

73

the faint movement at the jacket's front. I let out a quiet, satisfied breath.

"Enjoy your evening, Lord Thorne," said Prince Rowan curtly.

Thorne's posture stiffened at hearing the prince's words. Panic flashed across his face as he turned abruptly to catch up to my mother, the sound of crackling glass in his wake. "Wait," he said, voice tight with alarm. "Let me clear the pockets first."

I held my breath as Mother handed the jacket back. Thorne pulled out a small folded letter, the wet ink splotches visible even at a distance. The very same letter Mother had just placed there. Only the seal, which Lark had lifted from the original letter, was still intact. He ground his teeth and crumpled the ruined letter in his fist before stomping away toward the washroom.

I didn't need to follow to know what came next. At some quiet, unsuspecting moment soon, maybe even in that very washroom, a figure dressed in deep red would spring from the shadows and make Thorne's night even worse. I couldn't bring myself to feel sorry for him though, he deserved it, and we wanted him angry, vengeful.

"Miss..." the prince said, and I could hear the smirk in his voice before I even looked up. When I did, his impossibly blue eyes were twinkling with the same arrogance that both infuriated and charmed me in the warehouse. "I don't suppose you'd care to dance with a man you've robbed?"

I placed my hand in his. The palm was rough, callused, a reminder he wasn't just a pampered prince. My pulse quickened at the scrape of his skin against mine. He led me around the mess on the floor, his hold steady, my slippers leaving small wet marks on the marble that sparkled as I walked. On the dance floor, he drew me close. His hand at my waist was gentle and inviting, nothing like Thorne's aggressive grip.

A light touch on my shoulder stole my attention. I turned to find Raven stepping onto the dance floor next to us, leading Commander Silas Hawthorne by the hand. Relief flooded through me, if she was here, it meant that Wickham had taken the bait and left the ball. We were so close to the end now, and it seemed Raven was intent to have a moment of joy for herself. She met my eyes, pointing at the commander and mouthing one word to me. I nodded in understanding. The prince and I shared a look at the sight of the pair, brows raised.

For the first time tonight, I let myself truly notice the ball. Not as a part of some scheme or through the haze of adrenaline, but the beauty of the gathering. The chandeliers spilled gold over the crowd, gilding us in a soft glow that reflected off gowns and masks. The music swelled, smooth and lifting, wrapping us in a delicate melody. After hours of chaos and adrenaline, I could hear it, finally *feel* it. With my departure so near, I found myself grateful for the chance to hold a small piece of its beauty.

"You have something of mine," the prince murmured into the space between us.

"I do?" My voice softened into mock-innocence. Even this was so different from how I had interacted with Thorne, this wasn't calculated, it was fun.

"My ring," he said simply, but there was a weight to his tone, a fragile uncertainty.

"I'm afraid you're mistaken, Prince." He shot me a look when I used his title. "Rowan?" He inclined his head. "I'm afraid you're mistaken, Rowan." I let concern crease my brow, the picture of sincerity. It was difficult to keep up the pretense, to fight the small smile threatening to break free. "The ring you're searching for is tucked safely away... in the pocket of your vest. The small one. Right side, if memory serves."

His eyes widened then narrowed in disbelief before his hand slipped into the very pocket I described. He drew in a breath, relief flooding his features as he slid the ring home. His whole posture relaxed, as if he couldn't breathe without it.

His hand found my waist again, and I noticed he pulled me closer, a tenderness to his gesture that made me feel delicate and cared for. We resumed dancing, bodies moving together as if we'd done this before. His gaze lingered on mine with quiet reverence, and for a heartbeat, our surroundings quieted.

"You are truly magnificent," he said, voice full of conviction.

This time, I didn't fight the smile tugging at my lips.

"It was my mother's ring," he continued, softer now, and the open sincerity in his eyes hit something deep in my chest. "I can't bear to take it off. That's why I had it on in the warehouse. It keeps her close." He paused, letting his secret linger. "Thank you for returning it."

I could understand that ache all too well. It was how I felt about my hair. In quiet moments I ran my fingers through it, watching the strands catch the light the way my mother's once had. My throat tightened, and I forced a swallow. "You're welcome."

"Would you have let him strike you?" he asked, the question bursting from him suddenly, like he couldn't keep it in anymore.

"To save that boy?" I met his gaze, anger hot in my chest at the mention of Thorne. "Yes."

"I watched that monster touch you for almost an hour," he confessed, the fury in his voice mirroring my own. "I hated it. Hated myself for putting you near him." He hesitated. "I must have looked like a madman, trailing your every move while he dragged you around. But when he raised his hand..." He stopped, teeth clenched. "I couldn't let him. Damn the letter. I've seen what men like him are capable of when their rage turns on women."

His last words, spoken with such venom, struck me like a bolt of lightning. I wondered, were the rumors about the king's cruelty truer than I thought?

"But even though you didn't get the letter," he went on, letting out a long resigned sigh. "Keep the gold anyway. Go. Make your dreams come true."

I smiled at the thought that such a thing might actually be possible, that the coins Mother had retrieved from the washroom could change our lives. "Oh, I got the letter ages ago."

"You have it?" His voice was breathless, genuine shock written across his face. "Then what did Thorne pull out of his pocket?"

"Well, technically I don't have it." I tilted my chin to the side, where Raven glided in step with Silas. "Commander Hawthorne does. Thorne's carrying a fake, destroyed and smudged beyond recognition. I couldn't risk him realizing his letter was gone."

He froze, then set his hands lightly on my arms, as if he meant to pull me closer but stopped short. "I..." His mouth opened, then closed. "The spill." He breathed, looking down at my white, jeweled slippers, still damp from champagne. His gaze, full of wonder, collided with mine. The sight of him so frazzled was endearing.

Before I could tease him, however, a palace guard cut across the floor on quick feet. He interrupted the commander's dancing, speaking low, urgent words. My pulse jumped as I watched the exchange. After a clipped reply from Silas, the guard hurried away. Silas bent his head toward Raven, his much larger frame sheltering her as he murmured words meant only for her. I caught the faint flush rising on her cheeks, a gentle smile softening her mouth as she walked away toward the carriage that waited, toward our family and the freedom she'd earned. The last bit, the final piece of our plan, was mine to finish.

Silas lingered for a heartbeat, gaze following Raven. Fingers raked through his hair before he tugged off his mask and turned in our direction. He crossed to us with purpose, expression grave as he came to stand near his prince.

Rowan lowered his hands, and I felt the lingering warmth of his touch.

"Your Highness... Rowan," Silas bowed his head, voice dropping low, "there's been an attack on a noble in the east wing. Took a nasty blow to the head and was knocked out. He is furious." The words were precise, measured. Exactly what you'd expect from the prince's commander.

"Who?" Rowan asked, though the glance he threw in my direction suggested he already suspected.

"Lord Thorne." Silas's gaze found mine. "And Lady Thorne, the nosey detective that she is, claims to know the assailant. Insists he stole from her, something about a missing necklace." A knowing look crept across his face. "She suspects Lord Wickham."

I just stared back, brows raised.

Rowan nodded. "Thank you Silas, I'll be along shortly."

Silas flashed me a mischievous grin before striding off after the guard.

"Is this why you wanted him invited?" Rowan huffed a short, surprised laugh. "If Thorne suspects him, Wickham might not last the night. Thorne is that ruthless."

I leveled him a cold look, "I know." My study of Thorne had revealed plenty, grim stories about how he dealt with those who crossed him. I could only imagine the fate of anyone who actually caused him harm. The Heap had taught me there was always a bigger, more dangerous monster out there. Wickham had attended the ball after an official invitation was delivered to his home. His name was whispered among the guests, but none of that mattered, Thorne wouldn't waste time with questions.

"Let me go see the trouble you've caused, little thief," Rowan said, pushing the mask off his handsome face. "I'll find you after."

"Are you sure about that?" I asked, lips curving at the disbelief on his face.

"I am *very* good, remember?" he said with a wink before striding away. His steps were sure and certain, every movement radiating quiet authority.

Part of me wanted to stay, to let him find me, to see what that teasing grin would do next. A longing in my chest to be known, to be seen by someone who saw through all my masks. But midnight was only moments away, and my family was waiting. I slipped through the glittering ballroom. The swirl of masks and laughter, the hushed whispers of conversation, faded with each step I took.

The clock struck midnight, its deep resonant chimes echoing through the grand hall like a thunderous heartbeat. Each toll seemed to reverberate in my chest, marking the end of my old life and the beginning of another.

I hurried toward the castle's grand archway, my gown streaming behind me like a silken banner, the gentle rhythm of my footsteps echoing against the stone walkway. Only hours before I had crossed this same threshold, nerves buzzing, heart thrumming, every step a mix of hope and fear. That same intoxicating rush returned now, but this time my sisters weren't beside me. The thought of them waiting in the carriage propelled me onward.

Beyond the castle walls, I drew the cool evening air deep into my lungs. The sounds of the ball were gone, but the world beyond beckoned. I ripped away my mask, letting it drift to the stones in my wake. Laughter erupted from somewhere deep within me, wild and unrestrained, an exhilarating wave of joy flooding my body. Gathering my skirts in both hands, I broke into a sprint down the lantern-lit walkway. The flickering light caught on my gown in alternating bursts of sparkle and shadow as I ran.

In my haste, one of my shoes slipped free. I didn't turn back for it. I just kicked off the other and continued on, the stone cool against my bare feet. Noble ladies might not run, but I was no lady.

I would always be a thief of the Heap, and for the very first time... I was free.

BY ANY OTHER NAME

DEBBIE LYNN

Determined to prove himself as a botanist and earn his doctorate, Beau travels across the globe to study medicinal roses that have baffled countless other scientists. He has a chance to change the world with his findings and maybe earn his father's respect.

Upon his arrival to the secluded countryside manor, he's surprised to meet the reclusive owner, Ademina, and she's... not quite human. Talk of ancient curses, healing magic, and strange phenomena swirl as Beau stubbornly delves into his science. But the longer he stays, the more fantastical and undeniable the evidence becomes. Not only does true magic seem to sparkle through these roses, unexplained by science, but a budding relationship with Ademina may uproot all his plans.

"By Any Other Name" is a modern-day, gender-swapped fantasy inspired by "Beauty and the Beast."

At least I'd have time to study the flowers. After all, I'd risked everything to do so—my family, my career, my future. The letter my dad had written to me felt like fire in my pocket. I pulled it out and unfolded it once more. It had only been in my possession for two days, but it was worn and wrinkled from the dozens of times I had read it. I knew that doing so wouldn't change what it said or how much the words hurt, but I couldn't help myself. The pain those words caused was part of what Dad saw as the problem. I wasn't *man enough*. I was too *girly*. Only *pansies* studied flowers for a living.

> Beau,
>
> Your mother and I wanted more from you. For you. Let your sisters study flowers in Europe and get fancy degrees. You don't need to be called Doctor. Your place should be in the shop with me and your brother.
>
> If you leave for this trip, I don't know that I'll still have a place for you when you decide to give up on this silly girl's dream. Do the right thing, Son. Stay home. Meet a nice girl, give me and your mom grandkids. Be the man I raised you to be.
>
> I hope you come to your senses.
>
> Dad

The words stirred something inside me each time I read them. Yet I was here, halfway around the world with a beautiful view and fresh air, and I was going to make my research count. I'd return to my father with something the world had never seen and show him my dream was important, too.

Flowers aren't just for girls. They aren't just for looking at, either. They're majestic, living, harmonious, and often medicinal beings. And my studies had brought me to the brink of a scientific breakthrough regarding one particular strain of rare roses that was said to have healing properties. I hadn't believed the rumors at first, but enough respected scientists had touted their abilities that I needed to witness it myself. If I could figure out what made those roses so special, I could replicate that variable in a lab and cure millions of ailments around the world. Not only would I defend my thesis and earn my doctorate, but I would be at the forefront of my field. Everyone would know who I was. Maybe even my dad.

"Uh, kiddo?" the old man in the driver's seat grumbled.

"Yeah?" I hastily folded the letter and stuffed it back into my pocket, resisting the urge to correct the nickname. His white hair indicated he'd call most people *kiddo*, even doctoral students almost ready to graduate. I forgave him. It wasn't like I'd see him again anyhow.

His English was broken, and his Eastern European accent was thick. "You sure this is place?"

The taxi slowed as we drove through open wrought-iron gates, tall and ominous. The manor ahead had seen better days, or better years. It loomed over us with tall spires and steep slopes like a castle. I couldn't be sure what color it used to be, but it was an assortment of various grays now, as if it had been collecting soot for centuries. Was this really the place I was supposed to study for the next month? Could I really spend my summer this far from town, in a castle that looked like it was ready to crumble? Dad had been right about this trip taking me to the middle of nowhere. I hoped the state of my accommodations wasn't proof he was right about anything else.

Either way, this was the place. I mumbled in the affirmative to the driver. He shrugged and continued driving toward the building as I pulled out my cell phone. The screen read No Service, accompanied by the slashed-circle emblem. My device left no question about whether I could use it—even after spending money to upgrade and add the overseas calling and texting plan, none of which was cheap.

"This place haunted," the old man said.

Frowning, I glanced back up at him. "I don't believe in ghosts."

He gave an exaggerated shrug. "Still haunted."

I leaned forward between the seats to speak with him. "Why do you think that?"

The car slowed to a stop in front of the big main door, and he and I both got out. While we waited for my field leader to come out, we each grabbed a suitcase from the trunk of the taxi.

The driver eyed the manor house warily. "Hear it? Sounds like screams. Cries. That's why no one come here."

"I thought no one came here because we're two hours from civilization," I quipped, only half-sarcastically. All I

87

heard was a strong gust of wind whipping against the old building.

He shook his head sternly. "House cursed. It haunted. No one come close… except stupid Americans."

I chuckled. It probably wasn't the first time I'd be called a *stupid American* during my four weeks in the forgotten backcountry of Europe. Not that I'd see many people while holed up in this haunted mansion, dissecting parts of supposedly magical roses.

The roses crawled up one side of the manor on vines and sparkled in the sunshine. I'd learned that they didn't root into the ground and failed to thrive when planted. It was as if they lived to climb and sparkle. Reason number one the scientific community was perplexed by this variant. Reason number two was the roses' coloring, which ranged from bright pinks to blood-red to deep blue and royal purple. None of the hues occurred naturally in any one strain. Botanists worldwide were baffled by the shimmering, colorful flowers that could allegedly heal scrapes and colds, and maybe more.

"Your guy coming?" the old man asked, watching the door.

It was my turn to shrug as I forced my attention away from the manor. "She was supposed to come in last night. She probably just didn't see us arrive." Dr. Bardot, world-renowned botanist, was scheduled to oversee my endeavor. Because of that supervision, her name would go first on the paper I'd publish about the roses, regardless of how much she actually helped. No matter, though. I just needed my name on that paper, and to use the information in my dissertation. And get *Doctor* in front of my name, too.

"You go in," the driver said, urging me forward with his hands. "I go now."

Imposter syndrome and nerves hit me suddenly, and I wondered if I still had time to back out. Not go home to the shop, per se, but go home and away from this eerie place. I didn't believe it was haunted, but it had vibes that unsettled my stomach. Then again, I'd never had this experience before. I'd never been out of my state, let alone my country. I'd never been stuck without cell service, and I'd never been two hours from the nearest town. This was all new. Which made it exciting.

I grabbed a suitcase in each hand with a grin. "You go now," I agreed. "Thanks for the ride."

He nodded and rushed to the car, sparing an anguished look over his shoulder at the tallest spire before getting in and driving away.

With a deep breath, I rolled my luggage up to the massive door and knocked. And knocked again. After a third loud knock, I decided Dr. Bardot either couldn't hear me or wasn't in the manor. But, since the door was unlocked, it wouldn't hurt to let myself in. I'd either find Dr. Bardot or make myself comfortable while I waited for her.

I kind of hoped she was out for a while so I could relax. After all, I'd just taken a long flight across multiple time zones. Some food and a nap sounded appealing.

The foyer was in surprisingly better shape than the exterior, and I gaped in awe at murals painted on tall ceilings, floor-to-ceiling bookshelves—complete with a sliding ladder—and a statue in one corner, cut with exquisite detail. It depicted a prince holding a sword. I wondered if there were matching statues around the manor.

I left my luggage against the wall by the door and moved into the manor to explore. It was very well-kept for an abandoned building that saw very few visitors, save for curious botanists like me. Even the books lacked the amount of dust I'd expected. I reached for one that caught my eye, but before my fingers could touch it, a voice boomed from the staircase, causing me to jump backward in shock. My hip grazed the bookcase, luckily not causing an avalanche of books.

"Those aren't yours." The speaker was female but didn't sound like Dr. Bardot from our video and phone calls. Dr. Bardot sounded like my grandmother, with a slow, raspy drawl. This woman sounded younger and had an accent that seemed to be from everywhere at once.

"Sorry. I was just looking. I didn't know anyone was here," I stammered. As I gathered my bearings, I turned to look at the speaker. She definitely wasn't Dr. Bardot.

The woman—if she could be called that—stood at the railing on the second floor, overlooking the entryway. She wore a simple T-shirt and pants that ended at her calves. And she was... not human. At least, not like any human I'd ever seen.

I rubbed my eyes, blinking furiously. Surely, I was imagining things. I didn't think I'd hit my head when I stumbled, but maybe I had. Maybe this beast was the imaginings of a concussion. Or the foreign air was causing hypoxia, and I was hallucinating. Either way, the woman who was now descending the staircase appeared to be an animal of some kind, covered in long, shaggy fur, with large paws instead of feet. Yet, she walked upright and spoke like a typical woman.

"Like what you see?" she asked, a smirk appearing on her muzzle-like mouth.

My brain wouldn't form words. Definitely hypoxia.

"You must be Beau," she continued, ignoring my inability to respond. "I'd heard you were coming. Studying the roses just like the rest of them." Her head cocked to the side, reminding me of my dog when he was curious.

"Doctor... Doctor Bardot?" I managed to ask.

She laughed. "I'm not your doctor. She's not coming, anyhow." She stepped onto the floor and walked toward me.

I willed my feet to stay put despite every ounce of my body wanting to back away from the creature. "What do you mean? She was supposed to get in last night."

The beast stopped without getting too close, as if she sensed my fear. She reached into her back pocket with hands that, though animalistic, were surprisingly more human than the rest of her. She handed me a folded piece of paper.

I took it when offered and glanced at it quickly, not wanting to take my eyes off her. It was a letter, written in the same cursive style my grandmother used, announcing that I was on my own with the research, but she would sign off on it when I completed. Dr. Bardot had offered no explanation or apology, just two sentences she could have told me in an email or phone call. Instead, she wrote to the manor ahead of time, as if she knew someone would be here to pass the message on.

Which meant I was alone with this... whatever she was. For a month. Dr. Bardot had access to our stipend and car. Without her, I'd be cut off from everything. I'd have to rely on this creature for groceries and essentials.

But I would also be the sole author of the paper after I made a once-in-a-lifetime scientific discovery. I'd find the truth behind the so-called magic of the climbing roses and be the first to successfully reproduce their healing properties.

Their power was said to have been discovered decades ago by villagers experimenting with herbal and floral teas. The sparkles and colors had caught their eye on a trip past the manor, and they'd stopped to gather them. Legend said that drinking tea that included the petals fresh off the vine caused simple ailments and injuries to clear, but the roses wouldn't replant elsewhere.

Many had tried to recreate their power in the nearest village or major city, but each attempt ultimately failed. The roses refused to thrive anywhere but the walls of this manor. No one could figure out why or how they worked. I was skeptical the roses were true healing plants. If they were, though, I was confident I could determine how they worked and make them thrive outside this remote area. And now, I'd do it by myself, without having to bow to a senior scientist. No interference, no distractions. Except, well, the creature standing in front of me.

"I guess it's just you and me, then," I told her, my confidence returning. "Do you live here?"

"I do," she said, baring sharp teeth in what I assumed was a smile. She watched me with keen blue eyes, studying me.

"Then what should I call you?"

"My name is Ademina. People call me Mina."

Something about her demeanor prompted me to ask, "Do you prefer to be called Mina?"

She shrugged, her T-shirt raising to show a sliver of long hair on her abdomen. "Others do, when I encounter them. Which is not often."

"But which do you prefer?"

Her thick brows furrowed. "I prefer to be called by my given name. Some find it strange, so I've gotten used to being called Mina, Ada, Addie, even Demi. Anything but Ademina."

"Well, Ademina, it's nice to meet you." I offered my hand to shake.

Ademina stared for a moment then took it, her large, furry hand swallowing mine. "You too, Beau. Let me show you to your room."

The bedroom was as grand as the rest of the manor, with tall ceilings covered in intricate art and a large window overlooking a colorful garden. When I put my face to the glass, I could see rose vines on the exterior wall, close enough to touch if the window opened. Fascinating. "These roses," I began, still pressed against the window.

"Yes, yes, the roses," she answered, her tone bored.

I turned toward her. "How often do strangers show up here to study your roses?"

Her eyes widened. "Well, once or twice a year."

"That must be difficult for you, having people trample all over your home as if you aren't here." Something shifted in her eyes when I said that, and I continued. "They told me no one lived here, that the home is abandoned. Is that what everyone thinks when they arrive?"

She nodded wordlessly.

I didn't ask why she allowed the world to think she didn't exist. I was pretty sure I could guess the answer. Another question burned my tongue, but I didn't dare ask it.

Ademina cleared her throat or growled. It sounded like a growl. "I'm sure you're hungry from your trip. Settle in and come downstairs. I'll prepare a meal. None of the others have been this nice to me, so it's no problem at all."

"I'd love that," I told her, keeping eye contact so she would know I was honest and not just avoiding her. "But, as hungry as I am, I'm even more exhausted. If you don't mind, I'll eat a quick snack then turn in."

"Of course," Ademina said, those blue eyes softening. "How about breakfast?" She paused, her large eyebrows furrowing. "That is, if you don't mind dining with me."

The statement stirred something inside me, but I couldn't tell quite what. Ademina was strange but not terrifying, a curiosity but kind. "Of course not. I look forward to it."

She smiled, showing sharp teeth that turned my stomach a bit. "I'll see you shortly." She headed out of my room but stopped at the doorway. "Oh, Beau."

"Yeah?"

"Ignore any sounds you may hear. The wind whips through this old place like you wouldn't believe. Some say it's haunted, but it's just nature."

The taxi driver's words replayed in my mind. *Cursed. Haunted. Only stupid Americans.* Well, I'd show him I wasn't afraid, just like I'd show my dad I could do something worthwhile in my chosen field. I'd show everyone.

◆ ◆ ◆ ◆ ◆

The next morning, I awoke in a flurry of excitement, ready to start my work. Although the wind had kept me up most of the night, I only had twenty-nine days to discover the roses' secrets—at least, to see them heal and to get them to do so off the property. The rest of the research would be done back home, in a state-of-the-art university lab. But even the first phase of the study was a tall order. Twenty-nine days felt like both a lifetime and a mere minute.

After a quick shower, I put on my standard outfit—jeans, a T-shirt, and a plaid shirt over that. My grandpa's silver watch fastened around my wrist, because I didn't like smartwatches. They connected people to too much technology far too often. I preferred the simple feel of a metal clasp and heavy watch face. Plus, my grandfather's name was inscribed on the inside. It kept him with me long after he'd gone. I raked my hands through my short hair, not worrying about a comb or brush, and grabbed my favorite glasses. I barely needed them in daily life, but seeing details was necessary when working. With my notebook and kit in hand, I headed downstairs, intent on having a quick cup of coffee and a protein bar before going outside.

Ademina had different plans— the ones we'd made last night. She greeted me with a tray of pastries, fruits, and breakfast meats. "I'm glad you're awake, Beau. Did you sleep well? I hear the bed is very comfortable. I wasn't sure what you would like for breakfast, so I made a little bit of everything. Hopefully, there's something here you'll enjoy." Her words were rushed, her teeth showing in a strained smile and her brows knitting together.

I smiled at the way she tried so hard to please me. The roses could wait a few minutes. They'd be there when breakfast ended. After all, Ademina was isolated from the world, her only company arriving once or twice a year. When was the last time she'd had a friend?

We sat at a small round table with the tray between us. Everything was delicious. After a few moments of silence, I asked between bites, "How long has it been since someone visited?"

Her eyes cast downward. "Too long."

"It must hurt to lose friends that quickly and not make more for a long time."

Her lips pursed. "You think the people who come here are *friends*?"

I didn't miss the pain in her eyes, but decided not to comment on it. Instead, I bit into a slice of bacon and waited.

"They mock me, shun me, and want to leave early. You're the first one to treat me like a person rather than an animal.

That's why I..." She gestured to the breakfast spread as her voice trailed off.

"Well, I appreciate it, Ademina. The meal is amazing. But don't feel like you have to do this every day. In fact, please don't. I need to fit into the clothes I brought," I added with a laugh.

She smiled briefly. "I don't have friends, Beau. I have people who come here, expecting an empty manor and magical flowers, but find a freak instead. It's very lonely."

I reached across the table and laid my hand on hers. It was massive, both humanoid and animal. "I have a large family that doesn't understand me, and I live in a city full of people who ignore each other and go about their day. You can be lonely in a crowd, too. I know how you feel, in a way."

Ademina laid her other hand atop mine. "Thank you." After a moment, she removed her hand and smiled at me. "Now, I know you're itching to get outside. Go. I'll clean up after us."

She didn't have to tell me twice. With a grin, I headed outside to see the magical roses, determined to prove their powers were grounded in science. Magic didn't exist, after all. We weren't living in a fairy tale.

The garden was massive and well-kept, though not meticulous. This must be how Ademina spent her time, since she didn't have others to keep her company. The thought was sobering. I was certain the word *lonely* didn't fully describe how she felt.

Gently, I touched the petal of a bellflower, careful not to damage its delicate structure. This particular bellflower was uncommon, though not rare. I hadn't expected to see it here, where winters could be harsh and sunlight did not shine year-round. It didn't sparkle or change colors like the climbing roses, but it was an amazing find. I wondered if it was special like the roses.

Beside the bellflowers were mandrake, oleander, rare orchids, and even Orpheus flowers—which should not be growing in this part of the world. The climate wasn't proper for most of the flowers here. There was more to this flora puzzle than I'd expected. It was a botanist's dream.

I took my time studying each flower and bush, documenting everything that might be important in a new notebook. Perhaps something about these flowers could pertain to the so-called magical roses.

After three hours, I was ready to find the roses. I arrived at the side of the house and looked up at my bedroom window. The roses wove around the frame and sprawled across the façade. They simply clung to the brick as if they belonged there despite the lack of roots or connection to soil.

There weren't as many as I'd expected. Had the other botanists taken too many samples? Were new ones not growing? If these roses had healing powers, why didn't they propagate better? Having a finite sample didn't bode well for my plan, but I'd make do.

Most of the roses bloomed above arm's reach, so I'd need a ladder to grab them. Some empty vines crawled across the wall before me, evidence of previous researchers who had taken more than their findings were worth. I wouldn't do that. I would take only what I needed and find a way to grow more in their place. Whether they were magical or not, these roses were rare, and scientists shouldn't endanger them for the sake of research.

"Ladder later," I told myself, eyeing the distance to my second-floor window. I didn't particularly love heights, which was okay since flowers usually grew on the ground. This would be a new and nerve-racking experience for me.

"There's a shed beyond the trees," Ademina's voice said from behind me. "The ladder is there."

I turned to find her sitting down on a patio chair, book in hand. She raised it and said, "I hope it's okay if I sit out here while you work."

"Of course. It's your home, and I enjoy the company."

Ademina smiled briefly then turned her eyes to the ground. It was hard to tell, but she may have blushed. "How are the flowers?" she asked, setting her book beside her.

"Oh, I'm sure you know all about the flowers. I wouldn't want to bore you." I sat in a chair opposite her, grateful to rest my legs for a moment. I had been bending and squatting for quite a while.

"I tend to them, sure. But I don't know much about them. Those are purple, those are pink, those have thorns, those only bloom at night..." She punctuated each phrase by pointing a finger at a different section of the garden, then shrugged. "I couldn't name them or tell you anything special about them. I bet you could, though."

I grinned. "You have quite the collection, Ademina. Some of these flowers shouldn't even *be* here, given the climate. It's amazing. It's almost..."

"Magical?" she asked, quirking an eyebrow.

It was my turn to shrug. "I don't believe in magic. But something is definitely going on that defies scientific reason, and I'm excited to figure it out."

"Will you teach me about the flowers?" she asked. "No one has ever taken the time. I'd love to know what I have, and how to take care of them properly. When I was young, my grandfather taught me about some of them, but I couldn't tell you what he said anymore."

I nodded. "We can go for a walk later. I've made plenty of notes. I can share them with you."

She grinned, and her blue eyes lit up. They were a fascinatingly deep blue, framed by lashes most women would kill for. They were beautiful. I could get used to seeing those eyes for the next twenty-nine days, even if they belonged to a body that startled me.

The wind whipped around us, almost howling as it rustled the bush beside the patio. It died down as quickly as it had picked up. Ademina had mentioned the wind already, but it was still a surprise to hear it so intensely, like it was trying to scream.

"The weather's turning," she said, glancing toward the spacious garden. "It may frost soon."

My eyes widened at the thought of losing some of those rare plants, especially since many of them shouldn't even be growing in this part of the world in the first place. But there were so many. There was no way we could cover them all adequately. "Do you normally cover them?"

She shook her head. "I don't know what to do, so I just leave them." She glanced sideways briefly then looked back at me.

"Do you have cloth to cover them? We can at least cover the rarest ones."

She shook her head.

"Then we just wait and hope for the best," I said, my shoulders slumping.

She shrugged. "It's what I always do."

The garden was in full bloom, and there didn't seem to be any areas that had died out, so it was probably okay to not cover them. Unless the storm of the century moved in overnight, the average frost here was apparently not enough to kill the rare plants.

◆ ◆ ◆ ◆ ◆

She was right, as I suspected she would be. The temperature dropped drastically overnight and almost every plant froze. I stared in horror out the window at the limp blooms covered in white. There was no way they would all recover. The only ones unaffected were the roses, which clung to the wall outside my window, as vibrant and sparkling as they had been the previous day.

"Ademina, why are the roses safe?" I asked as I watched a harsh wind blow through the precious greenery. As before, it howled through the house, though not as loud as it had been.

"Magic," she said simply, as if she didn't know I was a skeptic. She sat at a small café table in the kitchen nook, watching me watch the wind.

I shook my head, sure I wasn't going to get any other answer from her. "It's freezing and windy," I said sadly. The frost had taken two days of research from me.

"Cut some and bring them in."

Shaking my head again, I glanced at her. "Normally, if you prune when it's too cold, the new growth can not only die from frostbite, but it can cause other problems. I know these roses are special, but I don't know if they're immune to root damage or dieback."

"Root damage?" she asked, raising a furry eyebrow.

I chuckled. The roses didn't have roots. Just as they clung to the wall, defying reason, they also began and ended on the wall, rather than the ground. I couldn't explain it with science, but I refused to call it magic.

"Why don't you sit and have tea with me? Then you can relax. Read a book, take a nap, whatever you feel like. You've been going non-stop since you got here, barely letting yourself rest."

She had a point. I was exhausted. The adrenaline from getting here and seeing everything I had to work with was finally fading. Even with the heavy frost, I'd been reading and exploring the manor, barely letting myself sit still. I sighed. "Yeah. I'll do that."

Ademina rose and poured me a cup of tea that smelled like lavender. "Do you like Scrabble?"

I nodded.

"If you decide to not nap, I'll play a round with you. It's my favorite game and I never get to play," she added, looking at her teacup.

"Get it now," I suggested. The idea of a nap had been appealing, but Ademina was so lonely. We both were.

She beamed and fetched the game from a closet.

We chatted as we played, keeping things superficial. She learned I had three sisters and a brother, that I played tennis in high school even though I didn't want to, and that my last relationship had blown up almost a year ago, though I didn't offer any details. I learned about her daily activities, which included a lot of reading and cleaning this huge manor, and that she had food and supplies delivered monthly. The last shipment had arrived just before me, and she had frozen the fresh foods to last the entire month. She didn't say it, but her eyes told me Ademina was dreadfully lonely.

I worked up the nerve to mention it and learn more about her than her favorite color and which produce she hated the most, but before I could say anything, she let out a triumphant yell.

Her blue eyes shined as she gestured toward the word she'd just played across two triple word score spaces.

For all my book learning, I'd never heard of the word before. "What is *quixotry*?"

"It's a real word," she said, her voice low.

"I don't doubt it. I've just never heard of it." I shrugged to show her I wasn't insinuating anything negative.

"It means acting romantically when it's not based in reality. Think of Don Quixote." She wrote her score down on the notepad—all 365 points. There was no way I could compete with that.

"I love learning new things. But my next word is going to pale in comparison to that, and I'd thought it was a good one. Actually, they will all pale in comparison to that."

She put a hand on mine. "I'm grateful for the game, regardless of who wins."

With a smirk, I said, "You say that because you're going to win."

"Well, yeah." She grinned at me, an expression full of excitement and joy.

I moved my hand from under hers to playfully swat at her then lay my 27-point word out. Not every move could be a big play.

To no one's surprise, Ademina won that game. I won the second game by two points and we stopped, though we both enjoyed it so much we decided to play again soon.

"Can I ask you a question?" she asked as she placed the lid on the Scrabble box.

"Of course." I sipped my tea and waited.

"If it's too personal, you don't have to answer."

I waited silently.

"I've seen you read something a few times now, a page you keep in your pocket. It seems important."

I nodded slowly.

"Is it from your ex?"

With a chuckle, I shook my head. "I wish. It would probably be less painful if it was."

She sat in silence, looking at her lap.

I definitely knew how to ruin a good time.

"You don't have to talk about it..." she said, glancing up at me through those impossibly thick lashes.

"It's from my father," I responded with a sigh. "He doesn't want me to be here."

She frowned. "With me?"

I laughed, a little harder than before. "Ademina, no one knows you're here."

"Oh." Her voice carried more sadness than I'd anticipated.

"I'm sorry." I reached across the table and placed a hand on hers. "I didn't mean it like that."

"It's true," she said, glancing at my hand.

I didn't remove it, and she didn't ask me to. "I'm glad I'm here with you," I told her.

"Me too, Beau."

We watched each other for a moment, then I pulled my hand back. "My father thinks studying flowers is for girls, and that there's something wrong with me for doing it. He wants me to work in the shop with him and my brother. Apparently, you can't be a real man if you don't have greasy nails and car parts everywhere." I curled my lip in disdain and resentment. "He basically vowed to disown me if I got on the plane. Which I obviously did. So, I don't know what I'll be going home to."

She nodded, as if she could understand the pain.

Maybe she could.

Ademina gazed at me with an intent expression, her eyes burning with curiosity and understanding. It appeared as if she wanted to say something, and I hoped I'd get to learn more about her. She'd been shut off so far, but maybe my small disclosure would let me into her world a little.

Instead, her face loosened, and she smiled. "This was so much fun, Beau. Let's do it again." She stood and grabbed the game box. "I'm going to take a nap, I think. I'll see you soon." Within seconds, she was gone, and I was left alone in the big kitchen, realizing there were two mysteries I wanted to solve in the month—the magical roses and Ademina.

The next morning was warmer, lit by bright sunshine against a cloudless sky. Stepping outside, I sucked in a deep breath, pausing out of fear of what I'd find. When I reached the garden, I discovered a third mystery. Every plant was perfect. No drooping, no limp petals; no discoloration; no lost limbs. The frost had moved out as quickly as it had come in, and every plant looked as if it had never gotten cold.

"Ademina," I called from the back patio. "Look at the plants!"

She strolled to the doorway and smiled, unsurprised. "Yes, strange."

The roses had been unaffected completely, but the other plants had been almost dead, then fine again. It made no sense. I rubbed my temples as I scanned the area but found nothing more than a couple of watering cans and my equipment. Business as usual.

That made three mysteries and just four weeks to solve them.

◆ ◆ ◆ ◆ ◆

Each day, Ademina and I took morning walks through the expansive garden, sipping tea while I educated her on the flora she'd been caretaking. We'd laugh so much, our bellies hurt and tears streamed down our faces. Ademina's blue eyes shined when she laughed in a way I hadn't seen before in other women. I could almost see through the fur and oversized features to the soul beneath, but occasionally she'd do something that reminded me she was, somehow, not quite human.

One morning, we strolled in a light rain. She never wore shoes, and her large paws made hollows in the wet earth as we walked. At one point, I looked over my shoulder at the indentations in the ground and was reminded of her beastly nature. I still didn't know why she was the way she was. I was afraid to ask, and she didn't offer.

Between botany lessons, we joked about a story we had made up, which was turning into quite the soap opera as we spoke fictional characters' parts to one another. It had begun as a random comment and turned into a running joke.

I put on my most dramatic voice. "The fruit of this tree will kill a person... if you get my drift." I touched the leaves of a definitely harmless berry bush.

She gasped, hand to her mouth. "I can't believe you'd suggest such a thing, darling."

In our skit, her sister had recently murdered my brother. Or something like that. Like a good soap opera, it was becoming convoluted, which was where the fun came in.

"I don't know what you mean," I said, raising an eyebrow.

Ademina grinned. "Well..." She looked to the side as her voice trailed off. "Aww, poor baby."

I followed her gaze to see an adult rabbit in front of a bush across the walkway. It was unmoving and a few flies sat on it. The poor thing was clearly dead. From where we stood, it didn't look like the rabbit had been bitten by a predator. Had it gotten into a poisonous plant? The thought concerned me. I'd been cataloguing the garden and hadn't identified anything dangerous. Perhaps my quip about the deadly plant wasn't really a joke.

Ademina headed toward the bunny, and I trailed behind her. Plants were my thing, not creatures. I had too much empathy; just the knowledge that the rabbit was deceased tugged at my heart more than I was proud to admit.

She squatted to look at the animal without touching it. "It got into something, but I don't know what's around here that could have killed it. Been dead a bit, though."

I stood beside her but didn't look at the rabbit. Still, it seemed like a solemn moment, so I touched Ademina's shoulder.

She looked up at me and smiled. It was a gentle gesture, but she seemed to appreciate it as much as I enjoyed it.

The thought stuck with me for a moment, only disappearing when she spoke again.

"You still don't believe in magic?" Ademina whispered.

"I haven't found anything to confirm that there's magic in the roses."

She made a frustrated groan and turned back to the bunny. "I'm going to prove it to you."

Unsure how to respond, I stayed silent. Part of me wanted her to prove the magic was real, but part of me would always be skeptical.

Ademina stood and headed for the house, pausing to clip a rose using my pruning tool.

I followed her into the kitchen and stood back to watch her work.

"You can use the roses in many ways," she said, setting the rose on the counter. "This guy didn't have any clear wounds to put a salve on, so I'm going to make a liquid. A tea of sorts."

"But he's dead," I said, more confused than ever.

She nodded and reached for a teacup, which she filled with tap water. She flitted around the kitchen, finding salt, a spoon, and a mortar and pestle. "The roses do the trick. You don't need much else." She ground a single rose petal with the mortar and pestle and added the small pieces to the water. A pinch of salt followed. "Come on."

Ademina seemed almost secretive, considering she spent so much time telling me to believe in magic. But I didn't bring that up. I just watched and waited as she put the items away slowly, as if she wasn't doing anything special. Once she had finished, I followed her outside.

In the garden, Ademina stood over the rabbit and handed me the teacup and spoon.

I stared at her, unsure of what I was supposed to do.

"I'll hold his mouth open, and you spoon some of the tea into it." She watched my face, apparently satisfied with my reaction. Then she knelt and gingerly held the bunny's tiny mouth open.

It felt disgusting. Wrong. Like we were desecrating this poor animal's body. But I crouched down and did as she asked. "Hey, little guy. Got a drink for you." I filled his little mouth from the spoon.

It only took a few seconds for the bunny to blink. In a few more, its legs started to twitch and then kick, as if it wanted to get away. The flies on its fur took off, uninterested in revived flesh.

Ademina held the rabbit tightly, letting me take in its vitality. "Was that enough proof?" she asked before releasing it.

The bunny hopped into the garden, not in the least bit dead.

My eyes met Ademina's, and she smiled. She didn't prod me to speak, but she appeared smug at the surprise I surely wore on my face.

"Okay," I said slowly. "I saw what happened. The roses clearly brought that rabbit back to life."

Her blue eyes lit up.

I started slowly. "But..."

She scowled.

"Maybe it wasn't magic. Maybe there was a scientific reason the roses worked."

"Beau." She only said one word, but she said it with disappointment.

I shrugged. "I'd love for the roses to be made of sunshine and sparkles and to usher in a world of magic and wonder. But it's more likely that they gave the rabbit something its body needed to get its heart started again."

She crossed her arms. "Like what?"

I panicked, because there wasn't anything in the known plant world with that ability. And any explanation I could try to use would be so convoluted, she'd probably think I was making it up. I would be. "Um, electrolytes?" I said finally, more a question than a statement.

"Beau. We didn't give it Gatorade. We gave it a magical flower."

"Maybe," I said. "We'll see."

Ademina's features lightened but remained serious. "You might want to start believing in magic if you're going to figure out those roses. Many before you have tried, and none have succeeded. Maybe their disbelief was their downfall."

I wasn't sure what I did and didn't believe, but after what I'd just witnessed, I was determined to find out. And if it took believing in the unexplainable to understand the flowers' secrets, that's what I'd do. Nothing would keep me from my dreams, including magic.

◆ ◆ ◆ ◆ ◆

The days rushed by, filled with Ademina's breakfasts and teas, exotic flowers, and roses that climbed on vines that anchored to stone without reason. I frequently remembered the rabbit, frustrated that I couldn't figure out the secret to saving his life. It was the roses, of course, but my PhD was in botany, not magic. I couldn't figure out how science saved him, and calling it *magic* was still difficult.

Halfway through my stay, I stood atop a ladder, pruning the roses beside my window. Inside, my bed was neatly made and my luggage was stacked in the corner. The room didn't appear to be lived in at all. But oh, how I'd been living.

I'd never met anyone like Ademina, and I didn't think I ever would. Knowing I'd have to leave her made my gut clench, but it also made me appreciate the time we had together. She was a great listener, a funny storyteller, and I found I could rest comfortably in silence with her.

She also helped with my research when she could. When I needed another set of hands or eyes, she was eager to assist. And since I hated ladders, she volunteered to hold the base, more for comfort than stabilization.

Atop the ladder, I trembled, both from the cool air and unease. The rain had turned into a mist. It wasn't unpleasant, but I hated being on ladders, regardless of who stood below me trying to distract me with horrible soap opera plots.

I glanced down at Ademina to deliver a line from my character with gusto. "It wasn't me, Sophia... it was my *evil twin brother!*" I gave a maniacal laugh, gesturing widely. A little too widely, in fact. As my hand left the ladder, I realized I had thrown too much of my body into the movement. It only took a split second to lose my footing and fall from the top of the tall ladder to the ground. The force of impact registered throughout my body.

Everything hurt. My head, my stomach, my leg, and my right arm. God, did it hurt. Turning my neck caused pain to shoot through it and into my head, but I had to look at my arm. The pain was so intense that I almost forgot how important that limb was to my work, my livelihood. Almost, but not quite.

"Beau!" Ademina screamed, releasing the ladder and falling to her knees beside me. "Where does it hurt?"

I couldn't even try to speak through the agony. Gritting my teeth, I forced my head to fully turn so I could assess the damage. Tears burned my eyes as I took in the sight. My right hand was covered in blood, likely from rose thorns rather than injury. More concerningly, my elbow bent the opposite way it should have, with bone protruding through my long-sleeved shirt. The sight made my stomach turn, adding nausea to my list of ailments.

My arm was not only injured, but it was devastatingly broken. The nearest hospital was at least two hours away, my entire body was wracked with pain, and my dominant arm was mangled. I was a botanist, not a doctor, but even this level of injury would require surgery with a cast or sling to follow.

My trip was over. I'd never discover the roses' secret and use it to save others. I'd arrive home without proving my father wrong. And I'd leave Ademina two weeks too soon.

She laid a soft hand on my cheek, gently forcing my gaze back to her. "Other than your arm, where?"

"Everywhere," I mumbled. Her face was becoming blurry. Was she leaning in too close?

"Oh, Beau."

My vision blurred around the edges like a vignette filter on a picture. Was this a concussion? Was that pain in my head a sign of something worse? Would I die here, in this strange, foreign land with this strange, beautiful woman holding me?

"I've got you," she whispered. She said something else, but I couldn't discern it. Ademina stood and bent to position her hands beneath me. "I'll be careful." Then she lifted me with ease and carried me inside the house like a child.

She laid me on a settee in the parlor, just off the main entryway, and stood back to stare at me. With a murmur, she disappeared out the doorway.

I tried to focus on my surroundings, but it was difficult. My vision was doubled and between the back of my head and my arm, the pain was torture. The rest of my body was on fire with aches and bruises.

It was several long minutes before she returned. When she did, her footsteps were softer than they should have been. She was taking care to be quiet for me, like she knew how much my head hurt. "I made a salve for your injuries," she said, setting a bowl on the table beside me. "But I need to apply it to your skin. I'm going to have to cut your shirt."

I mumbled a reply. If she could make this pain ease, even a little, I didn't care what she had to do.

Ademina produced a pair of shears from a corner table and carefully cut my shirt down the middle. She opened it and gasped at what I assumed from my painful breathing was a chest full of bruises. Gingerly, she traced a finger along my bare skin. Then she took the scissors to the sleeve with the broken arm, cutting slowly and carefully.

My head felt like it might burst at any moment. "Ade..."

"Almost done," she said. She cut in silence, wincing as she pulled the sleeve away from the visible bone. She reached for a bowl she had set nearby and dipped her large fingers into it. When she pasted it onto my skin, the contact made me want to jump, but the salve was cool and her touch was soft. Within seconds, the pain began to ease. Ademina rubbed the ointment across my chest, her fur caressing my chest hair. Almost immediately, it became easier to breathe. "I think you bruised some ribs," she whispered as she lifted her fingers.

My skin longed for her to touch it again. "Wow. I feel... so much better."

"There's still something I have to do. You may want to turn your head."

I frowned up at her, not understanding. I felt so much better already.

She placed a hand against my cheek again, warm and soft, and stared into my eyes with her deep blue ones. Her gaze was hypnotic. "Beau, I'm serious. Look away."

I did as she asked.

Ademina released my face, leaving an empty feeling where her touch had been. She grasped my broken arm, both above and below the elbow.

I barely had time to squeeze my eyes shut before she yanked it, producing a loud cracking sound. There was a flash of pain and pressure, but some of it released once she was finished. Still, I couldn't look at my elbow. It felt swollen and sore.

Her eyes found mine again. "It shouldn't hurt very long. The salve will take care of it."

"What's in that?" I asked, afraid to know the answer.

Her eyes flashed with mischief. "Electrolytes."

I groaned but chuckled, then immediately winced at the lingering ache throughout my body. Despite breathing easier, a reminder of the fall remained.

"Careful, Beau," she chided. "Give the roses a moment to work. Your injuries were severe."

I frowned. Of course, it was the roses. Those beautiful, frustrating, special roses. But what made them special?

Ademina interrupted my thoughts, her fingertips grazing my chest again. "How are your ribs?"

My skin came alive at her touch, and I stammered through a reply.

Outside, the mist gave way to rain that pelted against the windows, wind moaning fiercely. We could hear it through the walls, drowning out whatever she said next. The wailing had been louder lately, more intense, as if the wind was speaking to me. Every time I thought I'd grown used to it, I was surprised again.

Ademina kept her hand on my bare chest, and everything but her touch faded away, including the raging storm. Her eyes spoke more than words could. She wanted me in the same way I wanted her.

I hadn't known just what way that was until that moment. We'd enjoyed each other's company, laughed at inside jokes, and shared secrets. I knew I'd had feelings for her, but until she touched me and gazed into my eyes, I hadn't named the rest of the feeling. I wanted her, regardless of what she looked like or where she came from. I might even have started to fall in love with her.

Scooting myself upright, I brought our faces closer together. This beautiful woman was close enough to kiss. Her hand was on my bare skin. Her eyes were locked with mine. All I had to do was...

She cleared her throat and backed away, taking her warm touch with her. "Rest a bit, Beau. I'll come check on you soon." She patted the front of her T-shirt as if removing wrinkles or lint and forced a smile. "You'll be good as new in no time."

As she left the room, I realized there was, in fact, magic here. I just couldn't be sure whether it was in the plants, in the way we felt about one another, or both.

◆ ◆ ◆ ◆ ◆

My breakthrough with the roses came in the third week, on the same day Ademina told me her secret.

For the fourth day in a row, a storm raged outside, causing me to build a makeshift laboratory in a spare second-floor bedroom. Rain pelted both windows and the sky outside was dark despite it being mid-afternoon. Since the manor was old and not well-heated, I was bundled up in two long-sleeved shirts and my thickest pants. A headlamp adorned my forehead, and I squinted through magnifying glasses at the sparkling rose petal on the desk before me.

Ademina lounged on the couch, seemingly more comfortable than me in the cool temperatures. All that fur came in handy sometimes. She read a book, something romantic and magical, while I worked.

It was nice to have her here with me, and nicer that she didn't try to dictate my actions. She never did, letting me do the work I came here for without interruption.

I grumbled at the rose's response to my tests then slammed my fist against the desk. My equipment rattled.

"Not going well?" she asked.

"What am I missing?" I ran my hand through my hair in frustration.

Ademina lowered her book to her lap. "You're trying to quantify magic with science."

I growled at her words, causing her to raise an eyebrow. "I need to know how to replicate the magic, and for that, I need science."

She seemed to ponder something for a moment then moved her feet to the floor and patted the seat beside her.

Curious, I sat and waited for her to speak, which took some time. I removed the light and glasses in the pause.

She began slowly, as if choosing her words carefully. "Do you think I am this way because of science?" She didn't have to gesture or say what she meant. It was obvious.

"I..."

"No," she said sternly. "There are no more people like me in this world than there are young men named Beau who want both their father's approval and their independence and aren't sure how to attain both."

I forced a chuckle. We were both unique. Wasn't everyone? Then again, not everyone was a human-animal hybrid straight from a fantasy movie. I was pretty sure Ademina was truly one of a kind.

She continued. "This is the result of a curse, Beau. I wasn't born this way. I didn't develop some sickness that caused this. I was cursed. Magic made me what you see now. Not science, not humanity. Magic."

Of course, I'd considered such an explanation, having opened my mind to the idea of magic after the incidents with the rabbit and my own injuries. But this was beyond my realm of understanding. I could barely wrap my head around the healing properties of the endangered roses. Curses were another thing entirely.

"Can I ask...?"

"Why was I cursed? How did it happen?"

I nodded. The moment felt intimate, and I didn't want to ruin it with the wrong words.

She looked at her lap, where she fidgeted with long, clawed, furry fingers. "This isn't something I've shared in a very long time."

I waited silently, afraid that speaking would cause her to close up.

After a long moment, she continued. "Before I looked like this, I was pretty. Very pretty."

"You are now," I whispered.

Ademina smiled, however meekly, as if she didn't believe me. "I was pretty and popular... especially with men." She paused and shot a glance in my direction. When she didn't see me react negatively, she continued. "This was a long time ago, see, and the village didn't take kindly to an unmarried woman spending time with *so many men.* I wasn't ashamed of it, but they made me feel like I should be."

In the pause, I placed a hand on her arm. "You've said nothing that warrants shame. Plenty of people are popular with men or women. As long as you weren't hurting anyone, what's the harm?"

She flinched, almost imperceptibly. "Not everyone saw it that way. I'll admit, Beau, not all of the men were... unattached. And, as you can imagine, some people took issue with that." She glanced at her arm, where my hand remained. A small smile played on her lips. After a sigh, she continued. "They couldn't believe so many men wanted me on their own, so they decided I must be a witch."

"That's a far leap," I muttered.

The corner of her mouth quirked up. "Not for the times."

Her comment garnered more questions than answers. "I don't understand, Ademina. You're beautiful, young, and have this amazing manor. Why was it difficult to believe men would want you, regardless of their relationship status?"

She sighed again, pain freezing on her face. "Please don't think less of me, Beau."

I shook my head and squeezed her arm for support.

"There were beautiful and young women in the village, some of them with bigger and nicer homes. But they didn't get the attention I did. Maybe it was my attitude, or my body, or my reputation speaking for itself."

I couldn't believe magic and witches and curses were making sense. If my father heard about this, he'd surely exile me. Believing in the supernatural had to be worse than being *too feminine* or in a *girly profession*. Then again, maybe not.

I nodded in understanding. "So, since you had to be a witch, the only way to make you stop spending time with the men in the village was to turn you into..." I gestured up and down her body.

"Exactly," she said. If she was offended, I couldn't tell. "Mind you, no one had ever seen anything like this. Not before or since. I might be the only person in history to look like this. I don't know. I spent years trying to undo the curse. I traveled across countries seeking witches, shamans, or anyone who believed in something outside of science. That's how I came to use so many forms of my name; some tongues had trouble with *Ademina* and shortened it. I let them call me whatever they wanted, as long as they tried to help me. But no one could undo the curse. I'm doomed to live like this until I die. If I die." She looked away.

"Are you immortal?"

"I've lived many years, Beau. If I hadn't been cursed, I'd be dead by now."

For some reason, that astonished me more than news of the curse did.

"Is it too much?" she asked softly.

I shook my head. "I'm just sorry you had to go through that."

"I've never told anyone all of that before. Some people heard bits and pieces, but I've been too afraid to tell it all to one person."

My chest was heavy with mixed emotions—sadness that she'd never felt close enough to someone to share her secret and pride that she felt safe with me to do so. I leaned toward her, placing my hand back on her arm. "I'm honored that you let me in," I told her. And I meant it. The vulnerability it took to be that open was scary and difficult.

She tilted her head toward me. "Thank you for making me feel like I could. When I'm with you, I feel like I can be myself. The real Ademina, not the one who scares people and has to hide."

"Never hide from me," I whispered.

She smiled. Her hand found my shoulder, pulling us closer together. "I used to feel like your roses."

She called them *my* roses.

"Like the real Ademina was sparkling and magical, and the current Ademina is dried up, withered away. I lost my sparkle."

"You sparkle," I insisted. And she did. Ademina wasn't wilted and faded; she was fresh and vibrant, a force I'd never encountered before. She shimmered.

Something about that tickled my brain. I tried to remember the last time one of the roses had withered, but I couldn't come up with anything. Not only did they survive a major frost, but they didn't dry out on my table after being cut. They didn't even wrinkle. However, the one Ademina had used on the rabbit had turned to dust afterward. I hadn't thought anything of it in the moment—especially since I'd just seen an animal return from the dead—but now the memory played in my mind. There was something there, something I couldn't quite put my finger on...

was more at play here than mere wind. I
Ademina knew.

ackpack down and put a hand on her fore-
a." The sounds increased, so I spoke louder.
t's going on."

her head. "I told you what they thought of
y cursed me. These *things* are a reminder
did to me. Spirits, maybe. I'm not sure."
r head to look around the room, but there
visibly out of the ordinary. "They haunt me,

magine living with the howls all the time.
didn't have anywhere to go where she'd be
appreciated. Her curse wasn't to appear as
s to lack connection. To live her life alone.
ached at the thought, but the backpack
ll called to me. Ademina's loneliness was
to pay for saving the lives of millions of
h the roses' healing powers. Regardless of
her, I had to leave.

"

away, her blue eyes darkening. "If you're
, just do it. Your ride should be here soon."
back," I told her, not thinking about it
e back for you once I finish my project.
the roses' magic into something we can
then I'll return for you. We can live here
ve can go wherever you'd like." I reached
, and she let me grasp her shoulders. "I

I jumped up, startling Ademina, who pulled her hand away from my shoulder quickly. "I need to dry out the roses."

She shook her head. "I don't understand."

"Neither do I, really. But I think I need to get them to dry out."

I was right. It took days to determine the precise amount of drying necessary to isolate the magical essence. But when I finally did, I was able to capture a miniscule amount of glittery silver liquid from each rose. When I had drained the last drop of magic from them, they each crumbled to dust.

I had no way to explain it scientifically. Their magic literally kept them alive, and without it, they ceased to exist. With the right equipment, I could replicate the magical essence. I was going to save the world. And I'd do so with a combination of science and magic.

⋆ ✦ ◆ ✦ ⋆

I checked my watch again, the minutes drawing out. Each second that didn't involve a taxi pulling up the winding, narrow road was a second too long. Part of me dreaded the arrival of my pre-scheduled ride to the airport, but the other part was excited to share my findings with the world.

"In that big of a hurry to leave?" Ademina's voice boomed from the second floor. Though sarcastic, it held a hint of sadness.

We'd shared a month together, and I had a feeling she'd grown closer to me than to anyone else who had come to study her roses. The same was true for me. In another life, I might have stayed with this strange woman out of love and longing. But in this one, I had no choice. The amazing, miraculous flower would change countless lives, and the sooner I could get its magical essence to a lab, the more people would be saved. Despite my feelings for Ademina, I had to leave out of duty to others.

With a sigh, I turned toward her, ready to speak my thoughts. Everything on my mind flew away when I saw her.

Ademina stood against the railing overlooking the foyer, her typical T-shirt and pants traded for a sundress I hadn't seen. Though her frame was not that of a typical woman, the dress flattered her shape and accentuated her feminine curves. For a split second, my mind settled on those curves, but Ademina's tortured expression brought me into the present moment. She appeared as if she wanted to be nonchalant but was stricken with grief, which mirrored my heart and gut.

She ran a hand over the fur on her head nervously. "What if I ask you to stay?"

I shook my head. We'd had this discussion multiple times in the last forty-eight hours.

"Don't you feel something, Beau?" She gripped the railing again.

My eyes closed in a slow blink. "Of course I do, Ademina. How could I not, after the time we've spent together? But this is too important." I lifted the backpack, careful not to

jostle the carefully wrap
rose inside.

"It's always about the
all the same."

"Ademina..."

"I thought you were
about me."

I couldn't bring mysel
at her, hoping my expres
to hear.

"Beau," she said in a n
die."

"Don't be silly," I said.

Something flashed ac
pain.

"I didn't mean your fe
die. People don't really
Besides, we've only just
can't pretend this was n

She ran down the sta
"Tell me this was less th
Her hands grasped my s
eyes.

Any response I would l
howling of the so-called '
insisted I ignore. This t
by, echoing off walls an
seeming to center over
magic of the roses, I was
something more than ro

walls. There
wondered if

I set the b
arm. "Ademi
"Tell me wh
She shoo
me, why the
of what the
She rolled h
was nothing
Beau."

I couldn't
And Ademin
accepted an
she did; it w

My chest
at my feet s
a small pric
people throu
what I felt fo

"Ademina.
She backe
going to leav

"I'll come
first. "I'll co
I'll synthesiz
replicate, an
together, or
for her agair
promise."

Ademina tilted her head to the side in the movement I'd come to find cute. She appeared doubtful. "I don't know if I'll make it that long, Beau."

I leaned forward, our faces mere inches apart. "What?" The howling was too great.

"I'll die of grief before you return."

"Impossible," I told her, forcing a grin despite the ominous feeling in my gut. "You couldn't get away from me that easily."

She frowned, possibly confused by my attempt at a joke.

"Ademina, I'll come back. Give me time."

Her ear twitched. "Your car is here." She backed away, watching me sadly. "This was nice, Beau. Thank you."

I watched her walk back up the staircase, my head dizzy. She hadn't fought, hadn't insisted, hadn't begged. Did she really care for me as she said she did? Or did she care so much she was letting me go?

She did say she'd die of grief. But she'd been alone for a long time before I'd shown up, and the last scientists hadn't been as nice as me. Some had been afraid, or hateful. Did she love me, or did she love my kindness?

It didn't really matter, because I was leaving her, and despite my promise, I couldn't be sure I'd return. The thudding in my chest reminded me that I wanted to, but my scientific brain told me I couldn't possibly live the life of seclusion required to be with Ademina. Did I even really want to, or was I caught up in the companionship during an exciting but lonely time?

I scooped up my backpack and suitcases and headed for the door, unsure how to say goodbye. With a sigh, I opted to not say anything. It may not have been the best choice, but something inside told me that anything else would cause more heartache. There was already enough.

The grand doors opened without me—more proof of the supernatural elements in this place. That such magic existed no longer boggled my mind, but it fascinated me. Where else was it present? Had I grown up living alongside it without knowing? Was what we called *science* merely an extension of it?

My mind swirling with possibilities and confusion, I stepped outside and squinted against the bright sunlight. Everything seemed different now, knowing what I knew. The world was bigger. My life wasn't reduced to pleasing my father anymore. I needed to pursue magic, to bring it into the everyday world. To study and understand it.

Even if that meant never seeing Ademina again.

"Kiddo," the taxi driver said, surprise lacing his voice. "You made it."

"Of course," I responded as I handed him my suitcases. I'd keep my backpack close. "Why would you think otherwise?"

He nodded toward the manor. "Haunted, 'member?"

I nodded. It was haunted, all right.

"Go home now?"

Finally, I turned back and looked at the place that had taught me so much in four short weeks and housed someone I might have loved, if given more time. "Yes. I'm going home."

I settled into the taxi with a pit in my stomach. Leaving Ademina wasn't easy, but I had to live my life. My dad would probably be proud of me for *manning up* and choosing work over a silly concept like love. Then again, maybe not, since I wasn't choosing the work he thought I should be doing. I didn't really know what would make my father proud. And I wasn't sure it mattered anymore.

The thought kept me company while the old man sang along to the radio in a language I didn't understand. Trees passed by overhead, light beaming through in laser-like rays. The road wound through countryside and around a mountain, reversing the trip I'd taken before. But something felt different. My rapid heartbeat sounded in my ears, and the gnawing in my gut increased as we drove away. I wasn't excited to get home anymore. This was dread.

Ademina's words filled my head. *"If you leave me, I'll die."* Her pained expression was everywhere, whether my eyes were open or closed. *"I'll die of grief."*

"I'll die."

"I'll die."

Why wouldn't her words leave me? They haunted me like those things haunted her.

The trepidation grew, a quiet unease that permeated my skin like oil. An hour into our drive, the anxiety became too much. Something was wrong; I could feel it. My next thought was illogical and went against everything I'd flown around the world for, but I couldn't stop it.

"Driver," I said through gritted teeth, "turn around. I need to go back."

"Nope."

"Please." My word was drawn out, a wholehearted plea.

"I say no." His words were clipped and stern.

"I'll get out and walk," I responded, hand on the door handle.

He sighed as if we had been through this a dozen times already. "This what you really want?"

"Yes. Yes, with everything inside me."

The car slowed to a stop, and he turned to look at me. "Why?"

I couldn't explain it. A feeling of utter dread had taken over me, and I know Ademina wasn't exaggerating. Her grief would overcome her and she would perish without me. "I don't know."

"All the same, you flower people."

His words were strange, but I didn't bother to ask what he meant, as the discomfort had turned to pain. My skin crawled and burned, as if teeming with fire ants. I closed my eyes and breathed deeply, drowning out everything I could—the radio, the driver's profanity as he turned the car around, the sound of the wind against the vehicle and the tires on the road.

The pain lessened with passing minutes, though the emotions remained until the taxi pulled up to the spot I'd just been an hour before. The driver didn't get out or say anything. He put the car in park and shook his head.

I grabbed the backpack and ran for the entrance, not bothering with my suitcases. In my bones, I knew that every second counted.

"Ademina!" I called, pulling the straps of my bag over my shoulders. "I'm back! Where are you?"

Silence.

"*I'll die.*"

"*If you leave me, I'll die.*"

I shook my head against the memory of her words. "Ademina!"

The sounds began, as I'd expected, howling like a windstorm. I was probably going crazy, but it seemed like they moaned my name. Ignoring them, I ran up the stairs toward the main bedroom.

"Ademina," I said when I reached the door, "I'm here. I came back for you."

Silence.

"I'm going to come in now." After a pause, during which she didn't answer, I pushed the tall, heavy wooden doors open.

The room was grand, like the rest of the manor, but it was dark. Not just the lighting, but the décor. Walnut wood instead of the lighter stain in my room, dark rugs on the floors, and black drapes over the tall windows. Even the mural on the ceiling was painted in shadowy colors, and the story it told was a bit macabre—knights slaying beasts who looked too much like Ademina to be a coincidence.

Against the far wall was a four-post bed made of dark wood, so large it had to have been custom-made. Ademina lay in the center, rolled onto her side with her eyes closed. Her bosom rose and fell in shallow breaths. Too shallow.

"*I'll die.*"

I rushed to the bedside. "I'm here," I whispered. "I'm back. Don't leave me."

She moaned softly.

"What do you need?" I asked, grasping her hand. Mine was small against it, but it didn't matter. "Anything you need, my love."

Her eyes opened, glassy with a far-off gaze. Whether she saw me or not was questionable.

My mind was frantic, unable to hold onto a thought for long enough to form a solution. But it kept going back to one thing, the thing I'd been taught since I was a toddler that would fix this exact situation. Not that I'd ever expected to be in it. No one did.

True love's kiss.

Ademina's eyes closed again. Despite the sickness overcoming her—grief that I caused—she was more beautiful than I'd ever seen her. Through my eyes, she wasn't a beast or creature; she was a scared, vulnerable woman, who I loved.

I kneeled on the bed and leaned forward to reach her. The bag shifted strangely on my back, but I didn't take the time to remove it. I had been correct; every second counted. Without hesitation, I tilted my head and placed my lips against hers. I concentrated on all the feelings I had for her and the emotions this moment brought up and willed them into the kiss.

Nothing happened.

"Come on, Ademina," I whispered into her ear. "I love you."

Still nothing.

True love's kiss didn't work. The frenzy in my mind returned.

Around us, the shrieking intensified until I couldn't even hear the frantic thoughts. Meanwhile, Ademina's breathing continued to slow, the movement in her chest barely noticeable.

Paralyzed with indecision and lost in my emotions, I did the only thing left to do. I lay down beside her, lifting her arm over my side, and I held her. As she took her last breath, I told her I loved her and that I was sorry. Then I stayed there and sobbed.

The strange sounds around us grew softer until they were almost silent.

I shifted to cuddle her more closely, but the bag on my back made the new position uncomfortable.

The bag on my back.

The bag that held the rose and its essence.

The magical roses that could heal and revive.

Could they bring my Ademina back, also?

In a frenzy, I stripped it off my back and tore through the carefully packaged and arranged contents. I had only managed to fill one vial half-way with magical essence before I'd run out of sparkling roses. I'd saved one live rose to bring home and study. One rose and less than one vial were all that remained, unless the vines on Ademina's wall grew fresh ones in the future.

When I found the remaining rose, I held it gingerly in both hands and stared.

If I could replicate this flower's healing properties, millions could be saved. Billions over future generations. I could eradicate all disease.

Or I could save the woman I loved. This strange creature who'd captured my heart and died of grief over her love for me.

The logical choice was obvious, but I was compelled to make the decision with my heart. Whether by magic or love, I didn't know; it didn't matter. The wailing increased as I took the rose out of its protective case. I'd made my choice, and though I could turn back, I didn't want to. I was driven forward, called to place the petals against her fur. For the first time in years, I prayed, though I didn't know to whom I was begging.

I waited, but nothing happened. Why wasn't it working?

My eyes burned. I didn't want to lose her at all, especially not like this. Not when her last memory of me was walking away.

The flower itself wasn't enough, but the vial contained the purest form of magic available. There was no time to mix it into a tea or salve or potion or whatever else may get into her body best.

Holding my breath, I opted to open her mouth and dripped some of the essence onto her tongue.

After a moment that felt like eternity, Ademina's chest rose slowly and fell again. Her eyes opened, and she offered a small smile. "You came back." Her voice was hoarse.

"I did. And so did you," I added with my own smile. "I'm so glad."

She reached for my hand, engulfing it with her own. "I love you."

"I love you." I leaned forward and repeated the kiss, but this time, she reciprocated. My heartbeat quickened as her lips explored mine, and I leaned over her more fully, holding her by the back of her head. I wanted her closer to me. I wanted to feel her body against mine. Ademina may be a strange, cursed wonder, but she was my wonder. The kiss lasted a while, and when we pulled away, we were both panting. It was the best kiss I'd ever had, and if it was the last one I'd ever have, I'd be eternally happy.

We lay in each other's arms for several minutes, the sounds spinning around us, louder than before. I'd grown accustomed to them, almost missing them when they were gone. They didn't bother me, though I did still wonder what they were. The manor was certainly haunted, but that didn't seem strange knowing the owner was a cursed creature and the flora was magical. Ademina was magical. Her embrace, her kiss, her comfort... I realized I could be happy here forever. We didn't need to see the world or even my family. I didn't need to be called *Doctor* or make my father proud. How far would those things get me, anyhow? I would stay here with Ademina and I'd be more than satisfied.

◆ ◆ ◆ ◆ ◆

I woke with a start, confused because I hadn't realized I'd been asleep. Through the windows, the sky was dark and starless. How long had I been out?

Ademina stood over me, her expression unreadable. "You're awake." Her voice was almost robotic. She didn't sound excited or happy at the fact.

I yawned and stretched. "You're up. Are you feeling all right?"

She gave a curt nod.

"Is everything okay?" I sat up and watched as she paced the floor beside the bed. Whatever was on her mind caused emotions I couldn't pick out, especially since she wouldn't show me her face.

She mumbled as she paced, the words mostly undiscernible. *'Different this time'* and *'the one'* stood out, but the rest were jumbled.

My skin itched, and I felt foggy, but I sat up anyhow. Mistake. "I don't feel well," I told her, stretching my hand out. "Come to me."

More mumbling, more pacing. *'Not long now. I hate this.'*

What did she hate? And why wouldn't she look at me?

"Ademina, my love." My tongue felt thick. "Please."

She looked at me finally, her features sharper than normal, less soft and more beastly. "Lay back, love." She placed a hand on my forehead and guided me back to the pillow.

Something was definitely wrong, and she didn't seem concerned. "Why?" I asked, unable to form more thoughts or words.

She sighed and removed her hand, leaving a lack of warmth in its place. "My sweet Beau." She paused and glanced around the room, as if acknowledging something I couldn't see. When she spoke again, she was watching the moon through the window. "I told you why they cursed me."

I grunted in acknowledgement.

"I was beautiful, Beau. The belle of the ball. Coveted by men from towns away. I had my fun and didn't care who it hurt." She turned to me again. "Because it *did* hurt people, Beau. I hurt wives and girlfriends, men who fell when I didn't fall back."

"You told me," I managed. The room was spinning, but I wanted to hear her story. It felt important.

Ademina shook her head. "I did. And I never lied to you, but I didn't tell you the most important part of that story—they were right. I *was* the witch they accused me of being. I was vain and selfish and I ate men up and spat them out. The village was tired of it, and they found a stronger witch to place a curse on me. I've lived decades in *this* body," she said, grimacing as she ran her hands down her torso.

"Beautiful," I whispered.

"Horrendous," she countered. "You're the first person in all these years to treat me with respect, and I love you for that. But it doesn't change who I am, *what* I am. I'm a witch, Beau, and I'll be one until the day I die. Which, thanks to you, won't be for a few more years now."

I raised my eyebrows at her. My body itched badly, but I couldn't scratch it. My arms were too heavy.

She sat beside me, the bed creaking with the movement. "You know what? I wasn't sure if I wanted you to come back. My grief for you was more real than with anyone else. Then I'd hoped that the authenticity of my feelings for you would change things, and that your love for me would break the curse. But when I woke up in this body, I knew it was the same thing again. Either I'm doomed to repeat this forever, or you don't love me like you think you do." She paused, but I couldn't respond. With another sigh, Ademina continued. "Either way, I need your life essence to stay alive. And you might ask, as others have, why I bother to live this meager existence when I hate the body I've been given and I'm isolated most of the time."

She leaned in and whispered. "Because I have the chance to be beautiful again. To feel the touch of as many men as I want and take everything from them they're willing to give... and more. Because I've spent decades honing my magic, creating those roses you all love, and many things you never saw because you were too focused on the flowers. And when the time is right and I get my beauty back, I'll be stronger than ever." She leaned again, her lips grazing my ear as she spoke. "And I'll get my revenge. Oh, those who cursed me have been gone for generations. But they have descendants. The people who watched it happen without stepping in had children who had children. The witch who cursed me is probably still out there somewhere, ruining other lives. I'll find them all someday, Beau."

The howling around us increased, as if something sentient heard her words and wanted to fight back.

She sat up and waved a hand at the air. "Ignore those, dear. They're the spirits of researchers like you—not all of them, mind you, because then who would let the world know about my roses so more men would come? And I need men, as you know. Not just researchers, but plenty of others who've fallen in love and given their souls to keep mine alive. You'll be with them soon."

Tears pooled in my eyes, but I couldn't wipe them away. Even blinking was difficult. My vision blurred as I realized this really was the end. Ademina, who I'd returned for and sacrificed greatly for, had poisoned me—no, she had magicked me—and I was going to die here. I'd never be called Doctor, or work with my dad and brother in the shop. I wouldn't hug my mother or sisters or hold nieces and nephews. I'd certainly never change the world with my research.

All because I'd turned around for a woman. A woman who had manipulated me from the start. Did she ever love me? Did I ever love her, or was it a magical pull I'd felt as we drove away? If I had resisted the compulsion to return, as the taxi driver had warned me, would I have forgotten all about her and remembered only the beautiful vista and untamable flowers? Surely, that's what had happened to the others who had returned with tales of magic and wonder but no mention of a she-beast.

The edges of my vision darkened, and I realized I'd never know. My world would soon be relegated to wailing un-heeded warnings to strangers as they fell under Ademina's spell. The thought was sobering, and I forced my eyes to close and await the end.

When it came, it was peaceful rather than painful. One moment, I was itchy and dizzy in the bed where we'd held each other, and the next, I was watching from above as she cried softly in the corner of the bedroom, her back to me. Maybe her feelings were real, even a little.

I wanted to touch her, console her, yell and rage at her. But when I tried, the only sound I could make was the howl of a strong windstorm. It would be the only sound I'd make ever again, as I'd spend eternity watching the belle of the ball coerce naïve men into believing in magic and love. At least I'd have time to study the flowers.

CLEVER

HANA MAREN GODFREY

Armed with their mother's magic gifts, Leonora and her eleven sisters are determined to open a portal and escape their father, a wicked king who has banished sorcery from his kingdom (except the kind that serves him). Without proper training however, the princesses' task proves ruinous.

Henry, a guard magically bound to the king's will, becomes the tragic victim of the sisters' spellwork. Forever changed, his fate entwines with Leonora's and his loyalty to the king is shaken.

Together, Leonora, her sisters, and Henry must find a way to the lost queen's realm before the king imprisons, sells, eats, or burns them alive.

Clever is a fantasy mashup of "The Frog Prince" and "The Twelve Dancing Princesses."

Leonora

"Your cloak, Sister," Leonora whispered in the moonlight. She smoothed the invisible fabric over Berenice's petite frame, blotting the girl from view under its ephemeral gauze. "Hold it closed, here."

The child balled her fists around the seams, securing the two halves of the cloak together, and lowered her freckled face beneath the billowing hood. It was as though the night had eaten her. Yet Leonora could sense Berenice there, feel her younger sibling's warmth as she turned to follow their unseen sisters into the wood.

Leonora drew her hand inside her own invisibility cloak. She disappeared, all but the toes of her boots as she took measured strides into the darkness of the forest. Beyond the shadow of Castle Banebrook, she cast one last glance over her shoulder at the black stone façade. Two windows of the west tower were lit with the red glow of fire. Like wicked eyes, they peered over the rim of the parapet, searching for her.

Each night, swathed in their magic fabric, the sisters slipped unseen through a small gap in the eastern wall hidden behind thick tendrils of ivy. Forbidden as it was, they borrowed delight crossing out of castle grounds and into their sacred wood. It was the only place they dared to hope. Yet every morning, they were returned to their beds, with only tired feet and a secret disappointment shared between sisters.

One day, Leonora and her sisters would abscond from this place and never return. Perhaps tonight.

Leonora shuddered and turned to follow the way to the clearing. Ahead, her sister Carina whispered a spell enchanting mushrooms to emit a soft glow, lighting their steps as the sisters moved through the safety of the belly of the wood. Leonora quickened her strides. She fell in line behind Berenice, before the mushrooms darkened behind them once more.

The path was familiar, though with its treacherous roots and tangled underbrush, a preoccupied princess could easily fall. And so Leonora ignored the rustle of leaves as animals shifted in the shadows, dismissed the questions of owls, and kept count of the lights twinkling ahead of her.

Soon, the twelve princesses would step one by one into the Circle, the strangely symmetrical clearing in the center of the dense wood that wrapped the castle on three sides. Soon, Leonora would resume normal breathing.

Carina, the eldest at one and twenty, was the first to cross, leading the way as she tended to do. Then, as each princess was freed of the wood, they pulled back their hoods and peeled off their magic cloaks. They hung them carefully from a young linden tree. It would be dreadful to misplace the invisible things.

Leonora ensured the youngest princesses crossed the treeline, "as is your duty as the second daughter," Carina instructed her nightly. A mere ten months separated them in age—ten months and a whole spectrum of possible personalities.

"Are we all here?" Carina asked without turning to count for herself. She lifted a fair hand and with a choreographed flick of her wrist she illuminated the Circle with tiny flecks of starlight, seemingly borrowed from the sky itself. The shimmering orbs hovered, pulsing with an energy Leonora could feel thrumming in her blood.

"Twelve little ducks all in a row," Leonora answered.

The princesses were indeed in a row of sorts. However, the two youngest were shuffled around and the twins were huddled together as usual, whispering between themselves in a language all their own. Leonora was at the end rather than the start, which felt quite natural, given her circumstances. But it was unnatural. She could tell by the way Carina had a particular way of trying to order everything and everyone.

Leonora stepped behind the younger girls. She lifted the end of Berenice's flaxen braid and tickled the ten-year-old's cheek. "Switch with Delphine," she whispered through the side of her mouth.

Carina whirled around. Berenice clapped a hand over her mouth to hold in a giggle under the oldest princess's unyielding gaze.

"In order, now, girls," Leonora sang before Carina could bark the command. She strode to the start of the row touching each of her sisters on their blond heads as she went, counting them off by name youngest to oldest. "Berenice, Delphine, Ara, Caprica, Vela, Gemma, Ursa, Orian, Lyra, Eridana, and Leonora!" She curtsied for effect before taking her proper place, several of her own light reddish locks slipping from the twist of hair at the nape of her neck. She tucked the unruly waves behind her ear and smiled.

Carina did not. She was growing more tightly wound with each night that they remained in their father's realm, criminals right under his nose. To varying degrees, the princesses knew what would happen if they were caught using magic. The older girls had witnessed the fate of a sorceress with their own eyes and had elected not to shield the younger ones from the truth. Still, they'd all agreed. It was better to try and fail than remain at Castle Banebrook.

"Circle up," Carina sighed. Her consonants were sharp with a certain pressure on the *p* causing Leonora to wince.

The sisters ringed the clearing, extending their arms to grasp hands. Their nervous energy flowed one to the next, racing heartbeats felt in each other's palms. A circle was the most powerful form in the practice of sorcery. It could contain magic, or prevent a spell from breaking through.

Leonora observed a distinct temperature difference between the two hands she held, as though one sister had warmed hers recently by a fire and the other had shoved hers in a snowbank and left it there to blacken.

"Carina, are you quite all right?" Leonora asked, leaning down to assess if Carina's fingers were turning blue. It was difficult to tell in the light of Carina's stars, even harder when Carina jerked her hand free of Leonora's to swat her away.

"Do allow me some distance, Leonora," she bid.

Righting her posture, Leonora whispered, "Forgive me, Sister."

Carina smoothed her expression, daintily wrapping her long icy fingers around Leonora's.

Leonora shivered.

"Ready, sisters?" Carina addressed the collection of princesses.

They nodded their assent, and together they sang. Even Leonora chirped along as the circle moved around one way, the hems of their nightgowns twirling at their ankles, their feet skipping in a jaunty rhythm. Of course, her voice was merely that, a voice. Not an ounce of magic poured from her lips, not a single word of the spell she sang held fantastical meaning no matter from how deep in her belly she pulled the sound. It was great fun even so. The spell contained extraordinary lilting vowel combinations, and playful strings of syllables tried to tie the tongue over cresting waves of melodies. The lyrics were in another language, but she recognized enough of the words to know they sang of home.

Looping around, the twelve princesses twirled until Leonora was sure she'd dance right through the soles of her boots.

And then it began.

In the center of their ring a small light about the size of a chicken's egg blossomed, petals unfurling, stretching their iridescent fingers toward the princesses. It was, Leonora imagined, like watching the birth of a star.

This time it was going to work. The princesses had struggled to employ their young magic, but it hadn't stopped them from trying to follow their mother's final instructions. Carina possessed some skill and would lead them, guide their words and movements. And this time, yes, together they'd be strong enough to bridge the worlds, open the door, and find their way to the queen's realm. Together, as their mother had bid them.

Leonora sang louder, even knowing her contribution was magically worthless. It served to embolden the voices of her younger sisters. "*They need you*," her mother had told her, and so Leonora did what she could. Her voice arched over her favorite verse until her rich, warm alto stretched and curdled into a scream.

◆ ◆ ◆ ◆ ◆

Henry

"There!" Henry snarled in his throat where he waited, buried in shadow.

Though his eyes had been heavy with sleep the night before, they had not deceived him. He hadn't been mistaken. Here they were again—disembodied boots skittering across the ward, crossing into the wood. Tonight, there'd also been a small face, white as the moon and hanging like it in the night air. It'd been visible only for a second or two before disappearing beneath a veil of darkness.

"East," he muttered to himself. Whoever they were—fae, elf-kind, or worse—they were heading east.

Henry drew back his black hood and stepped from his hiding place in the stairwell spiraling through the eastern turret of Castle Banebrook. Striding across the battlement, he made his way to the west tower, to the king's chambers, where he bid His Majesty's personal guard a good evening.

"I must see the king," Henry said.

"He's busy, Watcher," said Riordan, a high-ranking man and world-class arse. He leaned against the wall sharpening his dagger against a whetstone. He wore the same black tabard emblazoned with the king's crest as Henry, but Riordan's tunic was white and blended almost perfectly with his sallow skin.

Henry tried again. "I've reason to believe there are magic-folk about the castle."

As if told Banebrook Wood was on fire, Riordan dropped the stone and sheathed the weapon. He pounded on the great arched wooden door.

"Enter," came the deep voice of King Ciarán.

Henry stepped into the room, and Riordan closed him inside with the King of Dorchada.

The king continued, "There had better be magic afoot, disturbing me at this late hour. Or plague. Yes, a plague would do. There are rather few acceptable reasons for entering the king's chambers in the dead of night."

As His Majesty spoke, Henry's gaze moved across the fire-lit room, tracing over endless bookshelves, fine, gilded furniture, and doors leading to other private rooms, until at last they settled on the king's form. Ciarán was seated behind a large, ornately carved wooden desk, a quill in his hand and a plush black evening coat draped around his wide shoulders. His dark blond hair was thick and streaked with silver, and it crawled from his head across his jaw, ending in a point on his sturdy chin. To his left, the king's reflection rippled in the magic mirror he used to talk with his lords, allies, and eyes throughout the realm.

Ciarán's quill scratched across a piece of parchment, forming thorny letters. Pressing a full stop into the document, the king spared a glance for his visitor. "What news, Henry?"

"Your Majesty." Henry moved before the king and bowed.

Bound to him as they were by magic, the king knew all his men by name. But the king did not need magic to recognize Henry. He had long been a resident at Castle Banebrook, and his startling blue eyes were a rarity in this realm. So rare in fact, he'd been tested for the ability to wield more than once. He possessed no magic by nature, but it did not stop people from wondering. "*From another kingdom,*" he often heard passersby whisper. And for all he knew, it was so.

He'd been found as a small boy by the head of the king's guard and was raised by the man until, at the age of five and ten, he was bound in silver bands to Ciarán in service. That was ten years ago.

One band was fastened around his wrist to prevent his hands from acting in opposition to the king. One around his neck to keep his voice from uttering a word against the king. And one was secured by magic around his heart to ensure its loyalty to the king. This was the law for all those in service to the king whether volunteered or otherwise engaged.

This practice was among the only legal forms of magic in the land.

Henry cleared his throat and offered his report in earnest. "I believe I have witnessed the use of illicit magic on castle grounds this night, sire. The criminals—"

"Criminals?" the king interjected. He did not look up from his parchment, though there was a note of surprise as he pinched the s between his yellowed teeth.

"Yes, my king. I am certain they move in numbers. I saw them from the eastern wall escaping into the wood." Henry stood straighter, shoulders pulled back. The blades nearly met behind him.

"I trust you, Watcher," Ciarán said, his ink pooling where his quill bore into the parchment.

Watcher. Henry's nostrils flared at the word, still after all these years. Having proven his devotion to the king, Henry had been named Watcher of the Keep, the king's eyes and ears about the castle. Ciarán would have him wear the title as a badge of honor. For Henry the title, the black regimentals, and hooded cloak he wore, were painful reminders of what he could not undo. And so he moved in the shadows unseen. He was the night.

He was the Watcher.

"With your permission, I can track them, bring their names before you for reckoning." He would need Ciarán to send him, to allow him to leave Castle Banebrook.

"Go." The king's voice seemed to lower by half to a haunting register. At last he turned his gaze fully upon Henry, his eyes as dark as the ink with which he wrote. "By any means necessary, discover who they are. I will be waiting."

"As my king commands." Henry felt a sharp tingling around his left wrist and circling his neck. The tightening in his chest bid him move. Compelled by his bindings, Henry hastened from the king's chambers, along the corridors, and across the bailey, until he passed through the gates of Castle Banebrook and into the night-drenched wood.

Eastward, his boots made nary a sound in the leaves and tangles of underbrush. While all guards were gifted additional speed, strength, and endurance, the collective magic in Henry's bindings gave him the enhancements he required to perform his duties as Watcher. He possessed stealth like a woodland wild cat and ears as attuned as the king's own hounds. Even in the dark, his vision was clear over long distances. He could track as well as any wolf, catching scents in the air.

A narrow path carved through the wood. Henry cursed. The criminals had passed here before, many times. How had he not discovered them sooner? Concealment magic could be very powerful he knew, but even so he prayed to the gods the king would not become aware of his failing.

Henry rounded a tree and paused. Yes. He had them now. Vanilla, something earthy, and the unmistakable hon-eyed scent of magic would lead him right to them.

There, he thought. Moving deeper into the forest, Henry chased the sound, faint at first, but then clearer. It was laughter, a song. He slowed, knowing how the magic-folk could turn a melody into a prison. He stayed in the shadows of the trees as he approached a lighted clearing. Stars hung in the air as though lured from the night sky.

Peering around a linden tree, Henry grimaced. He dragged a rough hand over his face in a futile attempt to clear the scene from his eyes. These were not fae or elven-kind. It was worse, much worse. Dancing around in circles were the king's own daughters, in their nightgowns, no less. All twelve of them were engaged in an enchantment. A light grew at the heart of the clearing, coaxed on by their singing.

Sorcery.

"What have they done?" he whispered into his palm. A familiar weight formed in his gut.

Suddenly the bands around his wrist, throat, and heart grew hot with his hesitation. Sweat pearled along his brow and lip and the clearing churned before his eyes. *The queen, the queen,* his mind looped on thoughts of the late Queen Celesta, and now her daughters, her foolish daughters.

Henry wretched into the underbrush.

His ears were ringing. No. That sound, sharper than a knife's edge, it was a scream. Henry righted himself and locked onto the second princess's gaze, the one with hair the color of honey and green eyes, like her mother's. Princess Leonora.

He couldn't move. He had no choice but to tell the king what he had witnessed. But when he did, what would become of them?

It didn't matter, he realized. The king's boundless wrath awaited them. Their fate was sealed.

Even if Henry had wanted to save them, his bindings burned, urging him to act. And so he stepped back—he stepped back—he tried very hard to step back, but *could not* move.

◆ ◆ ◆ ◆ ◆

Leonora

Leonora could only watch as fractions of fractions of seconds separated her sisters' uncoordinated movements.

Carina reached out with her magic and secured the scout where he stood.

Pulling deep, throaty syllables from somewhere in her belly, Eridana cast a spell.

Lyra spun in place, flung a hand in the man's direction, and cried out a series of piercing notes.

And Berenice charged the man, screaming something about the color green and waving her arms about like mad.

His gaze was fixed on Leonora, and she was certain she recognized him—one of her father's men, the distinctly handsome one with dark hair and eyes like the faint blue rings around stars.

As Leonora caught her youngest sister in her arms, the beautiful man disappeared from view behind a swirl of magic, a glistening pearlescent cloud.

Leonora's throat clenched tightly. For several long moments, her breaths were ineffectual. Had her sisters killed him? Or worse, maimed him?

"What have you done?" she asked, unable to peel her gaze from the concentrated mixture of magic cast by principally untrained, would-be sorceresses. The unfolding scene, an inevitably heinous magical crime, was captivating.

Berenice wriggled in Leonora's hold. "Unhand me, Sister!"

"I stole his voice," Eridana answered, her posture proud and pointed nose upturned. "He will never speak of this night."

"It matters not, Sister, as I have turned him to stone," Lyra said, arms folded over her chest. "He will make a striking statue to guard over the Circle."

"He shall not!" Berenice laughed maniacally. She broke free of Leonora and twirled, arms raised above her head in triumph. "For I have turned him into a frog!"

"Oh, by the gods," Carina groaned.

"There is no possibility this ends well," Leonora muttered, bringing a hand to massage her temple.

When the shimmering fog cleared, only one spell remained. Carina held in her magical grip a—well—a something, certainly not a gorgeous human man—floating a short distance from the ground.

"What is it?" Ara's lip curled in disgust.

Several sisters made sounds of unease, but no one moved closer.

Leonora rolled her eyes and stepped forward. Within a few strides, she determined the small hovering object was not slimy, nor green. It was grey like a stone. Maybe it was Lyra's spell which had taken. No. Stones are not furry as this phenomenon appeared to be upon closer inspection. It was some sort of creature rolled into a tight ball, its only movement a gentle tremor.

"Loosen your grip, Carina," Leonora tossed over her shoulder as she took slow paces to within an arm's-reach of the floating animal.

A moment later the creature gradually unfurled. A set of black pointed ears emerged. Its eyes were closed as it lifted its darling face and untucked its legs. From its muzzle to the white tip of its tail, the fox was covered in soft-looking stone-colored fur which darkened around its belly, face, and feet. But when it opened its eyes to look at her, it was clear this was no ordinary forest kit. Blue, like star rims, the fox's eyes set upon Leonora's face.

Then he opened his mouth and, in a rough whisper, said, "Princess Leonora, Your Highness."

◆ ◆ ◆ ◆ ◆

Henry

Princess Leonora leapt back, stumbled a bit, then regained her composure an extra step away.

"Leonora? Are you quite all right?" one of the princesses called from the cluster they formed behind the eldest across the clearing. "What's happened?"

"Perfectly all right!" Princess Leonora returned. "Fret not, Sisters."

Henry could only move slightly here and there, and even then, rather slowly. Over Princess Leonora's shoulder, he saw the eldest of the king's daughters had her arms raised, her face pinched with effort. He was secured by her magical workings, it seemed.

"I did not mean to startle you," Henry tried again, turning his attention to Princess Leonora. His voice felt like fine gravel in his throat. The magic which curled around him put such strain on his body, he could scarcely breathe. Or was it his bindings? He had never disobeyed them like this before. It was the understanding of every member of the king's guard that dereliction of duty would result in a death most painful. None had been strong or stupid enough to find out precisely what that meant.

"My stars!" Princess Leonora breathed, her mouth forming a perfect o. She studied him as though she'd never seen anyone like him.

He was used to this reaction. Despite having lived at the castle nearly all his life, this was likely the first time any of the princesses had bothered to look at him. Henry waited for her to reconcile any misgivings about the hue of his eyes. This usually required several uncomfortable moments of people studying him, or never happened at all.

The princess moved toward him again, this time stumbling over something lying in the grass. She bent to pick it up. Clasped between her delicate fingers, Princess Leonora held a silver ring.

Henry's heart doubled in speed when he recognized what it was. The king's crest was etched into the metal along with the symbols of the spell—the one that kept his hands from working against the king. It was one of his bands, the one he'd worn around his left wrist for a decade. But how? It was soldered on by magic, fitted exactly to him so it could never be removed. As he'd grown, built muscle, and broadened, the band had expanded with him. But this band in Leonora's grasp was miniaturized, roughly as big around as his dagger's hilt. How had it slipped off, shrank so? Henry's hands were too large to—his hands... *My hands?*

After a great deal of effort to adjust his gaze, Henry was looking down at them. They were covered in silken fur. He wiggled his fingers, or rather, the adorable, round digits tipped with claws.

These were not his hands.

These were not hands at all.

The band had slid from his slender foreleg, over his gods-forsaken *paws*. It'd fallen into the grass beside his crumpled black regimentals because he was *not* a broad human man. What had the princesses done? Henry tried to move his head, to look at the rest of his changed form. Was the band encircling his neck secure? His heart strained against the one in his chest—there was no question it had constricted to suit his new proportion.

What would happen to him without the third band? Henry felt feverish. His tongue lolled out of his mouth and he panted like one of the king's hunting dogs on a warm day. He needed his band returned to its proper place. By degrees, Henry put his paw out to the princess.

Princess Leonora shrugged and tossed the band into the forest.

Henry choked on a gasp.

"Something wrong?" Her voice was high and strangled as if she knew perfectly well something was wrong.

"Something? You tell me, Princess."

Leonora

"Ah, yes. You are... um, changed," Leonora decided. She leaned down to inspect him more closely, her hands resting on her knees. He was a decently sized fox with a thick coat of fur that almost completely hid the silver collar he wore. It appeared to have shrunk with him like the wrist band. There'd be no removing it even if she felt optimistic about risking her fingers to try.

"I must insist you allow me to fetch my band this instant, Princess." The restraint in his voice was thin. Were she not a princess, Leonora was sure all deference would be forfeit.

She studied his paw. For one moment she thought she might reach out and touch it. Rather, Leonora offered quietly, "You haven't a proper thumb to keep it in place." Then, when he bared his teeth, she added, "The one about your neck is still fastened. And perhaps you will hardly notice the absence of the other?" She smiled encouragingly as though telling a child who lost his toy bear that he might sleep better alone.

"I—" the guard-turned-fox tried, but instead tipped his head, considering.

"What is he?" Orian called across the clearing amid the huddle of princesses who were too frightened to see what they had done.

"He appears to be a fox," Leonora replied in her most polite tone so as not to startle anyone, most especially the fox.

"A fox?" the fox groaned.

"A frog?" Berenice called excitedly.

"Fox," Leonora repeated, emphasizing the *x*.

"Well, that is terribly disappointing," Berenice said.

"But how?" This was Vela.

Frog, fox... similar sounds? Leonora thought and shrugged once more, this time with a confused fold in her brow. She was perfectly aware her sisters, lovely as they were, were not the most adept sorceresses. All suitable mentors being in hiding, imprisoned, or dead had made it difficult to gain traction on their clandestine education, despite Carina's best efforts. But, really? How had *this* been the result?

"Is he green?" Berenice asked, and Leonora could hear the wishes in her words.

"I regret to inform you he's the color of stone." Foxes were much more charming in their customary reddish hues, but for his sake, at least he was not unnatural in color.

"Well, one of you got something right." This was Carina. It was also a snarl.

"He can't talk either," Eridana argued. "I have helped!"

Leonora winced. Clearly, she had been the only one to hear the creature speaking.

"He can't talk because he's a fox. Not due to any success of yours," Lyra spat.

"I'm letting him go." The exasperation in Carina's voice was matched only by her exhaustion.

160

"I wouldn't," Leonora cautioned.

"Pray, why not?" This Leonora heard in one ear from Carina's voice; in the other came the fox's hiss.

Leonora straightened and turned to face her sisters.

"He is not a frog. He is a fox. And while he is certainly stone-like in color, he is presumably rather fast, which is not like a stone at all. And, most surprisingly, he has not been silenced."

"He can talk?" Delphine clapped her hands together and giggled.

"He can talk?" Carina shrieked.

"He can talk," Leonora confirmed.

"Prove it. Say something, fox," Eridana shouted, a hand on her hip and wearing an expression of disbelief that wavered at its edges.

The fox looked to Leonora.

"Better do as she says," Leonora advised.

"Good evening, Princesses."

The girls leapt back, squealing in delight and fear in equal measure.

"Can we keep him?" Delphine pleaded, tugging at Carina's nightdress.

"We must kill him," Carina said matter-of-factly.

"No!" came a chorus of princesses, underpinned by a deeper, and understandably more frantic voice: the fox.

"He isn't a fox," Carina said. "He's a man, remember? A man under father's employ who witnessed us engaged in the criminal act of magic. A man who will surely run to Father and tell him all he has seen. A man who will need no proof at all, because he is the proof. He is a talking fox."

"You just said he isn't a fox," Berenice whimpered.

Carina groaned and stomped her foot. Her arms were trembling. "I cannot hold him here for all eternity. We must do something."

"I will silence him!" Lyra stepped forward.

"No!" her sisters cried, no one louder than Leonora.

"None of you will be conducting any more magic tonight. You're all in desperate need of more training. That much is quite clear." This was Carina again. "And my magic has been spent on restraining this." She tipped her head toward the fox.

Dark circles had bloomed under Carina's eyes. Leonora could not be certain if it was the cost of her magic or of being the eldest of twelve mostly magical sisters, the only gifted one who didn't pose an immediate threat to herself and others.

"What then?" Eridana asked.

Stepping forward, Carina wound a magic rope of stars. With it, she encircled the fox's muzzle, looped it about his chest, and left a length of slack which she placed in Leonora's hand. Carina lowered the fox to the ground. Her shoulders relaxed as she released her magic hold on the creature.

The fox tried to protest, but was unable to make more than a muffled sound that might have been a bark, but came across as a *harrumph*. He tried to run, but was leashed securely in Leonora's grip and only managed to tangle himself more tightly.

"There's something else I must tell you, Sister," Leonora said in hushed tones meant only for Carina. This man was not any man, fox or not. She had recognized him from the castle. He was the king's Watcher, the guard she could never forget... not since he'd broken her heart.

"Not now, Leonora. Manage the creature. We will figure out what to do."

"Of course, Carina," Leonora agreed. But as her sister turned and walked away, Leonora realized Carina meant the *magical we*, the *we* which didn't include her.

The eleven circled up a distance from her and the fox to whisper amongst themselves.

Leonora reached for the left sleeve of her nightgown, feeling for the small round trinket she'd sewn into the hem. Rolling it between her fingers, she sighed and sat in the grass next to the fox.

◆ ◆ ◆ ◆ ◆

Henry

"I don't have magic," Princess Leonora told Henry. "I come along to dance for fun, and because I'd hate to miss it if they managed to open..." Her eyes slid to Henry and narrowed as she allowed the unfinished thought to dangle between them. Feigning a cough, she continued, "I'd be useless trying to figure out what to do with you." She fidgeted with the hem of her sleeve, bringing both hands to her chest as though it might hide the way she manipulated the fabric.

Henry turned his large ears toward the group of princesses discussing his fate. He had excellent hearing as a bound man, but as a fox! Why, this was even better.

Except his captor was disinterested in the silence required for eavesdropping.

"Don't worry," Princess Leonora continued. She was watching her sisters as she spoke to him. "They won't kill you, probably. But we can't have you telling Father what we've been up to." She reached out, her hand hovering over him, and asked, "May I?"

"May you what?" he returned, but through the muzzle, it sounded a bit more like, "Mm-ym-hmph?"

Then she pet him. *Pet him.* On the head. Her soft touch glided through the hair—fur—on his head, scratching behind his ear. He leaned into her hand. It felt incred—no. No, no. No.

Henry turned his ears once more towards the group. But again, the princess spoke.

"My father is a particular man, you see. And rather against the use of magic. But you already know, do you not?"

Of course Henry knew the king's stance on magic—forbidden, unless it served the crown. Only the mage in King Ciarán's innermost circle could conduct magic legally, and this skill was primarily put to use binding people into service and inventing enchanted devices to aid the king.

"He would probably harm us if he ever found out. It wouldn't be the first time someone close to him was punished for using magic," Leonora continued.

Yes, Henry knew all too well the king's relationship to an offender meant nothing.

"He might let me live, since I can't wield myself. But I'm not sure I'd like living out my days under lock and key.

Aiding and abetting magic-folk is illegal after all." Princess Leonora shuddered, and closed her eyes tightly as though warding off visions of lifelong imprisonment.

Henry swallowed the lump in his throat. He did not like the idea of Princess Leonora detained. Curious. She had committed a crime after all. And criminals should answer for their transgressions. But he could not quite reconcile the idea. Maybe it was because she had her fingers beneath the band on his neck, scratching where he'd not been able to reach for many years.

"I wonder if he'd line them up in order or simply make one large bonfire and throw the whole lot of them over it. What do you think?" She turned her gaze on him at last. Her eyes were focused, but a thin line of water beaded her bottom lashes.

Henry felt sick again.

It's too late, he wanted to tell her. I've already told the king I sought magic-folk tonight. He'll be waiting. Even if he weren't muzzled, he doubted the band around his neck would allow him to reveal this.

"So you see, it's best if no one speaks of what happened here." She cupped Henry's chin in her hand, studying him intently. "For I do not want my sisters to die."

He wanted to at once stare into her green eyes forever and have his gouged out.

"Leonora." The eldest sister approached, her usual tightly-strung posture collapsed. "We are returning to the castle. Tomorrow is a full moon, better for our purposes. We will sort out then how to turn him into a stone fox or a speechless frog. Either will do," Princess Carina said, waving a dismissive hand in Henry's direction. Eyeing Henry with a narrow gaze, Carina leaned in to whisper in Leonora's ear, "Then we will finish what we started with the door."

Door? What door? Was the thing they were conjuring meant to be a door? These were pitiful sorceresses indeed if that was their intent. It had looked hardly big enough for a mouse to squeeze through.

"What of the fox until then?" Princess Leonora stood, dusting nature from her nightgown.

"We cannot leave him here. Without proximity to me I'm not sure how long the leash will hold. Bring him," Carina ordered.

Princess Leonora looked down at Henry. Henry looked up at her.

You cannot go back. He directed his thoughts toward her as hard as he could, as though they might infiltrate her mind if he willed it so. But for countless reasons, this was futile. Even without the muzzle he would not have been able to warn her. It was in this moment he wished the king had also bound his mind, for while his body belonged to the will of Ciarán, his conscience was fully aware of what he would and could not do.

Bending, Princess Leonora lifted Henry and carried him toward the linden tree. With the help of one of her sisters, she donned an invisibility cloak like the rest of the princesses. She tucked him inside like an infant against her warm bosom.

As they moved toward the castle, the bands around Henry's neck and heart grew warm. The collar compelled him to find the king and speak the truth. The band within his

166

chest insisted he remain loyal to King Ciarán. Yet the heart itself? Its desires felt far less certain.

Henry writhed, his thoughts and his bands warring.

"It's all right, kit. I won't let any harm come to you," the princess whispered, but Henry couldn't promise the same.

◆ ◆ ◆ ◆ ◆

Leonora

"It's blocked," Caprica said.

Leonora could not see her sister, but she knew each of their voices without question, and Caprica's quavered.

"Whatever for?" This was Berenice, her delivery smaller than usual.

With the ivy swept aside from the opening at the foot of the castle wall, Leonora could see their secret passage—the one Carina had worked very hard to coax from a crack in the foundation—had been sealed. Wet mortar between the stones glistened in the moonlight. No. Not moonlight. Fire.

"To put an end to this."

This voice wasn't one Leonora heard often in her waking life. Instead, it haunted her nightmares. Turning slowly, her cloak secured around her, Leonora looked upon the face of her father, the king. Torches in hand, a host of his guards stood behind him, each collared in silver, cloaked in onyx, and loyal to him alone.

"I should have guessed," the king muttered, smoothing a hand over his black surcoat embroidered with silver dragons. "You poor dears could not escape her curse." He almost sounded pitying. But Leonora knew it was false. "Magic about the castle grounds, no, I thought. Magic scheming *in* the castle, magic skulking about and up to no good at all. Magic leaking out of my own fortress, poisoning the wood. Just like her." He enunciated the last three words pointedly. Then, as though he could find her eyes through her cloak, his empty gaze caught on Leonora's face. "And sure enough, my suspicions were confirmed when my men found your rat hole in my castle walls." He pulled the word *rat* from the deepest part of his gut.

Leonora felt the fox tense in her hold. Though he clawed at her, she secured him more tightly. She knew he wanted to be among the guards. Wanted to? That wasn't quite right. It didn't matter what a king's man desired, only what the king compelled him to do. She was sure now that the Watcher in her arms had seen the princesses, reported them, followed them, and set this all in motion whether he'd wanted to or not.

"Father." Carina pulled back her hood, her head seeming to float disembodied in the air. Her face was like marble, until King Ciarán slapped her. The eldest princess's ashen cheek reddened instantly, her mouth gaping open in horror as a rivulet of blood trickled from its corner.

The king grabbed Carina by her throat and tore her cloak from her, spitting as he snarled, "I should have bound you all the moment I learned of your mother's treachery."

"Why didn't you?" Carina choked out.

He shoved her to the ground. "Insolent girl," he muttered before kicking her in the ribs.

Several of the princesses gasped, giving away their positions. The guards grabbed Lyra, Ursa, Gemma, Vela, Ara, and Delphine. It was enough. The rest of the princesses removed their hoods and clustered around their sisters in custody.

"I would have, had the mage not warned it might kill you!" the king bellowed, kicking his firstborn again.

Carina shielded her head with her arms, but refused to cry out.

"A blood bond and a magic bond cannot abide one another; like oil and water, he claimed. In hindsight, I should have found a way or annihilated you all trying. But even princesses have value," he muttered.

Leonora knew he did not mean intrinsic worth.

The king looked at each of his children. He placed his boot upon Carina's body which was curled and quaking. With disappointment he continued, "I thought watching your mother burn would have instilled in you the level of obedience I require. One would think my royal blood would have diluted any traces of magic with which she burdened you. I do hate to be wrong." He shifted his weight, pressing harder into Carina's back, flattening her. But she did not give him the satisfaction of crying.

The fox whimpered.

Leonora coughed to conceal the sound.

The fox whimpered louder.

Leonora broke into a coughing fit then doubled over and whispered down her cloak, "Hush, you!" Rising, she felt her father's eyes on her. They were darker than night. At least the night had stars.

"Are you ill?" The corners of the king's mouth sank in disgust, nearly reaching the curve of his jaw.

"No, Father." She shook her head.

"Unfortunate," the king muttered. Then, turning to his men, he shouted, "Strip them of these cloaks and lock them in the north wing." He gave Carina one last dig with the toe of his boot then turned to go, leaving a muddied print across the white fabric of her nightgown.

"Father." Carina found her voice once more. She pushed up onto her hands and knees and drew in a shaking breath. Speaking to the king's broad shoulders she asked, "What will become of us?"

The king turned his head, but the princesses could see only his profile, all hard lines and deep shadows. A wicked smile tested the crook of his lips.

"There are twelve of you," he observed, as though counting them for the first time. "So many opportunities for creativity. I couldn't possibly decide tonight."

The princesses let out a collective, shuddering breath.

At the gate, King Ciarán and his personal guard moved in one direction, while the remaining men led the princesses toward the north wing. They needed only to haul Carina by her arms. The rest followed. Little ducks in a disordered row.

As they went, one of the guards moved down the line jerking the cloaks away from the girls one by one.

No. Without her cloak Leonora would have nowhere to hide the fox. They would take him away, and he would tell them everything and... and it didn't matter.

Their father already knew the truth. He'd already begun to plot how to rid himself of them.

Leonora slowed her step until she was at the end of the group of princesses. She bent, set the fox down, and kept walking, her skirt brushing over his small form. Once Carina was far enough away, he'd be free of the leash and muzzle, and he could do as he liked. The king's mage could likely transform him back into a man, replace his missing band, and there could be one not entirely unhappy ending. She did not look back to watch him go.

When the guard reached Leonora she had already removed her cloak and folded it. She handed it politely to the man.

"Thank you," he said, surprise creating an upward inflection to his words.

The queen had taught Leonora that courtesy could be a form of magic, that if you treated people kindly enough, most would reciprocate.

"You're quite welcome. Do be careful with them, if you wouldn't mind. The fabric was our mother's and we have so little left of her."

The guard nodded uncomfortably, as though he would feel some measure of guilt in a few short hours, incinerating the garments at the king's behest.

The princesses were unceremoniously herded into the chambers in the upper floor of the north wing. Leonora felt a strange sense of relief, even as the key clicked in the lock. She took in the first drops of morning sun through the iron bars on the windows.

These were their mother's chambers. Situated in the corner where the northern and eastern walls met, they were rounded in shape. Leonora had not been here in four years. No one had. The air in the receiving room felt stale and smelled aged, as if it had hung there all this time, trapped in the moment it had first been vacated. The chaise and armchairs had been covered in white cotton sheets. But her mother's writing desk, since emptied of her correspondence—evidence, depending on who was asked—and personal treasures, was thickly coated in dust.

"*My dearest Leonora,*" she could almost hear her mother whisper. She strained her ears trying to catch more, but it became increasingly difficult amid her sisters' groaning.

"I cannot cast," Vela said.

"Everyone knows," her twin, Gemma, retorted.

"Try it," Vela said, her hands still lifted in a futile attempt to do something. Leonora was never sure what her sisters *meant* to do with their magic.

Caprica raised her hands, too, and tried to... Leonora could only guess, by her strangely punctuated murmuring.

"It's the iron," Carina said, her hand pressed to her ribcage. "It encircles Mother's rooms." She pointed to a continuous line of iron rods hammered into the base of the stone walls. "A ring of iron nullifies magic."

Berenice rushed to the nearest window. "If I think very small thoughts, I can squeeze through," she said.

"Berenice, no!" Carina cried, but it was too late.

Berenice had her fingers wrapped around one of the bars. She wrenched her hand back and wailed.

Rushing to her side, Leonora knelt to examine her sister's hand. Berenice's palm turned an angry shade of red. Leonora blew on the little girl's delicate skin and rubbed her back until the child quieted. She stood and helped Berenice to the nearest chair.

Gesturing to the bars, Carina said to her sisters, "These are pure iron. Do not touch them. Why do you think mother did not free herself of this prison when she was ten times the sorceress any of us could claim to be?" she grumbled.

"Mother would not have left us here," Leonora whispered, then added to herself, *That is why she allowed herself to be imprisoned.*

"And yet she did." Carina had heard her. She lumbered across the room stopping but an inch from Leonora's face. "She abandoned us here, with barely a decent caster among us, with nothing but some invisible fabric and a vague set of instructions to find the realm of her people. If it was so wonderful in Sunniva, why did she ever leave in the first place?"

Leonora backed up, her hand flying to the gold charm in the hidden pocket on the hem of her sleeve. She turned the ball in her fingers, her mind soothed by tracing the symbols carved on its gilded surface.

She too often wondered how her mother had found her way here, married to a monster. When Leonora asked, all the queen said was, "*He wasn't always this way, my darling.*" Maybe Celesta had loved her husband once. Fat lot of good it'd done her.

"It's you she left in the worst position," Carina hissed, drawing Leonora back into the present. "No magic. And yet you cling to her memory as though she can still favor you from the grave."

Another step backward and Leonora's boot found resistance as a small yelp met her ears.

She jumped, knocking her sister away from her, and found at her feet a stone-colored fox.

"Ah, good. You did something right," Carina sighed, resigned. She moved with as much grace as her injured body would allow to lie across the ornate settee by the iron-barred fireplace. "Now we won't starve."

♦ ♦ ♦ ♦ ♦

Henry

I have made a grave error, Henry thought.

"You cannot eat him!" Princess Leonora bent, then sat on the floor beside him. "He is a man."

"He is a fox," Princess Berenice observed.

"Only temporarily," Princess Leonora replied. She looked around the queen's receiving room. Henry's gaze followed.

The youngest girls sat together on the circular rug and watched Princess Carina and their older sisters, expressions full of hope in that way only children have the luxury of experiencing. The twins huddled in the oversized chair in the corner whispering intently, their fingers interlaced so tightly their skin reddened. The older girls avoided the gazes of the younger ones. One paced, another sat on a bench, her left foot pulsing wildly. A third girl was crying, while a fourth rubbed her sister's back and sang a soft lullaby slightly off key, her soprano voice feeble.

Princess Leonora wiped her eyes on her sleeve, then turned her attention to Henry with a weak but genuine smile.

"How did you end up here?" She gently swept away what remained of the muzzle's starry magic that clung to his coat. Enclosed in iron, Carina could not maintain the spell.

"I followed you, Your Highness," Henry said.

"But why? I meant for you to go," the princess said, even as she gently smoothed his fur where the harness had rumpled it.

"I—I am," Henry searched. "I am a man. One of you must turn me back."

In truth, Henry wasn't sure why he hadn't gone to the mage. He knew the north wing was a poor place to attempt magic. He also knew the princesses were terrible sorceresses. And yet, he had followed Princess Leonora, his dark gray fur blending into the shadows. It had been as though he'd been leashed to her hand... as though he were not bound solely to the king.

Without the band on his wrist to control his hands, which now operated as feet, he seemed to have more say in how they behaved. Still, it had been painful to follow her. His neck itched madly and his chest felt as though a great weight were expanding inside his ribcage. Perhaps he would turn to stone after all in a delayed magical miracle.

Henry's best guess as to why he'd been able to come here with her at all was because he didn't currently have any direct orders from the king. He had technically found the magic-folk. He had even delivered them to the castle... in a way (if one didn't think on it too hard). Possibly his heart was at least partially satisfied he was guarding her—er—rather, guarding the princesses by staying close by.

Regardless of the reason, Henry dropped to his haunches and scratched at his collar with his back foot. Unfortunately, the presence of iron was no match for the silver of his bands. The properties of silver opposed those of iron. Magic protected by silver was not easily undone.

"Turn you back? Oh, dear. I fear you have made a terrible error in judgement," Princess Leonora said, confirming Henry's own appraisal of the situation. "None of us can help you with your, um," she tilted her head, folded her lips between her teeth to hold in a laugh, then decided, "predicament. Least of all, me."

"Perhaps I can help you," he said, forcing his foot down and puffing his chest out as though he weren't dying a little with each breath. "I know this castle, I know the routines of the guards. I can help you escape." His collar burned with his defiance. Had he really just offered to help a prisoner escape? Henry hardly recognized himself, and not just because he was a fox. Without the complete set, Henry wondered if the bands' hold over him was weakened.

She tapped his nose lightly and scratched under his chin. "Why would I believe you? You are a fox. Foxes are known for their trickery."

"I am a man," Henry repeated. "I have only been a fox for mere hours thanks to you twelve dancing sorceresses."

"Eleven," she corrected, her fingers moving behind his large ears. "I am not a sorceress."

"Likewise, I am not a fox. I am a guard." Henry leaned into her hand as she caressed his head.

"And guards are known for their loyalty to the king," she replied.

"You will not trust me?" he asked, backing away, but remaining within reach.

"No, but I will protect you from my sisters. I quite like foxes and would hate to see you eaten." The princess smiled.

"That is... kind," Henry said. She was kind. Perhaps that was why he had quickly decided he preferred her company to any other person's in Castle Banebrook. The bar was low, he realized, but she exceeded it tenfold.

The day dragged on. When the sisters eyed him hungrily, Princess Leonora kept Henry close until bowls of something meant as food arrived, a small mercy from the king. She even offered to share her measly portion of colorless mush with him. He declined.

"You must have a name," Princess Leonora said sometime later while her sisters braided each other's hair with trembling fingers.

"Henry," he said, stretching in the pool of mid-afternoon sun warming the floor.

"Leonora," she replied.

"Of course, Princess Le—"

"Just Leonora," she insisted.

He lifted his head and looked at her. The sunlight played in her honey-colored hair which was half swept up, the rest dangling in her freckled face. She toyed with a golden ball, rolling it around in her hands, studying it.

"Just Leonora," he repeated. "Not a sorceress and not a princess."

At this, she smiled. It was warm and bright like the sun. He turned himself to face her fully, his legs tucked beneath him.

"What is that?" he asked her.

The light reflected off the gilded sphere as she held it out to him. "A trinket from my mother."

"Queen Celesta…" Henry wanted to say the late queen had been a kind woman, she hadn't deserved to die at the hands of the king, and he wished he could have done something to save her. But the band around his neck smoldered again and this time he stayed silent. Speaking well of the queen was equal to speaking ill of the king.

Leonora was content to continue. Lowering her voice, she asked, "Can you keep a secret? Of course you cannot. You are my father's man," she answered herself, which bothered Henry and made his heart itch. She went on, "But we are doomed so I shall tell you anyway. This sphere must possess some magic."

It was engraved with strange shapes he'd seen only once before, when the queen had signed her name in her own language to the book of the condemned.

"She felt for me, I think, being the only one born without her magical gift. Which must be why I cannot draw the magic out of this, rendering it as useless as I am." Leonora closed her fingers around the treasure and pulled it to her heart. "But, it is what she had for me. She gave me this and said, 'My darling Leonora, I have not left you with nothing.' And then they dragged her away. Because of you," she looked up, her gaze sinking into his. "You found her out."

The truth of this scalded more fiercely than his silver bands ever could. Henry had been the one to discover the queen's secret. He'd been the one to turn her over to the king. And that night he had become the Watcher.

The king himself lit the torch and set the kindling ablaze. And yet it felt to Henry as if he had been the one to burn the queen alive. The nightmares had not ceased. He could still hear her screams, smell the scorching of her flesh, and picture the pleading in her emerald eyes.

"Give that to me."

Henry and Leonora looked up. Princess Carina stood over them, her hand outstretched and shaking, her gaze fixed on the gold ball.

Leonora moved to conceal the object but the eldest princess bent and wrested it from her sister's hand.

Scrambling to her feet, Leonora cried, "Give it back, Carina! It is mine!" She tried to scale her sister, but Princess Carina held the ball high in the air, out of reach.

"It is Mother's. And so I shall give it to her." Princess Carina's voice was barely a whisper. She crossed to the window and shoved her hand through the gap in the iron bars, careful not to let them graze her skin. She pushed against the leaded glass panes, which parted easily. There was no need to lock the window when the metal rails prevented anyone from passing through. She heaved the ball out.

Leonora caught a sob behind her fingers.

Princess Carina had discarded the ball, Henry knew, in the direction of Queen Celesta's pyre.

◆ ◆ ◆ ◆ ◆

Leonora

"Carina, you beast!" Leonora cried, rushing to the window. She searched frantically for the ball but she had not seen where it landed. "Why? Why are you this way?"

"I swore to protect you all, Leonora. I promised Mother," Carina whispered harshly in her sister's ear. "You will not be found with an amulet in your pocket. It is a death sentence."

Carina turned on her heel, marched to the door of their mother's private chambers, and disappeared inside.

"I can get it for you," Henry rasped from his position at her feet. "I believe I can squeeze through the bars. The battlements are not so far down. I could jump."

"Then why haven't you escaped, Henry? Your fate is not tied to ours." Leonora scanned the grass far below for any sign of her treasure glinting in the sun.

"Because I want you to trust me."

Studying the fox, Leonora believed she found earnestness in his pointed features. "You may go." She bent to lift Henry and placed him on the window ledge, then turned her back to him. "But, please, do not come back."

Glancing over her shoulder moments later, she hoped he would be there. But he had gone. Leonora sank to the floor, her hand instinctively sliding over her sleeve for the golden charm, finding nothing.

"Oh Mother, what will become of us?" she whispered to a ghost and closed her eyes to hold back tears.

"*Gods protect them*," she heard her mother pleading in a memory. In Leonora's mind, it was the small hours the morning before the queen had been confined to the north wing. Queen Celesta prayed over her daughters as they slept, touching each of their heads with magic-spooled fingers. When she had come to Leonora's bed, finding her second daughter awake, she sat and said, "*This is my daughter Leonora. May she be brave and clever and solicitous all her days.*" She ran her magic through Leonora's hair, down her cheek, then cupped her chin. "*Gods protect her,*" she said, gazing into Leonora's tired eyes with her own rather sad ones.

"*Mother, is everything all right?*" Leonora asked.

"*Dream, Leonora, of Sunniva and worry not. Think of the hills edged in brilliant light, the azure river that flows north. My brother's palace overlooks the villages of the valley.*"

"*It's carved into the tallest hill and shines as though constructed from billions of stars,*" Leonora said. She and her sisters loved when their mother told them stories of growing up elsewhere. Each of them could paint Sunniva in their minds from their mother's vivid descriptions and the dreams she conjured for them with quiet spellwork.

Celesta smiled and tucked her auburn hair behind her ear. She leaned down to kiss her daughter's forehead, completing her blessing.

And then the queen sang her favorite lullaby, and Leonora did not see her mother smile again.

"Leonora," a slightly-garbled voice said, pulling her from her memories.

She dared not open her eyes for surely it was only a dream. But then she felt a small weight drop into her lap, felt fur brush against her hand.

Her eyes flew open to find Henry sitting before her, a grin stretched across his snout. In her lap, the gilt ball was nested in her pooling skirt.

"You foolish fox." She gaped at him but wasted no time securing the ball—somewhat slippery with saliva—in the hem of her sleeve where Carina wouldn't see it. *You foolish girl*, Leonora thought, knowing her sister was right to remove the amulet from her possession. She turned her attention to Henry. "What can I do for you in return?"

◆ ◆ ◆ ◆ ◆

Henry

"Turn me back into a man," Henry said.

"I cannot, as I have told you. I do not think my sisters ought to, even without the iron. However, in the unlikely event we manage to free ourselves, I'd be happy to request one of them make an honest attempt."

"I believe that *would* make me a fool," Henry said, and Leonora laughed. The sound was brilliant, like morning sun.

Henry cleared his throat and righted his shoulders; his tail curled neatly around his legs. "A kiss might do the trick," he suggested.

"Ah, but, as the storybooks say: only a true love's kiss can break a spell. Besides," she said and ruffled his fur, "I like you as a fox."

Henry winced as her words struck his silver-banded heart. *Winced.* Her words had hurt him. Really, she might as well have cut him. He hadn't expected this. He was a king's guard. There was no room in his heart for anything but his devotion to Ciarán. Yet he was here with her, an enemy of the king, and he felt no hatred toward her. It was strange, and wonderful, and extremely painful, but he was quite fond of Leonora.

"You might like me as a man," Henry tried.

"But what if I don't? Then I'm out a fox and burdened with a man." She laughed again and continued, "Oh, you did cheer me up, Henry. Thank you."

"Anything for you, Princess," Henry grumbled.

"Please, it's Leonora—"

The chamber doors flew open, banging against the walls on either side. The princesses yelped in terror as King Ciarán appeared amid a flock of guards. He reached for the nearest girl, Princess Berenice.

Leonora sprang to her feet and moved to put herself between them. The king raised a hand to strike her.

Henry took one step after her before he was cemented to the floor, the silver band in his chest compelling him to stand down. His heart painfully reminded him he was still loyal to the king.

"Father, please." It was all Leonora said as she sank into a deep curtsy, her head bowed reverently.

The king's hand fell to his side, and he nodded his approval.

"You. Line up your sisters." The king scanned them, his mouth moving as he counted silently. "There's another, is there not?"

"Berenice, will you fetch Carina?" Leonora asked without rising from her position of submission.

The youngest princess fled the room, disappearing to find Princess Carina in the private chambers. Moments later, the sisters emerged.

"In order, now, sisters," Leonora said sweetly, rising and taking her place. She looked over the younger ones to ensure they were in a tidy line.

The king appraised them, too. "You two, switch places." He gestured to Leonora and Carina.

"But Father, I am the oldest," Princess Carina said, a weak smile on her face, her tone a tight facsimile of politeness.

"And the ugliest," King Ciarán said, grabbing her chin and tuning her face to examine the discoloration of her bruised skin, the crack by her lip from where he'd struck her. He shoved his eldest daughter away, sending her stumbling into her sisters.

"Call in the maids. Have the princesses made presentable," he said to his guards. "They reek of magic, and I will not tolerate their filth in my hall."

The girls were led from the room to their mother's private chambers, Henry bringing up the rear because his bands bid him keep the princesses in line, and because his soul bid him to follow Leonora.

◆ ◆ ◆ ◆ ◆

Leonora

Under the watchful eye of their maids, the princesses were bathed and clothed in their best day dresses, all in shades of blue. Their hair was pinned in swirling golden arrangements on their heads.

Leonora was used to switching the gilded amulet from garment to garment each time their maids came to attend the princesses. Silver bindings compelled the servants to report any suspicious acts to the king. And so, Leonora would tuck the trinket in her mouth until she could sneak it into the sleeve hem of her new dress.

"Leonora, is he dressing us up to die?" Ara asked in a whisper as the pair of them donned their shoes. At three and ten, Ara's questions had become more pointed, less innocent. For a moment, Leonora longed for the days her sister wanted to know, "Why is it *always* cloudy?" or "Why are gemstones different colors?"

"I couldn't say," Leonora mumbled and patted her sister's arm.

"Have you got a candy?" Ara asked, tipping her head to the side and squinting as though she might be able to magically peer into Leonora's tightly closed mouth.

Leonora shook her head and almost swallowed the ball.

"That fox is following you," Ara observed over Leonora's shoulder.

Leonora turned. He was there in the shadows of the dressing room watching over her. Or watching her? She couldn't be sure. He was still mostly bound to the king after all. She noted he'd sat with his back to the princesses in their various states of undress. He had some honor about him, then. But still she wondered. Henry made for a good fox, and he might've been as clever as one. What if his friendship was feigned, some new ploy in the Watcher's arsenal to gather information? But then again, she knew nothing of use that the king had not already discovered. She was without magic, imprisoned, and possessed nothing... nothing but the golden ball. And he had returned her treasure to her when he could have laid it before King Ciarán's feet. Leonora pushed the thoughts from her mind. Henry would do as his bands required. To do anything else was suicide. There was no use pondering the Watcher's intentions.

"Princesses, His Majesty has requested your presence in the great hall," a guard called as he stepped into the room. He was fully armored in leather stitched with iron threads and outfitted with weapons as though heading into battle against a magic-wielding enemy force. His red hair peeked out from his helmet. The leather ensured the men could remain agile while fighting. The iron threads were an invention of the mage. They provided some protection against spellwork, though there were still plenty of ways a skillful or lucky casting could reach the man inside the armor.

"Do they truly think we're dangerous?" Ara asked, nudging Leonora, who gagged.

Inside a cough, Leonora spit the ball discreetly into her hand and slipped it into its pocket. Twice was two too many times to nearly choke on the trinket.

"Perhaps we are." Leonora winked and drew a grin from her sister's lips. They were no more dangerous than their mother had been—far less, all things considered, despite their numbers. But she preferred that Ara smile one last time.

Their hands were bound in tightly fitted iron manacles. Leonora's sisters complained of itching beneath the bands, but Carina assured them the iron was not pure. They'd be in agony if it were. It was enough to quell their magic, not enough to torture them.

They filed in their new order to the king's hall, a long room flanked with black flags bearing the royal crest, and portraits of the monarchs who came before. Queen Celesta's painting had not been added. In fact, her likeness could be found nowhere in the castle except her daughters' faces.

Down the long room they moved in a line until they were guided to stand in front of the dais facing their father on his throne. The chair was made from the wood of the walnut trees which grew in the forest and carved with grisly dragons. It was the largest chair Leonora had ever seen—three of her sisters could comfortably sit side by side across it. And yet, beneath the tall and broad form of King Ciarán, it was dwarfed.

"I have found husbands for three of you," the king announced. "I spent the day negotiating with a duke and two princes, neither in line to inherit, but their brothers

187

might die without children." He said this as though he could predict the exact likelihood.

Leonora envisioned her father seated before his magic mirror—an invention of his mage for communicating with allies—haggling over the best price for daughters. Considering she thought they'd all die at his hand, marrying them off seemed generous in a way that made Leonora's insides knot. She braced herself. There had to be more.

Carina leaned against her, and Leonora wondered if her sister felt sick as well. In fact, all her sisters appeared rather more anemic than usual, wobbly on their legs.

The king surveyed his daughters. By what criteria were they being assessed? Beauty? Demureness?

"You," he waved in Eridana's direction, "for the Prince of Tombé." Eridana gasped and shuffled closer to Leonora. "You will go to Prince Geoffrey in the north." He flung a hand toward Lyra, who let out a laugh of disbelief. She quickly sobered as the blood drained from her face. "And, you." He looked directly at Berenice, who shook her head, trying to look fierce—but this was undermined by her trembling. "You will do nicely for the duke."

"Father," Leonora stepped forward. Eridana and Lyra were of a marriageable age, but Berenice? No. Surely he meant one of the older girls—herself, even. As politely as she could, Leonora said, "Berenice is a child."

"I will go in her stead." Carina moved to Leonora's side, her manner far less genteel.

The king stood. He loomed over them from the dais. "Believe me," he snarled, "it is a better fate for her than what awaits you."

"I will do anything to spare them," Carina said, her voice barely a whisper. Her posture tightened as their father moved toward them.

"I cannot kill you all." King Ciarán's voice was measured. It sent something with a thousand legs crawling down Leonora's spine. He couldn't kill them, he'd said. But he might as well have issued their deaths, the way his words made her skin tighten and caused her heart to race.

The king continued. "The purpose of princesses is to build alliances. If neighboring kingdoms found out I'd burned the entire lot of my daughters do you think they would ally themselves to me? Trade with me? Come to my aid in battle? No. They would know I sired an entire generation of magic-folk and leave me to ruin." He paced across the edge of the dais, his large hands steepled at his chest. "But still, I must rid myself of all of you. So I will marry you off. You will go with your husbands and be good wives under the watchful eyes of your maids. And I know you will behave yourselves because if I receive an ill report about any of you, I will have you dragged before me, and I will light your pyres myself." Still he did not shout, but Leonora sensed an eagerness in him. The meager contents of her stomach churned.

The hall was still for a moment. Leonora could make out the tiny clicks of claws on the stone floor.

"Except you, Princess Carina." This the king said in low notes only his eldest daughters could hear. "You are too obstinate and homely to marry off in good conscience. Instead, you will stay behind and be bound in service to me." Carina's mouth opened to speak, but the king interjected,

189

"Ah, ah. My mage believes there's a way to stabilize the mixture of familial and magical bonds, though he cannot guarantee it won't be painful." He savored the last word.

Carina's face contorted into a snarl. Leonora thought her sister might lunge forward and bite the king, but he stepped back and raised his volume.

"To ensure you all understand," King Ciarán glanced down the line at each of his daughters, then turned his gaze on Leonora, "she will burn at dawn."

"Father, no!" Using her elbow and forearm, Carina shoved Leonora behind her own slight frame.

With a collective cry, the princesses flocked around Leonora. She could see their lips moving. Words like "love," and "gods protect" formed, but she could not hear them through the thick fog that filled her mind. She struggled to breathe. At once, her garments and skin were damp with sweat, and she shivered. It felt as though a dark hole grew inside her, and she thought for a moment it might be all right if she allowed herself to sink into it.

"Enough!" A loud crack shot through the din, reaching Leonora through the haze and pulling her back to the great hall. Her father's fist pressed white-knuckled into the back of his throne. The wood splintered, cleaving the face of a dragon in two.

Carina found her voice and raised it to their father. "Leonora has no magic. I am the eldest. It was I who led them into the wood and told them what to do. I taught the young ones how to wield when Mother was gone. It is I who should burn. Leonora is the most innocent among us, the most beautiful and kind. Surely you could find her an advantageous match."

"Ah, but you only prove it is as the maids describe." King Ciarán stepped down from the dais and leaned in close, his nose nearly touching Carina's. He spoke loudly so everyone present could hear. "She is the one you all love best. She is the one whose death will have the greatest meaning."

He waved a hand and in response, two guards seized Leonora by the arms, prying her bodily away from her sisters.

She did not fight them.

◆ ◆ ◆ ◆ ◆

Henry

Why isn't she fighting them? Henry silently pleaded for Leonora to do something. Stomp on the foot of the taller man, jab her elbow into the nose of the other. Anything.

From the shadows behind a cabinet—the only purpose of which was to hold the book of names of those executed for wielding magic—Henry prayed for the gods to intervene where he could not.

And then something happened Henry could not explain. A series of screeches let loose across the hall. The sounds burned. They burned? It was at that moment Henry realized the awful noise was emanating from his own body. He was barking, forming high pitched yowls easily mistaken for a scream. His silver collar scalded his neck as his voice

191

railed against the king. The smell of melting hair met his nose.

"Discover whatever it is making that unholy sound and destroy it!" the king shouted to his guards who had covered their ears as the barks echoed through the chamber.

It did not take long for the guards to find him. Henry wanted to run, begged his legs to give the guards trouble. But he could not move; his bindings would not allow it. The king had ordered he be found, and so he made himself accessible.

One guard reached to grab him. Defiance surged through Henry. He spun and lunged at the guard's hand, catching skin between his teeth.

The guard lurched backward and fell, wailing.

Henry's howls crescendoed. *Gods, it hurts.* The molten band, the drawn look on Leonora's beautiful face—Henry could not be sure which was more agonizing. He wrenched another cry from the depths of his small form.

And the collar shattered.

Splintered shards of metal flew in every direction, warning off the guards for a moment.

One moment. That was all he needed.

At once Henry felt lighter. He ran to Leonora amid the guards' cries of, "Cursed creature!" and "Unnatural!"

Had the gods freed Henry? Had his own audacity? He forced the questions from his mind as he sprang across the great hall, dodging guards. But it was King Ciarán who intercepted him, jerking him up by his tail.

Henry let out a yelp and writhed.

"Silence, foul beast!" the king commanded.

"Be still, my fox." Leonora's voice was reticent, but Henry's large ears did not miss the sound. "Speak and save yourself."

He obeyed the first of her commands, but hesitated over the second. Without his collar, he felt he could defy the king. He formed a few choice words for Ciarán, but he did not free them from his mouth. Speaking would reveal him as Henry the king's guard—hells, if Ciarán would simply look at him, he might be able to sense that it was his Watcher he held by his tail. Henry would be whisked away to the mage and transformed back into a man. He would either be punished for his incompetence or awarded a medal for his sacrifice, depending on the king's mood following the deportation, torture, and execution of his daughters. Then, as though nothing happened, he'd be fully bound once more and returned to duty.

But that was madness. He was changed.

Henry the Watcher would send Leonora to her death. But as Henry the fox, there was still a chance, however small, that he could do something. At the very least, he'd die with his honor intact.

Dangling from Ciarán's grip, Henry cried out in a howl he hoped Leonora understood.

Ciarán shoved Henry into Riordan's arms and said to his personal guard, "Take it to the kitchen. I will have it for breakfast."

A sob escaped Leonora. Henry tried to find her, to lock eyes with her one more time as Riordan obeyed his king.

"Take her to the south tower."

Henry scarcely heard the king's command as the door to the servant's corridor separated him from Leonora forever.

◆ ◆ ◆ ◆ ◆

Leonora

"Thank you," Leonora said to the guard who opened the huge arched door of the great hall and forced her into the castle's main corridor.

He loosened his grip.

The pair of guards led her through the castle and up the winding steps to the chambers at the top of the south tower.

The south tower quarters housed nobles when they had occasion to visit Castle Banebrook. Higher up, this room was smaller than her mother's and more sparsely furnished. The iron was not needed here. Its one window would not be locked either, nor the fireplace blocked. There'd be no need, not unless Leonora would rather die by falling than by flame.

"This will do quite nicely," she said to the guards and smiled. It was a prison befitting her station. She was aware of the alternative, a damp pit in the the bowels of the castle where not an ounce of starlight could reach. Here, she could spend her last night in a proper bed searching the sky for her sisters' namesake constellations to pass the time. "Thank you, good sirs."

The guards exchanged looks and allowed her to step inside the room with dignity.

The guard with red hair leaned forward and asked, "Is it true you don't have magic?"

"Not an ounce. Mother always said I had other gifts, though."

He winced at the mention of the late queen. Then, he reached for her wrists and unlocked the iron cuffs from her hands.

"You'll be more comfortable." He blushed, then cleared his throat.

Leonora nodded her thanks and rubbed at her wrists which were red from the tightly fitting manacles. As the guard stepped back, she wrapped her hands around his to steady herself and started, "Would you—"

"Yes, Princess?" The guard almost sounded somber.

"If you should see the Watcher, would you tell him..." She paused and chewed her lip. "Would you tell him he is a good man?"

"I will," said the guard.

"And my sisters..." Her thoughts caught in her throat.

The red-haired guard started to recoil, a grimace crossing his face.

"Please," she managed, and he softened to her once again. "If you can, tell them to look for my stars in the sky. I'll watch for them there."

He nodded again, though with some uncertainty. Patting her hands, he pulled away from her.

He couldn't deliver her messages, she knew. But for this one moment, Leonora believed that he wanted to. There was something in his warm brown eyes that struck her, something she hoped was empathy, but might have been its useless cousin, pity.

"What is your name?" she asked.

"Raff," he answered.

"Thank you, Raff."

Raff offered her one last kindness and lit a candle before closing the heavy door between them. She heard a latch click and wondered if it made guests of Banebrook uncomfortable knowing they could be locked into their chambers. Enemies abounded, she supposed, considering her father's point of view. Precautions were a signature of the king.

Pressing her ear against the door, she could make out only a brief, muffled exchange, followed by one set of retreating footfalls against the stone corridor. She wasn't sure if she'd rather Raff had stayed or had been the one to go, perhaps to look for Henry. She would never know.

Leonora moved to the window and pushed the panes apart, letting in the light of the stars. This vantage overlooked the bailey. Across the grounds she could see the north wing, its windows faintly glowing. It was too far and the angle was all wrong. She could not see inside. Guards were posted at the turrets, around the castle walls, by the gate, appearing like chess pieces her father had arranged. They were very still, as if they'd been ordered to do no more than breathe and blink unless trouble arose. All was quiet. She looked up, bathing her face in starlight.

Her mother loved the night sky. Leonora closed her eyes and let her mother's soft voice come to her again. *"It is the same here as it is at home. I can see the lion in mid-spring as though I am looking out from my window in my brother's palace. Leo, the courageous."* Celesta pointed, tracing lines between a handful of the brightest stars. "See? *It is for the lion I have called you Leonora."* Behind closed eyes, the memory from her childhood felt nearly real. It was as though, if she wished hard enough, she could step through to the past and curl against her mother's warmth one more time. But it was only that: a wish. She opened her eyes.

Sinking to the floor, she stared up at the sky and pictured her sisters dancing in the clearing. Without a thought for retrieving it, Leonora found the golden ball clasped in her fingers. She held it in the dwindling candlelight, studying the tiny carved symbols as she had when her mother had given it to her.

"*Take this, Leonora. It will help you find your way. They need you, do you understand? My darling Leonora, I have not left you with nothing. I have called you by the stars,*" Queen Celesta had whispered to her. Then she pressed the amulet into Leonora's palm, even as the guards were forcing their way into her chambers to drag her before the king for her crimes.

Leonora had only nodded. There hadn't been time to ask questions.

"It will help me find my way," she whispered, churning the words through her mind.

She felt along the ridges of the carvings on the golden ball, trying to make sense of them. But it was difficult to concentrate when one pervasive thought circled her mind: *They need you.*

♦ ♦ ♦ ♦ ♦

Henry

"I've not cooked a fox before," the cook, a round man with a freckled face and thinning blond hair, reported when the guard shoved Henry into his chest.

"Take it. Kill it. Cook it. Serve it to the king," Riordan said, his syllables clipped in impatience.

The guard had not taken his hands off of Henry because the cook had not relieved him of the fox. Instead, the cook stood there, arms limp by his sides, fox pressed against his chest, as he looked at Henry, brow twisted in confusion.

"He has paws," the cook observed, tapping Henry's foot.

"And big ears and a ridiculous tail," Riordan sighed. "What is your hesitation?"

"I don't think you're supposed to eat animals with paws." The cook patted Henry's head as though he were a very good dog. His hand fell to his side uselessly once more.

"Why would that matter?" Riordan snarled, his eyes rolling back in his head.

"We eat animals with hooves, and animals with feathers, and fish, but I don't think we eat animals with paws," the cook explained. Then, smiling at Henry, he added, "He's rather darling, isn't he?"

"Rabbit!" Riordan barked.

"Ah! That's right! We do eat rabbit on occasion, don't we? Well, not me. I just prepare it. The king and all those daughters of his, they're the ones who eat it. Me, I eat chicken."

"Cook it up like a rabbit, then." Riordan was growling as though he might eat Henry to save himself the trouble of this conversation.

"But what if he doesn't taste like rabbit?" the cook protested.

"Sort it out!" Riordan shoved Henry so forcefully into the cook's chest before releasing him, that he was sure he felt a rib pop. Henry whimpered and the cook caught him before he slid to the floor.

"Poor thing. I suppose I will have to find a recipe for you." With Riordan gone, the cook stroked Henry's head again. But Henry knew despite the kindness of the cook, he would find a way to serve Henry to the king. For he, too, was bound by silver to do the king's bidding.

The cook put Henry under an overturned and unceremoniously emptied onion crate and proceeded to consult his cookbooks.

While the cook muttered to himself, Henry assessed his predicament. The floor of the kitchen was made from stone like others of Castle Banebrook, but not the even, carefully laid sort one might find in the great hall. The crate rested skewed on the irregular cobbles allowing Henry to fit his paws beneath the edge of one side. If he could lift the wooden box enough to squeeze out from beneath it, there was an open window across the room. A quick scramble up a sack of flour would put him on the counter behind where the cook leaned on a table poring over his recipe books. With quick legs, Henry could leap over the sink, then slip silently to the window. The kitchen was on the ground floor. He'd be out and away before the cook could ever decide on a preparation.

Mustering all the strength he could find within his slight body, Henry tried to lift the crate. He was rather disappointed to discover foxes did not store as much power as one might hope in a situation such as his.

With a great deal of unnecessary commotion, the kitchen door burst open, allowing two guards admittance. They scanned the room. One jerked up the hatch in the floor leading to the larder and stuck his head in to have a look about. The other strode across the kitchen to peer into the annex where the cookware was stored, knocking over several stacks of apple baskets.

Henry pressed himself as far back into the crate as he could manage. Had the king decided he did not wish to wait till morning for a plate of fox? Perhaps he had designed an even worse fate in frustration having been unable to murder his progeny.

"You there, cook!" one of the men shouted. "The king requires an audience with the guard called Henry. Have you seen him?"

"No, only the one called Roy," replied the cook.

"Roy? There is not a guard called Roy," said the guard.

"Really? Began with an R anyway." Henry could almost hear the cook's shrug.

"You would know him. Unusually blue eyes, dark hair," the second guard described Henry—Henry the man.

"Who? Roy? Nah, he's as fair-haired as I am." There was the sound of a turning page, followed by the cook muttering something about mashed potatoes.

"The guard, Henry," the second guard replied, annoyance coating his voice.

The cook offered an equal measure of irritation in his own tone when he said, "I already told you, Henry's not here."

And he wasn't.

As soon as Henry's heart heard the king required him, it was obliged to obey. Henry had summoned the strength from his last silver band, lifted the crate enough to wriggle out from beneath it and had already leapt from the open window onto the grass below.

◆ ◆ ◆ ◆ ◆

Leonora

Leonora sat on the cold floor, the golden ball rolling between her palms. Even in the dark, the candle having faded out some minutes ago, she knew the sphere, all its symbols sunken into the gilded surface.

They need you.

She wrestled with the words. Of course her sisters needed her, as she needed them. Trying as they were, they were also magnificent friends, all she had in the whole world. They were sisters.

"What a stupid thing to say, Mother," she whispered to the queen's ghost.

No one answered but the wind whistling through the window.

"Berenice, Delphine, Ara, Caprica, Vela, Gemma, Ursa, Orian, Lyra, Eridana, Carina." She sang their names quietly to the tune of a lullaby she'd heard many times in her childhood, looping them over and over as she pictured their faces. All the while she wished she could get to them, kiss their rosy cheeks, wrap them all in her arms at once and never let go. She could almost feel the fire lapping at her skin, a horrific pain, but one which could not compare to knowing she would never embrace them again.

Rage brewed in her. Her sisters would be cast across the realm, sold to the highest bidder in neighboring kingdoms, used as nothing more than goods in a negotiation. And Carina would be trapped here. To be bound in silver to the king's will was a fate truly worse than Leonora's own.

"Oh, Carina..." she cried softly. It was all of them, from wild Berenice, sweet Delphine, and curious Ara. Caprica with her head in the clouds and always a pen to paper. Gemma who, with Vela, had invented an entire language. Ursa who loved to sing but usually did so just off-key, and Orian with her nose forever between the pages of a book. Lyra possessed a contagious laughter, and Eridana believed in herself and her sisters with all her heart even when they failed. And Carina...

Carina who had become mother to them all at seven and ten. Carina who had done her level best to keep them all in line so no one would notice when she whispered spells over her sisters' plates to make food taste better, when she dried their tears with miniature animals made of stardust, when she led them all into the wood at night to practice casting and attempt to create a way out of this shadowed place.

She pictured them all, trapped in the north wing. In her mind's eye, the room was as well-known as her own, her sister's faces as familiar as her reflection.

"Berenice, Delphine, Ara, Caprica, Vela, Gemma, Ursa, Orian, Lyra, Eridana, Carina. Berenice, Delphine, Ara, Caprica, Vela, Gemma, Ursa, Orian, Lyra, Eridana, Carina!" With the final syllable, a bellowing sob burst from her mouth. Leonora pitched the gilded ball away from her, a growl erupting from her belly.

When the ball struck the wall a light flared and the metallic *tink* stretched into a small but persistent ringing. A roughly circular frame of burnished gold grew out from the place where the ball had collided with the stone. For one brief moment, Leonora could see them. It was as though she were suspended several lengths outside the window of the north wing, the one from which Carina had cast her golden ball. It was still open. Through the iron bars she could see her sisters huddled on the floor in their mother's candlelit chambers, Berenice curled in Carina's lap, shaking with fear. Leonora's mouth hung open as she counted them.

"Eleven," she breathed.

Then they disappeared.

"No!" Leonora scrambled to her feet and charged the wall as though it might open for her and let her go to her sisters. When it did not, she slammed her fists against it, the rough stone angry beneath her skin. Sinking to the floor, she slid her hands across the surface until she came upon the treasure. It bore no dent from the abuse, but felt warm in her hand.

She threw it again, but nothing happened.

"Show them to me, you wretched piece!" she growled, repeating the action.

But it did not comply.

On the fifth attempt it occurred to Leonora she might recreate the exact circumstances of the first. She cried out, "Berenice, Delphine, Ara, Caprica, Vela, Gemma, Ursa, Orian, Lyra, Eridana, Carina!" and threw the ball. "There!"

The shimmering aperture opened once more, and Leonora could see them through the north wing window. "Carina!" she called, but her sisters could not hear her. "Carina, I'm here!" Carina only stroked Berenice's hair. Leonora could see her sister's lips moving, but was not close enough to read them. She reached out, but her fingers met masonry. It was as though the image was made up of light and cast upon the wall like sunbeams. She could not catch them. The golden frame blinked out of sight and it was dark once again, save the soft blue light of the stars.

"They are so far away," the princess sobbed, sliding to the floor to feel for the ball again.

With it in hand, she felt over the symbols. She knew the characters were in her mother's native language. Though she could not read them, she recognized a few from having seen Celesta's name written on letters from the queen's brother, Leonora's uncle whom she had never met.

There were two L's, two C's, an E, and an A written on the surface of the ball, along with six other characters. Twelve curving forms. Twelve daughters.

"Berenice, Delphine, Ara, Caprica, Vela, Gemma, Ursa, Orian, Lyra, Eridana, Carina...and Leonora," she whispered, touching the second L.

The ball grew warm in her grasp.

Standing, Leonora spoke the names of all twelve princesses and tossed the ball against the wall. The frame opened. She called out in a loud whisper, "Carina!"

At this, her sister's head lifted, looking about their mother's chambers. Again, Leonora called in a whisper, trying not to wake her siblings. Carina searched, scooting a sleeping Berenice from her lap so she could stand. She moved to the window and looked down, confusion crossing her face.

Leonora was about to call again, when she heard voices coming from below.

"Over here," said a man's voice. "We'll need to chop more wood."

Her aperture was suspended over her mother's pyre, she realized. Over *her* pyre. She heard the unmistakable sound of an axe cleaving wood, a man grunting with each heave. Her view was only of the exterior wall of the north wing and she could not adjust her angle, even if she possessed the courage. Instead she watched her sister, who watched the men below prepare the place where Leonora would die. Carina's hands covered her mouth, but there was another sound which could not be misinterpreted: her sister sobbing.

Leonora put her hand against the rock wall knowing so much distance and matter separated them, but she needed the aid to remain upright.

Carina's gaze caught on Leonora's movement. The eldest princess's eyes widened. Then her brow pinched and she mouthed Leonora's name.

Silently, slowly, Leonora formed the words, "I'm here. I'm coming."

Carina nodded her understanding and the aperture collapsed.

Using all their names was stronger. The magic opening had remained longer and allowed voices to pass through. Carina had seen her. The iron in the north wing, she guessed, prevented her from getting any closer, kept her magic frame from appearing inside the room with her sisters. But, surely the small amulet could do more. Her mother had been a decent sorceress and a clever one at that. If only there'd been more time to ask questions. Leonora could feel the phantom hands of the queen slipping from hers as the guards separated them. Between hurried instructions whispered to Carina, kisses for each of her daughters, and a stolen moment to give Leonora the golden ball, there hadn't been time.

"Take this, Leonora, it will help you find your way," her mother had said.

In the tower, Leonora deduced three things.

One, her mother had given her a treasure which, with the right mechanics, opened temporary windows to other places.

Two, her mother had given Carina a spell and guidance to open a door to another realm.

Three, neither of these worked well independently, and therefore it could be concluded that they were meant to be employed in tandem.

"I must get to them," Leonora said with renewed determination. Pacing, she talked aloud to herself. "They are on the north side of the castle. I am on the south. Perhaps they are too far." Leonora pinched the little ball between her fingers. "Perhaps I should think smaller, closer."

Her mother's rose garden was on the southern side of Castle Banebrook. No roses bloomed in the overgrown space anymore. But it was there, edged by linden trees with a small pond in its middle. Leonora knew it well. Picturing her sisters had been enough to call up their location through the gilded aperture. She envisaged the garden and said her sisters' names.

"...and Leonora!" She pitched the ball against the wall. Within the gilt frame appeared the decaying rose garden, the pond shimmering in the moonlight.

Leonora stepped toward it and reached out. The image rippled beneath her fingers. She was close enough now, she supposed. Her hypothesis held water; proximity had thinned the veil between the two points. With a feather-light press, her hand slipped through what she could only describe as a thin layer of mucus, like that on the skin of a frog.

She might've recoiled, except on the other side, she could feel the night air and it beckoned her. Immediately, she dropped to the floor to find the ball.

"Where are you, you blessed piece?" she pleaded as her fingers found nothing but coarse rock.

The frame was wavering. At any moment it would collapse.

At last she felt the ball beneath the heel of her hand and snatched it up. Leonora dove through the closing hole in the tower wall and fell onto the grass before the moon-bathed garden.

"HA!" she barked, then clapped a hand over her mouth, craning her neck to be sure no guards lurked nearby.

Quickly, she took refuge in the garden huddled behind dense brambles. From here, Leonora would need to make her way to the north wing unseen. How exactly she'd manage that was something she'd have to hope for rather than plan.

Peering up at the castle wall, Leonora could see the moonlight glinting off a guard's helmet. He was surveying the garden. She'd made too much noise. For several long moments she scarcely breathed, waiting for him to decide it'd been nothing more than an alarmingly large rabbit darting into the tangle of weeds. She realized, probably because she couldn't reach for them, that her wrists were still rather irritated from the snug-fitting manacles.

At last, the guard moved back from the edge of the inner wall, returning to his perch overlooking the castle's exterior. Gratified, Leonora scratched at her wrists. She moved to the edge of the row of bushes and assessed her surroundings. If she was quick, she could dart across the bailey to the shadow of the great hall. If she was quick? Leonora scanned the castle walls again, counting the guards she could see. There was absolutely no possible way she could traverse the castle grounds without being caught.

Then Leonora smiled. She could not traverse them, but she could hop hither and thither across them.

Eying the shadowy corner where the great hall met the inner wall, Leonora whispered the names of the twelve princesses. She dropped the ball straight down, opening a golden frame in the earth. Across the way, she could see a matching frame cast upon the exterior of the great hall. Grabbing the amulet, she slid into the hole and stepped out on the other side. The frames snapped closed behind her.

"Brilliant," she whispered, then began to plot her next target. The chapel was close enough, she decided. She repeated her careful movements and crawled out of the portal into the bushes beside the small structure's portico. She did this at precisely the wrong moment. The chapel's guardian, Brother Nial, stepped out into the night, just as the aperture cinched closed beside her.

"You're awake," she said as he stared down at her with wide eyes.

"I wish I were not, Princess Leonora," the priest replied quietly. He rubbed a hand over his thinning white hair, the silver band on his wrist peeking out from beneath the sleeve of his black robes. "I am to pray to the gods for mercy on your wayward soul in a few short hours. It is hard to find respite on nights such as these."

Leonora and her sisters were not allowed to attend services with their father, but she had witnessed the blessings Brother Nial bestowed on her younger sisters shortly after each was born, remembering Berenice's most distinctly. The last time she had seen the priest, he had been called to plead for mercy on Queen Celesta's soul four years ago.

The priest was like bookends, present to celebrate births and oversee deaths.

"I am sorry for your trouble, Brother. I, too, cannot sleep," she said.

"I—" the priest started. He shook his head, then tried again in earnest. "I am sorry... It is regrettable..." He extended a hand to her, whether to catch her or comfort her, was unclear.

"Yes, well..." Hot tears rolled down her cheeks, but still, she smiled and accepted his hand. "You will call the guard, but please, will you spare me one moment?"

He waited with her, their hands clasped, the princess still tucked into the bushes.

"When you were born, and your mother brought you to me to be blessed, she said..." He cleared his throat uncomfortably. The priest's hand was trembling around hers, but he forged ahead. "She said, 'Leonora is the antithesis.' A very strange thing to call an infant, I thought. But it's true, isn't it. You are singular. A bright star in a string of many."

She could see it pained him to say such things, to fight the band around his neck which would have him call the guard. But he did as she asked. He waited, he spared her, for as many moments as he could offer.

Raff, too, had shown her kindness when it was not in his best interest. Even her father had backed down when she showed him deference. But why? Because she'd said please?

"*Always be kind, Leonora. It is its own form of magic,*" her mother had told her.

Leonora believed politeness possessed enchanting properties as it always yielded positive results. The maids brushed her hair more gently. The cook left peas off her plate. Her sisters rarely argued with her the way they often did each other. But magic? True magic?

Kindness did not glitter. It did not require a song or particular gestures. It could be conducted in the open.

Brother Nial squeezed her fingers gently, and Leonora studied her hand in his. Her wrists were still rosy though the manacles had been removed some hours ago. Red, irritated, like Berenice's hand after she had grabbed the iron bar in her mother's chambers. Red, because somewhere in Leonora a small magic existed. A small magic that even iron could not subdue.

"Will you spare me my life? Please," she whispered. "Please," she said again, this time to the gods, inwardly pleading that this would work.

He locked eyes with her, tears pooling in his gaze. Brother Nial gave one swift nod, broke his grasp, and slid back into the chapel.

◆ ◆ ◆ ◆ ◆

Henry

Henry took three steps forward and paused. He took another step, but this time longer and in the wrong direction as he strained against his own heart.

He wanted to go to the south tower to save Leonora. His remaining band desired him to stand before the king. And so he had travelled this way—progressing and regressing—halfway across the castle grounds. At least, he observed, he was growing nearer to Leonora than he was the king, albeit painfully slow.

At once he caught a flash of golden light. A figure emerged from around a corner, ducking into the shadow of the north wing, but not before her honey-colored hair was illuminated in the light of a nearby torch. If they lived to see morning, Henry vowed to tutor Leonora in stealth.

"Leonora?"

At the sound of her name, Leonora peeked from her hiding place, squinting.

"Henry? Is that you?" she whispered.

"Who else would it be? I should hope there are no other talking foxes about."

"Well, you might have been an ordinary fox. Plenty of those exist."

But none so lucky as Henry to be wrapped up in these events.

"It is I. I was coming to rescue you," he said.

"I do not require rescue, but thank you all the same. I have saved myself as you can see, but I am pleased you are well and have not been eaten." The princess waved him over, disappearing once more behind the corner of the north wing.

"As am I." Henry started after her. Now he was with her, he found it much easier to ignore the band around his heart, its urging quieted by her presence. "Where are you going?"

"To save my sisters. Would you care to assist with their rescue?" Leonora offered.

"I suppose that will have to do," he accepted.

"Are you ready? I believe we are close enough." She glanced up at the north wing.

"Close enough for what?"

Leonora listed her sisters' names, ending with her own. She tossed something against the wall. When the object hit the stone, light radiated from the spot and an opening formed, revealing the torchlit corridor that led to the queen's chambers. Henry knew the passage well. A staircase was down the hall to the left of Leonora's golden window, while the doors to Queen Celesta's rooms were near the opposite end, tucked into an alcove. Beyond that only a few paces, another door led out to the eastern parapet.

"Very clever," Henry said, impressed and also filled with a sense of dread.

"I've been practicing." Leonora bent and snatched up the gold ball. "In you go," she said.

"In? In there?" Henry poked at the opening with his paw. It felt viscous. He cringed. "Perhaps I will take the stairs."

"We haven't time, Henry. Pardon me." With that, she picked him up and carried him through the aperture. "See, not so bad."

"Repulsive," Henry muttered, checking his fur for gelatinous residue.

The frame closed behind them. Leonora set him down and proceeded down the corridor towards the queen's chambers.

"Leonora, respectfully..." Henry made quick work of the steps to keep pace with the princess. "Have you lost your mind? There are guards posted at the door."

"Thank you for asking after my health, Henry, but I am perfectly well. In fact, I am filled with hope."

Henry had no choice. Trusting Leonora—or, rather, having no time to question her—Henry followed her, but stayed in the shadows, ready to pounce if the guards laid hands on her, even if it killed him.

They rounded the corner of the alcove. Leonora curtsied and addressed the guards. "Good evening, gentlemen."

The guards exchanged glances, their hands flying to their swords. Henry tensed and crouched as if spring-loaded, but the princess continued.

"Would you be so kind as to allow me to see my sisters? I would appreciate you unlocking the door and granting me passage, please."

Again, the men looked at one another. Henry's mouth dropped open when one of them gave her a nod and retrieved the keys from his belt.

"Thank you," Leonora said, stepping through, Henry on her heels, hidden by the folds of her skirts.

The door closed behind them, locking once more as if the last few moments had never occurred.

Henry had many questions, but before he could ask, the eldest princess spoke.

"Leonora?" Princess Carina sat up from where she'd lain on the settee.

"I have come to save you!" Leonora announced to her sisters.

They stirred from their places curled together on the rug, rubbing their eyes to be sure Leonora was not a dream.

At once, the girls clambered forward, knocking Leonora to the floor. Only Carina stood apart, hands on her hips, and a reluctant smile on her bruised face.

"Leonora! You are here!" Berenice squealed, wrapping her arms tightly around her sister, completely upending Leonora's attempts to stand. "As are you, little fox!" The child grabbed Henry, smashing him into the huddle of princesses. "You are not such a disappointment after all."

♦ ♦ ♦ ♦ ♦

Leonora

"We should go," Leonora managed from beneath her sisters. "Dawn is near and we must make haste."

"Go? How?" Delphine asked, looking down at her with wide brown eyes from her advantageous position atop the princess pile.

"I will show you, little ducks. Release me?"

The princesses moved off Leonora, and Eridana helped her to her feet.

"Stand back," Leonora instructed her sisters.

Picturing the castle grounds outside the eastern parapet, she said their names with feeling and hurled the ball against the wall.

Nothing happened.

"Well that *is* a disappointment," Berenice observed.

"It's the iron," Leonora sighed, stepping forward to pick up the ball. The black metal sapped the power from sorceresses and amulets alike. Only her personal form of magic and silver seemed to override iron. What good would cordiality do her in here?

Questions flooded her mind. Could she get away with politely asking the guards to let her and her sisters walk out? Perhaps, but she had no idea how far her abilities could stretch. When she'd been polite to her father, he hadn't struck her, but it hadn't stopped him from insulting Carina and shoving her. Why hadn't she asked the guards to leave? Truly, every move she'd made in the last few hours was strung together with hope and temerity.

"Why can we not use the door, Leonora?" Ara asked. "You did."

"I asked nicely."

A chortle burst from Carina's mouth. "You asked nicely, and the guards let you walk across the castle and into this room? How can that be?" She pointed to Leonora's hand which concealed the ball. "Is it to do with the amulet Mother gave you? I saw you, floating there in the sky like a ghost in a looking glass."

And so Leonora told her sisters and Henry about discovering the power of the golden ball, escaping the south tower, her exchange with the priest—everything that had led to this moment. She held up her red-ringed wrists as proof of her possession of magic. "I believe Mother meant for us to use the amulet and the portal spell together, that if we all pour our thoughts into one place, we can call it up. We can reach Sunniva... if only we can find our way out of this room." They stared at her, their mouths gaping open and closed like fish, unsure what to say.

"Ah, well, perhaps Father will burn us all," Carina concluded.

Leonora sagged, slinking away from her sisters to lean against the wall. She wanted to scream, but instead imploded, folding in on herself. "I am a fool," she whispered.

"Leonora?" Henry asked, leaping onto the window ledge beside her.

She shook her head, dispensing with her futile tears and smiled into the middle distance. "I have become rather disenchanted with princess rescuing. It is much harder than what they write in storybooks."

"Leonora," the fox repeated, pawing gently at her arm.

"Yes, dear Henry?"

"I can help." He dipped his head so that she had no choice but to look into his steady blue gaze.

"*You are a fox, known for trickery. You are a guard, known for loyalty.*" She had said words like these to him only hours ago when he first offered to help. And yet, his loyalty could not be questioned.

Henry had fetched her amulet when Carina flung it from the window. He had howled in the great hall in an attempt to distract the guards. And he had tried to come to her aid in the south tower. Despite his bands, he had been loyal to *her*.

He wasn't a fox.

He wasn't a trickster.

He was Henry.

"All right." She nodded. "You've proven yourself. What do you suggest?"

When Henry had whispered his ideas to her, Leonora stayed quiet, considering for several long moments.

"What do you think?" Henry asked, eagerly.

"It is a good plan. But there will be no turning back for you if you help us." When he did not reply right away, she urged him, "Please, Henry, what will you do?"

"I don't belong here," Henry said slowly. "I don't know where I am from. But, for so many reasons, this is not my home."

"Nor is it mine," Leonora offered.

"If I am able, I will follow you."

Leonora suspected Henry's disobedience might cost him dearly. She saw in his half-smile that he shared that concern.

"Leonora," Henry went on, "can you ever forgive me? Truly."

She knew what he meant. The betrayal of the queen. Leonora placed her hand on his shoulder. "Your actions were not your own, and you have atoned for it tenfold. Think no more of it." Her smile faded and she asked, "While we are sharing... I wonder, do you think my magic makes me like him? Like my father?"

Henry laughed, the sound erupting from his belly. "Are you mad?"

"I'm serious, Henry. I am manipulating people." She folded her arms over her chest. "I ask and they do as I say. How is that any different from the bands?"

"Leonora, I think you are at once incredibly powerful and yet not at all. In the great hall you asked me to speak. You said please. And even so, I was not compelled to do so. You are nothing but polite to Carina and, to my knowledge, she has not listened to you a single moment since this all began."

Carina had not listened to her a day in their lives. Leonora rolled her mind around Henry's observations.

"Your father commands, controls, collects people under his thumb," Henry continued. "You ask, and people are freed by your words, by your kindness, to do what they want for a change."

The antithesis, she thought. Where her father imprisoned his people, perhaps she could set them free.

And at that moment she decided. They would enact Henry's plan, but she had an addendum of her own, one which she kept to herself.

Leonora stood and called her sisters to her.

The princesses huddled around Henry as he laid out his plan. Several minutes and repetitions later, they set the strategy in motion.

"This could go rather poorly," Leonora said to Henry as they took their positions.

"It could," he agreed, "but we shall do our best."

"Ready, sisters?" Carina asked.

The princesses nodded and clasped hands. Carina led them in a song as they danced in a circle around the rug. It wasn't a spell, merely a lullaby in their mother's native tongue, but it was enough.

The two guards who'd been posted outside the door to the queen's chambers burst inside.

"Stop tha—" one started, but his jaw fell slack.

The other rubbed at his eyes and muttered, "My gods..." He pointed at Henry who sat in the circle's center appearing to glow.

That had been Leonora's touch. Placing a candle behind Henry made the edges of his fur shimmer, as though he had been produced by magic.

"But the iron?" the first guard managed to ask.

"There's so many of them. That's it. There's power in numbers, there is," the other said, his chin quivering. He pointed to Leonora. "We never should've let her in here. Sh—she must be the most powerful of them all!"

"Run, brothers," Henry said, feigning weakness and turning his head to give his comrades a clear view of his unmistakable blue eyes. "Lest they turn you, too."

Leonora sang louder, drawing up the voices of her siblings. The princesses focused their attention on the guards. Carina broke with Leonora, and the sisters slithered toward the men like a great snake.

One guard muttered an incoherent prayer and fainted dead away. The second scrambled backward, falling to the floor. He then crawled out of the room and took off down the torchlit corridor, calling for help in a high pitched screech rather unbecoming of a king's guard.

"That was much more fun than asking nicely." Leonora smiled at Henry, but made a note to apologize for frightening them later.

The princesses and the fox darted from the room, ducking out the door at the end of the corridor which led to the battlement.

Leonora ran across the wall until she could clearly see the place where her sisters had slipped so many times into the wood.

"Stop!" King Ciarán's voice boomed over the castle as he appeared, emerging with a horde of guards from the eastern turret.

The princesses and Henry obeyed.

"No magic?" Ciarán asked, directing his midnight gaze toward Leonora. "And yet you were clever enough to escape unnoticed from the tower. Too stupid, however, to disappear into the wood and save yourself. I knew we'd find you among them. Like sheep, you are, you move as one." He gestured to the princesses. They collectively flinched and stepped backward, only to find guards blocked the door they'd come through only moments ago.

Pinched as they were on the battlement, Leonora knew there would only be one chance to save them all.

"Now!" Leonora cried, bidding her sisters lend her their thoughts. Leaning over the outer wall she called their names and pitched the ball straight down, the Circle in all the sisters' minds, but no promise they'd be close enough for the amulet's power to connect them to the sacred clearing.

Below in the grass, the moonlit clearing appeared within the golden window. It was as if she were looking at it after crossing the treeline, a dizzying effect of which her eyes could scarcely make sense.

"Go!" Leonora said, turning to Eridana.

Without a moment's hesitation, Eridana climbed over the toothy crenels in the battlement's exterior wall and dropped into the opening. From where she landed safely on the grass of the clearing, she beckoned her sisters. One by one, the younger princesses jumped from the wall into Eridana's open arms.

For a moment, this display caught the king off guard. But after the fourth princess jumped, he started forward. "You will all burn for this," he thundered.

Carina raised her arms, one aimed in each enemy group's direction, and Leonora could see the magic swirling about her sister's fingertips.

While the twins took their turn jumping, Berenice, Ursa, Orian, and Lyra raised their hands, glittering with strands of unwieldy power.

The guards were suspended in fear. The king, however, did not stop.

"You may regret your current course of action, Father," Leonora said. "I bid you, please stop."

But the king was not swayed. His steps were long as he pushed past her magic. "It is you who will regret—"

"You see, my sisters are everything to me," she continued. "They are lovely. They sing and dance beautifully. But they are hardly adequate sorceresses. One never knows what the result might be when they cast a spell." Leonora tipped her head at Henry and smiled.

"Your Majesty," Henry bowed, stretching out his forepaws and lowering his head, but never taking his blue stare from the king's face.

The king slowed. His eyes grew wide, and his lips parted. "Henry?" King Ciarán recognized his Watcher at last. He studied the fox for a moment, then his expression tightened. "What have they done to you?"

Meanwhile, Carina tapped Ursa and Orian to break ranks and take their leap. They went and Lyra followed.

"Go, Berenice. We haven't much time," Leonora said to the child at her side.

"I want to help, Leonora!" Berenice argued, a pout on her lips.

"We're all going together," Carina said, her arms still outstretched, shaking. "Now."

Leonora turned and took Berenice's hand in hers. From the corner of her eye, she saw them too late. A pair of guards approached from behind, their swords inches from Carina's back. "Carina!" she cried.

Carina whirled on the men, forcing them back with the magic she'd collected across both palms. They crashed into their comrades, bringing them all down in a heap of groans and curses. She grabbed Berenice's other hand and mounted the wall, pulling the child up beside her. Leonora and Henry followed.

Over her shoulder, her father's heavy strides carried him too close, too quickly.

"It's too high!" Berenice wailed. "I cannot jump!"

"On the count of three," Leonora said, gently squeezing Berenice's knuckles. "One. Two." She took a deep breath. "Three!"

Her sisters leapt. Henry let out a bark. A hand seized Leonora by the arm, wringing skin around bone. Leonora's breath snagged in her throat as she hurtled backward, her grasp wrenched from Berenice's. She collided into her father's broad form. He coiled his thick arm around her neck.

"All alone, sheep?" he asked, his voice gravelly, stinging her skin as his hot breath moved over her.

But she could not answer.

◆ ◆ ◆ ◆ ◆

Henry

Henry watched Leonora, waiting for her to jump, for he would not leave her behind. When her body plummeted in the wrong direction, he followed, pouncing from his place on the crenel, closing the distance between himself and the king's grip on Leonora.

His heart clenched furiously; he was sure it would never beat again after this moment and yet, he was not bothered. His teeth sank into the king's hand, and he tasted blood.

Ciarán jerked away, releasing Leonora. Howling curses, he stumbled backward into the rows of guards. He shook his arm wildly to dislodge the fox's jaws, hurling Henry against stone.

Leonora screamed Henry's name.

Then everything went black.

◆ ◆ ◆ ◆ ◆

Leonora

"Henry!" Leonora cried. She lifted the fox, cradling his limp form as she felt his chest for a heartbeat. "There," she whispered, finding it still pulsing.

Holding him over the waning window below, she dropped him. He rolled in the grass of the clearing a short distance, but he was safe.

"Seize her, you fools!" King Ciarán shouted, clutching his bleeding hand to his chest.

Guards scrambled forward.

Climbing onto the outer wall, Leonora felt a hand at her ankle. Stomping on the wrist it belonged to, she leapt, knowing she'd run out of time. The portal had closed.

For a few merciful seconds the moment seemed to slow. She closed her eyes. It would hurt less if she unclenched, she thought, imagining the way marble statues of once-beloved queens fracture when felled.

Like a ragdoll, Leonora met the ground where the magic doorway had been, the breath forced from her lungs, her ankle searing with pain. She gasped like a fish drawn from water and pressed her aching body onto her hands and knees. Stifling a cry, she felt in the grass for the amulet, all the while the shouts of her father and the guards rang in her ears.

"You foolish girl!" the king growled.

At last, sliding the amulet into her sleeve, she limped hurriedly away from the castle walls, even as arrows and insults flew at her from the battlement.

Inside the wood, she hobbled as fast as she could toward the clearing. Impossible as it was to see, she dared not toss the golden ball in the dark. How many nights had the sisters wound their way through their glowing mushroom path?

Surely, her feet knew the way. But without Carina's magic, the blackness ate her steps.

Guards pursued her. They were shouting, bellowing like beasts in the forest.

In the distance she could hear her sisters singing, awakening the doorway to their mother's realm, but they needed her.

All along she'd been the missing piece. All twelve princesses were required to open the door. Celesta had given Carina the instructions. She'd given Leonora the key.

From both directions, the noises bounced off the trees madly; Leonora could not seem to catch them no matter how quickly she spun to track them. Turning, she tried to glimpse the stars to give her a sense of direction. But it was no use. Beneath the canopy of trees, she was parted from their light.

"They all burn at dawn!" the king's voice rumbled through the trees.

Leonora covered her mouth, holding in a sob.

Casting a glance backward, she saw torch flames weaving through the trees like dozens of terrible eyes hunting her. They'd find her soon if she didn't keep moving.

Her body shaking, Leonora trudged ahead in the miserable dark. She had to open the portal to Sunniva, send her sisters and Henry through. Then she would see her father dealt with. She would find a way to free the people he had bound.

Henry

Henry slid from a dream. He could feel lush grass beneath him, could hear the song of wayward princesses tickling his ears.

Kneeling beside him, Princess Carina jostled Henry and barked, "Wake, fox!"

Sitting up, he snapped at her fingers, narrowly missing them.

"Did you nip at me?" Her mouth was agape as she examined her fingers.

"I do apologize, Princess. I'm not sure what came over me," he lied.

She must have known because her scowl deepened.

Over her shoulder, nine princesses danced in a circle. Between them, a light bloomed, but sputtered like a candle in the breeze without Carina to stabilize it.

"You have to go fetch Leonora!" This was Princess Berenice who seemed to appear out of nowhere from behind Carina.

"Leonora," Henry breathed, scrambling to his paws. He looked around, even knowing she wasn't there. He could not sense her presence.

Princess Carina shook her head, darkly.

His heart seized. At this moment he knew it had nothing to do with his egregious disobedience against the king and everything to do with *her*.

"I will find her," he wheezed.

"Will you?" Princess Carina looked doubtful. "You look unwell."

"I will—" Henry collapsed. *I will lie here until I die of heartbreak*, he finished silently, clenching against the pain radiating from his chest. It overtook his small form, and his vision narrowed.

"Fix him, Carina!" Princess Berenice wailed.

"All right," she shushed the child. "I will do what I can."

Princess Carina passed her hands over Henry's body, a glistening mist settling over him. At once his pain subsided, seeming to retreat from his limbs, shrinking until it was a mere annoyance, an itch he could never reach.

"It won't last," Princess Carina said of her efforts. "The magic in your band is far stronger than mine. If you continue to fight it, it will win."

Henry stood. She was right. Part of him had known from the moment his heart chose Leonora to spite itself, he was damned.

"I've time to get to her, to deliver her to her sisters. Little else matters," he said with more confidence than he felt. He might die before he reached Leonora, but he had no choice but to take the risk.

"I'm sorry we..." Princess Carina searched for the words, then decided on, "I'm sorry we changed you."

"I'm not," Henry said.

The princess stood and took Berenice by the hand. "We will work to open the door."

"I will fetch Leonora," he vowed.

"Gods protect you," Princess Carina said.

"And you," Henry replied with a stiff nod.

The fox and the princesses parted ways. Henry plunged into the wood.

In the dark, Henry's vision as a fox was even better than as Watcher. While his ears were swarmed with the noise, he knew Leonora's scent, if only he could catch it in the night air.

He moved toward the castle in a zig-zagging pattern. If she had made it across the treeline, she would have started out all right on the path between Banebrook and the clearing. But she hadn't the eyes of a fox or Watcher, and she was likely somewhere off course.

A small wind slid between the trees, carrying her perfume and, at last, he knew how to find her. He raced through the wood so quickly his paws barely disturbed the carpet of fallen leaves. He leapt over a log, through an overgrowth of mushrooms.

And when he was close, he called to her.

✦ ✦ ✦ ✦ ✦

Leonora

A friendly voice cut through the din calling, "Leonora!"

"Henry? You're all right?" she panted, stumbling forward only to knock her shoulder into a tree. There she sank against the rough bark, closing her eyes to sort out Henry's call from the rest. "Where are you?" Leonora felt his fur brush against her fingers.

"I am here. I'm all right," he said.

Leonora stroked Henry's head. It was a comfort to have him near, to know the king had not killed him.

"Take me up and I will guide you to your sisters. We must hasten to the clearing."

His voice was thin, she realized. Had he run a long way to find her? How tangled in the woods had she become?

"It is lucky my sisters turned you into a fox and not some other creature which cannot see in the night," she said.

"It is merely a convenience, and I would prefer to be a man." Henry pawed her. "Up, Leonora. The guards are not far behind."

And she knew he was right. Their shouts were fervent, their loyalty to the king firm.

Lifting Henry into her arms, she trudged deeper into the wood. With careful instructions, the fox guided her along, avoiding trees and raised roots which he could pick out with his keen sight. Within minutes, Leonora could see the glow from the clearing ahead. Carina's stars shimmered, and the doorway at their center, though small, emitted a beautiful warm light.

Her ankle throbbed, sending shooting pains through her leg with every step, but she plowed ahead eager to be with her sisters, free of this place.

The princess and Henry tumbled out of the wood. Carina led the girls in a song and dance so familiar, so hopeful, Leonora felt tears prick her eyes. The sisters did not stop, not for a moment, as they coaxed the door—about the size of a cabbage—to open.

Holding Henry under his front legs, away from her body, his back paws dangling, Leonora looked into his arresting blue eyes.

For a moment she thought she might say something, offer him thanks which could never suffice. Instead, she brought him to her lips and kissed the top of his head.

As she set him down beside the pile of clothes he'd not needed as a fox, a twinkling cloud enveloped him in a gentle swirl. His eyes grew large before disappearing with the rest of him. The magic swelled, alive with an undulating incandescence. But Leonora did not have a moment to spare.

Turning from the cloud to where her sisters danced, Leonora limped forward and ducked beneath the intertwined hands of Lyra and Eridana. Inside the circle, the burgeoning doorway bloomed at her feet. At this rate, they'd be here for days attempting to open the passageway. With the guards drawing near, they needed a better way.

Leonora reached into her sleeve and withdrew the missing key. Shouting her sisters' names, she wound back her arm. "...and Leonora!" she called, heaving the golden ball down at the blossoming door.

It struck, and before them, the burnished frame rippled open, knocking Leonora to the ground, and revealing within it a beautiful kingdom, with rolling hills, a sapphire river weaving between them. In the distance there was a castle shimmering like treasure and carved into a hilltop, watching over a village in the valley below. It was as their mother had described. Where Dorchada was nothing but shadows, Leonora could feel the warmth of the sunlight shining over Sunniva.

The princesses' mouths hung open for several moments before a handful of guards broke through the treeline. At the site of the portal, they froze, the second wave of guards running into them. They were all mesmerized by the doorway to another world which glittered before them.

"All right girls, in you go," Carina said, pulling the youngest sisters toward the door. "Berenice? You goblin, where are you?" She searched, while helping Delphine and Ara through the door.

Leonora crawled over the grass toward the spot where the amulet had landed. Palming it, she watched as her sisters filed across the magic threshold.

"Leonora," Carina called. She pointed, guiding her sister's eye in the direction Leonora had left the cloud.

Only, there was no cloud.

There was no fox.

There stood a man with eyes like stars, the skin of his torso bared to the night as he'd only had time to retrieve his trousers before...

The king seized Henry's arms and wrenched them behind his back. Holding a dagger to Henry's throat, he laughed. It was a horrible sound, dripping with malevolence.

"Henry!" Leonora cried, trying to get to her feet. She stumbled and crashed to the ground again. "Let him go!"

Ciarán shoved Henry into the waiting arms of his guards and stepped forward. One of the men was Raff, who had the decency to offer Henry his black cloak.

"Trade yourself, and I'll consider sparing his life. Deliver your sisters to me, and I will let him return to service unharmed," Ciarán offered.

"You grossly overestimate her feelings for me, sire," Henry said.

"My stars, Henry. What a thing to say," Leonora scolded him.

"Leonora, take your sisters and go," Henry urged. "Don't worry for me." He smiled, but it did not reach his eyes. Resigned as he sounded, she could see he still strained against the hold of the guards. "Leonora," he said, nodding his head toward the door.

He'd only meant what they both knew. Her sisters, their freedom, nothing was more precious to Leonora. Feelings, friendship, whatever she held in her heart for Henry, they both knew it couldn't tip the scales. But what Henry didn't know was that Leonora had no intention of going through the door just now. She'd follow soon, she hoped... somehow.

"I surrender myself, Father. Let them go."

The king sneered. "Seize her," he commanded his guards. Then, turning to Leonora, he amended, "I shall kill you both."

"No! Henry!" Leonora's nails dug into the ground as she watched the guards pull him backward. Others came for her. "Please!" She locked eyes with Raff, and he let go of Henry's arm.

"Thank you," Henry said. Then he thrust his fist into the other guard's face, relieved him of his sword, and ran after the men heading for Leonora. They drew their weapons to face Henry.

"An unbound man? You are no match for my guards," the king hissed.

"That is where you are wrong, sire." His borrowed sword clanked against the blades of the other men. With a series of quick movements and impossible footwork, he disarmed one of the men and had the other stumbling to keep up. "I am bound by something far greater than your silver bands."

"Me too! I am bound by sisterhood!" It was at that moment Berenice tore out of the shadows and charged the king, screaming something about the color green and waving her arms about like mad. Magic streamed from her body and encircled the king in a sweeping emerald cloud of shimmering starlight.

"Oh dear," Leonora observed.

Those remaining in the Circle watched in horror as the magic cleared.

Where the great King Ciarán had once stood, was empty space.

"What did you do?" Leonora and Henry asked at once.

"I have turned him into a frog!" Berenice sang delightedly, pointing to the small creature hopping about and ribbiting furiously.

"Are we to do his bidding?" one guard asked another.

"Can you understand him?" returned a second guard, lifting the face shield of his helmet to scratch his temple, as though this amount of thinking for himself caused his brain to itch.

"Haven't a clue," the first said.

The man Leonora recognized as the king's personal guard bent to pick up the frog, cupping the creature in his hands. "Take him to the mage, I suppose?"

"Maybe not right away," suggested another.

"Perhaps not at all," Raff dared as he slowly retreated from the clearing.

Ciarán's man placed the frog carefully on the ground.

Then Raff reached for his own neck. With a slight tug, the band released.

Berenice has done it, Leonora thought, suddenly feeling far less heavy. The guards were bound no longer. No one would pursue the princesses to Sunniva, and perhaps the sun would shine on Dorchada once more. The princesses had rescued themselves and each other, and a castle full of people. Together they'd been strong enough. Together, as their mother had bid them.

Carina shepherded the remaining princesses through the door, taking special care to ensure Berenice was safely inside.

Then, kneeling beside her sister, Carina whispered a healing spell over Leonora's ankle, absorbing the pain into a cool mist. "There. Ought to hold for the moment. We'll get you to a proper sorceress when we arrive at our uncle's palace."

"Carina." Leonora reached for her sister's icy hand, but found it was warm, as though suitable blood flow had been restored now rest was within their grasp. "You are a proper sorceress."

Carina blinked rapidly, blushed, and said, "Tend to your guard, but do not delay." She helped Leonora up, kissed her sister's cheek, and passed through the doorway.

Having been abandoned by the king's guards in lieu of more pressing concerns, Henry said from behind her, "Seems it's undeniable, what the storybooks say: only true love's kiss can break a spell." It was a voice she knew well, giving her own words back to her.

"I truly love foxes," she replied, turning toward him, a smirk on her lips. She did love foxes, but perhaps she felt something for Henry which the magic understood better than she did.

"Will you take me as a man?" He moved forward, out-doing her with a broad smile. He had donned his tunic, left here the night of his transformation, but eschewed the regimental tabard that bore the king's crest.

"You are the Watcher." This time it was Leonora who stepped in his direction.

"No longer. Despite all my efforts, it is you who has rescued me." He lengthened his stride, closing the gap between them. "The last silver band which bound me to your fro—father," he cleared his throat as she stifled a chuckle. He continued, "It fractured the moment you kissed me."

"Had it not been for your absolute and reckless defiance, I'm certain this story would have a much different ending. We have rescued each other," she offered with a gentle laugh, fingering the thin cotton of his tunic. "Coauthors of our own storybook."

"Coauthors," he confirmed. Henry ran a hand through his dark hair as if to ensure the fur was gone.

"I miss you as a fox." She tipped her head and grinned. "But I will be glad of your company even so. Come. In my mother's realm there is no hurry, no burning at dawn, or fox for breakfast."

Taking him by the hand, Leonora led Henry to the door. She paused. Rising on the toes of her boots, she circled his neck with her arms. "May I?"

"If you don't, I will," Henry said.

And so she kissed him, soft and sweet. There was a small magic in it, she was sure, the way it shimmered and wound around her heart. "Ah, you are still a man then?" she asked, pulling back and eagerly examining the features of his human face.

"Yours," he said, his blue eyes steady and earnest. "Ever after."

"Very clever," Leonora whispered, as she and Henry stepped through the golden door, which sealed behind them.

Only an insistent ribbit broke the silence of the clearing.

ALL THAT GLITTERS IS NOT GOLD

CHARLIE MORGAN

Eira's days are filled with dirt and dust, but her dreams are dressed in gold.

As the eldest daughter, Eira loves her younger siblings, Hansel and Gretel, more than anything. After their father's death, she uses her skills as a scribe to help support her struggling family. But the cupboards remain bare and her skirts are in tatters.

When a beautiful stranger offers her a job transcribing fae scrolls for a handsome sum, Eira believes her luck is changing. But, as she works to recreate ancient alphabets and ornamentations, and earn gold for her family, she notices unsettling changes in her appetite. A dark craving churns within her and threatens to consume everyone she loves.

"All That Glitters Is Not Gold" is a fantasy horror origin story inspired by "Hansel and Gretel."

H er mother always said the fae were dangerous, wicked things.

But Eira had never seen a fae, and as far as she was aware, they only existed in bedtime stories. Tucked between thick pages and dried ink, the biggest threat they posed was heavy eyelids, hungry for sleep.

"From the corner of his eye, he saw a movement in the bushes. The boy knelt and peered into the darkness when two small glowing orbs popped into existence, nestled between the leaves," Eira said in a hushed voice. "He crept closer, his curiosity getting the better of him, twigs snapping under his feet." Her mousy brown hair fell into her face as she leaned nearer to the children. "The fae did not move. It merely stared back at him, unblinking." Her voice was now barely a whisper.

A fire crackled in the hearth, casting long shadows across the children's faces. On the bed, the smaller child, a girl with a round face, rosy cheeks and long, blonde hair, pulled a thick woolen blanket up around her shoulders. A shield from the monsters, fairy-tale or not. She shrunk beneath the heavy fabric as if being swallowed. Her twin brother pulled the small girl into a reassuring embrace as they listened to their older sister.

"The fae erupted from the bush." Eira jumped from the rickety brown stool, waving her arms. The children screamed and sank into the bed, the blanket gobbling them up. "It bared its sharp teeth and stood up on its long, spindly legs, towering over the boy. The boy turned to run, his hand on his iron dagger. But he was too slow. His screams pierced the night as the fae's sharp claws raked down his small, exposed back."

The door flung open, their mother storming into the house, a mess of long skirts and dust motes. "Stop it, Eira," Beth said after her eyes scanned the scene. The children hunched beneath their covers. "What drivel are you filling their heads with?"

"Eira's telling us a story of the fae," Hansel, the boy, said.

The wind blew inside, stirring up the fire and blowing out the candles before slamming the door closed.

"They'll never sleep! You and your scary stories. Nonsense," Beth scolded.

"The fae are not nonsense. You know it," Eira retorted.

"They haven't been seen around these parts in several years. Not since I was a small child when they snatched my cousin from the wheat fields. It's been a while since, no need to scare the 'lil ones over nothing."

Eira *harrumphed* and turned away from the children, her long skirts swishing around her ankles. Walking over to the hearth, she picked up a wooden split and set it aflame. She walked around the square room, igniting the wicks on each of the extinguished candles.

"I got the sheep locked up. Dark clouds are rollin' in. You can feel the charge in the air, like something wicked is coming," Beth said, placing a kettle on the grate over the hearth.

"Maybe it's the fae," little Gretel said from beneath the covers.

Beth *tsked* at the child. "All the fae are long gone, my child. No one knows where they went. Some say all the magic is gone from the land and it left with the fae. Others say a great wizard cast a powerful spell over the fae realm, freezing all the fae, and now they're trapped like statues—forever. But I say, good riddance. They weren't all magic and beautiful looks like the fairy tales claim."

"Vanya told me they had sharp teeth and long claws. And liked to feast on unsuspecting people," Eira said.

"Never liked that woman. What did she call herself? An astrologer? Old coot always blathering on about the stars and fortune tellin'. But that's probably the truest thing that ever came out of her mouth," Beth said. A second later, her cheeks flushed scarlet. "Look at you, Eira! Getting me spouting scary things in front of the children. Why don't you do something useful and start cuttin' some bread for us?" She spun, turning her ire on Hansel. "And you, grab the empty pot by the hearth. Rain clouds were rolling in over the hills. I expect we'll see it comin' through the weak spot in the roof."

Eira rolled her eyes, but this wasn't the normal eye roll of a temperamental child. No. Eira just reached her twentieth year and while her cheeks were full like a cherub, she was an adult. Most young women her age were engaged to be wed, but not Eira. She was stuck at home caring for her younger siblings and mother.

"Ma, are all fae bad?" Hansel asked, sitting up taller in the bed.

Eira trudged over to the rickety cabinet they called a pantry, retrieving some bread. On a plate, she arranged a slice, a few pieces of dried meat and a cut pear.

Beth shook her head and frowned. "Are all people bad?"

Hansel shook his head. "No."

"Just like people, the fae could lean more towards the dark or light. Nobody is born bad. Just like with us people, we are curious creatures. It's in our bones and blood. There is no fighting nature. It's like that with the fae, but their nature was to be tricksters. They couldn't help themselves."

Gretel's hands were outstretched in eager anticipation as Eira approached. She handed her younger sister the plate. "Make sure you share with your brother," Eira said, waggling her finger toward the blonde-haired child.

"I will!" Gretel screeched with annoyance.

Returning to the pantry, Eira frowned at what was left of its meager contents. She sliced another pear, placing half on one plate and half on another. After putting what was left of the meat away, she used a dull knife to cut through the remainder of the bread. Eyeballing the two slices, she huffed and put the largest slice on her mother's plate. Her belly grumbled with a fierce hunger. But she took her plate back to her bed without complaint.

After her father's passing, Eira, at only thirteen years old, went looking for work. Her mother, Beth, suffering from an all-consuming grief at the death of her husband, stopped working regularly and tending to the children. And even though seven years had passed since Eira's father tripped and fell onto his blade, a stroke of bad luck, she still felt like the brunt of the responsibility for maintaining the home fell onto her shoulders.

Sitting down on the bed, her plate in her lap, she picked at her food. She didn't want to rush through her meal.

When she ate quickly, it made her feel more hungry in the end, as her stomach wasn't yet ready to be done.

While she ate, a long strand of hair kept tickling her nose. She brushed it away several times, her frustration growing with each attempt. Using one hand, she twisted her hair into a knot on the head, and with the other shoved a loose pencil from her side table through its mass.

With her hair out of the way, Eira picked up a book and read while she continued to eat. She'd been meaning to sell the book but was enjoying the stories too much. Reading was a balm to her restless soul, which craved for so much more than the one-room hut she grew up in. While reading *Tales of the Small and Slight and Hidden in Sight*, she was able to forget the troubles of her small home and her even smaller dinner. And she escaped into a world where magic and the fae were real.

◆ ◆ ◆ ◆ ◆

Eira awoke with a jolt, her eyes flying open. Bright, unfiltered sunshine shone in through the window, hitting Eira squarely in the eyes. She jumped from the bed and gathered supplies. She shoved a mess of quills, inks, and scrolls inside her brown leather bag.

Like the last several days, she had no plan other than to look for work. Finding work as a scribe was not the easiest, as most commoners, like herself, barely knew how to read. But Eira had been blessed with a father who worked with a cleric. He thankfully taught her how to read and write before he departed from the world.

Today was different, though. In her gut, she felt a tug and a song in her head, as if someone were whispering in her ear. It told her to head north on the road out of town toward Farrington. It told her she would find work today.

Eira peered into the cracked mirror and her gray eyes stared back. The image was fuzzy from the residue and grime thickly coating its surface. She brushed out her long, brown hair before braiding it.

"You headin' out?" Beth asked from across the room. Her mother was sweeping the old dirt floor and opening windows in a flurry of motion.

"Yes. I have a good feeling in my bones."

"'Ey, I sure hope so. We could use some extra coin. The dried meat is runnin' low. I don't understand why you left that woman... the astrologer? She paid well."

Eira just shook her head, not wanting to go into detail about the strange experience with the sky scryer. But there she was, a week ago, using her one talent—scribing—at the astrologer's house, making these intricate, ornate and fussy charts for whoever wanted to know about their fate. Vanya claimed one could see—if one knew what they were looking for—their fate or destiny or whatever in the stars. Eira spent much of her time working for the woman looking up at the night sky. She wasn't sure she believed in such a thing, but decided it didn't matter if she did. As long as someone believed, she got paid to scribe the chart. She liked money, and being able to feed her family.

On the last day of her employment for the astrologer, Eira was scribing when she looked over at the woman and gasped. Vanya's eyes were normally brown. But as the peculiar woman stared up into the night sky, through a hole in her roof, her eyes went white like fresh milk from the cows. And the astrologer said,

"Beware the one with a silver tongue,
do not trust their poison song;
for they guide you to a place unknown,
until they have you lost and prone;
when you drink their sparkling light,
they will entrap you within their bite."

Then, in a singular blink, the astrologer's eyes returned to their normal, simple brown. Eira stared at the woman. Vanya returned to her work, as if nothing had happened. At that moment, Eira decided she would need to find a new employer. Vanya seemed to understand, paying Eira for her completed work without any grumbling.

Eira opened the front door to leave.

"But take these too, child," the woman cooed.

Eira turned around. The woman had her long, wrinkled fingers around three books. Eira reached out and took the books from the woman, examining the covers. They were beautiful. She couldn't help but admire the exceptional handiwork. Each book was wrapped in leather and embossed with gold lettering and fancy filigree decoration. The titles were, in no particular order; *Tales of the Small and*

Slight and Hidden in Sight, Encyclopedia of the Wee Ones, and *Stories of the Seelie and Unseelie.* Quite a common theme. Though Eira failed to notice it at the time. Her only concern was how beautiful they were and what price they might fetch her at the market.

Eira didn't bother recounting the experience to her mother. Beth wouldn't care. So, instead, she said, "she was a funny one."

Beth shrugged. "A gold coin from a funny peasant is the same gold coin from the king."

Eira crossed the small house and reached for the door handle. "It's hard to explain, Ma," Eira said, "but I promise to find a job. I'd really like some new skirts that are embroidered with gold thread."

"You always wantin' something. With your taste, you should've been born to a nobleman." Beth pulled the sheets from the children's bed and shook them out.

Eira ignored her comment. "I promise to be back before the sun kisses the hills."

◆ ◆ ◆ ◆ ◆

The sky was devoid of clouds. The birds chirped merrily in the trees while she walked along the north road out of town. If it weren't for the large branches and small sticks cluttering the road, one would never know a storm shook the world just last night. She kicked a few as she passed them.

In one hand, she twirled a pencil between her fingers. She always kept one close at hand, as pencils had many uses besides writing and drawing. The purpose of today's pencil was to help her pass the time, weaving it between her fingers, and sometimes tossing it in the air.

The road was no busier or quieter than usual. In fact, it was quite the same as always. The further she got from town, the fewer people she saw on foot.

Peering down, Eira looked at her dusty shoes and frowned. This was not a desirable state for a lady in search of an employer. One day, she'd have a horse and buggy to take her here and there, she thought. She daydreamed about serving rich clients who wanted enormous books printed with fancy gold ink, florals, and filigree, who'd pay her well.

The sun beamed down. A sweat broke out along her brow. Reaching a fork in the road, Eira stood there staring at the crooked sign, dumbfounded. Some time had passed since she last took the north road, and couldn't remember the way to Farrington, a large town just over the crest of a large hill. The rickety sign post indicated which way was east and which was west. But which way should she go? She crouched down to think but Eira's thoughts swam as if underwater. On an impulse, she headed east.

With each step she took, a twisting feeling, like a bramble of thorns, pulled at her gut. The same feeling one might get if they stood at the edge of a cliff and debated the merits of jumping off. This was not a good sensation—razor-edged foreboding. But Eira was determined to find work and continued down the eastern road.

"Where are you going, Miss? Are ya lost?" a deep, husky voice asked.

Eira spun on her heels. "'ello? Who's there."

A tall, dark-haired man with piercing blue eyes emerged from a small, hidden path behind a large oak tree. He leaned against a tree, tucking his hands into his finely tailored pants. "Good day, Miss."

"Oh, good day," Eira responded. She ducked her eyes, and nibbled on the top of her pencil.

"I'm Kazamir, was headin' to the next town—looking for a scribe. You wouldn't happen to be one?"

Eira looked up and saw his eyes glued to the pencil between her lips. Her stomach spun as her eyes lingered on the man, unable to break her stare. She knew she should mention being a scribe, but the words were lost on her tongue, running away before she could wield them.

Kazamir was devastatingly beautiful with his chiseled jaw, loose curls, and wide shoulders. She'd never seen a man who was such a picture of perfection. It was as if he'd been carved from stone by an artist who was blessed by the gods. But his gait was off, as if supported by the air itself, gliding with unnatural grace. The lilt of his voice was otherworldly, each syllable a song.

Aside from his beauty and unnerving presence, Eira knew he was a wealthy man. His doublet featured heavy golden embroidery and there was a general lack of dirt on his person, even though he walked on foot. His hair was well oiled. Along his jaw, his beard was manicured, as if trimmed by the royal barbers themselves.

A swirl of emotions coalesced within her—terror and curiosity. Unsure of what else to do, she said, "I'm Eira. I was looking for the next town, sir. Though it seems I've forgotten the way."

The man gave her a soft smile, his white teeth sparkling. Another sign of his riches. "Which town are you seeking?"

"Farrington. Going to find work. My father taught me how to read and write. I'm actually a scribe, sir," Eira said, finding her confidence finally.

"This is serendipitous, indeed. Do you have samples of your work?" Kazamir asked.

She kept her gaze downward to avoid getting lost in his magnificent eyes. Pulling her bag forward, she reached a hand inside. "I do, sir."

"I'd love to see your work. I have a feeling you are quite talented."

Eira blushed at his comment as she produced a scroll, handing it to him. She spun the pencil between her fingers, fidgeting away her nervous energy.

Kazamir clicked his tongue in approval. "Your decorative work is some of the best I've seen. How is it I've never heard of your name before?" Kazamir beamed. "I believe you'd be a great fit for my project, Miss."

Eira ducked her eyes but smiled, her pride ballooning. "Thank you, sir."

"Would you be interested in seeing the text in question? We could discuss pay along the way."

Eira's mind flashed images of gold coins, gold embroidered dresses, and golden quills as she thought of the money she'd earn. "I'd be quite all right with that, sir."

Kazamir waved a hand. "Please, call me Kazamir. If we are to be working together, I'd like us to be friends." He reached up and put a hand on her arm.

Eira finally looked up at him. Kazamir smiled, making her heart skip a beat. His eyes were like the icy lakes from the far north. It felt like they stared at each other for some time, several seconds too long. Kazamir shuffled his feet and cleared his throat, breaking her trance.

"Come, I'll show you to my humble abode. We can have some tea and look over that scroll. I think you'll quite like its artistry. I've never seen anything with such meticulous filigree." He offered out his arm.

Eira nibbled on the pencil some more, feeling unsure. Her mother always warned against strangers. Going scouting for a job was new for her. Normally, when she found work, it was through word of mouth, prior clients recommending new clients. She didn't know this man, but he was clearly a nobleman, or at least a very wealthy merchant. She was a young woman of twenty years and could manage on her own, could she not? Not too long ago, she batted off a vagrant who tried to steal her scrolls. She would be fine, she decided.

She linked her arm through Kazamir's and the pair walked along the twisting road while a soft breeze rustled the trees. The longer she walked alongside Kazamir, the more the uneasy feeling dissipated. It was still hard to behold his beauty, so she avoided eye contact as much as possible. They talked as they went along. Eira discovered he was a merchant who specialized in rare texts and antiquities. It was through his work he came upon an interesting scroll which a client desired a copy to add to his library.

⋆ ⋆ ◆ ⋆ ⋆

Approaching Kazamir's home, Eira did her best to school her features into neutrality. Tucked in the woods, a breathtaking three-floor estate stood against hemlock trees. A flagstone path led to the entrance, flanked by well-trimmed hedges. She admired the intricately carved pattern adorning the double doors. Only those with a large sum of money could afford such things.

Eira couldn't resist the thought which bubbled up. "Why do you walk? You look like a gentleman who could afford a carriage." The question was forthright—rude even. But her curiosity, as usual, won the battle over polite manners.

He smiled. "I enjoy walking. Keeps me youthful and prevents my joints from turning rusty. Carriages are for individuals who find walking above them, when really, they are lazy."

Eira blushed. She was glad her question did not bother him, but also appreciated his own forthright nature. It was easier to know where you stood with people who voiced their opinions freely. "If staying youthful is the goal, I'd say you've managed quite well. I'm sure all the noblewomen hound about which daily elixir you like best," she said earnestly because it was true. There was not a wrinkle on Kazamir's face, nor scars or pock marks, which was unusual even for the rich. Whatever he did to keep his appearance beautiful was working.

"Oh, you flatter me, Eira. So kind," Kazamir said, placing a hand over his heart. "Now, come, I'm very excited to show you this scroll."

He reached for the brass handle and pulled open the door. As Kazamir led her through the space, Eira's eyes darted this way and that. Every seat was made of supple leather. The side tables, desks, and counters were covered with heavy books and golden trinkets. She followed him into a cavernous room. Her neck craned upward to marvel at the exposed wooden beams which decorated the ceiling. The sight made her heart flutter. It was beautiful.

Along three walls stood heavy bookcases laden with various texts, scrolls, and tomes. It was a scribe's dream. At the far end of the room, the wall was covered in nothing but windows, allowing in vast amounts of warm light. No candles required. The view beyond the room looked over a picturesque garden filled with various wildflowers, walking paths wove around trees and statues.

"Oh my," Eira said, looking around the room.

Kazamir let out a nervous titter. "Yes, uh... this is my personal library and study. I've put a lot of care into turning it into a place I'd like to be in often," he said while striding toward two oversized desks in the middle of the space.

"I don't think I'd ever want to leave if I were you." Eira's eyes caught on a large leather couch placed in front of a fireplace, opposite of the walls of windows. Candles and books covered the end tables.

"Yes, it's quite peaceful. Please, have a look around. You may pull anything you like from the open shelves. Just do not touch anything from that case," he said, pointing.

Eira followed his pointed finger to a small bookcase by the fireplace. The front of the case was covered in glass. There was a small golden lock on the front. She nodded in acknowledgment even though her mind wondered about the possibilities of the treasures locked inside. Were they valuable? Ancient history? Stories of old?

"I'm going to warm up some tea for us." He crossed the room again, stopping next to Eira, and placed a hand on her upper arm. "Do you have a preference?"

Eira glanced down at his hand and blushed. His touch was warm against her skin. "Do you have anything with ginger?"

"Excellent choice. I'll be right back," he said.

As she stared at his retreating form, curiosity got the better of Eira and words tumbled from her mouth. "Do you not have any servants?"

Reaching the door, Kazamir turned around with a warm smile on his face. "I admire your sense of observation. Very astute for someone so young."

"My apologies for being so forward."

Kazamir shook his head. "No apologies needed. It is an apt question. I have had some in the past, but found I was always getting things myself even when I employed them. I didn't grow up with money, and so I am used to being of an independent nature. It's difficult to ask for help when you've always had to depend on yourself."

Eira knew this feeling all too well. It was why she didn't ask Vanya or any of her past clients for a recommendation, because asking for help felt wrong. Her father taught her to be self-sufficient and proud of her work. If she did, it would speak for itself. And in her experience, he was right. If she was organized, arrived on time, and produced work to the best of her ability, her prior employers gave her recommendations of their own volition. Soliciting for a job was new for her, and it indeed felt like going against her nature.

"I don't like asking for help, either," Eira said.

"Then we are of a like mind, you and I. Quite the pair we are shaping up to be!"

Eira's cheeks turned red at his compliment. This was happening all too often.

"I'll be right back with some tea. Enjoy the books," he said before exiting the room.

Eira stood for several moments, thinking about the chain of events leading her to this strange place. It seemed serendipitous, waking with the pull in her gut to head toward Farrington. Her thoughts drifted toward Vanya, the astrologer, and all her talk about the fates. Was it possible there was a greater, wiser force at play?

She looked around the room, overwhelmed by her present circumstance and the beauty of the library in which she stood. Kazamir had more books than most. She'd never seen so many texts amassed in a singular space. It was both unusual and quite magical.

She took tentative steps toward the glass bookcase. Stopping about a foot away, she peered inside. The case itself was short compared to the other ceiling-high bookshelves. The uppermost shelf was no higher than her head and held several scrolls, each tied shut with a thin piece of leather. On the next shelf was a thick brown tome with swirling lettering. She wasn't sure if it was the light playing tricks on her, but the book seemed to glow. It was lying on its side, and she was unable to make out the title. Its spine lacked any identification. The next shelf down contained several smaller books decorated in a language unbeknownst to her. There were also several thingamabobs. But generally, she was clueless as to their purposes.

The bottommost shelf held a dagger, gilded in gold. Along its hilt, ancient symbols were carved. For a long moment, she hunched over, staring at the object like a moth drawn to candlelight. In the surrounding silence, she swore she could hear the blade hum. A strange, otherworldly buzzing. But in the kitchen, something clattered. She bolted upright, leaving the thought and blade behind.

She glanced around the room. There was so much to look at. Should she go peer at the garden through the window? Or climb the ladder to see the many dusty tomes? The choice was difficult, so she gave up.

Eira sighed and trudged over to the large brown couch. She pulled off her bag, placed it next to the side table, and sat down. The piece of furniture was divinely comfortable. She sank into its soft depths, like plunging into a lake warmed by the summer sun. *I could get used to this*, she thought. Not even her bed, an old mass of animal skins and grass, was this plush.

Eira's eyes flew open at the sound of a spoon tinkling against a cup. Kazamir was bent over a short table in front of the couch, stirring tea. How long had she been asleep? Surely, it couldn't have been that long.

Kazamir glanced up and smiled. "You looked very peaceful there. I wasn't trying to wake you."

Eira shook her head, feeling disoriented and embarrassed. This was not her home. She shouldn't be falling asleep wherever she pleased. "I apologize. I didn't realize how tired I was."

Kazamir waved a hand in dismissal. "It's no problem. Do not trouble yourself. We walked a long way." He picked up a cup of the tea and passed it to her.

Eira graciously accepted it, thinking of Kazamir's words. Had they travelled far? She could barely remember the walk. Did they walk the eastern road? And what turn had they made to bring them to this estate in the woods? Her memory was like an old faded painting and she was stuck squinting trying to determine its original image. Hopefully, her slipping memory was only a symptom of a bad night's rest caused by the freak storm the night prior, and she could remember how to get home.

"Do you spend a lot of time here?" Eira took a deep inhale of the tea. The scent of ginger and something floral enveloped her, easing her nerves. "I heard the king has a library, too. Wonder how many books he has? You must have a lot to have your own library."

He nodded. "Indeed, he does have quite a collection. Mine is nowhere near as extensive."

"What about that glass bookcase over there? With the dagger? It looks ancient." Eira inclined her head.

"Oh, everything in that case is a relic of an older time. The most precious of my artifacts. The old stories say you could kill a fae with that dagger. But not sure how true that is," Kamazir said, shrugging. "All the other tales say only iron will do the trick, not gold."

"There is an old story I tell my brother and sister sometimes before bed. I don't remember where I heard it anymore, but it also mentions iron." Eira took a sip of her tea. The warm liquid was slightly sweet and fruity. "What's in this?"

"It's ginger and peach. Oh, and I added some honey. Is it all right?"

She smiled. "It's delicious."

"Well, now that you're comfortable, if you're amenable, might we speak of business?"

She sat up straighter in her seat. "Yes, of course. Go right ahead."

"Wonderful," Kazamir said, clapping his hands together. He stood from his seat and walked around the short table to the glass bookcase near the fireplace.

Eira's heart thumped like a wild hare in her chest. What text or scroll would he pull from the case? Any item he chose would likely be valuable. In the past, she'd worked with expensive pieces, at least to her. Though that didn't say much as the daughter of a courier.

"Would you mind clearing the table in front of you?" Karamir asked as he pulled a silver chain from beneath his doublet. At the end of the chain was a small key.

Eira eagerly jumped from the couch, setting her tea aside, and stacked the mess of books into a neat pile. Kazamir returned just as she finished, holding the large tome in one arm and a scroll in the other. She watched as he gently placed the items on the table.

Her eyes devoured the cover, inlaid with gold leaf. Two metal clasps held the tome shut. Brass coverings protected each corner. She could tell the text was old from its yellowed pages and the litter of pockmarks on its thick leather cover. From this angle, it didn't appear to glow like she remembered, and was probably just a trick of the light.

Kazamir took a seat next to her. His proximity set loose butterflies in her stomach. She was a young woman, with few prospects in her small village. Until this moment, Eira had never been so close to someone so beautiful. She could feel his elbow touching hers. It made her skin buzz as if she'd been struck by lightning.

He looked over his shoulder, his eyes roaming her face. "Ready to look inside?"

"Yes, please," she beamed.

Kazamir leaned forward and opened the tome. Eira gasped, her hand flying to cover her mouth. It was, indeed, glowing. The pages were not yellowed as she initially thought. They were emitting their own light, like the soft glow of the sun below the horizon before it broke for dawn.

"How does it do that?" Eira whispered, as if she might disturb the text. Ripping her eyes away, she found Kazamir not looking at the book, but staring at her. She ducked her eyes away.

"Uh..." Kazamir started, then paused to clear his throat. "Yes, it is quite magical."

"You don't mean actual magic?"

He nodded. "Actually, yes, I do. You've mentioned you're familiar with the fae."

Eira's brows furrowed. "Ma says it's just stories. They're gone now."

"She is correct. For at least three decades, there have been no signs of the fae in our lands. But there was a time they interacted regularly with our people. Traded with them even. This book belonged to the fae at some point. I came across it on my travels. I've received a request from a clerk of the royal court to procure a copy of the book and scroll for the king's library. However, I realize that is a large undertaking. I thought we could start with the scroll first and see how our working relationship develops before diving into the tome."

And it was a piece of actual fae history, oozing magic. What secrets did it hold?

"You want me...to make a copy of a fae relic?" she asked, wide-eyed. "For the *king*?"

"I do. You've shown me your work. I'm surprised you aren't working for a barrister or something similar. I'm willing to pay three gold coins per day that you spend on its creation."

Eira opened her mouth to speak but found nothing. She was entirely out of her depth. Tears lined the bottom of her eyes. She was both terrified of messing up the opportunity and incredibly grateful. Vanya, the astrologer, only paid one gold piece per day and now she was being offered enough to change her family's life for the foreseeable future.

She felt as if all the air in the room had left. It was difficult to find a breath when her lungs would not work properly. This was the job that could change everything. It would make her work known among the royal court. The king would know her name. The heavens were smiling down upon her today, perhaps her family's bad luck was changing.

Kazamir put a hand on her shoulder. "Eira, are you all right?"

She turned to face him, a tear falling down her cheek. He clicked his tongue as he reached up and wiped it away. A wave of nervous energy washed over her, goosebumps breaking out along her neck.

"Don't cry, dear Eira. You deserve it. Plus, I think the gods were at work today when we crossed each other's path. And we can't ignore the gods, now can we?"

She shook her head, then sucked down a deep breath of air. "No."

"Good. Now, why don't we put this away for the day? You can finish your tea and choose a book from my collection to take home for the evening. Then, we can get started on this project bright and early tomorrow. Does that sound like a plan?"

"That sounds wonderful. Thank you. And not just for your kindness, but for this job. For believing in me. I've dreamed of taking on a job for the king. I can't believe it's coming true."

"And I'm sure it won't be the last." Kazamir smiled.

◆ ◆ ◆ ◆ ◆

"Where were you when the sun kissed the hills?" Beth asked, her voice shrill. "It's dark out!"

The wind clung to Eira, ruffling her skirts as she walked in the door. Her steps felt light as if she was dancing upon the breeze which carried her home. She beamed at her mother. "I found a job!"

Beth's face rearranged itself into a look of surprise. "Really?"

Eira deposited her worn leather bag on the ground and walked over to the twins, who lay on their bed. Hansel was reading aloud to Gretel, albeit slowly as he was just learning how. He struggled with a word. "Al-uh-hhhhh," he said, his vowel hanging in the air.

"What's the word? Let me see," Eira said, sitting on the bed next to him. Her eyes scanned the page. "Oh, that's a big one. Alabaster."

"What's that mean?"

Eira pursed her lips, thinking. "Traditionally, it's a soft rock used for statues. But in stories like this, they use it as a way to describe color. It's nearly white."

"Al-uh-bas-ter," Hansel said, sounding out the word again.

"Well, are ya gonna just ignore me, Eira? Tell me about the job!" Beth screeched. She sat on a small wooden stool with a pile of knitting in her lap, and two needles, one in each hand. Knitting was about the only thing her mother did to bring in money. But it was summer, so she wasn't selling much at the moment.

Eira rolled her eyes and dropped a kiss on both the twins' heads, guzzling down their sweet scent. She stood and marched across the room to the old pantry, pulling out bread and some dried meat to cut for dinner. "There isn't much to say. I'll be scribing for a gentleman named Kazamir. I met him on the way to Farrington."

Beth's face twisted again. "How much is the pay?"

Eira shrugged. "It pays well—three gold pieces a day."

Beth gasped. "Oh goodness, the pantry will be stocked to heaven and back."

Beneath Eira's hands, the stale bread crunched as she sliced through it. Annoyance rolled through her like a crashing wave. It would not be Beth stocking the pantry, but Eira attending the market and carting the goods back home. "The twins need clothes. They've got holes everywhere. They look like they're street urchins."

"Oh, that's an easy repair," Beth said.

"I'd rather they have a fresh pair of tunics."

"But why waste the coin, when I can fix 'em? I just need some more string and a new needle. My current one is rather dull."

"Of course," Eira huffed as she plopped down on her bed with her meager dinner. She didn't feel like arguing with her mother. On her next trip to the market, she would purchase the twins new tunics, regardless.

Beth continued to prattle on about all the things Eira could buy to make things better around the house; a new broom, a sharpened knife, and lighter bedding for the summer. And of course, her mother was right. All these items would help. But Eira was more than the gold she provided. She was a person with feelings. It didn't surprise Eira at all that Beth didn't bother to ask any details about the job and was only concerned about the money. This wasn't anything new. With this particular job, it was probably better Beth was absorbed in the reward rather than the fae texts Eira would be scribing. Beth did not like any mention of the fae. Or of magic, for that matter.

◆ ◆ ◆ ◆ ◆

Eira slung her worn leather bag over her shoulder. The breeze was warm against her cheeks as she strode out the front door toward Kazamir's home. She'd awoken with a start, a smile on her face, and nervousness coursing through her veins. Since the bread and dried meat were running low, she forwent breakfast in favor of leaving some for the twins. But that was okay, as there would be more than enough food for everyone once she was paid for today's work. Hope was more than enough to satiate her until the evening.

Sometime later, she arrived on the flagstone path, but again, she wasn't quite sure how she made it to the large three-story manor. She vaguely recalled walking the road out of town, turning down the eastern road, and then... she wasn't sure. The memory faded like a drawing in the sand washed away by the tide, but that didn't deter her. The whole time she walked, she hummed an ethereal tune. Where had she heard it? She wasn't sure, but that tune carried her, and her feet, to Kazamir's home. She'd made it to her destination.

As she approached the front steps, one of the large wooden doors swung open. Kazamir stepped out with a warm smile on his face. The sight made her heart flutter. She returned his smile before looking away.

"Good morning, dear Eira. I've made us some tea. Have you had breakfast?" he asked.

"I have not. I was too excited to get to work," she said, beaming.

He gestured for her to come inside. "No worries, I have some bread and cheese I can set out for us. I'll be sure you go to work on a full belly. Come inside."

Eira meandered through the foyer, down a long hallway, and stopped at the large oak door at the end. With hesitation, she reached for the handle and looked over her shoulder, awaiting his confirmation.

"Head on in. The scroll is out on the desk opposite of my own. That will be your workstation while you're here. Get comfortable. I'll just be in the kitchen. I'll join you shortly."

"Many thanks."

Eira turned the handle and walked into the room. Leather and vanilla wrapped around her like a blanket. She took a deep breath, and her shoulders relaxed. If only that smell could be bottled, she thought. It would be quite lovely to walk around smelling of books and knowledge. There was nothing which smelled more beautiful to Eira.

With a few easy steps, she found herself in the middle of the library at a large oak desk. The surface was empty except for a singular thick scroll. She recognized the yellowed edges and the faint, golden glow emanating from the inside. She didn't touch it, not yet.

Preparing her workspace was an important step that could not be rushed. The act of setting up was meditative in quality, placing each item exactly so. The heavy jars of ink went to one side of the table. Directly opposite sat several quills, iron weights, a penknife and a small line marking frame. When all the pieces were in their places, she looked over everything with a satisfied smile.

"Wonderful. I'm glad to see you've made yourself at home. Have you taken a look at the scroll yet?"

"Not yet. That is the next step."

"Well, come over and eat some breakfast first. No one should work on an empty stomach."

Eira looked down at her desk. Her body thrummed with excitement. But Kazamir was right. She should eat. It was very common for her to start a project and forget to eat or drink. She nodded and crossed the room.

On the couch in front of the fireplace, the two shared a small breakfast of bread, cheese, and apples. Kazamir spoke about a device he'd seen recently called a compass—used for marking layouts and measuring. Eira had seen such a device at the market before, but she could never afford it, though she wished for one. It would make creating symmetrical designs a lot easier.

When they were both finished with breakfast, Kazamir gathered the teacups and the empty serving tray. The entire time he worked, Eira was irresistibly drawn to her employer's movements. He moved with such ease and grace like a swan moving through water.

When everything was picked up, he turned toward her, his piercing blue eyes landing on her face. Her cheeks heated, and she glanced away. She didn't want to get caught staring. That was unladylike. And she didn't want her new employer to think such things about her. She shot upward from her seat and shuffled over to her new workstation to prevent her gaze wandering further.

"Getting to work?" Kazamir asked from across the room.

"Yes. I should get started. You've been so generous. I don't want to waste any more of your time," she responded as she pulled out her seat. Looking down, surprise washed over her as she spotted a small, red cushion. That would make working for long hours much more comfortable. She sighed with gratitude.

"You're welcome. My home is your home." Kazamir waved, gesturing at the library. "I'll leave you be, but don't hesitate to let me know if I'm being too loud or if you need anything."

Eira watched Kazamir's back as he left the room. When he was gone, she finally felt as if she could concentrate. Her thoughts cleared, and her purpose became obvious. She looked down at the scroll with both wonder and determination.

Rummaging in her bag, she pulled out a pair of gloves and got to work. With gentle hands, she unfurled the scroll. A beautiful script flowed across the page. Along the left-hand edge was an ornate depiction of a vine with small, white, delicate flowers. It was some of the best craftsmanship she'd ever laid eyes on. She'd never seen anything like it. She placed several weights on the parchment to keep the scroll from curling up again.

Staring down at it, she had the urge to run her finger across it. She knew she shouldn't, in order to preserve the ink and artistry, but the urge zinged through her, unstoppable. She ran her finger across a line of text, and it shimmered. Her eyes widened, and her heart was in her throat. The scroll was magical, just like the tome.

In all the old stories and books she'd read about the fae, they used a variety of magic. The most common form was trickster magic, such as illusions or transmogrification, turning objects or people into things they weren't. Though it wasn't uncommon for them to use healing or protection magic, either. The problem was, Eira had no idea what sort of magic inhabited this scroll or how it worked.

She'd need to be careful.

◆ ◆ ◆ ◆ ◆

For the next three days, Eira awoke before her family stirred, gathered her things, and walked to Kazamir's house. She'd arrive with the sun cresting over the horizon and a readiness to work. Each morning, her employer was there at the door with a smile on his face and breakfast prepared. She found Kazamir was an excellent listener as she grumbled about all her challenges at home. And when he spoke of arcane magics and history, Eira devoured it all, having a voracious appetite for knowledge. Once breakfast was cleaned up, she'd set up her station and get to work. Hours would pass with her head buried in the work. It was peaceful and filled a void within her, creating beautiful things. It wasn't until nearly lunch each day that her trance would be broken.

"Are you hungry, dear Eira?" Kazamir asked.

"Yes, that sounds quite lovely." Eira came up for air, sucking down a deep breath and tearing her eyes from her work. Peering out the windows, she was surprised to see the sun was high in the sky. She didn't realize so much time had passed as she was so entrenched in her work.

He smiled. "Don't fret. I've just been preparing something for us. I'll be right back."

She continued working, not even acknowledging Kazamir. She was mesmerized by the fanciful brush strokes of the fae. They were dazzling, as if each one was made by the surest and most graceful of hands. It was difficult to recreate the strokes in the exact same fashion. She wasn't sure if it was the lack of tools, training, or maybe magic, but it engrossed her for hours on end. She practiced each on a separate piece of parchment before committing it to the ultimate piece.

"Come, have a seat. You must be famished," Kazamir said from across the room.

Eira's brow wrinkled. When did he come back into the room? She did not notice the sound of the door or his footsteps. The work entranced her. Though it was not unusual. She loved what she did. Ripping her gaze away from the glittering text and looking around the room, she found a sharp pain behind her right eye. A break from her task would ease the strain of staring so intently at the parchment.

Kazamir was already seated on the worn leather couch, pouring tea into cups. The lemon scent drifted over, and her stomach grumbled. Perhaps that was the issue with her head, she was hungry.

She took a seat next to him, his scent filling the space between him. It set her heart pounding in her chest, the same way it had the last few days. It was a mixture of caramel, cardamom, and amber. A unique mixture that she found quite intoxicating. Her body unwittingly leaned in closer to Kazamir to feel his scent all over her.

"How is the scribing coming along?" Kazamir asked as he passed over a cup of tea.

She took the cup in her hands. "It's going well. I'm happy with my ability to reproduce the vine flowers along the side. The script is a little more delicate and finicky. I'm having to take my time. I'm about a third of the way through it. If I'm being honest, I'm a little disappointed in myself at how slow that part is coming along."

Kazamir nodded. "The fae's writing is unique. I've studied it for some time. Their alphabet is longer than ours. And several of the letters are incredibly similar. Our alphabet is more up and down, whereas theirs is more like water. It flows."

"Yes, I've noticed. It does make me think about how the text was applied to the scroll. I wonder if it was not done by hand but with magic itself," she said.

Eira dipped her head and took a sip of her tea, a strand of golden brown hair falling into her face. Kazamir's hand reached up. Her whole body froze as he tucked the stray hair behind her ear. His hand lingered at the edge of her jaw for a second too long, causing her to blush.

He dropped his hand, but continued to stare into her eyes. "You know, I hope I'm not being too forward, but you're quite beautiful."

She opened her mouth to say something—what, she wasn't sure—but stopped, leaving her mouth agape. All the air in her lungs was suddenly gone. It had all evaporated at the thought he might be attracted to her as well.

Kazamir chuckled. "Please, excuse me. I shouldn't have said anything." He turned away to grab a plate of sliced, cured meat from the serving tray.

"No, no, it's quite all right, Kazamir," she said, sliding in her seat, closing the distance between the two of them. "I'm just unused to receiving compliments."

"Well, that is a shame. For someone with such talent and beauty, you should be positively drowning with both compliments and suitors."

Eira shook her head. "No. I'm too busy working, providing for my family."

He paused, setting the plate down, and turned. His face had relaxed, his mouth loose, and his eyebrows softening. "I do hope that this job will provide some relief for you and your loved ones. Just know, I feel very lucky to have stumbled upon you."

Her heart blossomed with appreciation and—something else. It was a feeling she couldn't name or place—something new. Was it admiration? Affection? "I never imagined finding someone quite like you, either. I'm so grateful for this opportunity and for welcoming me into your gorgeous home."

"It's nothing. A woman like you deserves so much more than what you've been given. Losing your father at such a young age, having to care for your siblings. I know you've struggled."

"It has been hard. And lonely."

Kazamir reached out and gave her hand a squeeze. "You aren't alone anymore, dear Eira. I'll make sure of it."

Eira didn't know what to say next. His outpouring of kindness was more than anyone had given her. She was not used to anyone freely giving away so much optimism and support. It was a strange thing to receive.

"Now, how about some lunch?" Kazamir said, breaking the silence.

The pair ate lunch, side by side, their elbows knocking the whole time. She enjoyed feeling close to him. He doted on her, serving her a meal and ensuring she ate all her food. She felt cared for, and that was a new feeling. As the oldest child, she'd spent most of her life taking care of others. Not the other way around.

The entire time she ate, she was lightheaded. It reminded her of spinning circles in the wildflower field as a child. It was an addicting feeling, the rush and exhilaration of not knowing when or how you'll land.

When lunch was over, Eira found herself lingering, but managed to drag herself back to her work. She huffed out a deep breath and pushed thoughts of Kazamir away.

While she was fussing over the next line of text, only a half an hour after finishing lunch, her belly grumbled. She looked down and frowned. She'd only just eaten. Her stomach was a traitor.

◆ ◆ ◆ ◆ ◆

Eira kicked up dust as she ambled home from the market, her arms laden with goods. She meant to visit the market sooner, but she was working long hours and getting home well after the sun retreated for its nightly slumber. But today, she made a point of leaving before the trees' shadows stretched like cats along the ground, as she wanted to surprise her brother and sister.

She walked home from the market with two piles of clothing thrown over her shoulder. To any onlooker, she looked as if a bale of laundry was dumped over her shoulders. But it would be worth seeing the looks on the twins' faces.

The walk from the market to their small home on the outskirts of the village was long. Even though Eira left the market with light on the horizon, she arrived with the stars twinkling in the night sky.

"I was wonderin' when you'd get home," Beth said from her bed. A pile of knitting lay in her lap again. "What's all that?" Beth gestured to the mess of clothing thrown over Eira's shoulders.

"It's for the twins," Eira said, beaming.

"What is it?" Hansel said, jumping from the bed.

Eira dropped her heavy leather bag, filled to the brim with cheese, dried meat and beans, onto the floor near the pantry. "Oh, these?" Eira said, tugging at the clothing. "Just something a little special for a pair of special children."

Gretel leapt from the bed. "I see pink!"

Eira chuckled as she approached the twins bed.. "Yes, pink for you Gretel, and blue for your brother. Now, get out of the way so I can lay them out."

The twins shuffled their feet, barely moving a few inches. They huddled around Eira as she worked to arrange the clothing. For Gretel, there were two pink dresses with simple ribbon work around the hem. For Hansel, were two sets of matching tunics and breeches; one a light blue, the other dark like the midnight sky.

"Didn't I tell you to get me some string and a new needle and I'd sew up their clothes?" Beth interjected.

Eira shrugged. "I was at the market, getting food for the pantry and spotted these out of the corner of my eye. I couldn't pass them by."

"A waste of money," Beth grumbled.

Eira ignored her mother and said to the children, "do you want to try them on?"

"Yes!" Gretel squealed, jumping up and down.

"Okay, well get changed while I prepare us some dinner," Eira said, moving toward her bag. "I got us some cheese."

"Oh, I want a big slice!" Hansel said as he plucked the dark blue breeches from the bed.

"We will have full plates this evening. Don't you worry, my darlings," Eira said, then turned to pull the spoils from her bag.

◆ ◆ ◆ ◆ ◆

It was difficult to turn down three gold coins per day. The money was greatly benefiting her family. In the last few days, she'd handed her mother two of three gold coins. Beth bought a few more chickens, more thread and needles, and arranged for repairs on their leaky roof.

But there was lots more her family could use like a new knife, a large stock of grain for the colder months, and new coats before the leaves started to turn.

So here she was, working on the seventh day in a row. It didn't bother her though. She loved her projects. While she labored over the scroll, a cold bead of sweat formed on her brow as she stared down at the beige practice parchment filled with sloppy marks. With her empty hand, she wiped away the wetness. The text ran together in her vision and squinted her eyes. She'd been staring at it for far too long, attempting to recreate a singular fae word. Her practice page was a mess. Nothing was looking exactly right.

Eira winced. A bolt of sudden cramping ran through her core. Breathing through the pain, she traced the feeling back down to her stomach. What was wrong with her? She'd only just eaten breakfast a few hours ago.

"Eira, are you hungry?" Kazamir asked, sticking his head through the doorway.

She nodded, but it only made her head throb with pain. Food would help. But how did he always know when her stomach was fussing? Brushing the thought away, she stood.

"Could I help you in the kitchen? I think stepping away for a moment would be good for my eyes. I'm straining, looking so intensely at the parchment."

"Yes, I can see you've worked up a sweat. Is something giving you trouble?"

As she trailed Kazamir out to the kitchen, she described the devilish fae word giving her a headache. It resembled a mish-mash of fancy j's, z's and g's in the English alphabet. But combining the curling and looping in a way that did the original justice was tricky. He nodded along, listening to her troubles.

"It sounds challenging, but you are a diligent worker. I trust you will figure it out," Kazamir said, giving her a reassuring smile.

A weight lifted from Eira's shoulders at the sight. His belief gave her a renewed sense of her ability to complete this project. Years had passed since she'd felt confidence in her talents. Being a provider to not only the twins, but also Beth, had worn her down.

"How can I help?" Eira asked, sidling up to the wooden counter.

"Would you mind slicing the meat?"

She nodded.

"The knives are there," Kazamir said, pointing to a drawer on her right. "The cured pig leg is at the end of the counter. I'll slice us some apples."

Eira procured a knife and went to work slicing thin pieces of meat. The meat fell away easily from the bone. A small pile gathered on the counter.

Engrossed in her task, Eira stood erect when a loud series of thuds filled the space. As her eyes landed on a few apples which had fallen to the floor, she hissed. A sharp pain seared across her hand.

Kazamir was bending to pick up the apples when he stopped mid-motion and rushed over. The knife in Eira's hand fell, clattering against the countertop. She lifted the opposite hand, examining her injury. She'd sliced her thumb open in the commotion. Her eyes caught on the thick line of bright red blood running down her palm. A sharp, metallic and almost floral scent wafted around her, and she felt spittle develop on her tongue.

When she looked up, she saw Kazamir's eyes open wide. His gaze locked on her hand.

"I'm so sorry. I've made a mess," she said.

Kazamir shook his head, as if being released from a trance. "You're fine," he said, smiling.

And when he smiled, Eira could have sworn she saw something there in his mouth—something pointed and unnatural. Her heart squeezed tightly with fear.

But when he stepped closer, putting a hand on her shoulder, and looked over her face with concern, everything was normal. He smiled again, and it was without anything unusual or scary. She'd imagined it in her heightened state, she realized.

"Let's get you cleaned up. Come over to the sink. I'll grab some fresh water and bandages," he said.

◆ ◆ ◆ ◆ ◆

Nearly a month passed with Eira returning to Kazamir's house each day. As she stared down at the now decorated parchment, she felt a swell of pride. She was sure she was done, or almost done. It was difficult to tell when all the t's were crossed and i's were dotted, in a figurative sense, with creative works.

As she set down her quill, her stomach tightened with hunger. A deep, wanting ache swelled within her. The feeling nearly sent her doubling over in her chair.

"It sounds like you're hungry," Kazamir said from his desk opposite her. "I'll go grab us lunch."

"Don't know why, but I've been so famished lately. It's so early," she said, rubbing her belly.

"It's all that creative work. It takes a lot of energy." Kazamir strode over to the library door. "I'll be right back."

If Eira was being honest with herself, the recent increase in her hunger levels was alarming. She was always famished, even after finishing a meal. It was as if nothing truly satisfied her any longer. Food itself was becoming less and less appealing.

A building pressure was developing in the confines of her skull, alongside the deep void in her stomach. Each morning she awoke, her head was clear and without pain. But as the day waned on and hunger grew in her belly, so did the ache within her mind.

She shook her head, then picked up her inkwells, quills, and other knickknacks, placing them back in her bag. When one neared the end of a project, it was best to step away, give it time to steep and come back to it with fresh eyes. If one kept fussing with it, it was possible to overwork the piece.

Kazamir slid back into the room. She joined him in their usual spot near the fireplace. He passed her a cup of tea with honey, and a plate with bread, a hunk of white cheese, and some berries. But all of it appeared stale and dull to Eira. The cheese, in particular, stunk of rot and twisted her stomach in knots.

"Are you going to eat, dear Eira?" Kazamir asked after she had sat and stared at her plate for some time.

Scrunching her nose, she looked up at him. "It doesn't smell right."

His eyebrows furrowed. "What do you mean? The bread is not molding. And the cheese I bought fresh from the market just yesterday evening."

She shrugged. "I don't know. I can't explain it."

"Well, why don't you try a bite and see if it clears up? I promise, it's all very fresh."

Looking back down at her plate, Eira frowned. All the food looked terribly unsatisfying. But maybe he was right—trying a small bit wouldn't hurt. She reached for the bread and took a hesitant bite from the thick slice. It tasted bland and dry, like sawdust in her mouth. She shook her head. "I think I will pass on lunch today," she said, placing the small white plate on the table.

Kazamir looked up at her, his features distressed. "I'm so sorry. Are you feeling ill?"

Eira stood up. "Maybe. My head hurts. And I believe I'm done or close to, anyway. It is best for me to come look at it tomorrow with clear eyes."

Kazamir smiled up at her. "This is excellent news!" He paused, clearing his throat. "The completion of the project, that is... not you feeling under the weather."

Her head throbbed, darkening the edges of her vision. She pressed a hand to her temple, willing the pain away.

"Are you all right? Should I join you on your walk home?" Kazamir asked.

Waving a hand, she turned away, walking toward her desk. "No. I'm okay. Don't trouble yourself. I just need some sleep."

◆ ◆ ◆ ◆ ◆

She'd been asleep since mid-afternoon. Her mother clucked over her when she arrived home, stating she looked pale as a spectre. Eira waved her mother away, hiding beneath the covers.

281

Darkness was all she could see when her eyes finally sprang open. The dark fabric of the night wrapped around her like a blanket. Now, she lay awake listening to the awful grumbling of her stomach. The sound was so loud. Eira was afraid it would wake the children. The smell of something had awoken her from her slumber. Her mouth salivated at some mysterious scent, it was bright metallic and floral—it smelled familiar.

Eira rose from the bed. Her feet glided across the floor like she was being guided by some invisible hand. She licked her lips at the delectable smell floating in the night air. Whatever it was, she needed to have it. Her heart fluttered, drawing her closer to its origin. Her hunger would be over soon.

Her feet stopped moving when she reached the side of Beth's bed. Looking down at her mother, her stomach moaned again. Cocking her head to the side, she could hear something. *Thump. Thump. Thump.* Her mother's thrumming pulse. And it was the most beautiful song she ever heard, like a gurgling stream just waiting for Eira to fall to her knees at its welcoming banks.

Kneeling down on the floor, she lifted her ear towards her mother. The pulsing sound consumed her fully. She stayed like that for several minutes, captivated. She imagined the liquid in her mother's veins flowing down her throat, warm and wet. The image sent a shiver running down her spine.

Thick strings of drool formed in her mouth as she listened. A frenzied feeling rumbled in her core and shot down her limbs. Her mind washed over with confusion as her body began to shake with need. Sweat broke out along her forehead, fear descending upon her. Her body wanted something it should not want. It craved the blood coursing through her mother's flesh.

But she could not stop herself. The feeling was too strong. She could not help herself from being pulled under by the storming tide. Her body convulsed as the sensation to feed, to eat, turned over every cell in her body.

And she felt herself change in that moment.

She leaned in towards her mother's neck, a plump vein pulsed there, ready for her to take. But a cracking sensation deep within Eira's jaw caused her to cry out. She felt her teeth rearranging. Searing pain ripped through her upper jaw and the taste of her own blood was thick on her tongue.

Beth jolted from sleep at the sound of Eira's shouts. Eira fell to the floor, gripping her head, attempting to soothe the ache radiating across her skull.

"Eira! What are you doing?" Beth asked, looking down at her daughter.

But Eira barely registered her mother's words. Horned, fiery pain filled each finger. She writhed in agony, a savage groan ripping through her chest.

"What is wrong, child?" Beth asked. She got out of bed and knelt on the floor. Reaching out, she grabbed Eira by the shoulders and hauled her up. "Are you all right?"

The pain faded quickly like a freak summer storm. Eira's head snapped up, cocking to the side. Beth gasped. In her peripheral, Eira caught sight of herself in the dirty mirror and saw her eyes glow in the dark, golden like pots of fresh honey. Her mouth was agape, displaying long, piercing fangs.

The hunger was overwhelming. The *thump, thump, thump* was like a siren's song. Eira couldn't ignore it any longer. She moved, like the wind, fast and silent.

Eira's sharp teeth sunk into the soft flesh of her mother's neck like it was butter. It was a most satisfying feeling, sending shivers down her back. The rush of blood was immediate. The hot liquid spurted up in her face, across her lips, and wet her tongue. Her eyes fluttered back. It was sweet. Oh, so sweet. The roaring hunger in her raged for *more, more, more.*

Beth tried to shout, but the sound was weak and strangled, like the dying squeals of a butchered pig.

"What's going on?" Gretel asked, her voice soft and cracking with sleep.

Eira was blinded by the luscious nectar. She barely registered the voice of her sister. The blood on her tongue was all she knew. It was all she could see and feel. She dug her teeth in further, *sucking, sucking, sucking.* It consumed her. The sinful liquid flooded down her throat, easing the burning hunger in her stomach as it filled all the cracks and crevices. It soothed over the ache she'd felt for the last two weeks. She continued to drink as she felt her face flush with life. Her vision became clearer with each gulp.

"Eira? What are you doing?" Hansel cried from across the room. "Eira! Stop! Leave Ma alone!"

But Eira did not notice her brother and sister, not until the hunger ebbed away. She stared down at the drained form of her mother with wide eyes and a knot in her throat.

Her eyes caught on the thick, bright red liquid coating her hands. At the end of each digit were not nails, but long, piercing talons. Fear jolted through her once again. What had she done? What had she become?

The rich, heady scent of more fresh blood drifted over to her and caught her attention, drowning the fear. She lifted her ear again, following the soft thump of heartbeats across the room. She could have more. There was still more. She stood up, dropping her mother's body to the ground with a loud thud. She wanted more.

She finally noticed the children huddled under their blanket, quivering in fear.

Eira pulled at her hair in anguish. *No. Not Hansel. Not Gretel.* She could not harm them, even if she'd become a monster.

"Eira," Hansel said and sobbed for a breath. "What's wrong with you?"

But they would taste so good. She could feel the thrumming of their blood inside of her. The constant beating of their hearts. They'd taste delicious.

No, no, no, she told herself. She thought of Hansel and Gretel in their beautiful new clothes, the smile on their faces when clean, fresh fabric touched their skin. A memory, like a hazy dream, of telling them bedtime stories of monsters just like her.

What had she become? *Not the children.* Her hunger called for more, but now, with her mother's blood filling her belly, she was able to fight it. But only slightly.

Grabbing her head in confusion, she cried out. Her screams pierced the night. The children scrambled back in their bed, pulling up the blankets. Her heart cracked at the sight—they were scared of her. How did this happen?

Eira threw open the door, ripping it clear off its hinges. She hurled the wood slab to the ground, and it splintered into pieces. "Run!" she yelled at the children.

The twins clutched onto each other, unmoving.

"Hansel, Gretel—out! I don't trust myself to not harm you. Go!" Her face was red with not only blood, but with the effort of holding back her hunger. "The neighbors will care for you." She backed away from the door, clenching her hands at her sides, her mouth salivating for more. "Get out! Please," she sobbed.

Hansel moved, then hesitated. But Eira continued to back away, curling herself into a ball in the corner, and the children dashed out of the door, crying the whole way.

When they were gone, Eira didn't dare move for several moments. She allowed the silence, the absence of the children, to wash over her. Tears welled in her eyes, in direct opposition to the dark, raging hunger swirling through her. But she knew she could not stay here forever. She needed to leave. There was no saving her mother, not now. But if she ran very far away, at least she could spare the twins. They'd be safe. Sadness clanged through her like a death knell. She'd never be able to teach Hansel how to read. And the thought tore her heart in two as she dashed into the shadows.

◆ ◆ ◆ ◆ ◆

There was only one place she could think to go—Kazamir. Something within the depths of her being knew it was his fault. This was the doing of magic, ancient and powerful. She could feel it coursing through her body, bubbling under the surface. And he was the only one who knew of such arcane things. Was it the scroll? Or the food he fed her each day? The prickling of magic was alive in his library. She'd felt it as she worked, whispering to her each day as she pored endlessly over the fae parchment.

Eira moved like a wraith through the woods, avoiding the roads. She didn't want to come close to another living being lest she put their life in jeopardy.

The speed at which she moved was inhuman. She'd become the surrounding darkness, a terror of the night. She was carried on the backs of shadows, arriving at Kazamir's door while the moon still hung heavy and pregnant in the sky.

For several long minutes, she stood there, staring at the ornately carved door, seething. Anger blazed within her, a raging fire in her veins. Why had he done this? What had he turned her into? The rage flickered, like a candle caught in the breeze—was it possible he didn't know the magic he'd unleashed upon her by giving her access to the scroll? But then, she stomped on the thought and the rage ignited once again.

Eira put her hand on the doorknob and found that the door was locked, but it didn't deter her. She stalked to the back of the home and into the garden. In the dark, the space looked devoid of life as if it had transformed in the presence of the moon. The trees were curled and knotted. The flowers were without blooms. It didn't resemble the bright, ethereal space she stared out into each day.

As she approached the large windows of the library, she caught a glimpse of herself in the reflection and flinched. Her skin was milky white, her cheeks sunken in, and her eyes were golden, like a feral animal. She opened her mouth and inspected her sharpened teeth. She had not imagined Kazamir's fangs. Disgusting. That was what she was now, something from her stories.

With a deep breath, she looked past herself and into the library. It looked just the same as it did when she was there earlier today. But in the gleaming moonlight, something caught her eye. In the case at the back of the room, a golden object glowed. The dagger.

There was a reason Kazamir had a dagger fabled to kill fae locked away. He was one of them. It was all an illusion. She could see it clearly now, as if the sun shined down, clearing all the fog lingering within her mind. It was not the food but the scroll, and the ancient words she recreated—it was a spell.

Eira took several steps back before launching into a run along the cobblestone path. She moved like the wind. Each step was light but powerful. Approaching the house, she sprang into the air and burst through the windows with a crash. Glass fell all around her and cut into her skin as she rolled across the floor. But there was no time to stop. He would hear the sound and come running.

She dashed across the room, passing the glittering scroll on the desk, and stopped in front of the case. She clenched her fists—anger, pain, and sadness coalesced like twisting vines in her gut. Thuds sounded overhead. He was coming. With a scream, she slammed her hand through the glass.

The door to the library swung open the moment her hand touched the blade. The pain was unbearable. Searing heat scorched her palm and ran down her arm like lightning. She crumpled to the floor.

"Eira, darling..." Kazamir said, striding across the room. "You need to calm down. Stop this."

Looking up, she saw it all now, clear as the moon that hung in the sky. He looked like her. The golden glow of life, which glittered across his skin, was gone. He still glowed, but he was pale like the moon which steals its light from the sun. She sneered up at him.

"Get away from me!" she screamed. "This is your fault!"

Kazamir stepped forward. "My dear Eira," he cooed.

"Do not use your sweet venom on me! You're a monster. A fae. You did this to me!"

He stopped several feet away and knelt down, looking at her. His brow furrowed and the edges of his lips turned down. "You do not understand, Eira, what it's like. It's so lonely."

"So, you changed me without asking? Without my consent? You cast a spell on me!" She dug her long talons into the floor, marring the wood.

He shook his head. "It's ancient magic that only works when written. You cast the magic yourself as you worked on creating the scroll."

The bottom of her eyes filled with wetness as a sob crawled up her throat. She screamed into the floor, banging her fists. She'd kill him. Looking up, she narrowed her eyes at him. "You had no right."

"You're correct. I did not. But the fae, before they disappeared, cast this spell on me. It was punishment for my greed, my thirst for riches. I'd stolen from them. They gave me a choice: become one of them or die. For decades, I've lived alone, and searched for a way to change it. To break the spell. And no matter how many fae texts or artifacts I found, none of them fixed the monster I'd become. Though, it did help me learn magic— illusions—to mask who I was so I could live amongst people again. But there was nothing to end the thirst for both blood or riches. And I couldn't keep on living like this by myself... and I felt the fates pulling me toward you. The fae magic pointed me to you... And when I met you on the road, so beautiful... I knew it had to be you." His eyes turned pleading. "I had a choice, but didn't extend that same kindness to you. I'm sorry, Eira."

As Kazamir talked, she seethed. Red hot anger boiled in her veins. Without another word, she wrapped her hands around the hilt of the dagger and leapt up from the floor. Pain coursed through her hand, but she didn't let go this time.

Before she could spin around, large hands wrapped around her shoulders and held her in place. "Put the blade down, darling. We don't want to do anything rash."

Her eyes flared, and she pushed against him, throwing him back. White hot pain zinged down her arm and lit up her torso. The magic from the blade was searing her insides like she'd swallowed hot coals. She wouldn't last long under the blade's magic. Kazamir stumbled back, and she spun on her heels, raising the dagger.

"No, Eira!" he yelled.

But it was too late—she was already moving. There was nothing he could do to stop her as the blade plunged downward, slicing through his chest. She stared into his stunned face, her eyes wide with adrenaline. His features fractured a moment later with a mixture of both anger and sadness. Baring her teeth, she twisted the knife.

All around the blade, light glowed. Letting go of it, she stepped back. The light grew in intensity. She watched the light fill his whole body, shining under his skin. His screams filled the room as he fell to his knees, grabbing his chest. Golden rays burst forth, out of his mouth and eyes, and filled his body. It was as if the sun was unleashed from a long slumber. Eira stepped back, covering her face with an arm.

Kazamir's screams trailed off several seconds later. The light disappeared. It was dark once again as something thudded to the floor. Dropping her arm, her whole body stilled as she looked down at what remained of the man. A pile of ash sat upon the wooden floorboards, and within their dusty center, the dagger glinted in the moonlight.

She fell to the floor, sobs racked her body. This was just too much. The weight and guilt of killing her own mother. The terrifying revelation she was now a monster and there was nothing, nothing at all to fix it, left her filled with dread. It was a heavy stone in her gut. She didn't know what to do or where to go next. But at least the children were safe from her ravaging hunger.

It wasn't until the shimmering rays of the morning sun poured in through the broken window that she peeled herself off the floor. Her body felt as if it was hollow and all she had left was a dark, all-consuming void. A swirling mass of sorrow making a home in her soul. If she still had a soul. She wasn't sure.

As she looked around the room at the destruction, her eyes caught on two things; the dagger and the scroll. She turned around and marched to the fireplace. Throwing in several logs, she ripped paper from a random book and used it as kindling. A small wooden box sat upon the hearth from which she pulled out flint and steel. Sparks ignited and danced in the air as she coaxed the fire to life. When the fire was blazing, heat dancing along her skin, she stalked across the room.

She stared down at the glittering parchment. In this new form, she could see the magic skittering across the paper. It was as if it was alive, swirling and moving across the page. But it didn't matter how beautiful it was—it was dangerous, just like her. She snatched up both the original and the immaculate copy she created, and turned back to the fire.

Without any ceremony or hesitation, she dumped the scrolls in the blaze. But she didn't stop there. She whirled around and snagged any book or scroll which was alive with any pulse of magic. They all became fodder, turning to ashes as the fire gobbled them up. The magic unraveled, crackling and hissing, as the flames roared to life.

When there was nothing left but mundane dusty books, she turned her back to the hearth, not bothering to put it out. She stopped and knelt in front of the pile of ash—all that was left of Kazamir's body. The dagger glowed from within the shallow mass. She pulled up her nightgown, and using her talons, ripped off a scrap of fabric. She didn't dare touch the dagger bare-handed again. Her palm was red and blistered. Through the thin slip of fabric, she felt the magic pulsing. It was still hot to the touch, but manageable, as she walked out of the room into the hall.

From the foyer, she stole a heavy cloak from a hook and threw it over her shoulders. After depositing the dagger in a pocket, she patted the blade. It would stay with her always. If she ever crossed paths with Hansel and Gretel again, this blade would be their protection.

Eira approached the front door, her eye catching on a host of gold trinkets on a sideboard, and she thought better. She whirled around the room, filling her pockets with any item fashioned from gold. If she could not be there to care for her brother and sister, she could ensure they at least had money to feed themselves.

With heavy pockets and a heavier heart, she walked out the front door into the daylight and didn't look back. The sun kissed her milky white cheeks.

And striding into the woods, a hunger for blood bellowed in her belly.

◆ ◆ ◆ ◆ ◆

On a moonless night, along a small gurgling brook, Eira stepped out from a small hut crafted from twisted branches, moss and overgrown ferns. The dark fabric of the night hugged her like an old friend. She moved deftly through the forest, never making a noise. After a year of living in the forest surrounding her old village, Eira had memorized all the paths.

At the edge of the woods, wrapped in a cloak, she peered at the bare farm where Hansel and Gretel lived. She stood there often, watching over them. During many of her visits, she left gifts and treasures upon their doorstep. Sometimes, Eira left a few coins stolen from the limp bodies of her victims, and other times, baskets of berries. She hoped it helped to keep their bellies full.

But a plague moved over the land in recent months. The sickness did not settle in the bones of people, but ate through the crops, rotting them from the inside out. People were starving, driving those desperate and without support into the forest looking for nourishment. These strays were a boon for Eira, who was rarely hungry.

Unfortunately, nothing good in life came without a price. She'd learnt that lesson the hard way.

In recent days, Eira found Hansel and Gretel meandering in the forest, foraging for whatever they could find—berries, mushrooms, nuts. Eira watched them from afar, never letting herself get too close. For if she ever caught a whiff of her siblings' sweet scent on the breeze, she wouldn't be able to resist.

Eira moved swiftly across the empty field. Against the dark, she was but a shadow, a trick of the eyes. She was greeted by the stone face of the house. Climbing the two front stairs, Eira hunched over and placed her hand upon the cold bricks.

"May the sun always kiss your cheeks," she said. She hoped her words carried themselves on the breath of the night and drifted into her siblings' dreams, warming their hearts.

Floorboards creaked. Eira bolted upright. The pitter patter of small footsteps grew closer, moving toward the front door. In a flurry of movement, she fled.

And on the doorstep, Eira left a golden blade and a note, baring a warning—

Beware the wicked fae in the woods.

CODE RED

C. P. ASHTON

An outbreak of deadly lunabelle flowers has engulfed the futuristic city of Three Oaks, plunging ten thousand people into a toxin-induced sleep.

As the foremost expert on the parasitic species, disgraced botanist Scarlet may be the only one with the expertise to formulate the antidote. With the help of two idealistic interns and one enigma of a barista, she'll need to infiltrate her old biotech firm to have any chance at developing a cure before time runs out.

But there's danger around every corner, a predator stalks from the shadows, and the further Scarlet strays into the dark underbelly of the firm, the more she realizes this outbreak isn't what it seems.

Code RED is a high-tech twist on "Red Riding Hood."

As the last sliver of moonlight winked into shadow, the city stopped.

Three Oaks was a glowing testament to the future of green technology. The city's glass eco-dome glinted gold through the starry nights, a faceted gem set neatly into the rocky desert landscape. Yet under a new moon no different from any other, as the desert grew dark and a cool breeze swept across the sand outside, the lunabelles bloomed within.

Across pavement and buildings, clothing and skin, microscopic spores that had lain dormant in the light of the moon suddenly sparked to life. They erupted into spidering roots, siphoning energy from everything they gripped. Curling vines wove and snaked over every surface while delicate, snowy blooms burst open, spewing countless spores into the air like shimmering, iridescent fireworks.

The citizens living in the North Quarter of the city slumped at their dinner tables. They crumpled in the streets and collapsed atop their desks as the lunabelles overwhelmed them. Children, already tucked into their beds, went unnaturally still. In the breadth of a heartbeat, ten thousand people slipped into a deep and dreamless sleep under the spell of the plants' toxins. All the while, the lunabelles slowly drained their bodies.

When the crescent moon returned the following night, the victims would wither and crumble to dust along with the rare flowers. The clock was ticking.

◆ ◆ ◆ ◆ ◆

Scarlet scowled at the objectively punchable face of Logan O'Connell—all twelve of them. The entire wall was lined with televisions, and Logan was on every single one as he prepared to hold an emergency press conference. She was far too hungover and not nearly caffeinated enough to deal with his bullshit this morning.

In the chaos and panic, no one had stopped Scarlet from entering the atrium of Herbatech headquarters in the heart of Three Oaks. The security guards sat at the desk, consumed by the news on their computer screens, and Scarlet had taken the opportunity to quietly slink off to the side of the lobby. Logan stood outside the front doors of the atrium on the black granite steps, but Scarlet didn't care to run into the press, and the view was better on the televisions, anyway.

The atrium of Herbatech headquarters was a sleek glass and marble showcase for the company's patented Phytogrid technology, the centerpiece of which was one of three genetically modified one-hundred-meter-tall oak trees in the city. It reached skyward through the back wall of the cavernous lobby, emanating a warm golden energy along its trunk. The light flowed seamlessly from the trunk into a series of manufactured roots, which wove across the floors and walls, embedded within strips of emerald moss in a wide inlaid hexagon pattern amid the polished marble. The Phytogrid harnessed plants' natural electrical signals to transmit power and communications. The revolutionary technology had put Herbatech on the map—figuratively and literally—about fifteen years previously.

By building a climate-controlled eco-dome and planting the fast-growing, power-rich oaks within it, Herbatech had been able to tap into a massive amount of steady, clean energy. Herbatech constructed the experimental city within the dome to put the tech to the test, not to mention launch the ultimate marketing campaign. Three Oaks and its eco-dome were one of a kind, but that wouldn't always be the case. Within a few short years, Herbatech had grown to a multi-billion dollar powerhouse with Logan O'Connell at the helm.

The television screens before Scarlet were rooted directly into the glowing grid. Typically, they would have been tuned to various business news and rolling stock market updates. But today, there was only one news story, and Logan's smug face was at the center of it on every channel. Of course, being a visionary tech genius wasn't enough for him. He was strategically positioning himself to come out of the current crisis as the city's shiny new savior. A news anchor spoke over the footage, recounting the same few facts they'd been reporting on loop since dawn, as the world waited for the conference to begin.

Logan ran a hand through his chestnut hair. He was one of those wolfishly handsome types—all sharp angles and piercing eyes. His crisp bespoke suit cost more than most people earned in a year. Sunlight shone off Herbatech's glass façade behind him, so he seemed to glow like a messiah for the cameras. Scarlet knew better than to believe it was a coincidence. Everything from Logan's expression to his statement to the position of the cameras would have been precisely engineered by Herbatech's crisis PR team—a group with which Scarlet had gotten all too acquainted in the last six months. She crossed her arms as if to hold herself together.

When he finally cleared his throat, the breaking updates that had been scrolling across the bottom of the screen were replaced with *Logan O'Connell: Herbatech Cofounder and CEO*. The rambling voiceover halted abruptly.

Logan's voice was clear and rehearsed as he spoke into the two dozen microphones mounted before him. "Shortly after four o'clock this morning, Herbatech responded to a regionalized environmental danger, or Code RED, in the North Quarter of Three Oaks. The airlocks were immediately sealed, and the quarter was quarantined from the rest of the Three Oaks dome to contain a large-scale ecological outbreak. At this time, we are confident that there has been no further contamination to other parts of the city. Our team has since positively identified the invasive species as lunabelles."

Scarlet failed to suppress an indignant *hmph*. Logan may have been a tech genius, but he didn't know anything when it came to the botany side of Herbatech's business. That was Scarlet's expertise.

Before dawn that morning, Scarlet's phone had vibrated incessantly until it skittered off her nightstand, knocking over an empty wine bottle. The phone hit the floor with a muffled *thump*. She'd groped for it in the dark, then squinted blearily at Logan O'Connell's text. *'What are these?'* he'd asked. The message accompanied a photo showing a clump of snowy white bell-shaped flowers. The telltale iridescent sheen over the dark foliage was enough to make Scarlet's blood run cold in her veins. 'Lunabelles,' she'd responded immediately. Then she'd caught the first mag-rail train across the city.

On screen, Logan's brow creased with practiced concern and determination for the news cameras. "Lunabelle flowers are extremely rare and parasitic. They bloom solely during the new moon and are almost always deadly as the crescent moon returns at dusk the following day. Herbatech has received emergency approval for our proprietary antidote, which has been in development for fifteen years. We are already mobilizing to manufacture as much antidote as possible and strategize a dispersal plan."

The reporters erupted, jostling forward and shouting over each other, lobbing incoherent questions until Logan eventually acknowledged one of them. "Kate?" The crowd immediately hushed in anticipation.

"Kaitlyn Hunter, Channel Seven," the reporter announced. "Has the spread of the spores been made worse by the air recirculation within the Three Oaks eco-dome?"

Logan shook his head. "On the contrary, if it weren't for Herbatech's revolutionary city design—with quadrant airlocks and full ventilation management—there's no telling how far the spores might have spread in an uncontrolled environment. Our staff's quick actions have already spared the remaining quarters of the city from this natural disaster."

Scarlet rolled her eyes. Of course he would never miss an opportunity to spin a story in his favor. Anything to control the narrative. After the events of the last six months, he probably had his rabid pack of lawyers on speed dial.

"You also mentioned lunabelles are extremely rare," continued the reporter. "How does an outbreak like this happen?"

"It's too early to tell where this contamination originated. For now, our priority as stewards of this city and as fellow citizens, is to come together to save as many lives as we can."

Again, there was uproar as the crowd volleyed another round of questions. The Channel Seven reporter attempted to slip another in while she still had the floor. "The North Quarter is home to just over ten thousand residents. Can Herbatech really manufacture enough antidote doses today to—"

Logan spoke over them all. "I won't be taking any more questions at this time. Herbatech needs to get to work. We thank you for your continued trust."

Scarlet chewed her lip, staring at the screens even after he walked out of frame. Logan didn't know the first thing about lunabelles, and she got the feeling he hadn't spoken to anyone else who did, either. Everything he'd said reeked of legal.

A tidal wave of reporters' voices surged, only to be smothered as the front doors resealed in Logan O'Connell's wake. Scarlet spun—her head throbbing in protest—just in time to see Logan march into the lobby, Italian leather loafers taking long clicking strides across the polished marble and the glowing Phytogrid which laced through it.

"Logan!" Scarlet's sneakers squeaked as she jogged to catch up with him.

He turned slowly and gave a huff of a laugh as he reached the elevators.

The guard behind the main desk did a double-take as Scarlet rushed past, and he scrambled to intercept her. "M—ma'am, sorry, but you can't be here."

"It's my building," Scarlet argued. "My name is still on the deed."

"It's also on the restraining order," Logan interrupted. He crossed his arms as she approached, puffing out his chest, but he waved off the security guard nonetheless. "And where do you think you're going this morning, my dear?" Logan snarled, teeth glinting.

"Having a picnic with my grandmother. What do you think?" There wasn't enough sarcasm in the world to do it justice. She glanced across the lobby at the roiling mass of reporters before she pressed her fingertip to the elevator button. "We shouldn't talk here." The cool xylem gel molded into every bump and crevice of her fingerprint, only to dim at her touch, rejecting her credentials.

Logan smirked and reached around her to press the button himself. She glared. Familiar icy silence crystallized between them. Logan examined his expensive wristwatch as Scarlet subtly tried but failed to straighten her wrinkled blouse and messy blond bun in the reflection of the stainless steel doors. None of it had felt important when she'd hurriedly dressed in the dark before rushing here, but

Logan's smug smirk had a way of wheedling into her mind and wreaking havoc on her confidence. A moment later, the elevator hissed open.

"Locking me out of my own damn building is a whole new level of petty," she muttered as she stepped inside.

"Basic security measures, especially considering your shaky legal standing." He followed her in and pressed the button for the eleventh floor. A gold flash acknowledged his clearance once more.

Scarlet folded her arms over her chest. "None of that is final, Logan. We haven't even signed our *own* damn paperwork yet."

He didn't respond. The second the elevator doors closed, he stalked forward, hands flashing up to slam against the wall on either side of her. She flinched and only managed half a step backward before her back collided with cold steel. Logan crowded her entire field of vision as the humming Phytogrid shuttled them smoothly upward between magnetic rails. Scarlet swallowed hard, her throat suddenly sticky. He had her caged like prey. A shiver clawed down her spine, every nerve in her body lighting up, instinct screaming at her to flee, but she ignored it, determined to stand what little ground she had. The sharp peppery spice of his cologne and the damp heat of his breath enveloped her as Logan leaned in close—too close. It was familiar in the worst way. She forced herself to raise her chin to meet his icy gaze with what she hoped would pass for a defiant glare. Eye to eye, nose to nose. He wanted her to know who held the power here. She was insignificant. The corner of his lip curled as that stark reminder furrowed her brow.

The elevator *dinged* to announce their arrival, and only then did Logan relax his stance. Scarlet's breath escaped as relief washed over her, though she tried to mask it as an annoyed sigh. Brushing his arm aside, she stepped out of the elevator, into the eleventh floor lobby, and straight through to the executive office. Every step, she had to force. She hated the way he could undermine her very thoughts without a word, but she hoped she could fake some semblance of strength.

"We won't be long," Logan told his assistant at the front desk. Then he closed the heavy office doors behind them.

The office was large, surrounded almost entirely by windows. The glowing white roots of the Phytogrid network laced across the office floor, embedded in emerald moss between the polished marble tiles, just like in the lobby. A pair of modern chairs sat before a glass desk, atop which stood a large computer display and laptop, rooted directly into the Phytogrid. To one side, a cabinet prominently displayed a series of gilded statuettes. Each featured a stylized hand holding a pointed leaf and recognized *Logan O'Connell* for *Outstanding contributions in the field of green technology*. Everything was sleek and minimalistic with the intent of drawing the eye to the most impressive feature of the room.

Above them, the glass ceiling barely brushed the canopy of the great oak. The tree's thick boughs extended out over the room and its leaves rustled in the eco-dome's circulating air. For visitors, it was magical, especially in the middle of the desert, but it was all performative for Logan.

He strode to the back of the room and turned to face her from behind the desk. "Surely you're not just out for a walk amongst the flowers, Scarlet. What are you doing here?"

"Come on, Logan," Scarlet sighed. "You're the one who reached out to me. There are ten thousand people who will die tonight if Herbatech can't get this figured out. I'm here to help."

He raised an eyebrow. "I appreciate the quick identification, but that is the only reason I allowed you to save face coming up here instead of having security throw you straight out of the lobby in front of the press. Again."

She ignored the dig and tried to push the events of that disastrous day from her mind. He was trying to get under her skin. Trying to shake her. That was the way he worked. "I'm the leading expert on lunabelles, and you know it. I was on the verge of developing an antidote, before…" she tripped over her words as he raised an eyebrow. "This spread is unprecedented. Are you sure this isn't some new mutation? Lunabelles usually bloom in small clusters, maybe infecting half a dozen backcountry hikers per year. They don't take over entire cities."

"That's what I thought, too, which is why I was surprised by your immediate identification of the species from a single photo with no context."

"I studied them for fifteen years, Logan. Of course I recognize them. CEO or not, you've always been the technology guy. No one expects you to know everything about the botany side of this business, but you're out there telling the press that you still don't know where the contamination originated."

"I don't see how any of this is relevant."

"That's the problem. Lunabelles bloom in very distinct generations. You have to sequence this specific bloom's genome to formulate the antidote, and the moment you do that, you'll know a lot about where it came from."

Something flashed in his eyes, and she charged on, hoping she was getting through.

"The antidote is a two part system," she explained. "There's the vector, which allows us to deliver instructions directly to the lunabelle roots, and then there's the instructions themselves—the catalyst, which is a fragment of DNA. It has to be precisely engineered. It latches onto the lunabelles' kill switch gene and short circuits it so that the plant dies back without killing the host. I think the catalyst must have been where my last trial went wrong, but I can help. The catalyst has to be manufactured and added to the vector within hours of use, or it breaks down, so we have time to do this right. There are too many lives at risk to not throw everything we have at this."

Scarlet's last flicker of hope that Logan was truly listening was snuffed out as his face twisted back to his signature smirk. "Herbatech is already manufacturing the antidote. We have this under control."

"How—?"

"By all means, go frolic through the North Quarter. Pick your own flowers." He sipped his coffee, and dread settled in Scarlet's stomach. "But considering your track record,

I'm not sure you know nearly as much about lunabelles as you seem to think, Scar."

Heat prickled up the back of her neck, her cheeks flushing. She set her jaw, determined not to let his barbs sink in, though they always left their mark. She closed the gap between her and the desk in three long strides and leaned over it, but he looked down his pointed nose at her before she could speak.

"I'm going to have to ask you to leave the premises now," he said. "After your last incident, Herbatech cannot afford to be in any way associated with our disgraced cofounder and her disastrous history with this antidote."

Scarlet stared, frozen, barely able to comprehend his words as he pressed the intercom button on his desk.

"Yes, Mr. O'Connell?" came a voice through the speaker.

"We're finished in here. Please show Mrs. O'Connell out."

Scarlet backed slowly away as he released the button, her skin crawling, hands shaking. "You know it's *always* been Dr., not Mrs., and paperwork finalized or not, I think it's safe to go ahead and start swapping that for Dr. Perrault instead of O'Connell." It had been almost twenty years since she'd used her maiden name, but so much had changed. Being in Logan's presence again today, she couldn't wait to reclaim it.

With a noncommittal shrug, he looked her straight in the eye. He knew he'd gotten to her. He always did.

A pair of security guards moved in through the door and approached her. It wasn't the first time she was being escorted out of this office. Her pulse raced, and it took everything in her to keep her breath from doing the same as adrenaline poured into her veins. She swallowed hard before she found her voice again. It came out softer than she wanted, but it was all she could manage. "What do you think I'm going to do, Logan? You can call off the wolves." Scarlet evaded the security guards' grasp.

"Can't be too careful." His teeth glinted. "The last time you were in this building, we had five people die at your hands."

"Logan, you son of a—" but she stopped herself. It wasn't just Logan and the security guards watching. Logan's assistant peered in from his desk, and behind him, the hallway teemed with health officials, board members, and reporters. She gritted her teeth, throwing Logan one last seething glare before storming out of the office.

In her rush to leave the room, she didn't think about the elevator. The button darkened at her touch, and so did her rage. "Damn it!" She could feel a dozen sets of eyes boring into her back. Just knowing Logan's smug smirk was among them made her blood boil.

"Excuse me!" A lanky, well-dressed twenty-something edged beside Scarlet, seemingly oblivious to the scene that had just played out. "Coffee emergency." They pressed the elevator button.

Seething, Scarlet followed them in. The kid was probably young enough that Scarlet could have been their mother, yet they had access privileges in her building. Scarlet wasn't technically allowed within a hundred meters. A scream threatened to burst from her lungs, but she settled for a shaking exhale as the doors closed. The coffee kid pressed the button for the cafeteria on level three.

She closed her eyes against it all. Finally, away from Logan's intimidating presence, Scarlet was able to focus on the science, and she was terrified that none of it made sense. The scale of the bloom was unprecedented. Lunabelles simply didn't bloom like they did last night in the North Quarter. When she'd studied them in the wild, she found them in small clusters in alpine forests. The only time she'd heard of them being found in an urban area, there were still only a few people affected at a single park. But no other city was encased in a dome like Three Oaks.

Logan was either clueless, or there was something he wasn't sharing. She didn't know how Herbatech could have formulated an effective catalyst without sequencing the genome, and if she couldn't explain it, she had a hard time believing anyone else could. She was the only one who had ever deemed lunabelles worth studying. They were rare, and an antidote was never going to be profitable, but that was the perk of owning a multi-billion dollar corporation like Herbatech. It had given her the freedom to pursue research others couldn't afford... until her research had not only failed, but killed.

Maybe Logan was right.

The thought halted as abruptly as the elevator. Scarlet stumbled, barely catching herself against the wall, her stomach groaning at the sudden jolt.

Her companion's hand was still clamped over the emergency stop button when they said, "Have a mint."

Scarlet blinked. "I'm sorry, *what?*"

"Look, we all love a buttery chardonnay, but this," they gestured vaguely head to toe at Scarlet, "is giving 'I fell asleep alone with a box of wine in a sad little apartment' vibes." They offered a tin from their vest pocket. "We're going to need you to pull yourself together in a hurry, because there's not a lot of time."

Scarlet narrowed her eyes. "It was *not* a box," she said. It would have been hard to drink wine directly from a box like she had the bottle. She took the mint.

"Right." They pocketed the tin. "You have to help us."

The kid was taller than her, lanky, and had their mousy hair pulled into a low ponytail. A crisp shirt, smart vest, and polished shoes made quite an impression. Scarlet was sure that if she'd ever seen them before, she would have remembered them. "I'm sorry, I've worked with all the interns across botany and tech, but... are you in accounts?"

"I'm Rye Thatcher," they told her, "and I'm not an intern. I make coffee for Mr. O'Connell."

"Oh." Of course that narcissistic asshole would have a personal barista. The only coffee her lab ever had was a thick pot of sludge that probably would have been more at home with the soil samples than on the hotplate.

Rye released the emergency stop and pressed the eight button.

"Delta Lab?" Scarlet asked. Her lab occupied the entire floor. Or at least it had been her lab before she'd been forced out.

"We need you to help us formulate the lunabelle antidote and cure the North Quarter before sunset."

"Wha—?" The elevator announced Scarlet and Rye's arrival on the eighth floor with a *ding* before Scarlet could argue otherwise. Her stomach squirmed. The courts were still hearing Herbatech's case against her after her failed antidote experiment. Scarlet's lawyer had laid out a clear path—very far away from Herbatech—and begged her to stay on the straight and narrow. Considering the current crisis, every scientist in the building would be working in Delta Lab right now. All of this was a very bad idea.

The elevator door opened, hissing along with the nervous intake of breath through Scarlet's teeth. But the hall was dark. The air was still. And the lab was nearly deserted, cleared of both staff and equipment aside from—

"Look who I happened to find upstairs," Rye announced.

"Oh, thank god!" A relieved outburst carried into the elevator.

Scarlet recognized the programming intern's unique raspy tone immediately. A stocky boy with a scruffy chin and an oversized hoodie emerged from a nearby stairwell, carrying not one, but two bags of cheese puffs. Mason Ward. Scarlet had previously worked with Mason on several R&D collaborations between botany and tech, and her nerves eased at the sight of his familiar face. "Mason, who let you into a lab?" she asked.

"Willow dragged me out of the IT dungeon," he joked. A blush crept up his full cheeks as he joined Scarlet's favorite biochemistry intern, Willow Palisade, at a table in the center of the otherwise deserted lab.

"Welcome back," Willow called, glancing up from her work as Scarlet and Rye made their way across the hallway to the main area of the lab. The glowing Phytogrid laced across the linoleum floor in a simple square grid. Separating the lab from the hall were triple-paned glass walls and pneumatic doors that would automatically seal off the lab from the rest of the floor in the event of an emergency.

Unlike Mason, Willow was exactly where she belonged. She had her black curls pulled up on top of her head and wore a rumpled white lab coat. Before her stood a complicated series of burners, flasks, and coiled tubing. A deep blue liquid bubbled through it. "Did you get the sample?" Willow asked Mason.

"Yeah. Uh, let's see." Mason fumbled with his crinkling plastic bags. "No, that one's actually cheese puffs," he muttered. "Here."

Willow reached a gloved hand into the second cheese puff bag, and for a split second, Scarlet froze, thinking Willow might reveal a lunabelle. Instead, what she pulled from the bag was a distinctly lacy-leafed plant in a sealed sample bag. Scarlet recognized it and silently raised an eyebrow as Willow carefully opened the bag and used tweezers to remove the dangerous specimen.

Rye wrinkled their nose. "Cheese puffs?"

"I took a detour for some essential IT equipment." Mason winked. "We don't have vending machines on the programming floor."

"Pretty sure that's by design, you know," Rye joked. "If you had vending machines, none of you would ever come out to see the sun."

"Well, it gave me the perfect reason to be loitering around Hydroponics long enough to snag the..." Mason waggled his fingers at the plant, "...leafy thing."

"Valerian root," Willow clarified. She discarded the sample bag and dropped the plant into the largest of her volumetric flasks, hurriedly clamping it shut again before an acrid yellow plume could waft out.

"Right. So." Scarlet crossed her arms and took a tentative step forward. "Do I want to know what you're planning to do with an incredibly potent sedative? And what does that have to do with the lunabelle outbreak?"

"It's a stealth mission," Mason said. "What if we come across security? They're not going to let us go wandering around the building like we own the place."

"Owning the place hasn't been very helpful this morning, anyway. But what? You intend to drug the security guards?" Scarlet asked.

Rye waved a dismissive hand. "Purely precautionary."

Scarlet's eyebrow threatened to disappear into her hairline.

They all watched as the angry yellow plume made its way through Willow's intricate system, snaking through the condenser coils and eventually dripping down into a tall glass cylinder as a violently purple liquid. Willow leaned in close. With a twist of a valve at the bottom of the system, she carefully dispensed a single drop each into a handful of miniscule glass vials. She sealed them and then handed one each to Rye and Mason, pocketing one herself before turning to Scarlet. One tiny vial remained between her thumb and forefinger. "Dr. O'Connell—" Willow started.

Scarlet bristled. "Let's just go with 'Scarlet.'"

"Right. *Scarlet*. Herbatech's whole lunabelle team is gone," Willow explained.

Scarlet's stomach sank. Knowing Logan, there had been a slew of forced resignations and non-disclosure agreements behind that. "That explains a lot about this morning's press conference. Logan clearly hadn't discussed the outbreak with anyone who knew anything about lunabelles. But how are you still here," Scarlet asked Willow. "I mean, you're brilliant, but…"

"I'm pretty sure temp employees are categorized separately in the database," she said. "They didn't technically fire me, so I just didn't leave. But that's beside the point. No one's worked on the antidote since you left. They're manufacturing *our* formulation." Willow's voice dropped low. "The one from the failed trial. I can't… I just can't… I feel responsible…"

"No." Scarlet's heart dropped. "Logan insisted they had this under control. He, of all people, knows that antidote failed. They must have revised it since."

Willow shook her head. "Everyone's gone. You have to help us."

Scarlet racked her brain. It didn't make sense. Did Logan really think it would be better to put on a show, churning out a bunch of worthless antidote just to say they tried? Was that really better than letting Scarlet try to create something new? "We know the vector worked, at least on previous generations of lunabelles, but there had to be something wrong with the catalyst."

"And if it was wrong for the strain we'd been working with in the lab, the odds that it will work at all for this other generation of lunabelle are practically zero."

Scarlet and Willow fell into a familiar back and forth. It was good to be back in a lab after all these months. "The strain that took over the North Quarter doesn't even proliferate like the lunabelles we were studying. For all we know, it could be a brand new mutation," Scarlet said.

Willow nodded. "We need to sequence them. Formulate a new antidote."

"And make sure the new version is manufactured instead of the old one," Scarlet finished.

Willow nodded, her face grim. "When the three of us heard about what was going on this morning, our plan was to do exactly that. We're not genius scientists or anything, but things really can't get any worse for the North Quarter. We knew we had to try. But Rye running into you... it feels like maybe we may actually have a chance. That is, if you'll help us."

Then three sets of eyes turned to Scarlet.

When Scarlet didn't immediately shoot them down, Mason chimed in. "So you're in?"

Rye pursed their lips. "We're doing it with or without you."

Scarlet sighed, realizing they'd tricked her into arguing herself into this. A hundred scenarios bounced through Scarlet's mind, and none of them ended well for her, her three companions, or the city. Willow, Mason, and Rye remained silent, their eyes filled with hope. That sliver of goodness pierced through Scarlet's heart, and she nodded before her brain could stop her. She smiled, mostly at the sheer madness, partly at the chance to learn where her past antidote trial had gone wrong, and at least a bit out of defiance.

Willow squeaked and threw her arms around Scarlet. "Thank you!" she cried. "Take this." Willow removed her lab coat, revealing a bright red faux leather jacket, which she peeled off and thrust into Scarlet's arms. "Gosh, I thought I was going to have to be the one sneaking around, but you need to disappear more than I do."

Scarlet cocked her head. "How would this help with sneaking..." But her thoughts veered as she recognized the jacket. "Wait. Is this—? You finished it?" Scarlet looked to Mason.

"He did," Willow said. "Mason's brilliant."

Mason's blue eyes flicked to Willow, a vivid blush blooming in his cheeks at the compliment.

Subtle, Mason, Scarlet thought, but she smiled in spite of herself.

"The Hood." Mason gave a devious grin once he regained his composure. "It may have somehow wandered out of R&D in the big corporate shakeup, yes. Try it out. It was all in the frequencies and filters. Once I figured that out, the programming wasn't too bad."

"Mason, you revolutionized phyto-communications. Why haven't I heard about this?" Scarlet asked.

"I tried to schedule a meeting with Mr. O'Connell, but he doesn't have time for an intern. I'm pretty sure he doesn't know I exist."

Wearable tech was meant to be the next generation of Herbatech's plant power revolution, and Scarlet had been working on this piece with an R&D team for the better part of three years when she'd been forced out. It was meant to take the smartphone out of the hand and weave it into the very fabric of the wearer's clothing—a seamless connection between the consumer and the Phytogrid for the first time ever. It was a wearable supercomputer built especially for residents of Three Oaks and future eco-dome cities like it. Unfortunately, they'd struggled to power it without being physically rooted into the Phytogrid or incorporating bulky battery packs. Until now.

As Scarlet slipped it on, a tingling energy drew up from the floor, channeling through her nerves like roots sucking water from the earth. Her very body had become a conduit between the tech and the Phytogrid. The jacket hummed to life with a subtle warmth and a faint vibration. It was a strange but somehow comforting sensation. Scarlet grinned.

"There's only one of these right now," Mason said, "but at least from my computer, I can be in your ear and you can talk back. I added some additional features, too. Download and upload information wirelessly via the grid, and there's a camera in the lapel, so I can see everything you're seeing."

As Scarlet pulled the hood over her head, her vision shimmered almost imperceptibly before her, and she froze. Her eyes flicked to the edges of the hood. Ever so slightly, the world seemed to crackle. A similar prickling sensation emanated from the cuffs at her wrists. "What in the world is this?" she asked.

"You know how they say 'it's a feature, not a bug'?" Mason started.

Scarlet eyed him, slightly concerned she may be about to burst into flame or start growing roots.

"It turns out the specific range of frequencies I had to filter out for the ambient energy to flow through the human body sort of filter out the human body at the same time,"

Mason explained. "You're invisible to the digital eye. Head to toe."

Scarlet's fingers traced the bottom hem of the jacket where it hit at her waist. "The security cameras can't see me at all?" Scarlet clarified.

Mason grinned. "Nope. Since your body is the conduit, the jacket is filtering out all of you so long as it's powered."

Rye gave a little laugh. "Because a bright red jacket is the obvious choice when you don't want to be seen."

"I didn't exactly have sneaking around headquarters in mind when I developed the concept. I chose red because it would stand out on stage against all the Herbatech green at the big launch." Scarlet shrugged. "All right, Willow. What's our first step?"

The girl's deep brown eyes grew wide. "Me?"

Scarlet nodded. "I don't even work here. You're the senior lab tech now, and you certainly had a plan before I showed up. What is it?"

Willow took a deep breath. "We need a sample of the North Quarter lunabelles."

"Good. Where are they?" Scarlet drilled.

"Live samples are in the special containment area of Hydroponics."

"That's beta-level security," Scarlet said.

Willow nodded. "Right. I won't have access."

"I can get in," Rye said, "but I don't know what I'd be doing down there."

Scarlet's eyes flicked to Rye. "You have access to the most secure area of Hydroponics, too?"

"I have access everywhere," Rye said.

"Have you had Rye's coffee?" Willow asked.

"It's like, *really* good," Mason chimed in.

Scarlet blinked.

Willow turned to Scarlet. "If you can go with Rye, I can try to get a dose of the vector so we can test it. We'll be twice as fast."

"The only thing is, Mr. O'Connell may call me back up at any moment," Rye warned, indicating a chunky pager on their hip.

Scarlet did a double take. "I'm surprised Logan even allows that antique in his presence."

"Coffee teaches us there is beauty in simplicity. This is how it's always been done."

"According to who?" Scarlet laughed. "Some ancient holy order of coffee brewers?"

Rye neither confirmed nor denied, and Scarlet was left to imagine a cloister of berobed monks jittering through a very caffeinated meditation session. "Okay, then." She shook her head and tried to ignore the absurdity of it all, getting back to the task at hand. "I can do Hydroponics, but if someone recognizes me, you'll be on your own," *and I'll be going to prison*, Scarlet finished in her head. "Where's the vector?"

"They're working on it on the manufacturing floor. They won't miss one vial—"

"No," Rye interrupted. "I was there this morning. The manufacturing floor is swarming. Every person in the building is there right now churning out as much of the vector as they can. There are cameras everywhere for quality control, not to mention multiple layers of security.

Going anywhere near the manufacturing floor would be absolute lunacy."

"Okay. Plan A is 'absolute lunacy.' Got it. What's Plan B?" Scarlet asked.

Willow paused, and Scarlet could practically see Willow's mind churning through the limited options. "We know they're manufacturing our old vector, so we can use one of our old samples. When they cleared out our lab, that all went to the Cryo Vault for long term storage. I should be able to get in there." She shot Rye a glance, seeking their approval.

They nodded. "Much better than the manufacturing floor."

Willow smiled, hitting her stride. "Then we meet back here in Delta Lab. We'll need to sequence the lunabelles. And then—"

"The Quiet Core," Scarlet finished. "Have you ever...?" Scarlet started and stopped. She knew Willow had never worked in the Core. "What was your plan before I showed up?"

"I watched you formulate a catalyst once," Willow said, "and I understand the science..." Scarlet stared in disbelief, and Willow trailed off. Desperation etched a furrow in her forehead. "It's really lucky we found you."

Mason and Rye exchanged a questioning look, then Mason cleared his throat. "Can you explain for the non-nerds?"

Rye stifled a laugh. "You're the biggest nerd in here, Mason."

"The Quiet Core is the only place we can design the catalyst," Scarlet explained. "When you're working on the genetic level, every byte of information represents a base pair in a strand of DNA. Any errant radio wave or spark of static electricity could mean a disastrous misinterpretation of the data. So, the Quiet Core is a concrete chamber in the basement, insulated from everything, including the Phytogrid."

"That means the Hood will power down." Mason looked worried now, too.

"Right," Scarlet said. "Once we go in, we won't have any communication out. Even the lunabelle data will have to come and go on a physical disc. You won't be able to tell us through the Hood if there's anyone coming unless you can reprogram it to work with the Core's isolated power grid."

"It took me months it to connect to the Phytogrid as it is," Mason said. "It would take some next-level genius to figure out how to connect the Hood to a totally separate power grid today. There's no way."

Scarlet nodded. Being disconnected in the Core wasn't ideal, but it was the least of her worries. She'd spent the last six months dwelling on her failed antidote, meticulously replaying everything she'd done, combing through her memories for any explanation as to why her patients had died. She was sure it had to have been the catalyst—the catalyst *she* had designed, but she had no idea what exactly she'd done wrong. She'd never had the chance to review the data before she was forced out of Herbatech. For Scarlet, this mission was as much about saving the North Quarter as it was a matter of proving to herself that she could formulate this antidote at all. If she were completely honest, she wasn't sure she could. But she couldn't just walk away, either.

"Scarlet?" Willow dragged Scarlet out of that dark corner of her mind.

"Right," Scarlet said. She stood straighter, forcing herself to appear confident. "This strain of lunabelles certainly grows differently than we've seen previously, but as long as they respond to the old vector, we just need to replace the catalyst formulation before the manufacturing team gets to it. They can't even begin to formulate that until they're ready to disperse it. It's too unstable to sit around."

Willow nodded. "Mason's good at that stuff, he can plant that info in the system once we have it." She placed a hand on Mason's upper arm.

"Yeah, I... I— I plant..." Mason sputtered a jumble of nonsense, a sheen of sweat breaking out across his forehead at her touch.

"Breathe, Mason," Scarlet muttered.

Moments later, the four of them piled into the elevator. Scarlet carefully tucked her hair behind her ears and adjusted the Hood to ensure she was completely covered. She knew it was silly. If the Hood was filtering out her legs, it would certainly cover a stray lock of hair, but she felt better shrinking into the Hood's shadow all the same. Beside her, Willow fidgeted nervously, shifting her weight side to side and wringing her hands. Mason stole very obvious glances at Willow, still blushing from her compliment. And Rye, the kid who likely knew the least about what was going on, stood tall in the corner, apparently unfazed by the whole situation. Scarlet did her best to smother her nerves over the group's fragile plan and the fact that she would undoubtedly be the one going to jail if they got caught.

Willow exited first on floor four to search the Cryo Vault for the old vector samples. Mason muttered '*good luck*' after her, though his poorly timed whisper was lost under the hiss of the elevator doors.

Then they rode down to basement level one for the lovingly-dubbed 'IT dungeon,' where Mason got off, leaving Scarlet and Rye. A tense, jittery silence descended while Rye held the elevator.

Scarlet looked to Rye in an effort to break the tense silence. "So how do you fit into all this?"

Rye shrugged. "Well, for starters, Willow and Mason are the only ones worth hanging out with here anymore. My friend at Channel Seven says there are ten thousand people at risk, so, I mean obviously I have to do something. And, to be completely honest, it sounds like an adventure, and I'm always up for a good adventure."

"At the risk of being fired and/or arrested for trespassing and tampering with Herbatech's antidote?" Scarlet clarified.

"Let's just say that after a run-in with the dictator of a certain country over a prized antique Persian coffee pot, this is nothing." Rye winked.

Scarlet wasn't sure what *certain country* she was meant to assume or what sort of *run-in* could have possibly transpired over a coffee pot, but there wasn't time to ask. Mason finally patched into the Hood's communications from his computer. Static crackled in Scarlet's ear for one brief second before Mason's voice rang through, crystal clear.

"Okay," came Mason's voice, streaming directly to the Hood. "Testing, testing. Over."

Scarlet grinned broadly. "Wow, Mason, this tech is amazing. It sounds like you're still standing right next to me."

"I think you're supposed to say 'roger,' or something," Mason corrected.

"Wow, Roger, this tech is amazing." She rolled her eyes.

"No, uh—" Mason started to explain, but Scarlet cleared her throat. "Yeah, okay." He sighed. "Let's see. Pulling up live security feeds..." Mason's keyboard clacked in Scarlet's ear while she and Rye waited. She tried to steady her nervous breathing, not sure how sensitive the Hood's microphone was and whether Mason could hear her.

"You're clear on Hydroponics," Mason told them.

Scarlet caught Rye's eye and nodded. Rye released the elevator, pressing the button for the second floor. It rose under them with a hum, and anxiety did the same in Scarlet's chest. A moment later, the doors opened with a *ding*, and hot, humid air flooded in as a visible wave.

Much like stepping back into Delta Lab, being on the Hydroponics floor again after months away felt like coming home. Even before she and Logan had founded Herbatech, she'd spent her time wading through rainforests and marshes, studying every bit of flora she could get her hands on.

The trickle, spray, and drop of water on leaves was a many-layered symphony in the maze of miniature greenhouses. Herbatech's hydroponics technology was not only state of the art, but extensive. Plants grew in vertical foam columns and in hanging channels. Glass enclosures provided separate climates, perfectly catered to the species within. Around the outer wall, a variety of conventionally beautiful species—those that weren't likely to kill anyone—climbed two stories up. The third floor cafeteria overlooked them, and on a normal day, jabbering voices would have drifted down from employees having lunch or excitable school kids on field trips. Today, it was silent, and it only added to Scarlet's unease. Silent until—

"Are you buzzing?" Scarlet asked Rye.

"That would be your lovely husband. It's coffee time." Rye paused just long enough to silence their pager. "Let's make this quick. I have to hurry."

"You're seriously going to go running just to get him coffee?" Scarlet asked.

"Mr. O'Connell sans caffeine? Something tells me I don't need to explain precisely how terrible that scenario would be for everyone in the building."

They didn't.

"This way. Don't touch anything." Scarlet sighed and shook her head as she and Rye made their way through the maze of specimens, their shoes splashing through the occasional puddle.

Mason made a sound of disgust in Scarlet's ear, "Why is it that every plant I've heard about today wants to drug or kill?"

"Most of the plants aren't dangerous on their own. Even the valerian root you managed to snag earlier would have been in one of these easily accessible enclosures. The real dangerous ones are kept behind more security, in a sealed chamber, in their own boxes. Nothing gets out of there by accident."

She and Rye finally reached an area sectioned off with thick concrete walls and an airlock. A control panel was mounted to the outside and the screen glowed as they approached, reading *Alpha-Level Clearance Required.*

Scarlet stopped in her tracks and groaned. "Mason, when did they upgrade this to alpha-level? Only Logan would have that clearance. If we set off an alarm down here, all hell is going to break loose. Can you do the hacking thing, maybe?"

"'Do the hacking thing,'" Mason scoffed. "No, I cannot spoof alpha-level security. That's a bit above my pay grade, though I'm open to discussing that if you want to put in a good word for me with your ex about a promotion."

Scarlet groaned.

Rye wasn't listening. They brushed past Scarlet and pressed a forefinger to the xylem pad. Scarlet gasped and flinched, anticipating blaring claxons and flashing lights, but they didn't come. The panel flashed approval a second later. Scarlet sputtered.

"When I said I have access everywhere, I meant everywhere," Rye said.

"Wait. Mason says I'm invisible on the cameras, but clearance or not, aren't the guards going to think it's a bit weird when they see you in this highly classified area, of all places?"

Rye waved a dismissive hand. "I'm developing a handful of new coffee cultivars, which, as I'm sure you understand, are the absolute highest security. I'm down here all the time. There's just something magical about a medium roast Guatemalan arabica, ground perfectly, and brewed at precisely the right temperature, you know?" They pulled the airlock door open.

She eyed them. "I really don't."

"It's already noon," Mason urged in her ear. "Willow is getting close to Cryo. I can see her on the cameras. We should hurry before someone else sees her and starts asking questions."

Scarlet followed Rye into the airlock.

As soon as the door sealed, the decontamination cycle started. The air around them rushed out, sucked down through the purifying green algae floor with a bubbling gurgle. It was quickly replaced via the vent in the ceiling, cool and dry. The Hood buffeted around her face in the gust. Then a brilliant white light flared from their right and left for five full seconds. Scarlet tried to blink the stars from her eyes, her vision still dark and bleary, when the lock clunked open on the opposite side. The door hissed, pressure equalizing with that inside the containment unit, and she and Rye both pressed through to the dimly lit space.

"Um," Mason said as Scarlet and Rye blinked away the lingering blindness from the flash. "Why are you two in a closet?"

"We're not in a closet," Scarlet argued.

"Small dark space. No plants. That's is definitely a closet."

Scarlet approached the lone computer on their side of a glass barrier, her fingers fluttering over the familiar keys as she navigated the catalogue. "The samples are stored underground and accessed via this robotic retrieval system so there's minimal chance for biological cross-contamination."

Mason cleared his throat, and his voice came in a squeak. "Underground where, exactly?"

"Basement level one, next to the IT dungeon," she said.

"Excuse me?" Mason's voice escaped in a raspy squeak.

"Just the most dangerous ones." A grin played at Scarlet's lips as she continued typing.

Lunabelles would be stored under their taxonomic name, but as Scarlet navigated to *Aconitum lunarus* and scrolled through, she frowned. There were dozens of samples listed, each with the location of their origin, the date they were stored, and what portion of the plant had been preserved. "Huh."

"What's wrong?" Rye stepped beside her and watched over her shoulder.

"What are we looking at here?" Mason asked.

"The most recent sample is dated the day before my last antidote trial. I can see it was accessed last week, but there's nothing new catalogued since this morning's bloom." She shook her head. "I know Logan didn't bother sequencing them, but surely they got samples from the North Quarter this morning."

"What's a lunarus? I thought they were called lunabelles," Mason asked, reading her screen through the Hood.

"They are, but..." Scarlet stopped herself. "Wait, do you programmer types really not know this?" An idea struck her. Scarlet scrolled back to the search bar to type 'luna'. A single entry for 'luna bells' appeared on her screen. It was dated this morning and listed the North Quarter as the origin.

"Absolute hacks," she muttered. "And this is the crack team Logan's assembled to save the North Quarter?" She rolled her eyes but selected the entry to be retrieved by the system. At her click, the area behind the glass lit up, and phyto-magnetic rails on either side hummed to life much like the elevators. A moment later, a clear case rose from under the floor. As it stopped before her, a crooked label bearing the hand-scribbled name 'luna bells,' came into view. She scoffed, but inside it were the samples she needed—a handful of dark green plants with spidering roots and white, bell-shaped flowers.

Rye recoiled, horror twisting their features as they backed as far away from the samples as possible.

Scarlet slipped her hands into the thick rubber gloves that reached into the containment area, placing three sample vials into a stand on the opposite side of the glass before pressing the spring-loaded door mechanism on the lunabelle box. Her breath fogged against the glass as she carefully snipped burgeoning white blooms, rife with spores, into three separate vials. Then she sealed the sample case. With the press of a button, the 'luna bells' box disappeared again under the floor, and the vials were sent through the glass barrier via a miniature airlock.

"Okay, Mason," Scarlet said. "We have—" Alarms screamed out of nowhere, a red beacon flashing on the wall over her head. She jumped and nearly dropped the lunabelle samples. "Holy— What's going on?"

"I set off the alarm, not you," Mason said, "but you need to get out of there now."

"Why the hell did you set off the alarm?" Scarlet screamed over the din.

"*He* set off the alarm?" Rye shouted. They got up close to Scarlet, partly so they could hear Mason, but mostly so they could yell at him. "What the hell, Mason?"

Scarlet stuffed the lunabelle vials unceremoniously into a pocket of the Hood and tried not to imagine what would happen to her and Rye if the glass broke in this tiny room.

"I was watching Willow on the security cameras, and she was going to get caught by a pack of Mr. O'Connell's corpo-bros. I panicked. I set off a bunch of other alarms as a diversion."

"Mason!" Scarlet screamed.

She and Rye both turned to the airlock and peered through it together.

"I had to think fast!" he said.

Rye exploded. "Can you think with your *brain* next time instead of with your—"

"Don't go out the airlock!" Mason interrupted. "Security's coming. They'll see you."

"We're in a closet, Mason!" Scarlet looked around frantically, her heartbeat ramping up. They were trapped. "There's no hiding in here."

"There are only two of them," Mason said, a nervous waver in his voice. "Can you take them?"

"'Take them' *where?*" Scarlet asked.

"Um, *out?*" Mason suggested.

Rye threw up their hands. "We're going to jail."

Scarlet ducked to the side of the airlock access, crouching out of view behind the concrete wall. She pulled Rye down with her. Her heart raced. It took everything in her to drown out the noise and stay focused. "Mason, I need you to seal this place up as soon as the airlock releases. Can you cut power to the door or something?"

"Uh..." Mason's frantic clicking met her ears.

The muffled voices of the security guards were barely audible under the blaring alarms as they neared the airlock. Outside, the control panel beeped. Scarlet listened closely as two sets of footsteps crossed into the airlock. There was the rush of wind, and then Scarlet averted her eyes for the blinding flash.

"Hell, that's bright!" one of the guards grumbled in the airlock.

Beside Scarlet, Rye cursed, blinded as well. In retrospect, she probably could have explained the plan a bit better.

Then the door hissed open. A rush of cool air rustled their hair and clothes as the guards blindly felt their way into the room. They squinted and tried to blink their sight back. The effect wouldn't last long. Scarlet thrust her foot into the doorway to stop the magnetic locks from sealing.

She held her breath as the door bumped silently against her sneaker.

"What the—?" one guard muttered.

The guards could hardly see, but they were still right on top of Scarlet and Rye. Scarlet scrambled as the guards wheeled around. She shoved Rye bodily into the airlock and threw herself in after. The two men lunged forward, but Scarlet wrenched the door closed, barely evading the security guards' grasp. The powerful magnets engaged as the door sealed, trapping the guards inside the containment area. Normally, the decontamination cycle would run within the airlock, and the door would release fifteen seconds later, but the routine never started. Mason had managed to cut the power, so the inner door remained locked.

Scarlet and Rye both doubled over, catching their breath.

"Oh my god, it worked?" Mason asked.

The guards inside banged on the door, their angry red faces shouting noiselessly.

"I don't like how surprised you sound," Scarlet said between quick breaths as she and Rye sprinted away from the trapped guards. The prisoners shouted into their radios, but they were sealed in a concrete box, and Scarlet doubted their signal would make it out. She'd make sure someone found them before tomorrow. Or if she got arrested, maybe in a week.

Mason groaned in the Hood's speakers. "The elevators are locked down and there are security guards all through the stairwell."

"So we're trapped down here?" Scarlet asked.

Scarlet and Rye slowed amidst the foggy greenhouse compartments and looked around, as if some other way out would manifest if they just looked hard enough. Rye stood close to Scarlet so they could listen in on the Hood.

"How about the service elevator?" Rye asked.

"It's clear," Mason said, "but it doesn't connect to Hydroponics."

"No, but it connects to the kitchen on the cafeteria level," Rye said.

Scarlet followed Rye's gaze to the outer wall where the second floor Hydroponics level was open to the third level cafeteria mezzanine. There, the showiest and least deadly plants grew out in the open, two stories tall against the wall. Trees towered and vines wove, all with broad, fanning leaves and vivid blooms wider than Scarlet's hands. Her eyes floated all the way up the wall.

"Can you climb?" Rye asked.

"Can *you* climb?" Scarlet eyed Rye's crisp collared shirt and vest. "You don't really strike me as the type."

"With my expertise, I could work anywhere. There's a reason I chose Herbatech. Plants are fascinating." They grinned, removing their cufflinks and rolling up their sleeves. "I once spent a month trekking through the jungles of the Amazon in search of a coffee variety that was previously thought to be extinct."

Scarlet smiled, a warmth settling in her chest. "That sounds a lot like what I used to do before Logan and I founded Herbatech."

"Really? I ended up kidnapped by a cartel and eventually bargained my way to freedom by making espresso on the yacht of a billionaire oil heiress. Maybe we can exchange stories over a cup of coffee some time." Rye winked, then dove into the plants.

Scarlet blinked, not sure her experiences cataloguing slime molds would quite compare, but she sidled into the foliage after Rye.

It was so dense that the plants completely surrounded her. The damp leaves brushed against her and dew pattered onto the moist ground around her sneakers. She took a deep breath of the earthy air and grabbed hold of a thick vine, pulling herself up amid the leaves. Being amongst the branches and vines, she was reminded fondly of climbing into the rainforest canopy decades ago. Her knees, however, were less than nostalgic. Scarlet couldn't imagine running from a cartel like this, but as the glass lunabelle vials clinked ominously in her pocket, she briefly wondered if the cartel would be preferable.

The wall made for remarkable camouflage as she and Rye scaled it. Rye was only a meter from her, but she couldn't see them at all—only the gentle rustling of leaves.

Rye made it to the top first and leaned out, peering through the dense growth. "Come on." They grabbed onto the top of the third floor glass railing where it met the vegetated wall, flinging a leg over it to a far corner of the overhanging cafeteria floor. Then they reached back over to take Scarlet's wrist and help pull her over, too.

Breathing a bit more heavily than she'd like to admit, Scarlet steadied herself on solid ground and looked around the cafeteria. "Any other day, this place would be packed at this time," she muttered. But the tables stood empty, chairs still pushed in. Not a scuff on the polished floor. No one had been here all day.

"Everyone's working as hard as they can," Rye said.

Scarlet hoped they could get them the right formulation in time.

"There's staff in the kitchen, but you still need to hustle to that elevator," Mason said in Scarlet's ear. "You've got someone coming around the corner in the cafeteria."

Scarlet and Rye dashed across the abandoned cafeteria toward the kitchen. A set of free-swinging kitchen doors stood in a small alcove, and Scarlet crouched in the corner of the little nook, out of sight of both the cafeteria and the kitchen. She may have been invisible to the cameras, but the brilliant red of the Hood would stand out like a beacon to anyone who physically glimpsed her.

Rye peered into the kitchen through the window in the door. "When I walk in," they said, "you need to be fast. Stick with me, but stay low. The elevator is in the back. So we're going to have to keep you out of sight as we go through."

She didn't have time to respond.

"Let's go," Rye whispered.

They pushed the door inward, and Scarlet scrambled, following Rye as quickly as she could, crouched toward the floor. Only a couple meters into the kitchen, she reached the cover of a prep table and let out a breath. Adrenaline coursed through her veins. Her legs itched to move—to jump and dart for the elevator. It took everything in her to stay still.

The whole place looked to have been doused in liquid metal. Every surface, every appliance, every vessel was shining stainless steel. The aroma of fresh bread wafted from the industrial ovens, and a mountain of boxed lunches weighed down a nearby cart.

"Hey, George," Rye raised a hand toward the chef who—Scarlet could only assume—was somewhere on the opposite side of the row of prep tables. "Some day, huh?"

"You're telling me," the chef replied. His voice was far too close for Scarlet's liking. "Everyone's having meals in the building today instead of going out. I'm taking everything up to manufacturing, and they go through it all faster than I can make it."

"Let me take the cart up for you," Rye said. Below the level of the table, Rye gestured toward the cart. Scarlet edged toward it, still hidden from the chef's view. "I just came down for some more coffee beans, so I'm headed up, anyway."

"That would be great!"

"Let me just get that coffee." Rye moved ahead of Scarlet, disappearing into a pantry.

A sharp intake of breath came through the Hood speaker. "Don't move," Mason whispered.

With a labored grunt from the chef, the tower of sandwich boxes next to her head shuffled as yet more lunches were piled on the top of the heap. The bottom row sagged, and the stack teetered. Reflexively, Scarlet's hand shot up over her head to brace them before they toppled. If they fell, she'd lose her cover, and the chef would see her for sure. Her breath froze in her throat. A split second later, the chef steadied the stack as well.

"Excellent catch!" Rye said, rushing from the pantry to help. They wedged a small bag of dark roast Sumatra in amongst the sandwiches, and helped the chef right the stack while Scarlet withdrew her hand and let out a shaking breath. "I'll take these right up."

"Thanks." The chef breathed a sigh of relief.

That was too close.

Rye slowly rolled the towering cart between gleaming prep tables and past walk-in freezers to an oversized elevator in the back of the space. All the while, Scarlet crept alongside it. At the end of the kitchen, Rye opened the elevator and they both moved inside as Rye pressed the eight button for Delta Lab.

"After you get out on eight," Rye muttered to Scarlet, "I'll take these up to manufacturing and then see Mr. O'Connell. I'll get back to you all as fast as I can."

Then a new voice called through the kitchen. "Hey, Thatcher!"

Rye shoved Scarlet to a corner of the elevator, out of view. Glass vials clinked in her pocket, and they both drew in a sharp breath. There was no leaving the elevator without being seen, but the door took its time. Scarlet pressed herself as tightly as she could to the wall, deeply regretting the vivid red she'd chosen for the Hood.

"Rye! There you are!" Scarlet recognized the voice as that of Logan's assistant. That must have been the person Mason warned them about in the cafeteria. "I saw you on the security cameras. Mr. O'Connell's been looking for you the past thirty minutes. Is your pager dead? Who were you talking to just now?"

"Go help Willow," Rye whispered. Then they plastered on a shallow smile and stepped out of the elevator before Logan's assistant could get any closer. Scarlet stayed hidden in the corner. "I just came down here for some more coffee beans. Did you know it's proven that if you speak kindly to them, they're less bitter? But I think I made a terrible mistake with this Sumatra. It's definitely more of a Kona day, don't you think?" Rye swept back into the kitchen, steering Logan's assistant away from the elevator.

Scarlet peered out from around the corner, watching Rye's back as the elevator doors finally closed.

Mason cursed in her ear.

"That about sums it up," Scarlet muttered.

She arrived at Delta Lab moments later, leaving the sandwich cart in the elevator. As she entered the lab, she found Willow pacing nervously. Willow's face was anything but triumphant. "What's wrong?" Scarlet asked.

"I couldn't get the vector from Cryo. I thought they were going to catch me. They all went running when a bunch of other alarms went off, but then everything got locked down and I couldn't get in." Willow finally faced Scarlet. "Where's Rye? Do you have leaves in your hair?"

Scarlet groaned and raked a hand through her bangs, removing a surprising number of twigs and leaves. "Rye and their famous coffee got waylaid by Logan's assistant."

Willow nodded. "Yeah, that makes sense. Everything pauses for Rye's coffee."

"So it seems. But we did get the lunabelle samples." She withdrew the vials from her pocket and handed them to Willow. It was a weight off her chest to know the samples were finally in a lab with an automatic quarantine routine, instead of banging together in her pockets as she scaled the walls. "You stay here and sequence these. That should take about an hour and a half. That will put us at about two o'clock. I'll get the vector."

"But the Cryo Vault was totally locked down," Willow said.

"I'm not going to Cryo," Scarlet said. "It's going to have to be Plan A."

"Didn't we agree Plan A was insane?" Mason asked through the Hood.

"I believe the phrase Rye used was 'absolute lunacy,'" Scarlet corrected.

Mason groaned. "I hate Plan A."

◆ ◆ ◆ ◆ ◆

Manufacturing occupied the entire tenth floor, and would be clogged with people. The elevators led directly into the main hallway where any number of former colleagues might recognize Scarlet. Even the new people would know her face from the tech magazine articles. Unfortunately, those were focused most recently on the devastating antidote failure and Scarlet's subsequent removal from the Board. Even the gossip columns had covered her and Logan's messy separation on top of it all. The elevator was out of the question. Instead, she wedged herself into an air duct in the wall outside of the lab at Mason's direction as he scoured the building's HVAC plans on his computer. It led up through the ninth floor wall, and into the space between the ninth story ceiling and the tenth story floor.

"Huh," Mason said. Scarlet could hear the rattling of ice in a drink through his microphone. "These vents always look a lot bigger in the movies. And brighter. And cleaner."

"Ha," was all Scarlet could manage between labored breaths. Her elbows squeezed against her ribs, and her hips were uncomfortably snug to the cool silver walls. With every move she made, the faux leather jacket stuck to the galvanized surface and her shoes squeaked. She could only hope that no one was standing too close to a vent. She struggled to point her tiny flashlight ahead of her and move at the same time. She could just imagine Mason kicking his feet up on his desk as he watched the ridiculous display on his screen. "It's not far, right?" she asked.

"After that last right turn, it's only about twenty more meters or so."

"*Only,*" Scarlet grumbled, shimmying along bit by bit. "You got eyes on Rye?"

"No, after they left the kitchen, they disappeared somewhere in the Treehouse," Mason said, referring to the corporate level. "There aren't any cameras in the boardroom or Mr. O'Connell's office, so I don't know."

"No cameras? Since *when?*"

"Since you left."

"Unbelievable."

A moment passed with the only sound being Scarlet's struggling through the tight vent, her sneakers squeaking against the aluminum with every bit she managed to scoot forward. She was going to go crazy well before that if she didn't get her mind elsewhere. "Mason?"

"What?"

"Can I ask you why you're still here at Herbatech? Why do you want to work for someone who doesn't know you exist?"

He sighed. "I mean, because Mr. O'Connell's a genius. Even just having the idea to harness plants' electrical signals was revolutionary. And the fact that he figured it out? And built a city on it? The programming I've learned while I've been here has been unlike anything anyone else is doing. He's just the best. I can't turn down an opportunity like this one, even if Herbatech loses some of its luster when you start digging through the air ducts."

Scarlet frowned. The kid wasn't stupid. Of course he would learn a ton here, and just having Herbatech on his resume would set him up for any career he could ever dream of. "Why risk all that for this crazy plan, then?" Scarlet asked.

"Because I'm not evil?" He said it like it was the most common-sense thing in the world, and Scarlet's heart warmed. She hoped Logan's environment wouldn't change these kids for the worse. "Willow told us what was happening, and, uh..." he stumbled, "I really like... um, the uh, snacks here."

Snacks. Right. Scarlet grinned, but Mason piped up before she had a chance to needle him about *who* exactly the 'snack' was.

"That vent right there," he said.

Her thoughts snapped back to her task, finding the vent above her head and twisting onto her back. "Are we clear?" she whispered before clenching the flashlight between her teeth. She worked out the four small screws that held the vent cover in place using a test tube clamp swiped from the lab.

"It's the women's locker room," Mason reminded her. "Something tells me there would be complaints if we had security cameras in there. I'm blind here."

"Right." Scarlet popped the last screw out of place. Then she held her breath and listened. There were voices—lots of them—along with the rustling of plastic suits and the squeak of rubber boots. Above all that was the clank of steel carts and the tinkling of glass vials, but it all sounded muffled and distant. "I think all the noise is from the actual manufacturing floor. There's no one in the locker room."

Mason blew out a breath. "Good luck."

With that, Scarlet lifted the grate off the top of the duct and shimmied her way through the hole in the floor. She was met with a sea of shining epoxied concrete, surrounded by tall green lockers. It all smelled of rubber and cleaning solution.

"We're clear," Scarlet whispered.

"What exactly is your plan here?" Mason asked. "Because there may not be anyone in the locker room, but we know there are hundreds of people just through that door, and everyone knows what you look like."

"Oh, I hadn't thought of that," she joked, searching locker after locker down the row. "Did you want to swap places?"

He gave a sarcastic laugh. "Red's not my color."

She finally found what she needed—a hazmat suit. "I'm hoping to hide in plain sight."

"You know, I saw everyone wearing those. What's the deal?"

"While not technically dangerous, it's a live virus they're breeding in there, so hazmat suits are required as a precaution."

It sounded like Mason spat out his drink. "What?"

"And that's why we usually use the term 'vector' instead," Scarlet said as she pulled the suit out and stepped into the legs, slipping the grippy rubber boots over her sneakers. "People tend to get a little antsy when you tell them your plan is to infect them with a virus."

"Ya think?"

"Viruses are just DNA messengers," Scarlet explained, "and DNA is just a string of biological instructions. We're able to make the viral vector carry our custom-engineered DNA catalyst directly into the lunabelle's cells, sending a precise electrical communication to the plant to stop drawing energy and let go of its host."

Mason made a noise of disgust. "I think I prefer the computer variety of virus, thanks."

Scarlet shook her head and grinned as she pulled the hazmat suit's voluminous plastic hood down over her face, securing it with a zip.

"Can you still hear me?" Mason asked.

"Yep."

"Okay, good. I worried the Hood may not be able to connect to the grid. Still, there's no way it's going to mask the whole hazmat suit from the cameras. You're going to be a ghost inside it, so don't get too close and personal with any security feeds."

Scarlet was much more worried about the hundreds of physical eyes that would be on her. Safety goggles and a medical mask covered most of her face within the plastic shield of the bulky suit, but if anyone looked too closely they would surely recognize her. Not only would Logan have her arrested, but she'd never see the inside of Herbatech or any lab again. Scarlet could probably cover for Willow, Mason, and Rye, but ten thousand lives was more than Scarlet would put on anyone's shoulders. She needed to keep her head down.

With a deep breath, she pressed through the locker room doors, and through the airlock that led to the manufacturing floor. Scarlet walked out from under a mezzanine, her bulky hazmat suit rustling and squeaking with every move.

The air crackled with a frantic energy. At the center of the space, a team of scientists worked with microscopes and pipettes, carefully measuring out diluted samples into vials. They swirled the vials with special solutions and then set the mixtures aside before they were whisked off by another team. That team transported the vials to the incubation room, and from the incubation room to a team working the centrifuges and spectrometers, overseeing final bottling and quality control. Of all the whorls of chaos, that team seemed to be struggling the most. The vials came out of incubation faster than they could finish them, and the small trays piled high around their workstation.

A monstrous new display hung from the ceiling over the manufacturing area. It looked like something that belonged at a basketball arena, but it displayed in large, colorful text *Origination, Incubation,* and *Synthesis.* Under each of those, a number ticked up with each dose they finished, and beside it, a bar graph displayed the current 'leader' was *Origination.*

"Holy crap, Mr. O'Connell gamified the manufacturing floor?" Mason's tone betrayed a lingering admiration for the man.

"Everything's a game for him as long as he thinks he can win," Scarlet muttered, careful to ensure her voice didn't carry. But her stomach twisted the longer she watched. Even with everyone in the building bustling at this assembly line, Herbatech was in no way set up to manufacture ten thousand doses of this antidote in twelve hours. She estimated it was taking three hours to make a dose, start to finish, and most of that time was in incubation. That process couldn't be rushed. Looking at the tickers on Logan's display, they'd be lucky to have about a thousand finished doses by the time the crescent moon appeared that evening, and even that depended on whether Scarlet, Willow, Mason, and Rye managed to formulate an effective catalyst.

Mason continued to ramble in her ear. "Mr. O'Connell gamifies a lot of projects for the programming staff. It totally works, but that's way too many people. Give me my IT dungeon any day. I'll be happy all alone."

Scarlet went for the Synthesis station, where she could best hide amidst the chaos. She chose the scientist who had the largest stack of incubated vials backed up in front of him, and she nudged him out of the way. "Take a break," she ordered, waving him off.

He happily backed away, and Scarlet got to work.

"Are you sure you'd be happy *all* alone?" Scarlet spoke softly so only Mason could hear her, lacing her words with insinuation.

"I..." Mason swallowed, coughed, and took a breath. "I guess some people are okay."

Scarlet made quick work of the vials, practiced hands setting each smoothly into a slot in the centrifuge, before turning to a second set of vials with her pipette. It was work that she'd done a thousand times, and muscle memory kicked in. For the first time that day, Scarlet felt comfortable, and it was easy for her to carry on her conversation. "Anyone in particular come to mind?" She quickly completed three full trays of doses, popping one sample from each into the spectrometers in front of her. "Maybe a brilliant young biochemist?"

She grinned as she heard Mason stutter before he tried to change the subject. "Aren't you supposed to be doing something?"

Scarlet's spectrometers all flashed green, indicating her three batches met the pre-programmed standards. She took the samples out and completed her tidy, organized rows in the trays, surreptitiously slipping one vial into the single pants pocket of her suit just as a buzzer rang out overhead. Everyone else on the floor turned toward the large monitor for the results of the competition, but Scarlet continued working, loading another round into the centrifuge. "Just tell her how you feel, Mason. What's the worst that can happen?"

"Mr. O'Connell—"

Scarlet cringed. "Okay, yeah. Logan is absolutely the worst case scenario, but Willow—"

"No, I mean he's right—"

A hand came down on Scarlet's shoulder. "Could I have everyone's attention, please."

Scarlet's blood ran cold. She knew that voice, even through the plastic.

She looked behind her, and there stood Logan, wearing the same suit he'd used to dazzle the reporters, a hazmat mask over only his face, as if the power of his presence would be enough to fend off any contagion. Idiot.

He turned away to look at the crowd of workers. "This round goes to the Synthesis team! From last to first in the last few minutes, thanks to the efforts of—" For a second, Scarlet felt certain that she was going to be found out, but Logan's eyes only passed over the nametag on her chest. "—Dr. Little! We still have a ways to go, but we will save this city! Two thousand dollar bonuses for each member of the Synthesis team!" He took a few steps away from the lab tables and fanned out a wad of Herbatech-emblazoned checks in his un-gloved hand.

The Synthesis team cheered and rushed to form a line. Scarlet folded her arms and rolled her eyes, hanging back.

"You too, Dr. Little," Logan called over the rest of the line. "Don't be shy."

"Are we busted?" Mason whispered into her ear.

Scarlet reluctantly shuffled into line with the other floor technicians on her team. She watched nervously from the back as one by one, Logan folded a check and slipped it into each team member's pocket. "Not yet." But she braced herself as she moved forward. She knew as soon as Logan placed the check in her pocket, he was bound to find the vial she'd stashed there. Maybe he would believe it was a mistake? She clenched her teeth behind her mask as the person in front of her gathered their check and returned to their workstation.

Logan raised an eyebrow as she approached, folding the last check in half and holding it up between his index and middle fingers for her. "Ah, Dr. Little. I'll admit you've caught my eye around the lab before this, for... various reasons." His eyes roamed as if he could see any hint of a figure inside the oversized suit. "I'm impressed." He flashed a smile, taking a step toward her. Scarlet had to suppress her instinct to recoil. Instead of putting the check in her pocket, however, Logan slipped it into the back waistband of her suit before his hand trailed downward. "Very impressed." He gave her a squeeze through the thick plastic, winked, and then walked away.

Scarlet's face flared hot, fury boiling inside her. She couldn't have hidden her reaction even if she had remembered to try, but Logan either didn't notice or didn't care as he turned again to the rest of the room.

"All scores are reset!" Logan announced to the floor. "Let's keep this pace up. For the next thirty minute period, bonuses are doubled! Get to work!" He clapped his hands and moved toward a side door, removing his mask and fixing his hair before he even walked through it.

Scarlet fumed, glaring at his back.

Mason's voice snapped her out of it. "Scarlet?"

She shook her head as everyone on the floor hustled back to their stations. The buzzer rang out again, and the time started ticking down over their heads. She took the opportunity to retreat to the locker room in the scramble.

"What was that about? Do you think he recognized you?" Mason asked.

"I don't think he was looking at my face, Mason." Scarlet found Dr. Little's locker and stripped out of the suit.

"Sounds like a great success, then," Mason said.

"That bastard grabbed my ass! He's married!"

"Yeah. To you."

"He's not allowed to do that to *me*, either!" She put the suit back in the locker, along with the check. It wasn't near enough compensation for what poor Dr. Little would have to deal with when she next ran into Logan.

"So... did you get the virus?" Mason asked.

"Who *knows* what viruses I've got. Apparently, I need to go get tested, if that's what Logan's up to."

"Um..."

Scarlet sighed. "Yes, I got the *vector*."

"You're right. 'Vector' does sound better."

Scarlet plucked the vial from the suit pocket where it hung in the locker and glanced at their prize. "Mason, what day is it?"

"The fourteenth."

"Why do I have a vial with an origination date of the seventh, if the lunabelles just bloomed this morning?"

Scarlet didn't get an answer. At that moment, the doors opened again, and she closed her fist around the vial. Her heart jumped into her throat. The Hood might have hidden her from the cameras, but not from the naked eye.

"Dr. Little?" Logan's voice called from the other side of the locker room. "The floor supervisor said you headed this way. I wondered if I might have a, uh... *moment.*"

Scarlet was hidden behind a row of lockers, but there was no time to wedge herself back into the air vent in the floor, and she didn't have time to put the hazmat suit back on either. There were two doors out of the locker room—the one Logan had entered led back into the manufacturing area while the door on the opposite end of the room accessed the main hallway. She bolted for the hall.

As soon as she closed the locker room door behind her, she muttered to Mason as inconspicuously as she could, standing in the hallway with a bright red jacket pulled over her head. "Get me out of here." Panic crept into Scarlet's voice as she hurried away from the locker room.

"The elevator and the stairwell both require fingerprint ID," Mason said.

"Can't you just IT magic that?"

"I can't just open doors."

"Why not. You hacker types do all that stuff in the movies."

"These are *your* paranoid security measures, not mine! Submit an IT ticket. Your request will be answered in the order it was received," Mason grumbled, still clicking away.

"Let me pull up the building plans. Um..." He typed and clicked on his computer. "The door to the right of the elevator is maintenance access."

"Sure. That's the cooling column for the tree, but I still don't have access, unless you want me to use the axe," she joked, eying the fire axe in the glass case beside the door.

"Wait." Mason's typing paused abruptly. "There's an axe?" His voice trailed excitedly upward at the end of his sentence, betraying a bit more enthusiasm than was strictly reasonable.

"I mean, yeah. On every floor, in case of fires. The tree's hot. But I think it would be less conspicuous to just go back and give Logan a big kiss than to chop through the door."

"Right." Mason sounded disappointed. "The lock on the maintenance door isn't a fingerprint pad, is it?"

Scarlet examined it. "No, it looks like it takes a keycard."

"Yes! It's easier to transfer a card to whoever's doing maintenance on a particular day, than it is to map every individual's fingerprints. That I can deal with!"

"So you *can* just magically open doors," Scarlet pointed out.

"I may have some tricks up my sleeve," he said. "Or, up your sleeves, at least. Put your hand on the card reader."

This would be perfect. The maintenance column had access to every floor of the building. She placed her palm on the cool surface of the card reader and waited.

"Okay," he said, "this is older tech. It uses a radio frequencies to..." he trailed off as he worked.

"Just hurry." She risked a quick glance over her shoulder. Logan was presumably still skulking around the women's locker room. The door hadn't opened since she left. A second later, Scarlet felt a surge through her arm. She pulled her hand from the card reader with a yelp as it zapped. At the same time, the lock before her clicked. "A little warning might have been nice!"

"Sorry. Honestly, I've never done that before, but hey! It worked!"

"You just shot electricity through me, and you've never even tested it?"

"I shot *radio waves* through you. Big difference."

Scarlet bit her tongue. There wasn't time to argue, and she was relieved to escape the hall. She slid into the maintenance door and closed it with a soft click behind her.

The room was reminiscent of an elevator shaft—small, but stretching several stories above her to the roof and deep underground to the root of the great tree. Along one side, the tree rose the entire height of the space and out the top of the building, partially embedded in the wall. Golden energy coursed through the wood, and a low thrum of electricity reverberated against her eardrums. Between Scarlet and the trunk flowed a thick stream of clear fluid. It ran down from the roof, along the length of the trunk in an unnaturally smooth column. Only the rush of the glittering bubbles within it betrayed the speed with which the fluid thundered past.

Above and below her, doors punctuated the wall on every story, each opening onto a small area of grate flooring. Yet when she turned to climb down to the next floor, the fleeting elation she'd felt when Mason unlocked the door evaporated.

"Mason, what in the actual hell is this?" Scarlet shouted over the hum of electricity.

"Um, the maintenance column?"

"There's no ladder. I specifically designed this area with a ladder between each floor. I put it on the plans myself."

"The floorplan I have says that the ladder was value-engineered by the owner during construction."

"Logan nixed my ladder to save some money? He spends more on his hair in a month than this ladder would have cost." Scarlet fumed. "I'm tired of being trapped in my own damn building."

"Can you swim?"

"You have got to be kidding me." She tucked the vector sample into an internal pocket of the Hood, eying the rushing fluid.

"Looks like it should be a, uh, 'hydrogenated plasmatic coolant solution'?" he read.

"It's water jelly," Scarlet translated. "It's pumped from the basement up to the top of the building in a pipe, then it runs down along the length of the trunk. The gelatin helps it flow without the need for a pipe so we can maximize contact with the tree. It keeps the tree from spontaneously combusting due to the heat."

"More deadly plants. You're seeing the pattern here, right?" He snorted softly at his own joke. "At least that doesn't sound nearly as toxic as the hydro-plasma-whatsit. Lucky you."

"Lucky me," Scarlet echoed, reaching out a hand to test it. Her fingers cut into the stream, and the force of the cool fluid dragged her hand downward. When she withdrew her hand, it was clean and dry. The gel was so thick, it stuck only to itself. She wondered if she would even be able to move in it.

"You only have to go two floors," Mason said. "Below you, floor nine is office space, then you hit Delta Lab on floor eight..."

Scarlet's mind veered from their careful plan at the mention of the office level. For months, she'd wanted a chance to review her old files and comb for any explanation for the antidote failure. Now, she had a vector that had inexplicably been manufactured before the outbreak. Willow had said work on the antidote had stopped when everyone was forced out, but if that was the case, the manufacture date on the vector sample didn't make sense. She could only assume Logan was up to something, and she would never have another chance like this one to investigate.

Mason's voice drifted back into her consciousness. ". ..just don't overshoot. I don't think there's any swimming upstream."

"Yeah," Scarlet muttered absently. Before her, tiny bubbles glittered as they rushed past. Warm light from the trunk refracted through the jelly, and the whole thing resembled a sparkling beam of sunlight, piercing through from the ceiling and shining all the way down to the earth at the trunk's base, deep within the lowest floor of the building.

With a deep breath, Scarlet stepped into the flow. The cool gel enveloped her, sucking the heat from her body just as it absorbed the heat from the tree. It pressed on her from all directions, threatening to squeeze the breath from her lungs. In an instant, she was rushing downward in the stream.

She had just seconds to escape, unless she wanted to be spat out at the bottom, below the building. She tried to move her arms, hoping to pull herself through as if she were swimming, but they were pinned to her sides by the thick substance. Instead, she kicked through the jelly with both legs. Her sneakers connected with the glowing trunk, and she pushed off of it with all her strength.

She burst sideways out of the flow and hit the grate flooring hard, gasping for air.

The door beside her bore a large white number nine.

Mason must have seen it through the Hood's camera. "Nine?" he asked. "You're supposed to be on eight."

"Well, I'm on nine. How do the security cameras look? Is it clear?"

Mason fumbled. "Uh, yeah, but—"

Scarlet wasn't listening. She stood and cracked the door open, carefully peering out into the open office. It was a sprawling maze of desks and computers, but aside from the dimly glowing Phytogrid, everything was dark.

"Which of these computers can you get me into?" Scarlet asked.

"Aren't you going to Delta Lab? You and Willow are supposed to figure out this catalyst thing. Isn't this kind of off the trail?"

"I've got half an hour until Willow's got a sequence we can work with. I want to pick through some lunabelle files and figure out where this vector came from."

"Is that info we need to cure the North Quarter? Or is this about something else?"

"Just get me a computer."

Mason groaned, resigned. "They're all rooted into the Phytogrid and the servers. Pick any computer."

Scarlet removed one of her sneakers and carefully propped the maintenance door open with it—anything to avoid serving as Mason's experimental radio antenna again. She darted for the closest workstation. Within seconds, Mason was logged in remotely through the Phytogrid, and neon code spilled across the display as she watched. The entire office was bathed in the electric blue glow from the screen.

"Okay," he finally muttered.

"Thanks. Keep an eye on Willow."

"Yeah." Mason's voice was clipped, nervous.

Scarlet ignored it. They had plenty of time. She took control of the computer, digging into Herbatech's manufacturing database. She keyed in the catalogue number for the vector from memory. As she searched it, information for every manufacturing order anyone had ever made for it filled her screen. There were dozens of entries, and she sorted by most recent. The top line listed an order for twelve-thousand doses, placed just after five this morning by O'Connell, L. Progress listed just five percent.

Scarlet chewed her lip.

"What are you expecting to find here?" Mason asked.

The screen flickered before her, and so did her resolve. "Honestly, I kind of hoped to catch Logan doing... something," she sighed. "I don't know why they would have been manufacturing the vector a week ago, but I can see he didn't order all these until after I identified the lunabelles for him this morning."

"What's that next one?" Mason asked. The next line down showed another order for a hundred doses placed a week ago by O'Connell, L, ninety-five percent complete. "Maybe he was running some sort of clinical trial?" Mason asked.

Scarlet shook her head, unsure. "They wouldn't have needed a hundred doses for that, and Willow said they'd stopped research," she muttered. The display flickered again. "What is going on with this screen?" Scarlet asked.

"Did you try turning it off and on again?"

"Does that *ever* actually fix anything?"

"No, but it keeps people occupied while I search for the real answer," Mason joked.

"I knew it."

Mason gave a half laugh. "It could be that the Hood's affecting it. You're drawing a lot of power in close proximity. Or maybe it's just a power surge. Hard to say."

Scarlet sighed, her eyes trailing further down the page. "What is this?"

The next entry in the database was an order for five doses, placed by O'Connell, L., six months ago, completed. But while it listed the same vector number, the catalyst number was different from all the others near it. Something clicked in Scarlet's mind, like a gear shifting into place.

"You said the Hood can download information, right?" she asked. "How?"

"Just put your palm on the computer."

Scarlet rested her hand on the machine as she kept reading. A second later, she felt a surge of energy, similar to when Mason had sent the radio wave to open the maintenance door, though that had been from her hand. This time, she could feel the tingling energy entering her hand from the computer and winding up her arm.

"There's something here," Scarlet said, "I just don't know what." Her eyes flicked over the data, analyzing each entry in the log until something else caught her attention. "What—?" The word had barely left Scarlet's lips when the screen went black with a tiny electrical *pop*. The flow of information into her palm halted with a sharp zap of static electricity, and she snapped her hand back with a gasp. "Wait! Mason, bring that back. That was important. It could be—"

"We got a problem," Mason cut in. "Delta Lab. Willow!" Mason shouted, the volume of his voice overloading the Hood's speakers and coming through with a crackle.

"Shit." After six months wondering what had happened in her antidote test, maybe the answer was here the whole time, but she tore herself away from the computer, sprinting back to the maintenance column. She'd be back.

She entered the towering room again. The roar of the coolant flow and the thrum of the tree were deafening after being in the silent, abandoned office. This time, she knew what to expect. She crouched and gripped the edge of the grate flooring, easing off the edge into the flow without letting go. The force of the water column pulled at her, dragging her downward, but she held on tightly, working with the momentum this time to swing out of the

361

flow and onto the floor below. She landed on her feet—one sneaker and one sock—on the eighth floor grate. Then she wrenched the door open without waiting for Mason's all-clear.

When she emerged into the hallway outside Delta Lab, she found Willow in the middle of the glass-enclosed lab. Her hands were raised over her head as a pack of Logan's security goons surrounded her.

Scarlet's nerves jolted like lightning, yet she stood paralyzed outside the lab, watching, waiting. She desperately hoped Willow could defuse the situation. Unlike Scarlet, Willow worked here. If Scarlet intervened, the security guards would recognize her, and they would know there was something bigger going on.

"This area has been locked down," one of the guards said to Willow. "You're not authorized to be here."

"I was just getting some samples to take down to Beta Lab," Willow lied. "They're right here." She held up a vial of the lunabelle samples Scarlet had brought her earlier.

In a tabletop enclosure before her, Willow had already grown a lunabelle from another of the samples. Its dark vines twisted around its host—in this case, a stray cheese puff from Mason's snack earlier. Dark leaves splayed out from the winding stem, and little bell-shaped flowers dangled down in cascading sprays. Everything within the container was dusted with the iridescent spores, but those spores hadn't spread and multiplied out of control like they had in the North Quarter.

Scarlet frowned. These samples had been retrieved from the North Quarter just this morning, so why weren't they growing the same way? What variables had changed? Her mind bounced back and forth between analyzing Willow's work and the escalating situation with the guards.

"You still can't be in here. Move it." The guard turned to one of her colleagues. "I thought this lab was secured."

"I thought so, too." The other guard frowned.

"Check that control panel out in the hall. There have been some weird security malfunctions today."

The second guard nodded and turned. As he did, he locked eyes with Scarlet through the glass, where she stood in the hall. "Hey!"

Everything happened at once. In front of Willow, a light flashed on the containment case as it finalized its sequencing routine. She slammed her hand down, pressing the button to export the information to the Herbatech servers.

The guard who'd spotted Scarlet rushed toward the open hallway door, but the remaining three guards all lurched toward Willow at her sudden movement.

Willow backed away out of their reach, but her eyes went wide as she saw the guard going for Scarlet. For just a moment, Willow met Scarlet's gaze through the triple-paned glass. "Go!" Willow shouted.

The guard who'd seen Scarlet darted around the last lab table, just meters from the hallway door where Scarlet stood, but Willow was faster, and she knew how this lab worked. Scarlet realized it a split second after Willow did.

"Willow, NO!" Scarlet screamed.

Willow smashed the lunabelle vial on the floor. It shattered, the bloom within bursting into a glittering cloud of spores at her feet. In a flash, the heavy glass doors all around the lab slammed closed, sealing with a pneumatic hiss as the emergency quarantine protocols triggered. The guard slammed into the door right as it locked, barely a meter from Scarlet, but there was little to celebrate.

The spores drifted to the floor where the illuminated Phytogrid thrummed with power. In an instant, they latched, rooting down onto the grid and sprouting. Vines snaked upward, twisting around everything they could reach and growing heavy with buds. The buds expanded, pulsing with energy drawn straight from the grid, then the white blooms burst open, showering yet more spores over the scene. And the process repeated, the plants taking over every inch of the lab.

"Willow!" Mason screamed in Scarlet's ear, but his voice was nearly drowned out by the rush of her own blood as her heart slammed against her ribs.

Scarlet threw herself at the door, pulling at it in vain.

Inside the lab, Willow and the guards scrambled away from the spread. They climbed atop tables and backed into walls, but the toxins in the spores slowed them. Their heads lolled slowly on their shoulders, their eyes glazed, and they stumbled as the vines groped at their legs and wrapped around their arms, dragging them down into the roiling sea of white blossoms. Scarlet pounded on the glass as Willow crumpled and was swallowed up by the writhing plants. All the while, alarms blared around her. A recorded voice ordered, "*Evacuate eighth floor,*" over the speakers.

The lunabelles spread over everything, turning the lab into a dense forest. They spread and multiplied until the

364

plants choked each other for space to take root. Only then did the growth finally cease.

Scarlet's hands shook as she backed away, and bile burned in her throat. The guard that had come for her was pressed against the glass, unconscious. The spidering roots of lunabelles covered every bit of his skin and clothes, and they pulsed as they drew energy from him.

Mason's voice quaked in Scarlet's ears. "Oh my god, Willow..."

Scarlet closed her eyes against the quarantined lab, but even then, her mind was flooded with the sight of the writhing parasitic plants. It was horrible. It was grotesque. She'd never seen lunabelles grow like that. Yet just last night, thousands in the North Quarter had succumbed, just like Willow.

Willow...

The realization lit up Scarlet's mind as everything finally slammed into place. Willow's original sample had grown normally in the containment box. Scarlet had seen that. It drew organic energy from the host cheese puff, and remained a single stem. Only one variable had changed.

"We only have a few hours," Mason muttered, "and we haven't figured out anything."

"Yes, we have. Willow just told us everything." Scarlet turned, nearly slipping on her sock, and sprinted for the main stairwell where the access panel displayed EMER-GENCY. The door had automatically unlocked when Willow triggered quarantine protocol, allowing staff to evacuate the floor. "It's not a mutation. Willow's sample behaved just like I've seen other strains behave in the wild outside the eco-dome and in other cities. The only thing that changed in the lab just now is the Phytogrid. Get the generation code Willow just uploaded to the server, and meet me on basement level three."

"Th—The Quiet Core?"

"Yes. Hurry."

There was a sniffle, then a clatter in her ear as Mason dropped his headset. Then she launched herself into the concrete stairwell. Voices jabbered and footsteps scuffed through the tower above her while a claxon outside the eighth floor door blared through the cold space. Scarlet took the stairs down as quickly as she could. She didn't meet anyone below, but even as she sprinted, gripping the rail and flinging herself around the corners, she adjusted the Hood to ensure her face was hidden from anyone who might glimpse her flash of red. All the while, Scarlet's head raced. She knew what they needed to do. Ten thousand lives depended on it.

Scarlet slowed as she reached basement level three. Mason stood on the landing, just outside the door to the level that housed the Quiet Core. His arms were hugged around himself, and his head hung.

"Mason, I..." she whispered.

When he finally looked up, his eyes were red, his cheeks wet.

"Oh," Scarlet pulled him into a hug the second she reached the landing. He was shaking. "Listen, Mason. Willow quarantined the lab because she knows you're going to fix this. She trusts you."

He pulled away, nodding feebly and sniffing.

"I'm going to go in there and formulate a catalyst," Scarlet said. "I'll upload the information as soon as I get out with the disc. Herbatech still doesn't have enough doses of the vector, but the vector is just a messenger that delivers instructions to the lunabelle root system. It's just an electrical signal," she said. "That's how the Phytogrid works, and exactly why the lunabelles are attracted to it. Their entire life cycle revolves around finding an organic energy source. They're feeding off of the unlimited energy in the grid, which is why they've exploded so much more than they do when I've studied them anywhere else. The entire eco-dome is connected via the Phytogrid, but we can use that."

Mason caught on before she finished. "We need a digital virus that communicates to the lunabelle roots the same way that the vector does. Add the right catalyst information to the code, and we can cure the entire North Quarter with an electrical signal."

Scarlet managed a smile. "You're brilliant, Mason. Exactly. You really need to reconsider working for my ex." She withdrew the vector vial from her pocket and handed it to him. "Can you work with this?"

He nodded. "Yeah."

Voices entered the stairwell above them, and Mason opened the door to the Quiet Core level so he and Scarlet could slip out of view. For a moment, they stood in silence on the opposite side of the door, their breath heavy as they listened.

"Are you okay?" Scarlet asked. Mason didn't deserve to be in this position.

"I don't know." He frowned, clutching the vial in his fist. Worry etched a deep crease between his brows. "Are you okay?"

"I—" Scarlet exhaled. "I haven't been okay in a long time, Mason."

Voices echoed through the stairwell. Their eyes shot to the small window in the door, but no one came down this far. The bang of a door somewhere above them stifled the conversations, and all that was left was the echo of the alarm.

Scarlet straightened. "What's the generation code Willow sent?"

"Um…" Mason fished in his pocket and withdrew a crumpled paper with a scribbled code. "It's 015.782.7."

Scarlet read it several times, muttering under her breath to memorize it. "Okay. Go," she urged. "I'll upload the catalyst to the database for you as soon as I get out of the Core. You'll use that same number to access it."

"Got it," he said. "Good luck."

"You too."

With that, Mason turned and left, stranding Scarlet with only her thoughts and the echoes of her breathing. Her face was hot and damp from the run, and her heart was still racing. Willow had done her part—far more than she should have ever had to do. Surely Scarlet could do hers.

She would never be able to right the mistakes of the past. Whatever had happened in her antidote test was still a mystery, but the weight of ten thousand lives now rested on her shoulders, and she had to try. A part of her knew this was also her chance to prove the value of her research to

Logan and to the world. And somewhere, in a dark recess of her mind, Scarlet knew this was her last chance to prove it to herself, too.

Around the outer wall of the hall, a single strip of the Phytogrid cast dull golden light unevenly through the space. Three meters wide, three meters tall, and completely empty, the hall made a complete loop around a concrete box of a room—the Quiet Core. Unlike any other place in the city, the Quiet Core was isolated from the Phytogrid to prevent ambient energy from interfering with the sensitive information within. Digital information had to be carried in and out on a physical disc, which was why, in the wall just beside the stairwell door, an optical storage writer stood ready to pull information down from the Herbatech servers before entering the Core.

As Scarlet neared it, the screen lit up. She keyed in the lunabelle generation code Mason had given her, sending a silent thanks to Willow. With a buzz, a laser flared to life behind the wall. She watched through a small tinted window as the genome for the North Quarter lunabelles was etched into a quartz disc the size of a coin. It was finished in seconds.

The little piece of quartz was still warm in her hand, wafer-thin, but precisely etched in three dimensions through its crystalline structure. As she closed her hand around it, the crackling energy of the Hood enveloped the disc, reading the information, downloading it with a surge of energy into her hand and up her arm, just like when she had tried to download information from the computer moments ago. But she'd still need the disc within the Core. As soon as she got inside, the Hood would power down.

Disc in hand, Scarlet turned and crossed the hall to the Quiet Core.

The room was small and dimly lit, and once the door sealed behind her, it was silent. Eerily silent. Scarlet's uneven footsteps were oddly dampened, the sound stopping at the source, muffled before it began. The Quiet Core was the only place in all of Three Oaks where the Phytogrid didn't hum under everything. Its absence was deafening. But the thing that struck Scarlet most was the Hood going suddenly still and cold. She'd grown accustomed to the gentle vibration, the subtle warmth of the energy channeling through her, and especially to Mason's voice in her ear. Now she was on her own.

A slender steel pedestal stood alone in the center of the space. Scarlet let out a quavering breath, pressing the quartz disc with the lunabelle sequence into a shallow indentation in the top of it. As soon as she did, there was a hushed hydraulic sigh. The pedestal sank down, then lights erupted all around her as the system read the disc.

Beams of golden light shone from the floor and the ceiling, converging in the air before her eyes to form a spiraling holographic model of a double helix—Willow's genome for the North Quarter lunabelles. It stretched across the length of the room, each gene section segmented and labeled. With a flick of her hand, Scarlet zoomed down its length. The helix sped across her field of view, glinting and flashing and swirling until she found the gene she needed and plucked it out of the sequence. A tap brought her chosen section forward.

She took a deep breath, willing herself to believe she could do this and trying to push out the sinking doubt and the guilt that had festered inside her for the last six months.

She unzipped the two halves of the hologram. The tiny glowing filament bonds snapped, one by one, allowing her to splay both sides out before her. Then she got to work. She twisted the lunabelle sections and examined them. Knowing what this gene included told her how to communicate with it and how to break it. To the side, she began crafting another structure.

Both hands moved through the air, tentative at first, but soon falling into a familiar flow. Her fingers remembered the intricate gestures that allowed her to control the hologram before her mind could comprehend. One base pair at a time, she carefully worked her way around a brand new golden structure, choosing genetic building blocks from a virtual palette of light. New bursts of gold popped into existence before her eyes.

It was a process that had taken Scarlet and her team over a decade to develop. Even after she'd theorized about the method, it took years to design and build the necessary tech. It took even longer to formulate a genetic structure for the catalyst that might inhibit the lunabelle lifecycle. Since then, she'd built a generation-specific catalyst like this a dozen times. They'd tested the method and eventually had huge success with it. Until the first human trial.

For months, she'd done nothing but rack her brain for answers. For anything she'd done wrong. She couldn't explain it. Why couldn't she explain it?

Logan's voice surfaced in her head, then. *"Considering your track record, I'm not sure you know nearly as much about lunabelles as you seem to think, Scar."* She blinked back tears. What had she done?

She chewed her lip and focused on the task before her, hands shaking. The catalyst took shape from the inside out, as Scarlet wove delicate bonds into snowflake-like patterns, specifically designing each to latch onto portions of the lunabelle gene beside her until it formed a glittering starburst.

Connecting the last piece with a shimmering thread of a bond, she blew out a breath. She stepped back, double and triple checking the structure. Her eyes combed over every glowing strand, every glittering sphere, desperately searching for some fatal flaw—whatever had killed her patients six months ago. Had she fixed it? Or was it still lurking like some silent killer, and she just didn't see it? She couldn't get Logan's voice out of her head. *"The last time you were in this building, we had five people die at your hands."*

She tried to convince herself of everything her own expertise was telling her. There was nothing wrong. Scarlet swallowed, squeezed her eyes shut, and took a deep breath. *There was nothing wrong.*

Then she reached out to the catalyst structure, holding the hologram between her hands, and gently lifting it toward the ceiling. A moment later, the computer in the floor hummed, scanning her work and engraving another piece of quartz with the new formulation. The steel pedestal emerged from the floor again, presenting a new little quartz wafer. Scarlet plucked it up. As soon as she got it uploaded to the server, Mason could insert this code into his program. Only then would she know if she'd done it right.

Clutching the precious disc in her palm, she turned for the exit, but there was a heavy metal clunk before she reached the door. Scarlet's nerves jolted. "Mason?" she called, but of course, he couldn't hear her. The disc dropped from her hand to the rubberized floor as she rushed to pull at the door. It was locked. "No, no, no..." she muttered, her heart leaping into her throat. She gripped the handle again, bracing herself with her socked foot against the wall and wrenching at it with all her strength until her sweating fingers slipped from the slick handle, and she fell backward with a guttural cry. It wouldn't budge. Her shout was snuffed out like a feeble candle in the strangely dead air, and she found herself shaking on the floor.

And then a crackling static came through the Hood. Scarlet spun frantically, as if she would find the source in the room with her, but deep in her gut, she somehow knew exactly what she would hear.

The Hood came to life again, power surging through from the Quiet Core's isolated grid, humming with an overwhelming surge. When a voice finally came through, it was Logan's wicked laugh. It sent a shiver down her spine as if he were standing right beside her.

"Logan—"

"I've been waiting for you to finally make it down here."

"What are you doing, Logan?"

"This is a nice little gadget you have here. All the better to hear you with, my dear."

"Logan—"

"I've got people headed to find your accomplice, too. We were able to follow him on the security cameras after he met you in the stairwell. Very interesting that we couldn't see you, but whatever you're using to hide from my security has quite an interesting power signature on the Phytogrid."

"The lunabelles—" Scarlet pleaded. "It's the Phytogrid, but we can use it to—"

Pain cracked like lightning through her skull as a piercing electronic tone blared through the Hood straight into her ears. In one last moment of clarity, she found the disc containing her catalyst formulation on the floor and closed her fist tightly around it. She screamed, but she couldn't hear her own voice, couldn't feel her limbs. Nothing else existed outside of the shrill tone as it stabbed through her ears and ricocheted through her head. Her vision flashed red and then faded to a deep, empty black.

◆ ◆ ◆ ◆ ◆

When the world started to take shape again, the first thing Scarlet noticed was the darkening sky. The sun was setting, painting the backdrop an ominous bloody red. Her pulse quickened. Hours had passed. Night was falling. She moved to check her watch, but zip-ties cut into her wrists behind her back. Twisting and struggling in the chair, she found her ankles bound as well. The Hood had been pulled from her head, hanging limp around her neck. Her eyes flicked around the room. Above, the boughs of a massive tree rustled in shadow across the red sky.

"I've been waiting for you, my dear." Logan smirked as Scarlet met his icy gaze across the glass desk. He sat with his back to the darkening wall of windows, his face illuminated electric blue in the light from his computer. "I'll admit, your little red hood is rather clever, hiding you from my cameras. Though once I noticed the computer downstairs spontaneously turning on and digging into old lunabelle records, I knew something was going on. And who else would be dredging up those old records but you? I cut the Phytogrid connection to the computer, and then I saw it—a mysterious energy draw on the grid. Mobile. Intriguing. I traced the energy fluctuations and watched the security feeds when doors opened with no one around. I followed your every move from the office level to Delta Lab, and from there, into the stairwell where I watched your accomplice speaking to *no one*. When he unlocked the Quiet Core and left, it presented the perfect opportunity to hack into the mysterious device."

Mason's words from earlier in the day surfaced in Scarlet's mind as she fought to keep bile from rising in her throat. "*It would take some next-level genius to figure out how to connect the Hood to a totally separate power grid today.*" Of course, that's exactly what Logan was.

"We're running out of time to disperse an antidote," Scarlet said.

"What's done is done."

"We have to try. People are going to die. But I have a new catalyst. Just take it. You can have all the credit. I—" At that moment, she realized that her hand was empty. "Where's—?"

Logan produced a small quartz wafer from the inner pocket of his suit coat. It glinted in the blue light before he dropped it on the marble floor and crushed it violently under his shoe.

"No!" Scarlet screamed. Even if Mason had managed to write his virus, it was now worthless without the catalyst portion. Every hope they'd had of saving the North Quarter was shattered under an expensive Italian loafer. "Logan, why?"

Logan's temper flared. "Do you realize how hard it was to have you tossed out of here earlier this year? I can't have you coming back now, looking like some hero."

The words woke her up as much as his hands slamming against the elevator wall had earlier this morning. She locked his gaze. "What did you do?" Her voice came out as a whisper.

He smirked, but something flashed in his eyes behind the usual arrogance. He hadn't meant for her to hear that.

Scarlet was used to tiptoeing in his presence. Not anymore. She braced herself, balling her trembling hands into fists. "What did you DO, Logan?" This time, she found her voice, and it echoed through the stark room, charged with all the pent-up anger of two decades under his thumb.

But every hint of uncertainty in his eyes vanished in a blink, his expression hardening. He laughed that infuriating laugh—the one that always made her feel tiny and worthless. Deep inside her, a smoldering ember of doubt glowed red hot.

"I'm getting you out of my city the moment this is all over," he said. "You're a disgrace to your field, a black mark against this company, and you're going to rot in a cell for your incompetence."

He was changing the subject. Distracting her. But she wouldn't let him control the conversation. "You tampered with my antidote trial six months ago."

Logan leaned over the desk so their noses were nearly touching. His breath was hot on Scarlet's face. "That sounds like the desperate coping strategy of a delusional failure."

Her head screamed that Logan was playing games, trying to break her. This is what he always did. She knew that. But that realization didn't keep his teeth from sinking in. "I saw the manufacturing records," she said, as much to convince him as to convince herself. She couldn't let him undermine her, no matter how much he gnawed at her nerve. A fire raged in her head, but she forced out her accusation before the words were consumed by uncertainty. "You ordered antidote doses with a different catalyst formulation right before my test." She'd seen the evidence with her own eyes.

"Manufacturing orders are placed everyday, Scar. Any competent scientist would have checked the codes on the vials before administering to patients. Surely you did?"

"I—" Her thoughts blazed, and her confidence fluttered away like ashes in billowing smoke. She searched through her memories, desperately trying to recall the details of that day. He was wrong. Right? She had to have reviewed the labels. She always reviewed them. Had she gotten complacent, reading the number and not comprehending? Just going through the motions? Had the vials gotten mixed up without her noticing? Or was it her antidote that killed those patients? Her stomach twisted.

"The only thing we can be sure of," Logan continued, "is that you administered the lunabelle spores personally. And you administered the antidotes. It's all in your notes. I didn't kill those people, Scar. You did."

Scarlet's eyes stung as he continued, and she shrank in her chair, collapsing in on herself under the gravity of his words.

"I only ever wanted the project dead, but you bared your throat to the wolves, my dear. After the tragic results of your little experiment, it was easy to convince the Board that the only problem was you. Especially after I showed them my own tests, and we knew Herbatech finally had a functional antidote."

"What? How?" she asked.

He ignored her, arrogantly barreling onward with his story. "Here's the kicker, though. After you were out of the way, even with an antidote in my hand, I had to play damage control with the Board. Herbatech had still sunk our investors' funding into this niche research that was never going to turn a profit. You can count on one hand the number of people who come into contact with lunabelles in a year. So," he shrugged, "I set out to create a market for our new product."

Scarlet's jaw fell slack. "That's why you ordered antidote doses last week. You infected the North Quarter on purpose. And that's why you didn't bother to sequence them. You already knew exactly what strain you spread."

He grinned darkly, radiating pride over his clever scheme. "You said it yourself this morning. Sequencing the lunabelles would eventually lead investigators to the source of the contagion. My plan had been to destroy the lunabelles in the North Quarter before anyone had the chance to determine their origin. But what should have been a few pockets of infections spread like wildfire," Logan clenched his teeth. "We ended up taking a sample just to ensure it wasn't some mutation, but when the tests showed they grew just as we expected in the sample container, we started producing our antidote. We'd never be able to make enough, but I would be remembered as the hero that did everything possible to mitigate a tragic natural event. Herbatech would avoid a PR nightmare and get to show our shareholders the fruits of their investment after our antidote formulation worked."

Scarlet strained against the zip-ties. She wanted nothing more than to leap across the desk at him. "Your PR nightmare is the lives of ten thousand innocent people. But I can speak your language, Logan. I can see the headlines now—Herbatech fails to save North Quarter. So-called 'city of the future' in ruins. They'll dissolve this company before they even clear the dust out of the streets, and you'll have no one but yourself to blame."

He huffed softly into his coffee cup and took a sip. The puff of steam wisped away as he breathed into it, shimmering in the neon blue light of his computer. "That's not how this is going to work, Scar." His teeth glinted. "No one is going to gut Herbatech when they realize that this entire infestation came from the stores of a certain disgruntled former lab director. One who indeed had more knowledge than anyone about this species. One who identified the lunabelles within minutes from a cell phone photo with no context. One who disregarded a restraining order and disappeared from our security cameras shortly before our facilities were contaminated with that very same strain of lunabelles today."

Scarlet's stomach twisted and heat rose in her face. "You're framing me for the outbreak?"

He smirked, and when he spoke, his voice was a low growl under his breath. "Why else would I have told you about the flowers in the first place, Scar? I didn't need an ID. I planted them. But we all know lunabelles are your precious pet project. When everything went to hell this morning, I knew you would come running if I texted you. A field of wildflowers was all I needed to lure you in."

He'd trapped her, but that hardly mattered right now. Time was running out to save the North Quarter. Scarlet couldn't think straight. Her head was hazy, and she squeezed her eyes shut against it. In the back of her mind, she knew there were still files on the Herbatech servers that could implicate him. Of course, now that he knew she had seen the records, it was only a matter of time before he wiped the evidence from the system. If she could access the servers tonight, maybe she could prove that Logan had ordered the antidote a week before the outbreak.

Her antidote.

He'd ordered *her* antidote.

When she opened her eyes again, Logan was right in front of her, sitting back against the front edge of the desk, a fresh smirk pulling at the corner of his lip. "I'm going to eat you alive, Mrs. O'Connell."

She met his gaze. It was as if he'd finally removed his disguise, and she was seeing clearly for the first time in nearly twenty years. She'd been right. This whole time, she was right. And more, her catalyst had worked. He'd ordered her antidote, because that's the one he had tested and taken credit for after he forced her out. She was still zip-tied to the chair, but she felt like she had finally burst free from the belly of the beast.

"You swapped the labels," she said, the truth solidifying in her mind.

His smirk turned sour, his eyes narrowing. "When it's your word against mine in court," he threatened, "whose do you think will hold up? I'm the alpha wolf, and you're just—"

"*Shut. Up.*" She could suddenly see him through the dark forest of lies he'd coaxed her deeper and deeper into for so many years. His words pinged off of her. Nothing he said could hurt her anymore. "Wolf packs don't have alphas," she said. "That myth was disproven ages ago, you ignorant, insufferable bastard."

His eyes darkened dangerously, but then his face went unnaturally slack. His eyes glazed as his grip relaxed on his mug. It fell to the floor with a clatter, splashing hot coffee over both their feet. Then his head lolled, and he toppled sideways, hitting the floor with an unceremonious thud and a sickening crunch.

Scarlet watched, eyes wide. Then a voice spoke up behind her. "I thought he'd never drink that."

"Rye?" Scarlet twisted in the chair, craning to look over her shoulder. Rye rushed up behind her and cut the zip-ties at her wrists with a pair of scissors. "I put the sedative Willow gave us in his cup."

"You drugged your coffee?" Scarlet asked.

"Yes. And I'll have you know that was fair trade organic arabica, too. Sacrilege." They cut the ties at her ankles. "I thought I was taking a risk putting it in front of him before you woke up, but Logan was just *'blah blah blah.'* Damn, that man likes to hear himself talk. What did you ever see in him, anyway?"

Scarlet rubbed her wrists and pulled the Hood back over her head. It felt like a warm hug. "Mason?" she asked.

"Right here the whole time," Mason said in her ear.

"Logan said they're searching for you. Are you safe?" Scarlet asked.

"This place is solid." Mason's familiar typing clicked in the background. "I'm working on the code right now."

"But the catalyst is gone," she said.

"The Hood downloaded the catalyst information while you were in the Core, after Mr. O'Connell connected it to the Core's power grid," Mason told her. "I saw the file as soon as they hauled you out, and you were back on the Phytogrid with the rest of the building."

Scarlet faintly remembered reaching out to grab the disc before she was knocked out in the Core. Her heart leapt. Maybe they had one last chance at this.

"Tell Rye to get on Mr. O'Connell's computer real quick," Mason said. "I'm sending over another file."

She did, and Rye rushed around the desk to Logan's laptop.

"Be quick. We have to get out of here," Scarlet whispered to Rye.

Scarlet rushed to slide a pair of heavy chairs across the floor, barricading the doors against the security guards who would certainly be posted out in the hall. Metal scraped against the tile. Then she scanned the room and chewed her lip, looking for any other way out.

Above them, the boughs of the great oak tree rustled in the gentle artificial breeze outside the glass ceiling, and an idea struck her. She marched across the room and seized one of the statuettes from the display case. Then she climbed onto Logan's desk, her single sneaker squeaking on the pristine glass. The award was heavy in her fist, and her eyes narrowed at the plaque: *Logan O'Connell* for *Outstanding contributions in the field of green technology.*

"Watch your eyes," Scarlet warned Rye.

"Yeah," Rye said absently. Their fingers flew over Logan's keyboard. "Scarlet, what are you—"

Scarlet squeezed her eyes shut as she reached, thrusting the statuette skyward until it pierced the glass ceiling. A million spidering cracks wove across the pane in a blink before it shattered. The fragments crumbled and rained down over them as Scarlet and Rye both ducked, hands over their heads. Beads of tempered glass pelted the Hood, plinked over the desktop, and bounced across the marble floor where Logan still lay unconscious under her. But as fresh evening air poured into the office, Scarlet took a deep, clarifying breath. "Let's go."

Rye grinned broadly and hit one last triumphant key on the keyboard. "Finished."

Scarlet slammed the laptop closed and ripped out the glowing Phytogrid connection before cracking the whole computer on the edge of the desk. It bent, whirring fans and humming drives turning to whining, mechanical groans. Scarlet flinched as a metallic jolt of static drove through her ears, the connection between the Hood and Logan's computer severing, banishing Logan's voice from her head once and for all. The electronic screech dissipated just as quickly as it came on. She shook her head to clear it, and then she held out a hand, hauling Rye atop the desk beside her.

Rye reached up, gripping the vacant skylight frame, tiny fragments of the glass cutting into their hands. They pulled themselves through the ceiling before plunging a hand back down to grip Scarlet's wrist, helping her up in turn. Rye and Scarlet were on top of it all.

"Mason, what do you have for us? Did you finish the code?" Scarlet asked. Rye stood close behind her where they could listen in.

"I'm... Woah. Are you two on the *roof?*" Mason blurted out.

"Focus!" Scarlet snapped.

"Right," Mason said. "Rye, hang back in the office. Let security think Big Bad Scarlet did this all on her own. I need you to meet me downstairs after all this."

"On it," Rye said.

Rye flashed Scarlet a grin before they expertly dropped back down through the broken glass panel like some hero from an action movie. She wondered whether Rye had done that stunt more than once over the course of their various outlandish misadventures, and she grinned.

But the sky was darkening by the second, and the crescent moon would appear soon. They were running out of time.

Mason cleared his throat and got back to clacking away on his keyboard. "I'm debugging the code now. Should be ready to run in a few min—" A *bang* issued through the speakers in the Hood, and Mason cursed.

"*The door's locked!*" came the muffled unknown voice through the background of Mason's audio.

"What's going on?" Scarlet asked.

"*There's someone in there!*" shouted a second unknown voice.

"Security found me," Mason whispered.

More blows crashed against the door through Mason's microphone. "*Open up or we're knocking the door down.*"

"Not by the hair on my chinny-chin-chin, assholes!" Mason shouted. He lowered his voice to Scarlet as the banging turned into crashing. "Look, this door might as well be a brick wall. There's no way they're getting in here, but I can't upload the virus from here. It's got to be uploaded directly to the tree, near the roots so it has the best chance to go out through the Phytogrid to the North Quarter."

Scarlet's heart hammered in her chest, and she dashed across the glass ceiling as quickly as she could. "Can you upload the virus through the Hood? Like you did the radio frequencies?"

"Um, yeah. I think so. But we've got to get it to penetrate into the tree if it's going to get through all the cyber security. We need to embed it deep."

Scarlet reached the glowing tree where it emerged from the top of the building and peered down. The tree plunged clear through the building, deeper and deeper into darkness. Alongside it, the water gel coolant emerged from the pump to course down the entire length of the trunk within the maintenance column. Her eyes flicked to a fire axe mounted near the access door. The glow from the trunk glinted off the steel blade.

Mason's excitement was thinly veiled. He was clearly watching the video feed from the Hood. "Are we—?"

"You focus on the software." Scarlet lifted the axe from its mount and tested its weight in her hands. "I'll deal with hardware."

"Oh, hell yes," Mason chuckled.

Scarlet peered down the column. This was final. She knew that when she jumped down there, she was diving into the wolf's den, getting herself cornered where she couldn't escape. She'd be locked in, just waiting to be arrested, and just as Logan had threatened, she'd go down for everything, because Logan would wake and delete every shred of evidence from the servers. But there was no way around it. She gulped in a deep breath and jumped into the column.

The gel coolant didn't splash—it swallowed her. She plunged down into the thick substance, and the shock of the cold this high up in the system nearly made her gasp, though she couldn't have if she tried. Everything hummed and vibrated. A deep reverberation rattled through her chest and her skull like shockwaves underwater. She clung to her axe, trying to count the floors as she passed them. Nine, eight, seven? She fell faster and faster, and the floors turned to blurs in the rushing coolant. All she could do was hold her breath. She was moving too fast to escape the flow. Darkness crept in at the edges of her vision.

But she realized the coolant was heating up. The further down she traveled, the more heat the gel drew from the tree. She had to be getting close, so she held on. Her lungs ached. They felt like they might burst. Her body begged her for breath until at last, she plunged into a shallow pool.

The thick liquid dampened her fall, but she still hit the bottom under the streaming torrent. She found the grated floor and kicked off of it, her face bursting from the surface of the pool with a desperate gasp.

"—arlet?" Mason's voice drifted in through the crackles in the Hood's audio like a tuner finding a radio station's frequency. "Scarlet, can you hear me?"

"Roger," she managed between gulping breaths.

"Who's Rog—? Oh, ha ha," he laughed dryly.

The faintest hint of a grin tickled at the corner of her mouth as she hefted herself out of the pool and onto the damp earth. She was in the depths of the Herbatech building. The lowest level was cavernous, and her quick breath echoed. Massive concrete caissons rose in a grid from the soil to support the building above, and in the center of it all, the great oak rose up out of the ground, its trunk a massive fifteen meters across. To one side of the trunk, the coolant gel flowed down into a collection pool before being pumped back up to the top of the building again. At her feet, thick roots extended out from the tree in all directions, connecting to the Phytogrid, and carrying energy to each quarter of the city. The entire room hummed with the golden glow of the power channeling through the tree.

Scarlet approached the tree, the axe heavy in her hand.

"You have to drive it deep," Mason reminded her. "And you have company."

"Security?"

"No, police—" His words were drowned out as alarms blared once again.

"Upload the code," she told him.

Mason's program came through like a lightning strike, surging up through her body and into the Hood itself. Before her eyes, the world went fuzzy, crackling out of existence and fading back in, the images refining slowly from meaningless pixels back into physical reality. Ghostly lines of code flashed across her eyelids when she blinked. Every bit of her hummed, and brilliant white light streamed from the Hood, over her hands, through her fingertips, and across the surface of the axe. It shone like moonlight.

Her hands shook as the reality of it slammed into her. This was it—her catalyst and Mason's virus were the only things that could prevent the final death knell for the city she and Logan had founded.

"Stop right there!" Police flooded into the space from the elevator and the stairwell behind her.

She didn't turn around. She tightened her grip on the axe. "*Drive it deep.*" Mason's words echoed in her head, pushing her forward. This would work. It had to. She charged toward the tree, hauling the glowing axe over her head and bringing it down in a sweeping arc as she reached the trunk. The blade sliced into the coursing gold wood, sending a forceful shudder through her arms, but it wedged deep within the trunk. She held fast, gritting her teeth as Mason's code surged through her from the Hood. The white moonlight burst from the head of the axe, carrying up and down through the trunk. It emanated outward through the roots, surging from the tree to the rest of the city.

Bulky arms ripped her hands free from the axe a second later, pulling her bodily from the trunk and shoving her to the dirt. A knee came down heavily in the center of her back, pinning her as police yanked her arms roughly behind her. She didn't care. She'd done everything she could. An officer wrenched the axe free from the trunk, but Mason's code continued to spread outward from the wound.

"You did it! I think you did it!" Mason celebrated.

As the last flicker of brilliant white light faded from the Phytogrid, Scarlet and the police were left again in semi-darkness.

◆ ◆ ◆ ◆ ◆

The officer's voice droned behind Scarlet's head. They had rattled off a laundry list of charges as they hauled her out of the basement, but she wasn't listening. The police steered

Scarlet out of the Herbatech atrium and onto the black granite steps. They emerged into a frenzy. Lights flashed. Everywhere, police and paramedics rushed around, barely holding back a sea of media crews and curious bystanders.

Camera flashes popped, glittering in the dark like Scarlet was walking some sick red carpet with one lone sneaker. Her face, dirt-smeared and disheveled, would no doubt be the top story on every channel in the morning, the front page of every news site. She wondered if it would be these photos or the mugshot.

She'd never see a lab again—that much was certain. Her life's work. Her passion. But none of that mattered right now. If they'd managed to save Logan's victims, she'd do it all a thousand times over.

Scarlet desperately needed to know whether their cure had worked. Was Willow okay? The North Quarter? Scarlet halted abruptly, and though the police tugged at her arms, she resisted, staring up at the crescent moon. Outside the eco-dome, the inky purple of night slowly spilled across the sky, and the thinnest shining sliver of the moon shone out near the horizon. It was over. The fates of everyone in the North Quarter and in Delta Lab upstairs were sealed, one way or another.

"Wait." Scarlet looked around for any sign, peering through the shoulders of the crowd. "The lunabelles. Is everyone...? Did they...?"

As if in answer, the lobby doors were pushed open behind her again with a faint hiss. "Medical coming through," an EMT called. The crowd parted for them. Scarlet was jostled around in the mix, and she twisted against her arresting officers to see.

Every possibility flashed through Scarlet's mind in a disorienting whirl. Would the medical crew come through pushing gurneys? Carrying body bags? Or just wearing grim, sorrowful expressions. Scarlet's escorts dragged her aside as a brigade of paramedics moved slowly out of the building. Half a dozen patients walked out with them, and the crowd exploded into cheers.

"Willow!" Scarlet's heart leapt at the sight of her. Willow's umber skin was pockmarked ghostly white where the roots had latched into her, but she was alive and strong enough to walk. Scarlet attempted to rush forward and hug her, only to be reminded of her arrest by a rough yank backward on her handcuffed arms.

But Willow heard her, and she spun to find Scarlet. Even as she nearly toppled sideways, a wide smile spread across her face. Once she regained her balance, Willow pulled free of the paramedic who had been steadying her at the elbow. She shuffled sideways on uneasy legs against the stream of people exiting the building, and when she finally reached Scarlet, Willow threw her arms around her just like she had earlier in the day.

"Ma'am, you really shouldn't—" one of the police officers warned Willow, but she ignored them.

Willow beamed, and Scarlet leaned warmly into her in a sorry attempt at a hug with her arms handcuffed behind her back. Just feeling Willow's breath against her cheek, Scarlet had to bite her lip to hold herself together.

"You did it," Willow said. "It was the Phytogrid, wasn't it? The power from the grid is what caused the uncontrolled growth."

Scarlet nodded, marveling at her. Even as Willow had been overwhelmed by the spreading lunabelles in the lab, she'd been observing, analyzing, deducing. Someday, Willow would have her own name on some bit of revolutionary science and on all the awards that came with it. Scarlet was sure of it.

"Scarlet!" Mason's voice shouted over the crowd. "We did it! The whole North Quarter! It's amaz— Willow!" He rushed over to them. His eyes combed over Willow's injuries, but a relieved smile pulled at his lips.

"I'm okay," Willow told him, grinning broadly.

"Oh my god. I'm— I—" Mason stumbled over his words, a blubbering mess, as he struggled to process everything at once.

"Your antidote code worked, Mason," Scarlet said. "You're a hero."

"Antidote code?" Willow's eyes went wide as she comprehended what Scarlet meant. "You coded a *digital* cure?" she asked Mason.

Behind Willow's back, Scarlet cracked a smile.

Mason blushed and nodded sheepishly. "It's all just electrical signals," Mason muttered.

Willow beamed and kissed him on the cheek. He turned, if possible, even redder.

"That's amazing! Mason, you're amazing!" Willow gushed.

A silent tug at her arm pulled Scarlet out of the sweet moment. She turned and met the eyes of the officer beside her. He nodded his head toward the street. "Time to go." Scarlet took a deep breath, nodded, and quietly turned to walk down the steps. She didn't want to interrupt Willow and Mason in this long-overdue moment, but Mason saw Scarlet turn.

"Wait, no! You can't..." his voice trailed off, and he looked around wildly, scanning the crowd.

"Mason," Scarlet sighed. "I knew what I was getting into when I agreed to help today. I knew the risk I was taking. Just knowing what we accomplished... knowing that we saved people... knowing that we were able to formulate that antidote against all odds... We pushed the boundaries of botany and tech today, and it was all worth it."

"But you can't—" Mason muttered.

Scarlet looked him in the eye and smiled. "I'm okay, Mason." A long-absent sense of peace warmed in her chest. She'd formulated the catalyst. She had proof. And no one—not Logan, not the police, not the courts—could take that from her. Her work had broken new ground and saved lives, and that's all she'd ever set out to do.

"Here they are!" This time, it was Rye's voice that rose over the crowd, and they all spun to see Rye pointing to them over the heads of the throng.

A second later, Rye arrived with a reporter and the chief of police in tow.

"Officer, let her go. There's new evidence," the police chief announced.

Both Scarlet and the officer who held her arm stared. It was Mason's turn to smile.

"Kaitlyn Hunter. Channel Seven," the reporter introduced herself. "We received an email directly from Mr. O'Connell's computer which proves that Dr. O'Connell is innocent."

"Dr. Perrault," Scarlet corrected out of habit. Then she did a double take. "Wait, what?"

"The video details Logan O'Connell's blatant confession to infecting the North Quarter and seems to imply sabotage of the lunabelle antidote study six months ago," the reporter said.

"Mr. O'Connell confessed everything right to the Hood's video," Mason said.

"You were recording everything?" Scarlet asked.

Mason grinned.

"Mason sent it over," Rye said, "and I just dropped it in an email to my friend here before we left. I knew Kate would be able to get the word out to the right people."

The officer released Scarlet's cuffs, and she rubbed her wrists, still in shock. She'd been so sure she was going to jail and would never get a chance to dig up the evidence on Herbatech's servers after Logan had her hauled off.

The lobby doors opened again, and the crowd burst into chaos. It was Logan, still looking drowsy, his clothing uncharacteristically rumpled and coffee-stained, his nose broken and swollen from his fall. Half a dozen police officers steered him through the crowd in handcuffs.

"Logan O'Connell, you are under arrest on charges of premeditated homicide, five counts, and domestic terrorism…" The officer's voice was drowned out as they pressed down the stairs and through the crowd.

Scarlet's phone buzzed a moment later, and she pulled it from her pocket.

"Who's that?" Rye asked.

They all turned to watch as she read the message.

"It's the Herbatech Board," Scarlet told them, hardly believing the words as she spoke them. "They're begging to have me back and want me to call right now."

Willow lit up. "Scarlet, that's great!"

But Mason raised an eyebrow. "Are you going to?"

Scarlet glanced down at her phone again, then up at the three of them. "I want to be wherever you want to be. I could start fresh, and obviously you'll all have job offers as soon as I get up and running. Or I could answer this call, and make sure you're brought on full-time. Promotions and pay raises, of course. I want to create a whole new innovation team dedicated to doing the nonprofit research no one else deems worthwhile. What do you think?"

Willow grinned. "I'll learn amazing things from you no matter where we are."

"Herbatech's not perfect," Rye said, "but it's yours, and you could turn it into whatever you want."

"What *we* want," Scarlet corrected.

"Does that mean we could get vending machines on the programming floor?"

"Um, I mean, I guess?" Scarlet said.

Mason's face was dead serious. "I'm not going without the vending machine. I know my worth."

Scarlet laughed. "I'll work it into the contract."

"You know," Willow said, "the lab could really use—"

"Maybe we should discuss all this over coffee," Scarlet suggested. "I think we've earned a break, and I'm told Rye's coffee is pretty good."

"'*Pretty good*,'" Rye scoffed. "It's life-changing. A remote village in the Alps founded a new religion after I worked at their café one winter. I was stranded there for a few months when the mountain pass was cut off by an avalanche."

"I'm sorry, what?" Scarlet asked, hardly suppressing a laugh.

Rye grinned, but didn't elaborate. "Didn't you say the Board wanted to talk right now?"

Scarlet smiled and pocketed her phone. "The Board isn't going anywhere. They'll wait." She looked around at Willow, Mason, and Rye, standing a little taller, knowing the team they'd formed—full of hope and brilliance and goodness. Together, they could pursue the things that truly mattered, and for the first time in a long while, Scarlet knew she had the power to make it happen.

About the Authors

◆ ◆ ◆ ◆ ◆

Ash Whitaker | instagram.com/booked4adventures

Ash is an avid traveler and coffee fiend. She has been lost in books for as long as she can remember. From hiding beneath desks during reading time to getting lost in countless stories since, her love of books has shaped how she views the world, making it a brighter, bigger and more adventurous place. She lives in Indiana with her husband and two sons. Her contribution to *Not Your Ever After* is her debut story.

Debbie Lynn | debbielynnwrites.com

Debbie is the author of the urban fantasy series *Unveiled.* She is also a therapist and yoga teacher, pizza lover, and she's been told she enjoys the color orange more than is healthy. She is a sucker for characters with emotional trauma and friends who become lovers. Outside of writing and working, Debbie watches too much Disney with her young daughter, argues with her teenager about what to eat for dinner, and adds to her To Be Read pile. She lives in Indiana and dreams of living somewhere near the ocean.

Hana Maren Godfrey | hanamarengodfrey.com

Hana writes darkly whimsical, sometimes poignant fantasy and science-fiction stories. She fully believes in magic, science, and the transportive power of storytelling. When she isn't weaving plot lines and heartstrings, Hana is fond of crocheting magical creatures and listening to audiobooks. She lives in North Carolina with her husband and one little bookworm.

Charlie Morgan | charliemorganwrites.com

Charlie is a neurodivergent author writing about the ghosts that haunt us and women doing bad things—she loves a villain story. Before switching genres to fantasy horror, she published two spicy romantasy novels known as the *Wickedly Ever After Series*. In her free time, she is hanging out with her sons, thrifting treasures or playing video games.

C. P. Ashton | cpashton.com

Author by night and engineer by day, C. P. Ashton entertains readers through fantasy, sci-fi, and contemporary fiction. C. P. is a sucker for witty banter and high emotions, especially on the backdrop of a fantastical adventure. In rare quiet moments, C. P. enjoys playing cooperative board games and video games, baking sourdough, and soaking up the Colorado sunshine with the fam.